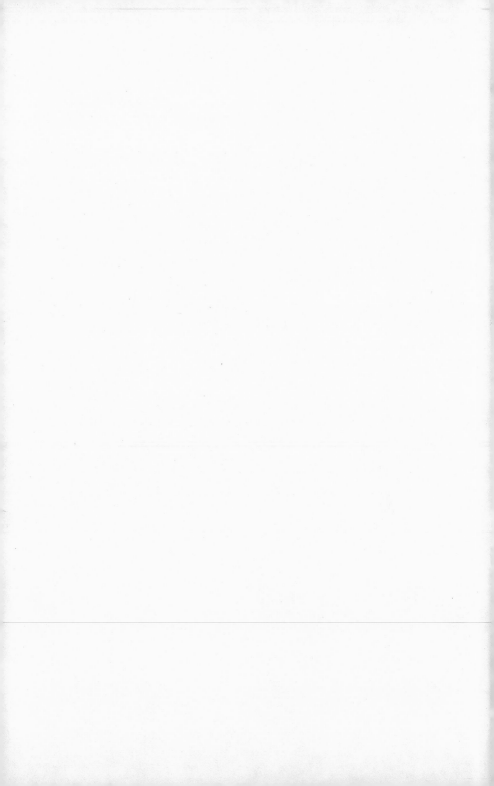

DIANA'S ALTAR

DIANA'S ALTAR

Barbara Cleverly

**SOHO
CRIME**

Published by
Soho Press, Inc.
853 Broadway
New York, NY 10003

Library of Congress Cataloging-in-Publication Data

Cleverly, Barbara, author.
Diana's altar / Barbara Cleverly.

ISBN 978-1-61695-664-6
eISBN 978-1-61695-665-3

1. Sandilands, Joe (Fictitious character)—Fiction.
I. Title
PR6103.L48 D53 2016 823.92—dc23
2015037547

Interior design by Janine Agro, Soho Press, Inc.

Printed in the United States of America

10 9 8 7 6 5 4 3 2 1

For the two Juliets, at stroke and bow:
Juliet Burton, agent
Juliet Grames, editor
Ladies, my admiration and gratitude!

～

Upon that day either prepare to die
For disobedience to your father's will,
Or else to wed Demetrius, as he would,
Or on Diana's altar to protest
For aye austerity and single life.

—Shakespeare,
A Midsummer Night's Dream,
Act 1, scene i.

DIANA'S ALTAR

CHAPTER 1

Adelaide Hartest reminded herself sternly that she was a doctor. A doctor of medicine. A scientist, she would have claimed—one who believed in evidence gathering and cause and effect. In reason.

So why was she standing here at dawn, one indecisive hand on the latch of the gate of All Hallows Church, suffering a very particular set of symptoms? Her mouth was dry, her hands were trembling, her teeth were trying, unbidden, to hold their own chattering conversation and, interestingly, the hairs really had risen at the nape of her neck. Briefly she explored the inches of skin between her hat brim and the collar of her cape. Her fingers encountered warm dampness and a palpable, unnatural bristliness there. She pulled up her woolly scarf to fill the gap and looked about, seeking some external reason for the current of cold air that was trickling down her spine. There was no sign of a breeze; the few golden leaves left clinging to a solitary ash tree hung motionless.

Homeostatic mechanisms, of course! This was merely Nature clicking in faithfully after the brisk cycle ride back from a grim all-night stint. None grimmer. Emotionally disturbed, professionally challenged and physically threatened by her case, young Dr. Hartest had expressed her frustrations by vigorously pedalling over country roads in the dark back to Cambridge. She'd become overheated and her body was responding obligingly by kicking in with its cooling-down devices. Simple. No—that wouldn't quite do. Adelaide was trained never to accept the immediately obvious without question. Autonomic body temperature adjustments didn't go halfway to accounting for the mental and physical state she was experiencing.

She made her diagnosis: good old-fashioned fear. It wasn't a feeling that had troubled her often in her twenty-seven years. Standing almost six feet tall in her silk stockings with a head of hair that impressed by its auburn luxuriance, Adelaide was blessed with a confidence that rebuffed danger. At the sight of her smile and her long stride, Danger crossed the road and slunk past on the opposite side. Danger with a human face, at any rate. But what natural cause of terror was there—other than human—that might possibly lie in wait to ambush her? Earthquakes, floods and volcanic outpourings were completely unknown in the centre of civilised Cambridge at six o'clock on an autumn morning.

She was alone here with her turbulent thoughts, come to seek a solace which most probably wasn't available to her.

The Market Place, only yards away, was silent. None of the traders had arrived to set up stall yet. No barrows rumbled over the cobbles, no merry banter rang out. She hadn't even spotted the beat bobby who usually lurked under the gas lamp by King's College, lighting up a Woodbine and ready to greet her with a cheeky, "Morning, Doc! Give it ten! You're winning!" when she cycled by.

The crowding medieval rooftops enclosing the tiny square where she was standing were taking on a sharp silhouette against the brightening sky. The ancient church of All Hallows, squat and square, blotched by damp, bore witness to the passage of every one of its thousand years. It conjured up the image of a discoloured tooth shakily attached to decaying roots, but having nerve connections all too vigorous and snaking down to draw strength from some deep past.

Adelaide reined in her imagination. Fatigue and anger were weakening her defences against fanciful thoughts. She was in the wrong place at an inconvenient time and ought not to be loitering here. Though she had by now identified the source of her unease. The poisonous miasma floating, undetected by the usual senses, all about her—it was All Hallows. The church building itself. It was resenting and resisting her intrusion.

If there were few willing to penetrate the first defences of evergreen foliage that encircled the ancient stones, there were fewer yet who would enter the dim interior in spite of the enticements advertised on a billboard at the gateway: the skull of Saint Ethelbert, a page from a prayer book of Queen Isabella and an oak lectern once pounded by the fist of a dissenting preacher.

Adelaide found their lure perfectly resistible. She had other business at All Hallows.

She was intent on having a serious word with the Lord. Bearding the Almighty in his den. She reasoned that, just as she listened with care to the patients who made their way into the privacy of her consulting room, confident that they would be telling her nothing less than the truth and expecting nothing less than an honest answer in return, the Lord—if he existed—would show similar good manners.

Consultation was a game for two players and imposed its own etiquette. In the stillness of a deserted church in front of his own altar, Adelaide had initiated such conversations many times before. God, in her simple estimation, was a Gentleman. If he wasn't, she couldn't be doing with him. She had always left whatever sacrosanct surroundings she had chosen to witness her outpouring of emotion feeling more at peace with herself. Unwelcome truths and difficult decisions were more swiftly dealt with on one's knees on a lumpy hassock.

There were two responses to fear: flight or fight. Rush for the cliff's edge or loosen your sword in your scabbard and take a stand. She had a decision to make, and her self-imposed time limit was almost up. In three hours she would lift the telephone and ask the operator to connect her with a London number. She would wait for the familiar voice, warm and expectant. She would deliver her decision. Her life would change forever.

Adelaide never made detours and she never ducked out of any situation. She had playground scars to prove it. She swung the gate open and paused for a moment to take a torch from the pocket of her cape. The battery was running low—she'd almost drained it during her nightmare excursion into the Cambridgeshire countryside—but it clicked on valiantly and the narrow beam lit up the paved path beyond.

It had been swept clean of leaves. Visitors were clearly expected. Adelaide decided to take this as an omen. An invitation. Steadily she moved towards the west door.

In the English tradition, the House of the Lord was always left unlocked. When she lifted the latch of the heavy oak door and pushed, there were no metallic squeaks to break the silence. It swung open with ease on oiled hinges. Adelaide hesitated, her attention caught by a postcard pinned neatly to the door at eye level. It was handwritten in scholarly calligraphy.

All Gallows' Eve
Tuesday, 31st October
Vespers
By invitation only
Please apply to the Rev. Sweeting for admission.
The service will be followed by a symposium on
the darker issues of modern life:
* Distrust   * Doubt
* Depression   * Death

"Pompous prats!" was Adelaide's muttered response to this. A group of self-indulgent soul-searchers egging each other on to plumb the depths of melancholy on Hallowe'en? Well, they were just looking for trouble, and she rather thought she was better qualified to comment on the four Ds than any academic sensation seekers.

Something about the wording of the announcement struck her as strange. No times were given for the service. Just: Vespers. The evening service. But this was the house of God, open to all at all times, not a private chapel where invitations might be issued to the specially chosen. The Reverend Sweeting seemed to have taken on the role of God's maître d'hôtel. When she met him, Adelaide would have a question or two to put to the reverend. Crossly, she tugged the card from its moorings and put it in her pocket. Someone should hear about this.

Just in case "Vespers" had turned into "Vigil" she put her ear to the door and listened. Bursting in on a coterie of depressed souls further debilitated by a night of philosophising in a minor key was not a tempting prospect. All was silence and she risked peering in.

Signalling to her through the musky darkness, a solitary candle flickered a welcome. Soft as a sigh, a breath of air lightly scented with incense invited her inside.

CHAPTER 2

A six-foot bobby having a quick pee at the end of his shift is not easily concealed in the centre of a compact city, but the still-thick canopy of leaves on the chestnut in front of King's College Chapel was up to the task. Police Constable Risby thoughtfully buttoned up the flies of his uniform trousers and listened to a cracked college bell sounding the hour. He was trying to make sense of what he'd just seen. He'd had the central city beat entirely to himself since three o'clock. A good, quiet spell of duty it had turned out to be. He'd expected worse: "Mischief Night," they'd always called All Hallows' Eve when he was a kid before the War. There was a craziness that got into folk these dark evenings after the clocks went back an hour. Even the governor had thought to remind him of the date. "Last day of October, Constable! Witches, ghoulies and long-leggety beasties—you may expect a selection of various frightful apparitions about the town tonight. Put a spare pair of handcuffs on your belt and stand no nonsense. Haul 'em in and leave 'em to sleep it off down in the cooler. I'll deal with any spirits that have missed the witching hour myself when I get in. I've booked the magistrate."

He'd thought the students at least would have been up to something, but if they had, he hadn't spotted it. A few drunken party-goers in masks and costumes had joked with him in an amicable way, and he'd managed to hang on to his helmet and his truncheon—always the targets of trophy hunters. His last contact with student revellers had occurred just before three o'clock when he'd warned a group of young men that a college Bulldog was on the trail and advancing at a brisk pace down the passage. Good-humouredly, he'd given them a leg up over the tall, wrought-iron fence in a secret place where he knew the spikes had been tampered with, and had seen them safely inside the college grounds before the official came puffing along. Risby didn't care much for students, but he cared far less for self-important college policemen.

And that was it for excitement until, in the middle of his pee, he'd noticed the cycle light wobbling towards him down Trinity Street. He'd just been able to make out the flying nurse's cape and woolly hat of that new lady doctor. The big, good-looking redhead who'd joined the medical practice in Trumpington Street only yards from where he was loitering. She was going at quite a lick on her Raleigh tourer, he noticed. Returning to base after working the night shift? Risby wanted to know how anyone could think that was acceptable. It was no duty to give a woman! He had a fellow feeling for anyone grafting through the small hours and watched her as, abruptly, she turned off the main Parade and dived down the snicket into Peas Passage. Now why would she do that, at this time of night—or was it day?

Risby was uneasy. A rum place, that little square by the church. Bad feeling to it. He always found himself patrolling at a quickened pace through those little alleys surrounding . . . now what was its name? All Hallows! That was it.

Making the connection, Risby was suddenly alert. This was All Hallows' Eve. The constable shuddered, remembering his superintendent's lip-smacking evocation of the sinister goings-on one might encounter on this night—some rubbish about malicious spirits tearing through the thin veil that separated the living from the dead. Load of superstitious codswallop, but PC Risby reckoned that if—if!—any veil-tearing was to occur in Cambridge, that would be just the spot for it.

And on this night of all nights, his duty was to check the church surroundings, open the door and take a quick look inside. They still kept valuables in there, trusting to the sanctified aura to protect them. Fools.

He vaulted over the wall into the Parade, pulled his truncheon from his long pocket and, grasping it firmly in his hand, crossed the road. A single woman could scare herself silly or even come to real harm down there, and it wasn't going to happen on his watch. Be it Old Nick the Devil or Old Dave the Dosser—anyone he found causing mayhem or offence would feel the weight of twelve inches of English oak across his skull.

NO REVEREND SWEETING shimmered forward to check her invitation, but Adelaide stood motionless at the door, giving her eyes time to adjust to a different degree of darkness, and getting her bearings.

As colours and shapes began to emerge, she stepped over the threshold, sensing a soft carpet under her feet, her focus on the east window ahead of her. The huge space above the altar was filled with stained glass and was beginning to come alive inch by inch with shards of kaleidoscope colour, revealing a seductively beautiful and mysterious scene. The old stones had retained the unseasonal warmth of the day, and the air seemed to be still reverberating with the music, the incense, the devotions and farewell kisses of a just-departed gathering.

The intimate space was filled by ranks of oak pews in deep shadow. They were divided down the middle by a red runner laid over the stone paving slabs. Her torch swept down this path to the altar, locating the single candle that had survived the night's ceremony. The flame bobbed again, acknowledging her presence and luring her deeper inside.

As she stared steadily ahead, her eye was caught by an imbalance. She traced this to a thickening and bulking of the shadows in the pews to the right. And, floating a foot or so above this dark shape, she saw a shimmer of silver-white, highlighted by the candle flame. A bone-white, head-sized pool of light. She blinked and looked again. Was she seeing the full moon through a window she hadn't suspected was there? No. She reminded herself that she had already seen the full moon set that night in a fiery gold over the sheared wheat fields.

Adelaide drew in a shuddering breath. With a stab of relief, she remembered that the decapitated head of Saint Ethelbert was reckoned to be about the place on display somewhere. Could someone, in a fit of donnish humour, have positioned it at head level to surprise and entertain the visitor? She had no wish to shine her torch into a pair of empty eye sockets or a mouth sagging open in bony rictus grin.

Obeying the childhood rule that if you turned to look at the Devil you gave him leave to appear, she kept her gaze focussed on the altar. From the corner of her eye, she saw the patch of light begin to move. It advanced an inch or two towards her, seemingly of its own accord. It steadied then moved again, making a slight inclination in her direction. A formal bow? A nod? Was some ghastly spirit of this place introducing itself?

The remaining candle was already guttering with that last treacherous surge of brilliance which defies but inevitably precedes its extinction. A flash of golden warmth that threatened to plunge her into darkness.

Soft as a sigh, a voice lightly tinged with humour invited her inside.

CHAPTER 3

"Do come in! I say—you're an early bird! But what bird are you, I'm wondering? Raven or wren? Messenger from Heaven or the Other Place? You'll find me over here in the first row of the pews, to your right. Do excuse me if I don't get up. Not feeling too good, I'm afraid."

The voice, which had been suave and academic, degenerated into a gurgling cough.

The surprise of meeting not with the remains of a medieval saint but the flesh and blood presence of a man was swiftly followed by a stab of resentment. Was there no place in this city where you could be truly by yourself with your thoughts? Good manners chased away irritation and she managed to greet the sole occupant of the pews: a slumped, grey-cloaked figure. It would be rude, she thought, to shine torchlight in his eyes, so she kept it tactfully averted.

"How do you do, sir? And good morning to you!" Her voice had taken on its customary professional briskness. A sick elderly gent was something she knew how to react to. "But—no Raven, Harbinger of Death—that's just my shiny black cycling cape. Sorry! It must look a bit sinister in this light. I'll take it off." She proceeded to do that, revealing the sensible skirt, angora twin set and Hermès scarf of a lady doctor on duty. "Wren, perhaps? Bustling and cheerful? I'll settle for that! Adelaide Hartest. Doctor Hartest. If you're not feeling too sharp, perhaps I can help? Let's have a bit of light on things, shall we? I'm sure it would take me an age to find the electrics in here, they will hide the switches in cupboards, so I'll do the obvious."

A box of Swan Vestas and a bundle of tapers came neatly to hand on the altar and she proceeded to light four more fat wax candles.

"That's better! Now, tell me if I may be of help. My bag's just outside in my bike basket. I have everything from sticking plaster to a shot of morphine. Ambulance perhaps? If you're walking wounded, I can whistle up a taxi home. There's bound to be one waiting in the market place."

Further to reassure a potential patient, she pulled off her hat, shook out her hair and approached the motionless figure in the pews. He extended a trembling hand from the depths of his cloak, gave up the attempt at greeting and began to cough again. Adelaide's heart sank at the sight of a trace of blood trickling from the side of his mouth. Tuberculosis? In her London hospital posting she'd seen many cases of this killer disease. The stranger could well be in the last stages of consumption, poor fellow. What on earth was he doing here? Was he a leftover from last night's gloom-and-doom soirée? Deserted by the rest of the congregation?

She hurried to his side and captured the hand to take a pulse rate. The hair she had taken for silvery-grey in the candlelight was, she noted as she came closer, an ash-blond colour, the thick, shining hair of a young man. The old-fashioned garment she had assumed to be a Hallowe'en get-up or an opera cloak was, at close sight, a tweed overcoat slung about his shoulders. It was hard to guess his age from his features since they were twisted into a mask of pain, though the eyes were unclouded and sharp as he returned her quizzical gaze.

He steadied his breathing and managed a few more words, "Not raven. Not wren. It would appear I've been sent the services of a golden eagle. They used to release them over the forum at the funerals of Roman emperors, you know, to give those undeserving scallywags a lift up to heaven. Are you my soul bearer?" His expression of earnest enquiry thawed into amusement and Adelaide realised that she was looking at a very handsome man. "You'll be needing a strong pair of wings! My soul comes with heavy baggage, I'm afraid. Whatever you are and whoever sent you, you're welcome, my dear. At the last, it's good not to be facing the void alone."

"No one's facing a void, sir. I won't hear talk of voids! If this is consumption you're suffering from, we can do wonderful things for it these days . . ."

The brazen lie was accepted for the groundless but well-intentioned reassurance it was, with a knowing eye and an ironic twist of the mouth. "I'm not consumptive though I fear I am dying. Here, give me your hand."

He grasped her wrist and, with his remaining strength, began to draw it beneath the folds of his coat towards his heart.

It took all of her determination not to recoil from the touch of his cold fingers as they guided her unwilling hand deeper below the layer of tweed to slide over a silken waist-coat and, though she had never given voice to surprise and horror in the presence of a patient before in her life, Adelaide knew she would never come closer to uttering an expression of revulsion than at this moment. Her fingers had come to a halt against the handle of a knife sticking out of the man's body.

"Don't take hold of it!" he whispered urgently. "If you pull it out, you're like to drown both of us in a fountain of blood—though, of course, you must know that. Just be aware that it is there. I don't want you to handle the implement. The police will doubtless decide to test it for fingerprints—they're sharp fellows, our local plod—and I want them to be certain that they find only traces of the person responsible." He took three shallow breaths before he could go on. "Which is to say: my own prints. I have left no letter of confession behind—events outpaced me in the end—so I would be very grateful if you would hear this as my oral suicide statement. I wouldn't wish anyone else to be sought in connection, as they say." His voice was growing ever more uncertain but the urgency to communicate was unabated. Adelaide murmured encouragement, held him gently by the shoulders and leaned closer, doubting that he had the force to continue.

He took another painful breath and, eyes holding hers, started on his confession: "Mea culpa! My sin. My crime. Suicide is still held to be a crime, I think, in this benighted country of ours? Am I getting this right?"

She nodded her understanding.

"My God is my witness to this, his . . ."

The words stopped abruptly. A last flash of appeal from the ice-blue eyes before they closed and he was gone.

An unbearable moment. The body's gallant struggle for one more breath, the mind's impulse to make contact with another mind even on the verge of extinction—all human energy was gone in the fall of an eyelid. In a very unprofessional way, Adelaide tightened her grip on his shoulders to shake him back to life, unwilling to accept that the irreversible moment had come, desperate as ever, to stand toe to toe, fist to fist with Death and beat him away from his victim.

"I'LL BEAR WITNESS to that too, miss . . ."

The voice, shockingly loud in the sudden stillness, but measured and reassuring, came from behind her and to the left.

Risby took a hasty step back, seeing the doctor's reaction to his tap on the shoulder. She gasped and shuddered and turned terrified eyes on him.

"Oh sorry, I didn't mean to startle you!"

"Constable!" Adelaide regained her composure and gave him a shaky smile. "It's all right! I'm really pleased to see you! Don't be concerned—nothing else could startle me after this. When—how . . . ?"

"I followed you down here. Not the best place for a young lady to be, especially not at this time of year. Constable Risby of the Cambridge Police Force. You were so busy with the gentleman, you didn't hear me coming in. That's a thick carpet. Is he a gonner, doc?"

"He is, indeed, a gonner, Constable. A lucky gonner, too, you might say, with a doctor and a policeman dancing attendance in his last moments."

"Don't think lucky's the right word, poor bloke, if I correctly heard all that stuff about blood and fingerprints."

"Well, no. Not when you've got a knife handle sticking out of your chest and you're confessing to having put it there yourself. I think you'd better take a look under here, Constable."

"Thank you, miss." He turned his own flashlight on the scene. "Stabbed in the chest area. Dagger handle protruding. Five inches. Silver. I'll put that in my report. Do you recognise the deceased?"

"I've never seen him before. I've been away from Cambridge for years. I know no one outside the practice."

Risby stared more closely at the dead man. "I think I've seen him somewhere . . . that hair . . . around town perhaps, but I can't put a name to him. With a coat like that, he's definitely not a rough sleeper or one of the drunks who lounge about in the parks. Not that they would venture inside a church anyway. I wonder who he is."

"Are we supposed to search his pockets to find out? Or should we avoid disturbing the body? What on earth do we do next?"

After a moment of uncertainty, Risby's training took over. "What we do is—you nip along to your surgery and phone the nick. Um . . . police headquarters in St. Andrew's Street. I'll give you the number. It's well after six now. I should be clocking off but the super may be there already. This is definitely one for him to sort out. Tell him what happened and say I'll stay here by the body awaiting his orders. Can you do that, miss?"

"Ten minutes, Constable. And I'll come straight back to tell you what he says." She cast a glance at the features visible beneath the helmet. Thin, drawn and very young. "I say—will you be all right? I mean—in this spooky place, left alone with a dead body?"

"I worked the Midsummer Common Killings last year, miss," he offered cryptically. "Kind of you to ask though."

"Well, good luck! Crikey, what a night. Two corpses through my hands in as many hours!"

"Goes with the job, I suppose, miss," Risby commented, seemingly unsurprised. "Yours and mine." He shuffled uncomfortably, feeling a need to say something more, something to alleviate the pain and exhaustion that quenched her pretty features. "No one wants to die alone, even if they did bring it on themselves. The gentleman seemed pleased to know you were there, holding his hand at the last."

"Fat lot of use I was!"

"Oh, I don't know . . . I'd say you brought him the only comfort available to him in his situation." And, greatly daring, "Can't think of a nicer face to be looking at when the lights go out, miss. He did have a bit of luck there. Another few minutes and it could have been mine."

CHAPTER 4

"**S**uperintendent! Superintendent Hunnyton!"

The landlady knocked again on the door of the first floor set of rooms. The sound reverberated down the corridor and risked rousing all the inhabitants of the respectable Victorian boarding house, apart, it seemed, from the superintendent himself.

Mrs. Douglas sighed in exasperation at the continued silence from the CID man's quarters, and she looked anxiously along the row of closed doors. Police activity on the premises, no matter how legitimate, was bound to create a bad impression. She didn't want her paying-guest establishment to acquire an undeserved reputation for dawn raids by the constabulary. "I've got someone with me. Someone you ought to see," she hissed, all too aware of cocked ears behind doors, then added coaxingly, "Come on, Adam! Show a leg! You're wanted."

She opened the door an inch, put her ear to the crack and was rewarded with a cheery bellow, "Well, that's always nice to hear! But hang on a minute, Hannah, while I chuck these two floozies out. You'll have to wait your turn."

Thumping and banging and theatrical yawning went on for a minute or two and finally, clad in a brown velvet dressing gown, Hunnyton appeared, scratching and snuffling like a grizzly bear awakened in mid-sleep. He flung the door open and blinked out at the startled face and gangly frame of the uniformed constable waiting to see him. Alternately snorting and giggling, Hannah Douglas, duty done, was already making for the stairs.

"Ah! Good morning, young man! It's PC Risby, if I don't misremember? Won't you come in?" The voice was deep but warmed by a geniality at odds with the bear-like appearance. "Glad to see you survived the night, lad. I'm not normally at home to the police before breakfast. To what dire emergency do I owe the favour of your company this bright A.M.? I say—it is a bright A.M., isn't it? I haven't had time to peek outside."

"Sorry to bother you, sir. It's nearly seven and the sun's just up. Looks like we're in for another good day." Risby ran out of conversation and stood awkwardly, eyes riveted on the inspector's bare feet. It was kinder, he felt, not to look at the dishevelled hair, the unshaven chin and the blue eyes blinking away sleep.

"Well, as you're here, Risby, you might as well make yourself useful. Step inside. Go and draw the curtains back and let the day in while I put my socks on. And while I'm doing that, you can tell me why I awoke to a police knock-up instead of an arousing tickle from rosy-fingered Dawn."

The constable swallowed. To his embarrassment, he found his eyes had betrayed him by skittering beyond the open door to the tumbled bed, in dread of detecting the presence of a leftover tart flexing her fingers. Well, he'd fallen for that one! Better watch out. He reminded himself that this bloke was known to be a strange one. Oh, a cracker at the job—none better—but a teaser. Spoke in riddles.

Sometimes even in a foreign language. Thankful to have an excuse for turning his back on the superintendent, Risby crossed the room and set about attending to the curtains and heaving sash window panes up and down. "First things first, sir. Mrs. Douglas said as I was to be sure and tell you she's put the kettle on and the stove can cope with a fry-up in five minutes."

The superintendent grunted. "And the second thing? Which, if I'm not mistaken, will cancel out the first?"

"Ah, yes, sir. Immediate summons to the city centre. There's been an incident requiring your attention. Sorry about the breakfast." He paused for a moment, his eyes slipping dreamily out of focus. "And she had a basket of fresh mushrooms on the table . . ."

Hunnyton ran a concerned eye over the officer's scrawny limbs. Hardly any flesh on those bones. In these days of depression, the land was still far from being awash with milk and honey and pay was not good in the ranks. He guessed that the lad could count on a slice of bread and dripping at best when he got home to a cold stove after ten hours on the beat.

"I'm just coming off night duty," the young copper explained, aware of Hunnyton's appraisal. "Quiet shift considering it's been Hallowe'en. No hijinks on the river. No malarky of any sort. But, on my way back to the station to clock off, I encountered something a bit odd going on at All Hallows Church . . ."

"There's always something a bit odd going on at All Hallows," the superintendent commented dryly. "Especially after dark. It's an odd church. Not exclusively university, not civilian either. An uneasy mix of Town and Gown, I'd have said. The clientele don't welcome police intrusion into their devotions and idiosyncrasies. They're a law—possibly even a religion—unto themselves. So long as they don't draw too much attention we look the other way. The occasional black candle on the altar isn't going to trouble anyone. Certainly not God—if he's looking—and, more pertinently, not the Cambridge CID. Unless someone's defrocked the vicar and hung him from the flagpole, I don't want to hear about it."

The constable refused to be discouraged. "It's worse! And I wouldn't want to keep Doctor Hartest waiting about with a dead body in that creepy hole, sir . . ."

"Hang on, lad! You've missed a page! Doctor Hartest? Adelaide Hartest?" Without thinking the superintendent found himself miming abundant hair and generous curves and stopped himself in mid-gesture.

Too late. He had earned the constable's scorn. "Yes, sir. That Doctor Hartest. A very recognisable lady," he replied, delivering a prim rebuke.

"What in hell was she doing in the church at this hour?"

The superintendent's question was automatic and not directed particularly at the constable, but the reply came swiftly: "I didn't presume to enquire, sir. It's a free country. If the lady wishes to attend early morning mass it's no concern of the Cambridge Constabulary. Which doesn't stop me from casting a watchful eye, however."

"You've made your point!"

"She was just coming off duty. She's been on night shift this week—like me. A man has died, sir. Death witnessed by the doc who was on site attending to him at the time. She confirms the deceased died of a dagger blow to the heart or thereabouts." He used his hands to indicate the position of the fatal wound. "Difficult to be precise seeing as how the victim—if you can call him that—was sitting slumped over in a pew."

Hunnyton's reaction was all the constable could have hoped for: "Good God! Is she all right? What in hell was Adelaide doing getting mixed up with that louche bunch of scoundrels? Well come on lad! Spit it out! What's going on?"

"She's all right. No evidence of scoundrels in the vicinity, sir. In fact, no evidence of foul play. But suicide is what's been going on—and that's bad enough. I was in attendance in time to hear the gent's confession . . . No, sorry, sir, he's not been identified. Died in her arms before he could tell us." A frown and a hesitation followed then, wondering, "Funny, that . . . It's as though he expected us to know who he was. Anyhow . . . I didn't interfere with the body or the scene, sir. I stood guard and asked Miss Hartest to phone the station from her surgery. It was the nearest telephone. She nipped off to that house in Trumpington Street where she works—"

"And lives," supplied the superintendent. "She's got a set of rooms up on the third floor."

"Well, she got hold of Inspector Jukes, still on duty. He decided this was no case for uniform. He wanted it done discreetly, not on the phone with telephonists and landladies listening in, and said we ought to get you down there straight away, seeing as you are the one who handles these toffs. Erm . . . liaises with the upper classes, sir."

"A toff, eh? How do you know he was a toff, Risby, if you have no ID for him?"

"Posh voice, nice manners, fifty-quid coat . . . even the dagger hilt sticking out of him was silver. Hallmarked. I got the flashlight on it. It had one of those little lions stamped in the metal . . . you know . . ."

"Constable, you don't need to intrigue me with hall-marks! I don't care if the weapon was purveyed by Asprey of Bond Street or nicked from the local Woolworths' hard-ware counter. A dagger in some poor bugger's chest gets my attention, whoever put it there. We'll go straight round and you can fill me in on the way. Seems the best use of our time." Hunnyton noted the constable's expression of weary compliance and added, "Now listen, lad . . . Fancy a bit of overtime? An extra hour? I'll sign for it. Look—you've done a full shift and had no breakfast as yet. While I'm stirring about in the bathroom and getting dressed, I want you to go down to the kitchen and order up a cup of tea and a bacon buttie for two. Best white bread, not the gritty stuff I had yesterday. Oh, and tell Mrs. Douglas some fried mushrooms in there would be appreciated. Sharp's the word. We'll eat them as we go. Doctor Hartest is a tough young lady, but . . ."

"S'all right, guv! The inspector was sending a bobby or two straight round to help out. Orders to relieve the doctor and secure the scene. They should be there any minute now."

Risby was taking the weight off his feet in Mrs. Doug-las's armchair, halfway down his mug of tea and halfway through an account of the film he'd enjoyed at the Tivoli on Friday night, when Hunnyton joined him in the kitchen. Risby fell silent and passed an anxious eye over his boss. The governor's dark suit, college tie, shining city brogues and brushed hair made a favourable impression on the young policeman. The appearance of a ready-packed Gladstone bag—his "murder bag"—in his hand was a reassuring indication that he was taking the matter very seriously. Risby could not hold back a smile of approval.

"Will I do?" Hunnyton asked, noting this, and he turned sideways to strike the jaunty pose of a man in a knitting pattern, chin jutting, one hand on hip, the other holding an imaginary pipe.

Risby knew exactly what his mother's reaction would have been: "Fine figure of a man!" and she would have fluttered her eyelashes.

But it was Hannah Douglas who replied, in a voice quietly holding back amusement, "Oh, yes, you'll do, Adam. Whatever you've got in mind."

She turned quickly back to the kitchen table and handed them each a bacon sandwich wrapped in a brown paper grocer's bag. "Eating on the hoof!" she tutted. "You'll ruin your digestion. Now, don't let anyone we know catch you scoffing this in the street. I don't want people to think I'm running a whelk stall. This is Maids' Causeway, not the Market Place!"

THE CAMBRIDGE POLICE presence at the scene stepped forward and saluted as they approached the church. "Morning, sir. There's another constable with me. PC Batty's inside with the lady doctor and the deceased. We got here ten minutes ago."

"Good man, Hinton. Stay right where you are while I assess the damage. Come in with me, Risby."

They were greeted with less formality by a second PC, who was clearly glad to see them.

"Sir! She won't leave go of him!" He tried unsuccessfully to deliver his concern in a subdued tone. "I've tried to persuade her to let the body flop down sideways onto the bench, natural-like, but she seems to feel she's got to support him." Anxiously, in a whispered aside, he added, "And she keeps talking to him. An' him dead this last hour! That can't be right, can it?"

"Constable, I wouldn't like to be the one to explain the finer points of doctoring to Doctor Hartest. If you want to criticise her technique and don't mind having your ears torn off, you can give it a go."

Hunnyton hurried to the front of the church and put a firm hand on Adelaide's shoulder. "Well done, old girl!" he said. "You've made it! Now just let me and Constable Risby attend to the gentleman. We'll make him a bit more comfortable, shall we? You can let go now. We've got our hands on the tiller . . . Risby?"

Risby instantly came forward to grasp the body by the feet and, with Hunnyton at the shoulders, they had it laid out the length of the pew in a second.

"Adam! Thank God you could come! I don't know who this is. He didn't have time to tell me his name," Adelaide whispered. "There was so much I wanted to hear but all he could tell me was that he was unhappy with the state of his soul and he'd killed himself using the dagger you'll see still in position in his chest. We both heard his confession, Constable Risby and I. I think he was trying to say . . ."

"That's all right, Adelaide, love." Hunnyton surprised the constables by pulling the doc up off her knees, folding her in a hug and murmuring in her ear. "Shush, shush now! Risby filled me in on the way here. No need to say any more for the moment. We'll keep it for the statement, shall we?" He released her and handed her down into an adjacent pew.

"Now just sit there and hold still while I give this the once-over, will you? I'll be treating it as a suspicious death until we know otherwise—that's the routine—so you may find my procedures somewhat pernickety and time-consuming. I can assure you there's method and good sense behind all this palaver." He broke off to shout in exasperation, "Batty! Find the switches and let's have some light shed on this medieval scene!"

He took a pair of rubber gloves from his murder bag and handed a second pair to Risby before starting his check on the body. A search through the pockets of the greatcoat followed. As he removed articles of interest, Hunnyton named them one by one and Risby, who seemed well able to anticipate the detective's every move, made a list in his notebook and packed the items neatly in a folding paper carrier that Hunnyton produced from his bag.

"I hardly need to look in here," the superintendent admitted, drawing out a wallet. "I know this man's name." He looked inside and gave a confirmatory nod of the head. "Aidan Mountfitchet. Sir Aidan Mountfitchet I suppose I should say these days. Cambridge man. St. Benedict's, I remember. Before the war." He was silent for a moment, head bent, eyes turned away from his audience. "I'll have him taken down the road to Addenbrooke's. We'll use the hospital morgue. They have much better facilities than we have and they're right on the doorstep, so to speak. There'll be many people to inform . . . Not least, I'm afraid: Joe. He's not going to be pleased." He took off his gloves, coming to the end of his investigation. With a sharp gaze at Adelaide, he asked casually, "Is he with you? Joe?"

"What! With me? Of course not!" was the swift retort.

"At seven o'clock on a Tuesday morning in Cambridge? Why would he be? He's in London doing London things. Probably having a shave before catching a taxi to the Yard. I'm sure you're more familiar with his habits than I am."

Hunnyton smiled, seemingly pleased with the reaction he'd provoked. "Well, perhaps you could alert him? Go and ring him for me, will you?"

"Why should I? What's it got to do with Scotland Yard? The suicide of a Cambridge man in a Cambridge church?" She gave him a shrewd look. "The deceased would seem to have been an interesting man but surely of no concern to the Metropolitan Police? What's more, I would have thought . . ."

He stopped her flow of protest by putting a finger over her lips. "That'll do, Adelaide! Look—this here isn't a case for the Cambridge CID, I'm afraid. You'll have to take my word on it. I'll do the necessary for now but this is Joe's man. He'll soon come swanning in, taking over. I hope so! This is one wasps' nest I don't want falling on my head." In a louder, more official tone he added, "I'll be requiring a statement from you, Doctor Hartest, but it can wait until later this morning. You look done in. Why don't you go put your head down for an hour or two? I'll have you paged if need be."

"Very well. But while I still have my wits about me and can get my jaw to work—there's one more thing . . ." She stood and faced him formally to give emphasis to her words. "I should like to report a second death."

"Eh?" Hunnyton was startled into running a fearful eye over the pews he had unthinkingly assumed to be unoccupied by the living or the dead.

"No, not here. And, in fact, a first death if we take them

chronologically. It's been a busy night. I was on my way back from attending a patient—not one of mine, one of Doctor Easterby's. In Madingley village. The lady is dead and I don't believe her death resulted from natural causes or accident. I think her death was most probably premeditated and prepared. I mean to say—she was murdered. A Cambridge woman. In a Cambridge village. Would that qualify for your attention or will you be wanting Joe to look into that too?"

Hunnyton blinked and sighed. He did what she was beginning to expect from him: he returned a soft and joking response to her rudeness. "And things are done you'd not believe /At Madingley, on All Hallows' Eve! To misquote my favourite poet," he grumbled. "Rupert Brooke would rap me on the knuckles for that superfluous syllable in the second line."

And, wearily—"Get your notebook out again, Risby!"

CHAPTER 5

A delaide checked that she had Easterby's office to herself. "Operator, can you get me a London number, please? It's Flaxman 8891."

"Give Joe a ring for me, will you?" Hunnyton had asked. Wasn't that a little unprofessional? Adelaide could only guess the Cambridge police would be making all the correct approaches themselves, and if the superintendent assumed she had a special line through to the office of an assistant commissioner of Scotland Yard, he was mistaken. Sandilands was one of those active officers who refused to be desk-bound and was frequently out of reach of a telephone. But he had given her the number of his flat in Chelsea. If that proved fruitless she would have to leave a message.

As she waited through the beeps and buzzing for her connection, Adelaide tried to conjure up a picture of her friend Joe Sandilands. She saw him rarely and found it increasingly difficult to recall his features, let alone visualise his movements and surroundings. Of course he was probably on his way to the Yard in the back of a staff car, sliding through the heavy traffic on the Embankment or already sitting behind his grand desk on the third floor of his airy office overlooking the Thames. She pictured him: sleek, suave, smiling and ordering up a cup of Jamaican coffee in a

Worcester china cup to stiffen the sinews before sanctioning the assassination of a Communist Party cell boss or
an IRA terrorist. She probably exaggerated his powers;
arrest was more likely than clandestine killing. Though
you could never be sure with Joe. She had guessed at
official powers he never disclosed. Not even—perhaps
especially not—to her.

The responsibilities he was free to declare were impressive enough: authority over the Metropolitan Detective Force,
the Flying Squad and, his biggest headache, the Special
Branch. He jokingly referred to them as his "bunch of patriotic scoundrels in trench coats. Lively lads! The cream of the
detective force. Twenty-six languages among them, guns in
their armpits and fists like steam hammers. I try not to annoy
them!" He wore his power lightly, uniform sparingly, medals
hardly ever, but Adelaide remembered with a shudder that
she had had a glimpse early on in their acquaintance of the
man below the charming exterior. In the company of a dozen
other witnesses last summer, she'd watched helplessly as he
put in jeopardy—calculatedly, though not without pity—the
lives of a whole family and household in a bid to flush out
the killer in their ranks. Throughout the process, he'd main-
tained the righteous authority of an ancient prophet. A stern
and devious man whose company she would have fled had
she not, by that time, been completely in love with him.

She had thought to try his Chelsea flat first. Her preferred option. To her delight and relief, Joe picked up the
phone at once.

"Adelaide! How wonderful! But this is an hour and six
minutes before I expected to hear your voice telling that I'm
about to be made the happiest of men!" The jocular

confidence in his tone faded and he added, "I say—is everything all right?"

"Not really. I'm ringing from Doctor Easterby's office and he's likely to put in an appearance any minute now. Look, Joe, this is official business, not personal. I'll keep it short. Where are you? Not got one foot out of the door, umbrella in hand, have you?"

"No, no . . . I've been having breakfast for the last hour. You catch me slumped at the table, covered in crumbs . . . Ah, well, I made the mistake of opening up a book I've just bought for young Jackie before I wrap it up and post it to him. Bad move! I've been stuck here ever since, enraptured— smiling and snuffling by turns and much admiring the new illustrations . . . *The Wind in the Willows*. Do you know it? I'd marked a bit to read to you when you rang." He paused, hearing his voice rattling on as he sometimes did when he was nervously trying to stave off unpleasant or unexpected news. Having plunged in, he struck out further, "A not-very-subtle bit of heavy-duty persuasion—you won't be deceived!—but it so took me back to our first romantic outing on the Cam last summer . . . the picnic hamper, the willows, the ducks a-dabbling. Listen.

"Ratty is telling his friend the Mole that he doesn't talk about his river but he thinks about it all the time. And Mole says: 'Shall we run away tomorrow morning, quite early— *very* early—and go back to our dear old hole on the river?'"

Into the lengthening silence he murmured with the low Scottish roughness that always broke through and betrayed emotion or uncertainty, "That was your cue, Adelaide. Are you still there? I'm asking you for the umpteenth time to run away with me. Your river or mine? It needn't be tomorrow—today will do. Just say the words. There's only four: 'Joe, I'll marry you.'"

"Joe! For God's sake! Stuff the ducks! You weren't listening. I'm not ringing to give you my decision—I'm speaking on behalf of the Cambridge CID. There's been a death. Hunnyton says it's one you will need to work on personally. The dead man is what he called 'one of yours.' Whatever that means. So, yes, for quite the wrong reason, I'm saying get over to Cambridge as soon as you can. Sorry, Joe. No canoodling on the river this time, I'm afraid. You'll have to put 'Adelaide' away in your pending tray for a bit."

His recovery was instant. "The name of the dead man?"

"Aidan . . . um . . ."

"Mountfitchet?"

"That's right. Mountfitchet."

"I'll be down on the 10 A.M. from King's Cross. Tell Adam to send a car out to that godforsaken station, will you?"

The line went dead and the operator spoke in her plummy voice: "So sorry, madam. Communication seems to have been interrupted."

"You're not kidding, miss. Thanks anyway . . . No, don't bother to try to reconnect. The party I was calling is no longer available."

"AIDAN MOUNTFITCHET, WERE you saying?" The voice was tetchy and dismissive. "Did I hear correctly? I know a person of that name in Cambridge. He's not on our list, I believe."

Dr. Easterby had entered the room and was thoughtfully putting his overcoat and bowler onto the hatstand.

Adelaide was in his office, using his telephone. She could hardly resent him listening in to her conversation, but she was taken aback. "You don't need to be on our list to die," she said bluntly. Easterby always brought out the truculence of a rebellious schoolgirl in her. "I came upon him in his last moments and offered ... not sure whether it was first aid or last rites ... a friendly face at any rate. He committed suicide in All Hallows Church at some time in the night. Stabbed himself rather clumsily, hara-kiri style, and lingered in agony until I happened by. I made all the right communications with the law and Superintendent Hunnyton instructed me to call an assistant commissioner at Scotland Yard to come down and take over the case. You heard me passing on the message."

"Hara-kiri? The case? The Yard? Sounds as though someone's making a three-act melodrama out of it." And, shrewdly, "Suicide, you're saying? A rather, er, flamboyant exit, wouldn't you agree? At All Hallows on All Hallows'? A scenario, one might suppose, deliberately staged to titillate the headline writers of the local rag. Hmm ... Nothing like it since the Bursar of Bede's defenestrated himself and died, speared on the wine cellar railings, thirty years ago. The claret, as they said with ghoulish glee, flowed. Mmm ..." Schoolmasterly humour turned skittishly to schoolmasterly reprimand. "Suicides aren't usually heralded by a blast on the Metropolitan trumpet. A discreet enquiry and a death certificate signed by an understanding physician is all that's normally required. What are you not telling me, Doctor Hartest? Come now! You must account for your role in this Grand Guignol. Meddling again, eh?"

"Meddling? Yes. If that's what you'd call trying to save a stranger's life."

He sighed wearily. "The deceased may not be connected with our practice, but as you were there officiating in a medical capacity at the end, we must be to some extent called upon to accept a modicum of responsibility and provide the officers of the law with at least a statement. I insist on being kept informed. I shall need to know how to answer questions." Without pausing to hear a reply, he chuntered on, "I shall need also to hear your report on the legitimate business I entrusted to you last evening. I anticipate a favourable and preferably undramatic account of the outcome."

He checked the time swiftly through the back window of his gold half hunter and slipped it into a pocket of his waistcoat, smoothing down the chain that held it in place. He began to rock his considerable bulk backward and forward, heel to toe, in the annoying way he had of indicating that he was being kept waiting. His heavy ginger moustache bristled with impatience.

"Very well, Doctor Easterby. I'll start. And I'll stop when you've heard enough or when I drop from exhaustion, whichever is the sooner. Though, as I shall tell this story backward, you may like to stay with me until I reach the intriguing bit where I recount my adventures at the beginning of my shift. The bit where I try unsuccessfully to treat the female patient you sent me out to attend. The patient who, I do believe, was unlawfully killed by person or persons unknown—to me at least. You may have better information. If you have, you may want to order your thoughts—and your files—before Superintendent Hunnyton makes enquiries of you. Or the editor of the *Cambridge Gazette*."

～

ADELAIDE WOKE UP at her usual time and with the usual reason for waking after an all-night duty—at lunchtime with a raging hunger. She opened her eyes to see a mug of tea on her bedside table. Disoriented and sleepy, she reached out a forefinger to test the temperature. Hot. Someone had placed it there only a moment before. Mrs. Gidding? Phoebe Gidding, the daily cleaner, was a good-hearted woman and might well have struggled with the gas ring and put the kettle on, but she worked the early bedders' hours imposed by Easterby and had been on the point of leaving, her hat on, her duties done, as Adelaide made her way upstairs. And Easterby would never have hauled his bulk up three flights of stairs to the room of an unmarried woman even if the idea of indulging his youngest partner had occurred to him. She peered over the eiderdown and focussed on movement at the hearth.

Joe was on his knees, busy lighting the fire. Overcoat and black fedora had been abandoned over a chair and he was working in his shirtsleeves. Adelaide watched him silently. Capable hands assembled firelighters and a pyramid of sticks above them in the grate, followed by the remains of yesterday's half-consumed pieces of coke, the edifice topped off with fresh lumps of coal from the scuttle. He took a lighter from his pocket, clicked it and sat back on his heels to admire the enthusiastic rush of flames up the chimney.

"I thought you'd need a cheering blaze after the night you've had. And I can offer other comforts! No, nothing too intimate, sadly, our friend Hunnyton is about to descend on us any minute now. Though there's a kiss coming up the moment I can turn my attention from this. There, that's going nicely! I always find that if you put in twice the recommended number of firelighters, it takes hold at the first attempt. Starting a love affair or lighting a fire—give it all you have right from the off, I say. Oh, I called by Fitzbillies on the way here and got a bag of sticky buns, a couple of chocolate éclairs and some ham sandwiches. Or, seeing as it's really lunchtime, we could just nip out to the Eagle and have a pint and one of their steak and kidney pies."

"All of those, please! In any order—so long as the kiss comes before the sticky buns. So good to see you, Joe! Pass me my dressing gown, will you, and tell me how on earth you managed to get past Easterby. I had very strict instructions about the house rules concerning 'gentlemen callers' when he offered me these rooms."

"Well, I made him understand that I'm no gentleman! I pulled my fedora down, flourished my warrant card and threatened to arrest him for obstruction if he barred my way. He had at least half a dozen clients queuing for his attention in the waiting room so he'll be occupied for a while yet. Plenty of time for me to squeeze a confession out of you. Though I'll let you finish your tea first."

While Adelaide scuttled off down the corridor to the bathroom, modestly clutching an armful of clothes to prepare for the day, Joe looked about him, deciding his next contribution to domestic comfort. He sighed. She deserved better than this. The long, low-ceilinged room must once have accommodated a company of house servants, sleeping in ranks cheek by jowl, shivering in the winter and steaming in the summer under the leads. The single space was arranged for living, working and sleeping and managed to be at once too large and too small. Unsuitable, he reckoned, for a twenty-seven-year-old professional woman leading a gruelling and lonely life. Where were her comforts? He smiled to see Adelaide's efforts to make it her own. The pretty quilt on her bed was a patchwork one from her father's house, he guessed, the pictures on the walls an odd mixture of amateur—but good amateur—watercolours of the Suffolk coast and gallery prints of famous and favourite paintings. Among them was a daring Klimt featuring a red-haired woman who could have been Adelaide. Given to her by some admirer who'd noticed the similarity, no doubt, he thought with a stab of disapproval. He reminded himself that he knew very little about her and that a girl with her looks and character could not have reached her late twenties without attracting a good deal of attention.

But this was here and now—Joe's moment. He set about laying the kitchen table for two, grinding coffee beans and putting the cafetière on the stove. He arranged piles of cakes and sandwiches on a fresh chequered cloth and stood back to admire his work.

"Neat and quick and the crockery all lined up and on parade, handles to the right," Adelaide said appreciatively, appearing behind him. "Now there's a soldier's table! I shall expect a salute from the coffee pot."

THE DOCTOR WAS an excellent witness, Joe noted— not for the first time. Sitting opposite him at the table, cup in hand, she told her tale simply and concisely with no superfluous personal opinions or observations.

He had started her off with the disturbing encounter in All Hallows Church, realising that this was the third time she had given her story to the ear of authority. He decided to give out a little information in reward and at

the same time to divert her from offering polite condolences.

"Aidan? Yes. I know him. Rather well. Not a bosom
friend but a man I have known for some years and whom I
admire. I suppose I should now acknowledge his death and
say 'admired.' We fought in the War. He was always a rank
ahead of me."

Enough in that dry little speech to close off any expression of sentiment. Women knew better than to enquire into
a man's military history and relationships. Out there lay a
No-Woman's Land, fenced about by tradition. Adelaide
would spare him any effusions of sympathy for the loss of a
friend in the knowledge that he had spent almost two
decades hardening himself to death and disaster.

"I'm sorry. I'm sure you'll find a more suitable time to
honour his name. Forgive me; I only knew him for a few
minutes, but I can truly say that I mourn him and will for
quite some time."

She had meant it to sting. Joe tried again. "We were out
of touch for years—apart from occasional sightings at
reunions. His life took him on a very different course from
my own." He caught her expression and acknowledged that
he was being evasive. He gave an apologetic smile. "In fact,
the man was what my sergeant would call 'a right villain' at
times. Qualities that were valued in the front line—daring,
cunning and optimism—lose their currency in the sober
world back home. Aidan was ever the charming companion.
The best of educations: Radley and Cambridge, I think.
Witty, free-thinking, a womaniser, a teller of stories so fan-
tastical you might be excused for assuming they were not
true. Incredibly, on investigation, most of them turned out

to be nothing less than the truth and, sadly, some a great deal more. He was an instigator, a plotter, an activator, a joker ..."

"He sounds hell," Adelaide commented.

"You weren't seeing him at his best moment exactly," Joe pointed out, quick though inconsistent in defence of his friend.

"Quite. Though I have to admit some very special quality shone through in his last minutes of life. Gallantry? Humour? He must have been in agony—of body and soul— and yet he tried to put me at my ease ... take an interest ..." She looked away for a moment.

Joe smiled. "I'm glad his last encounter was with a pretty girl he could charm. There's no way he could have arranged it, but that's the kind of luck the old rogue had. Consistent to the last. But why he should have chosen that place, that night and that method of doing away with himself I have no idea."

"It's always the brightest-burning candles that gutter out first," Adelaide said sententiously. "According to my grandma. What was he doing in Cambridge, Joe? Adam said that he was 'your man.' Are you free to tell me why you had this fire-cracker on a lead? Or was it a noose you had about his neck?"

Once again, Adelaide had got straight to the nub of a problem. And she was a difficult girl to lie to.

"Noose, actually, is nearer the mark. He owed me a favour and I had a particularly unsavoury undercover job that needed doing here in Cambridge. Luckily, 'unsavoury'— for Aidan—would always be something of an attraction. He had the background, the status, and the reputation which qualified him for a spot of infiltration into a group of gentlemen whose activities risk becoming more than just a political and social scandal. They may constitute a Threat to the Realm."

Joe realised that Adelaide was laughing at him. "In Cambridge? Joe, can you be certain of that? Frisky dons running amok? Dirty deeds in deserted churches? What is the place coming to? You must write a letter to the editor of the local paper and warn him."

"There's more than debaggings and dunkings in the Cam going on, you know. Always has been. I'm talking about a convergence of wealth, privilege, intellect and evil that could gain momentum and harm society. Possibly even bring down the government."

Joe watched her bite back a saucy comment and then ask soberly, "And we are now to conclude that his involvement with this group may have led your friend to take his own life? That you, Joe, are holding yourself responsible for putting him into a lethal situation? Are you allowed to tell me who's at the heart of this conspiracy . . . nexus . . . whatever it is?"

"No. Not professionally. But—what the hell!—you're involved now, though I'll try to keep the effects to the minimum. I'm going to ask—with a declared personal interest: are you acquainted in any way with a bloke called Pertinax? Gregory Pertinax, baronet and all-round bad character? He holds an estate in Cambridgeshire, I understand . . . Adelaide?"

She had fallen uncharacteristically silent, staring at him in disbelief. Finally, "Yes, Joe," she said. "He's on our list, as Easterby would say. I've never met the man but I remember the name. Well, you would, wouldn't you? Once heard, never forgotten. Can it be real? I made a point of inspecting the practice's list of clients before I signed up for the partnership. It's a very impressive lineup, Joe. The old goat's surprisingly popular. Whenever I have the office to myself, I look through the records to familiarise myself with the cases. I've got as far as the letter 'S.' So, yes, I have seen Sir Gregory's case notes. No, I'm not allowed to reveal the contents to you without a court order or a gun to my head. I will only say that, aware of the scandalous information those notes contained—I mean, really dire—I was doubly on my guard yesterday evening when Doc Easterby sent me out to respond to a call for medical attention in the village of Madingley, just west of here. A house call was urgently required by the lord of the manor. I cycled out there and spent a hellish night at Madingley Court. Sir Gregory Pertinax's country seat."

TO HIDE HIS agitation and distress, though unconsciously betraying it, Joe leapt to his feet and went to poke energetically at the fire. There was no point in alarming the girl further by communicating his own fear, and he would do well to master his urge to hold her close and croon comforting nonsense in her ear. Staring into the flames, he composed his features, even managing a slight smile, and went back, wearing it, to join her at the table.

She looked at him intently. "Oh, dear! What a face! I really did have the bad experience I imagined I was having, then?"

"You're here now, safe and sane and within arm's reach, Adelaide. Nothing else matters. Well, it does, though . . . *Easterby* is going to hear from me. I shall require him to account for his criminally careless behaviour in sending a young woman out by herself at dead of night into the . . . lair of an infamous scallywag." Joe tried to keep his tone light. "You read the medical notes and that must have been warning enough! The man who composed those notes— Easterby—we must presume to have had full sight and intimate knowledge of the depths of the man's turpitude!"

"It's all right, Joe. I didn't even shake hands with Pertinax let alone get a sight of his turpitude. I was never granted an audience. *He* wasn't the patient. The patient was female. I only saw the butler who admitted me, the sick woman herself and a terrified little maid the whole time I was there.

"The call came through, unfortunately for me, right at the change of shifts—as far as we have shifts. You can't run a medical practice entirely by the clock. Doctor Jones, Easterby's second in command, had been on duty in the morning and was spending his afternoon on the golf course. Easterby was just coming to the end of his afternoon and looking forward to his evening meal and bridge party. I had arrived, bright-eyed and bushy-tailed and early for the night hours. Easterby was talking on the telephone when I went to his office to clock on. He waved me to a seat and sort of invited me into the conversation he was having. You know . . . lots of: 'so you're telling me that . . .' and, 'have I got this right?' and concluding with, 'I believe I may have the solution to your problem, Sir Gregory,' with a beaming smile at me. 'No, no. That's well understood. Many females actually prefer the attentions of a lady doctor. We have recently engaged the services of such a one to cover these occasions.'

"Well, the upshot was—I was despatched on my bike. Easterby doesn't trust a woman to drive his Bentley—and there is no practice car. I was told I was to attend the house-keeper, who was complaining of stomach pains."

"Stomach pains? Would that be a pressing concern? Serious enough to send someone out at night to treat it?"

"Clearly it was. You don't call out the doctor on the night shift lightly. Oh, not out of concern for us medics! Such a visit would be charged at a sum more than the price of an upper servant's wages for a month. And those symptoms can be a sign of a much more serious condition, so we would always be alert. I assumed the latter in the light of over-encouraging advice to me before starting out. It was a bit strange, Joe. Easterby usually waves me in and out without bothering to look up from his desk. On this occasion, he asked me to check the contents of my medical bag. 'Make sure you're armed with a bottle of Milk of Magnesia and a death certificate. That'll get you through.'

"He warned me to try at all costs to avoid summoning an ambulance. The party concerned was of high standing in the county and would want to avoid any display of emergency. They kept a Rolls-Royce, he told me, and an old game van and either would be perfectly capable of making a run in to Addenbrooke's depending on the condition of the patient, should it come to that. But that would be a last resort, he warned me. 'Discretion, Doctor Hartest!' he advised. 'Our client moves in the very highest circles. He is known to entertain members of the royal family as well as politicians and foreign gentlemen of ambassadorial rank.' Then, having frozen me with fear, he relaxed, probably realising he'd over-steered. This would turn out to be no more than a case of female hysteria, judging by the symptoms described, he said, suddenly offhand. The wretched female had probably had a difference of opinion with the butler and this was her way of showing her displeasure."

Adelaide smiled to see Joe's raised eyebrow, ignored it and carried on. "So I arrived, feeling very chirpy after my ride. Cycling is invigorating. Everybody does it in this town. There was a good road, a bright full moon, no one about. It only took me fifteen minutes. The house was easy to find. Almost in the centre of the village. Just off the road behind a wrought-iron fence and gate. Splendid house. I'd like to see it again in the daylight. By night, in moon shadow it looked a bit creepy. It's very old and has pediments, even a cheeky turret or two. But it's hardly the Castle of Otranto.

"The gate was standing open. I went in and parked my bike discreetly in the shrubbery out of sight of the lineup of very posh cars. There was a Hispano-Suiza, two Bentleys, a Dodge . . . others . . . I'm not very good at cars. There was definitely an evening do of some sort on. Most of the rooms were lit and the place was humming. Someone was playing jazz piano—rather well—women were laughing . . . My first thought was: what a rotten time for the housekeeper to come down with something nasty."

"Your second?"

"I hoped it wasn't anything catching! Housekeepers, like the cooks, have their fingers in every pie. The thought of a whole house party coming down with food poisoning was alarming."

"Who greeted you?"

"The butler, of course."

"Name of butler? Did you . . . ?"

"Yes, I asked him. I always do. He's Mr. Jennings."

"Mmm . . . like a thousand other butlers . . ."

"Herbert Jennings."

"Like a hundred others."

"That *would* be bad news! This one is cold, silent and hostile. Perfectly correct in everything he said and did—well trained, all right—but I didn't take a shine to him and he, clearly, would have been happier to admit me at the tradesmen's entrance. He accepted my card and studied it without comment, then he rang a bell. A young maid appeared, still wearing her afternoon uniform and looking rather dishevelled. He gave her her orders, 'Collins, this is Doctor Hartest here to see Mrs. Denton. You will take her to the housekeeper's room and stand by to fetch anything she needs in the way of equipment.'"

"Was there electric lighting out there in the country?" Joe thought to ask.

"Oh, yes. The corridors were all lit and the room—to the side and rear of the building, well away from the company rooms—was well-illuminated. A typical housekeeper's room. A combination of work and living space. Nothing unusual."

Adelaide frowned as she remembered the sight that had greeted her.

She cleared her throat and began again firmly. "The stench from the doorway was warning enough that something was terribly wrong. Unpleasant, but you learn to analyse and use the elements you detect in your diagnosis. Having something to work on takes the edge off . . . Sorry, Joe! I don't need to explain. You've encountered more than a few obnoxious stinks in your working life . . ."

He smiled and nodded. "These elements were . . . ?" he prompted.

"A cocktail of vomit, diarrhoea and sweat. With a musky, foreign undertone I couldn't at first identify because it was so out of place. The room had the usual layout of office section—desk and filing cabinets—in one half and living quarters in the other. Luckily, it also had the benefit of a small bathroom attached—housekeeper's perk, I suppose. We would never have managed otherwise. There was an armchair, a dining table and a bed. The patient was lying on the bed. Not in it. On top of the coverlet as though she'd collapsed there or been placed there. She was a woman somewhere in her late thirties, I guessed, with fair hair, marcel-waved but so messed about and damp with sweat it was hard to tell. She was bent into a hairpin, arms clasped around her abdomen, groaning and barely conscious."

"Was Jennings any help? Did he fill you in?"

Adelaide narrowed her eyes. "No! The fiend just turned on his heel and abandoned me with a muttered, 'Collins will be your runner . . . tell you anything you need to know . . .' Joe, there's sometimes a moment—less often, I'm glad to say—when, confronted by a problem of a gross nature, I still think, 'Help! Someone fetch the doctor!' Then I remember someone has and it's me. I roll my sleeves up and get on with it."

"Did she manage to communicate her problem? Did she speak to you?"

"No. She said not a word. She was aware of me. Aware that I was trying to help her as I went through the usual diagnostic procedure, but the pain and the struggle were draining her strength. I think she knew she was dying and was not able—or was afraid—to tell me how she came to be in such a terrible situation. When I moved into her orbit I caught again the smell I'd detected from the doorway. It was on her breath. Joe, she was breathing out a strong odour of garlic."

"Oh, Lord!" Joe muttered. "I feared as much."

Adelaide chewed her lip for a moment then went on, uncertainly, "Something else struck me as being very odd right from the start of my examination. I loosened her clothing—it was constricting her breathing—and took off her soiled outer layer. She was wearing a very smart dress—off the peg but good quality—from a London store. Fenwicks of Regent Street, according to the label. A dinner dress in magenta satin. Her underwear was equally good. Silk, not Celanese. Stockings silk too. Not the lisle or wool a house-keeper would wear."

"Her shoes? Were they on view?"

"Calf skin, high heels."

Joe pulled a face to indicate his puzzlement.

"I have a confession to make," Adelaide said without the slightest trace of guilt. "Just in case the lady was subject to an existing heart or gastric ulcer problem she'd been wanting to keep quiet from her employer, I found her bag and searched it. It's routine in an emergency. It can save hours of uncertainty if you find a neatly labelled box of prescription pills in a patient's pocket. No pills in there, on prescription or otherwise—just a pack of aspirins in amongst the female clutter of hankies, powder compact, cigarette case and such-like. But she did have a small bottle of her perfume. *Rêve de l'Orient.*"

"Dream of the East, eh? Sounds rather racy! . . . Never heard of it."

"I'm glad to hear that. I wouldn't like to think you knew

the kind of lady who uses it. Joe, this Mrs. Denton—who should have smelled of Yardley's Lavender and been dressed in sober skirt and blouse and lisle stockings—I've no idea who she was, but she wasn't the housekeeper."

CHAPTER 6

They heard it at the same moment: large feet pounding athletically up the stairs and then suddenly beginning to clatter where red wilton gave way to the uncarpeted treads that led to the third floor.

"Adam! Thank goodness!" was Adelaide's reaction.

"Hunnyton! Damn it!" was Joe's simultaneous outburst.

"Adam will take over all this nonsense now. Sorry, Joe! He's your friend, of course, but I really don't see why you have to concern yourself with his local affairs. You're far too grand for that. A suicide and the death of one female servant sixty miles from the capital? Bring on the honest copper! Let Adam deal with them both. Leave the police work on his desk where it ought to be, and we can spend the rest of the day together."

The superintendent came in, riding a bow wave of energy and bonhomie.

"Allo, allo, allo!" he said, affecting a music hall comic policeman's greeting. "Got your feet under the kitchen table at last, I see, Sandilands!"

Joe might have expected a formal, "Good afternoon, Commissioner. So glad you could come down so quickly, sir!" Why the lack of deference? Joe could only speculate. Showing off for Adelaide? Perhaps. She was herself direct and not one to stand on ceremony. But Joe thought the reason ran deeper. Perhaps the secret knowledge that you had held a superior officer's life in your rifle-sights but shot wide, and had held his career in your pocket but destroyed the evidence, granted you the right to indulge in a certain playful intimacy. Joe was not normally a stickler for ceremony, but he was irritated by the man's intrusion into his quiet moment with Adelaide.

"Superintendent Hunnyton," Joe said, nodding. He pointedly remained seated, officiating at the coffee pot. "So sorry to drag you from your investigation." His stiffness thawed swiftly in the face of Hunnyton's beaming geniality and outstretched hand. "Why don't you join us? I'm sure we can find space for your size twelves if we shuffle up a bit. May we offer you some coffee? I think I can squeeze another one out. Where are you in your day?"

"I'd rather have tea, please. Your kitchen tea will do me just fine, thanks, Adelaide."

"Milk, one sugar?" Adelaide reminded herself of the formula with a smile as she jumped to her feet and headed for the kettle.

"Oh . . . this is quite a spread I see before me! One or two of those sandwiches wouldn't come amiss to a bloke who's not had his lunch yet," Hunnyton said with a hopeful smile.

Joe filled him in with the brevity required of one copper by another as Hunnyton munched his way through the pile of sandwiches. The superintendent listened attentively, his only question being, "Have you got any mustard?"

"So, that's you up to speed with Adelaide's story, Hunnyton. We have a woman named Denton—who could well not be the housekeeper—discovered in her last hours of an agonising death, which could well not be natural. Over to you."

Hunnyton's voice took on a crisp, professional edge. "Right. Got it. You're going to tell us, Doc, that the lady was dying of some sort of poisoning? Let's eliminate the obvious first of all, shall we? A step you've already taken, Adelaide, I suspect. Forgive me for dotting the i's. Mushrooms? It's that time of year. Fungus fortnight. We've had two cases already this week. Poor folk who forage for whatever's edible in the fields fall victim. Cooks in posh country houses know their Puffballs from their Poison Pies or else they leave it to a greengrocer who does. But there's always the chance of a sneaky little Angel's Bonnet making its way into a pheasant casserole, I suppose."

"I did think to ask. The maid couldn't say. No such thing had been served up below stairs. They'd had scrag of mutton stew served at five o'clock before their evening duties began. But the gentry . . . well, they ate some strange muck, fish eggs and suchlike. Nobody else above or below had been taken ill as far as she knew."

"Mmm . . . Well, I'll tell you what the symptoms are saying to me—and I think to you, Doc. That smell of garlic . . . ? I don't suppose in the circs you had time to . . ."

"I did. The maid told me it couldn't be garlic. Cook wouldn't have it in the house. But it was strong on her breath."

"A clincher, then? Arsenical poisoning. Thought so." Hunnyton scratched a note in his book. "How very Victorian! We don't get so many of these since they got a handle on it. Still, cases do crop up. Usually as an accident rather than through evil intent. It's tasteless and odourless and generally appears in a white powder form looking for all the world like something you'd cook with." He shrugged. "Once the previous generation caught on to the fact that the wretched stuff was lethal, freely available for tuppence an ounce over the counter, and killing thousands of old ladies and unwanted spouses, they took steps to suppress it. Inadequate, belated and quite barmy steps in some cases. Hiding the stuff in a tin labelled SUGAR and stowing it away on the top shelf of the pantry isn't such a good idea in a hungry, underfed, food-hoarding country. I don't exaggerate! Only last month a bedder at St. Anthony's found a packet of white sugar hidden away from before the war—would you believe it?—in the bottom of the grandfather clock in the college pantry. Poor lass sneaked it home in her pinny and cooked up an apple crumble for her six children. Three of them survived. Did you get anything further out of the girl?"

"Very little. I'm sure she'd been told not to speak to me about the patient. She only gave me information about the garlic because I implied it might have a bearing on the illness. She was scared out of her wits, poor little soul! She can't have been more than fourteen."

"Was there anything more you could have done to save the sick woman?"

"No. All I could do—all anyone could have done—was offer nursing services of the most basic kind while murmuring useless reassurance. I gave her a painkiller. The one or two who have survived a bout say that the pain is unbelievably bad—like having a ball of fire in your insides. Even if she'd been taken off to hospital the outcome would have been the same. Death within hours."

"Why didn't you tell them to call for an ambulance? Shift the problem on?"

"I did. I sent the maid off with a written note as well as a spoken request to send for one at once."

"And?"

"She was away for half an hour and came back, totally confused, saying that she'd told the butler who'd refused to alert the master. Collins—I managed to establish that her first name was 'Daisy'—turned out to be one of those girls who can't be doing with reported speech. It tumbled out verbatim, even with changes of voice to convey Mr. Jennings's brusqueries. It was all, 'So I says . . . Then he says . . . Mardy old trout!' I'll summarise for you. The dinner was in full swing—a 'personage' was present and the master wanted no fuss. Jennings wasn't going to upset his master's appetite between courses. A soufflé was on its way up from the kitchens and you don't keep a soufflé waiting. They could manage without Mrs. Denton. In the maid's hearing, the butler went to the telephone in the hall and phoned the hospital. He waited about a bit then put the phone down."

Hunnyton raised an eyebrow and made another note.

"'No ambulances available tonight, Collins,' he told the maid. 'They're all out at an accident on the Huntingdon Road. And there's no one to drive her in. Chauffeur's got the night off. Tell the doctor she'll just have to stay at her post and do what she can for Mrs. Denton. I'm sure that's what Doctor Easterby would expect of her. Contain the situation. State the lady's in, she'd be a gonner anyway by the time they could get out here from Cambridge.'"

"I'll have that phone call checked. Pressure, Doc, did you detect?"

"No doubt about that! I was very scared. Adam, they were virtually holding me prisoner! I hesitate to say that because it sounds so shrill—like a line from a Bulldog Drummond thriller. You know ... *What are those fiends doing to Phyllis?*"

"Topping gel, Phyllis Drummond!" Hunnyton commented, selecting his alarmingly upper-class voice. "Quite the strider but—really—barely house-trained."

Joe knew what the man was doing: using humour to sidetrack a confession of weakness she would instantly regret and bounce her back onto the main line. "Jolly uncomfortable to have around—a girl who carries a gun in her reticule and a cosh in her knickers, I've always thought," Joe added lightly.

Adelaide smiled, undeceived. "Anyway—I can't be absolutely certain I was under restraint because, unlike Phyllis, I didn't test out the boundaries at Mystery Manor. I could have made a dash for my bike, I suppose, and that would have made them show their hand, but I would never have deserted my patient. They knew that. Duty was more effective than a pair of handcuffs. But that's not the worst of it!"

"Go on."

"Well, she died. It seemed to take forever. Poor woman! I made her last hours as comfortable as I could, but there wasn't much I could do. Finally, when she died in the middle of the night, I sent Daisy off with another message. There was a further time delay—for which I was quite grateful, in fact, as it gave me a chance to ... um ... do a bit of tidying up. Jennings appeared, still in his evening uniform. He checked she was dead and offered to countersign the death certificate.

"Under his stony gaze, I filled in the details as far as I knew them. 'Just the name will do,' he said. 'Clarice Denton. I haven't got her home address by heart. I'll enquire and fill it in later. Just leave it with me.'

"He checked the form and exploded when he saw that I'd filled in 'Cause of Death' as arsenical poisoning.

"'What's this rubbish?' he yelled. 'Do I have to get Doc Easterby up in the middle of the night and ask him why he sent us an idiot? You were told what to do! Stomach troubles. Now wrap that up in whatever technical terms you like, but do it! You've wasted enough of our time fannying about.' He tore up the form and sort of loomed over me. He didn't need to add, 'Or else!' He was truly frightening, Adam. No threat is somehow more chilling than an overdramatic suggestion of, 'or I'll break your bones and boil you up for soup.'"

"Indeed?" said Joe, with a sudden show of interest. "I'll try to remember that next time I have a hard case under the spotlight."

Adelaide was not to be mocked. She pushed on with her explanation. "The thing was, you clown, he left it to my imagination. My fevered brain and overwrought emotions were doing his work for him. I was very certain at that moment that I'd end up squashed on the road on the way back to town if I didn't comply. You can imagine—'Poor lady! Dreadful accident in the dark! That tight bend by the oak tree—how many victims has it claimed? Exhausted, of course, after her all-night vigil tending the sick. Such a tragedy!' So I complied. I gave him exactly what he expected."

"He wasn't suspicious?"

"Of course not. In his world women are obedient creatures. They exist to carry out his orders. I tried to show no fear. Just grumpy compliance. I even offered to add a note and a flourish of Latin to make it convincing. He watched every word I wrote over my shoulder as I filled in a fresh form."

"Glad you didn't resist," Joe murmured. "There are times when you have to retreat, gather your allies about you and reform the company. It worked for us on the Marne."

"Right," agreed Hunnyton, his face severe. "Buggers! And I'll tell you the next chapter, shall I? With the second certificate in their hands . . . what does it say, by the way, your revised version?"

"It says, *Cause of Death: Perforated Peptic Ulcer.* I added in explanation, *Delayed presentation resulted in subject being moribund on examination and too far gone to sustain operative treatment.* And, underneath, a bit of Latin to impress: *Hoc mendacium est. Non bene decessit.* And I signed it V. C. Hartest."

"Gawd!" Hunnyton spluttered. "You were chancing your arm, girl! *The above is a lie? She died a bad death?* You were confident this thug wouldn't be able to work it out?"

"Yes. He had to ask what 'moribund' meant as I wrote it, so I thought 'mendacium' would be beyond his ken. I dismissed the phrases as ritual doctors' Latin to confirm my bona fides with the coroner, the equivalent of swearing on the Bible."

"And what's this V. C. stand for—Violet Christabel? What have you been holding from us, Miss Adelaide?"

"Oh, I read that in an Alexandre Dumas novel, I think. It stands for *Vi Coactus.* 'By force constrained.' It's supposed to nullify a signature. 'I'm signing under duress.' I made the mistake of telling my brothers! They always used it when they signed their pocket money IOUs when we were children. I didn't take any notice of it then and I don't suppose anyone would now, but it made me feel better at that moment! In fact it still does! I didn't relish taking orders from that gorilla."

"I look forward to hearing that read out in a court of law," Joe muttered uneasily.

"It will never make it to a court of law," said Hunnyton. "As far as Clarice Denton is concerned, we must prepare ourselves for a bad outcome. A dead end, you might say. The moment he had that in his hand, he'd have rung his preferred undertaker and made arrangements for a swift and discreet burial—cremation, most likely. The room will have been scrubbed clean and all traces of the deceased removed. Fat chance of any suspicious coppers rootling about in there, helping themselves to incriminating evidence." He sighed. "I'm most awfully sorry, Adelaide, that you suffered as you did and all to no avail."

"Oh, come on, superintendent! Don't be such a weed! There's always something one can do. Do you really think I was going to stand by and let them get away with such bad behaviour? I suspected more or less what you've just surmised might happen as soon as she was dead . . . out would come the mops and buckets and all traces of the night's events would be removed." She went to pick up her medical bag and put it down carefully on a bench before opening it. "I was left to my own devices for long periods and I took the opportunity to remove some evidence."

"What? But—"

"I know. I know it would never stand up in court—break in continuity of evidence keeping, would you say in the trade?—but I thought it might just give the police an inkling, even if unofficial, of what was going on." She took two specimen bottles from the case. "Disgusting but useful! On the left: vomit. On the right: a blood sample."

Hunnyton waited until she had placed them back in her case before leaping up and enveloping her in a congratulatory hug, growling his approval.

Joe frowned. He wished Adelaide would discourage such displays. Hunnyton seemed to think his overtures had the unquestioning welcome of those of a soppy, great Labrador retriever—which he much resembled, Joe thought bitterly. He had the same trusting eyes, floppy fur and big feet of Adelaide's father's dogs. Instead of being confined to barracks in the rear of the house, like any other working dogs, that pair of hooligans had the run of the house and the freedom to welcome guests in their own all-overish way, heavy paws pinning even strangers to the wall to be covered in slobbering affection. Small wonder Adelaide seemed to feel at ease in Hunnyton's company.

"We can get those straight off for testing," Joe said. "We should have the answers back in a couple of days. Perhaps sooner, if Hunnyton has influence at the labs."

"Tell you what," Hunnyton said, smiling with triumph, "it's not the labs we need at this moment, it's what's her name—your cleaner, Adelaide."

"Mrs. Gidding?"

"Where does she keep her cleaning equipment? Soap, detergent, bottles of cleaning fluid?"

"In a cupboard on the landing just outside, but . . . Oh, got it! Ammonia? I'm sure she's got ammonia in there. A spot of it turns blue in the presence of arsenic—have I got

that right? I'll go and have a look. But hang on a minute.
You can take these away and do your chemistry somewhere
more suitable. I don't want to turn my bedroom into a stinks
lab. There's more—I've got another piece of evidence up my
sleeve."

She reached under her bed and pulled out a brown
envelope. "Not so much up my sleeve as down my front! I
smuggled this out of the death room under my jumper." She
tipped the envelope on its side and a blood-red piece of silk
slithered out onto the floor. "I cut the label and a surrounding inch or two of fabric out of the soiled dress. The store's
details are there and the name of the model. This dress was
'L'impératrice,' apparently. You can see why. It's just the sort
of decadent, figure-hugging style that Empress Josephine
would have worn while reclining on one of her gilt sofas. It's
a long shot, but Fenwicks may be able to help. It looked very
recent to me in style and wear. She may well have bought it
just last week for her trip down to the country."

"Expensive enough to have been paid for with a cheque.
And that, complete with name and banking details, might
well be moving slowly through the system. A system we can
tap into somewhere along the line." His smile even broader,
Hunnyton poked the fabric back into the envelope and
pocketed it.

"There are other questions you could ask but haven't
concerning that dress," Adelaide pointed out.

"Well, go on, then," Hunnyton encouraged. "What have
we missed?"

"That the woman, Mrs. Denton, was not of the working
classes. The clothes are smart and quite expensive. A housekeeper's wages wouldn't pay for such a dress even if she could

get up to London's West End to spend her money. But this type of dress isn't bought by the very rich either—those ladies would have designers' names on their labels: Worth, Dior, Chanel . . . So I don't imagine the lady was one of the guests that evening. Then there's a middling-upper class of woman who wants smart things but can't afford the top names. She might choose just such an off-the-peg dress at a West End store, then cut the label out and pretend it was haute couture."

"Blimey! And here was I, thinking I was an expert on the British class system!" Hunnyton exclaimed, mystified and exasperated. "I don't know the half of it! The twaddle that must get talked in women's cloakrooms! You show me your label and I'll show you mine . . . Joe and I don't have these problems. Now, explain: does this leave *anyone*—and if so, precisely *who*—to buy just such a dress in this shop and leave the label intact?"

"Middling well off, good fashion sense but not a slave to fashion. Independent minded. Someone like me. I can imagine myself choosing that model—if not that colour. Though I would never be invited to quite the right occasion to wear it. Ladies' Night at the Conservative Club? I'd cause a scandal and ruin my escort's reputation! It's lovely but . . . a bit flamboyant. It says: look at me! It's a show-off dress."

"Hang on a minute! How old did you guess Mrs. Denton to be?" Joe asked. "Housekeepers in my experience are formidable women of mature years."

"Thirties? Too young to have risen to the top of a household hierarchy. But too old to be wearing low-cut magenta silk. Too Hollywood starlet by half! Though perhaps, in health, she was a good-looking woman and could carry it off. Who can say? Marlene Dietrich gets away with it . . . And this lady took care of her appearance—her hair had been freshly marcelled, I'd guess by a skilled coiffeur in London. She had one or two pretty but flashy rings on her fingers—costume jewellery. No wedding ring. Her feet and hands were manicured and polished. Her armpits were shaved and . . ."

"Got it!" Joe exclaimed.

"Lord!" Adelaide sighed. "I thought you'd never get there! You made me work for that. I was wondering just how far and how deep I would have to go. And to think it was the armpits that did it! Should I be concerned that you know your way around the armpits of London, Joe?"

Joe grinned. "I don't, but I know an inspector who's not a complete innocent. He worked the Victoria Vice desk for years. I'll ring him at the Yard. You, Superintendent, can go off and have a cosy chat with the buyers at Fenwicks." Joe got to his feet, signalling that the session was over. "Oh— don't forget to take your blood and vomit away with you. The Met spends an afternoon investigating the death by suicide of a gentleman known to the Intelligence Services while the Local CID delves into a suspected murder—the two cases could well be connected. There, at last I've stated the obvious! Let's go our separate ways, as far as they are separate, but remain alert to the possibility that we may have to work closely together to solve our problems."

"As you say. I don't believe in coincidences either." Hunnyton turned to Adelaide, pocketing the bottles she was handing him. "Thank you, Adelaide, for all this. My chief inspector couldn't have done better! My mother couldn't have done better and she was a resourceful lady!" He hesitated for a moment, then, flashing a conciliatory glance back at Joe, "Look, I'm going to take it upon myself to issue a friendly warning. I say again: Sandilands and I mistrust coincidences. Two mishaps, seemingly related, merit our attention but no action. A third oddity has us checking that our guns are loaded. In this case we have Aidan Mountfitchet and Mrs. Denton dying in one night. Both victims known to Sir Gregory Pertinax. Intriguing enough. But linking them at the crime scenes? The doctor present at their deaths. Why you, Adelaide? I don't know. But I know I don't like it. I don't like Easterby. I don't like the tasks he piles on your shoulders, the hours he makes you work. I bet you haven't told Joe the half of it or he'd be carting you off back to London, kicking and screaming. Can you take some leave and go and stay with your father in Suffolk until Joe and I have sorted this out?"

"Leave? What leave? I've only just got started!"

Hunnyton failed to see the warning signals and plunged on, making plain his intention to beard Doctor Easterby in his consulting room before he left and tell him to organise a replacement for Adelaide on the coming night-time shift for the rest of the week. She was a material witness and would be expected to remain available at all times of day or night to respond to the needs of the CID officers enquiring into the case.

"Oh, Adam! Let me suggest a rephrasing of that last bit in the interest of preventing Easterby from instantly tipping me out onto the street. You're as fussy as my pa! Let me get your hat."

As Adelaide went to the door with the superintendent, Joe wondered, whilst keeping an eye on the consoling and reassuring pats that accompanied the farewell, if he could ever tell her the truth about Hunnyton. At least, for now, any animosity between the two men was easily—and by common consent—disguised as gallant rivalry of a lightly sexual nature in so far as Adelaide was concerned. She seemed to enjoy a warm relationship with both of them and, sensing without understanding the rivalry between them, she happily ascribed it to competition for her affection and was quite capable of mischievously playing one off against the other. He knew that. Could he—should he?—tell her that Hunnyton was probably anything but his friend and that in Joe's book—indeed, in Joe's recent experience—the friendly Cambridge copper figured as schemer, blackmailer and calculating killer?

CHAPTER 7

He'd remain silent, of course. Joe's role in Military Intelligence during the war and his present-day duty as nominal head of the Special Branch—with all the cooperation that involved with the various offices of the Secret Services—ensured that he spoke with care. He confided in no one, not even the woman he'd asked to marry him.

His association with Hunnyton had arisen through policing, which had thrown up a regrettable personal element. No, in honesty, it was the personal element that had led to his involvement in a double murder case. He'd been drawn in by both Hunnyton and the man he was stalking, each one attempting to use him. Joe had emerged battered and angry, feeling as though he'd gone ten rounds in a boxing ring where he'd been set to referee a bout between two heavyweights, only to discover that both fighters were prepared to knock *him* to the canvas as readily as their opponent. His fleet footwork had saved him but only by inches. He'd emerged with an uneasy mix of mistrust and admiration for the Cambridge man but any remaining interest in his affairs could, in no way, justify professional surveillance.

Assistance perhaps? The Metropolitan Police at Scotland Yard with their superior laboratory facilities and their high-grade, hand-picked detective force were frequently called on for assistance by their CID counterparts in the county forces around the land. No shame intended, none suffered in the exchange, in spite of the flames of competition which the local newspapers chose occasionally to ignite and feed. Joe thought he could leave the handling of the press to Hunnyton. Cambridge was his town. The case, whatever would prove to be the reality, would and should reflect his talent and the sooner Joe could extricate himself, the better. The man was working his way with faultless footwork to the top of his particular ladder. He'd end his days as chief constable for the county if he avoided blotting his copybook and ingratiated himself with the right people. With his advantages of character, there was every chance that he'd manage that; Joe had watched him charm, win over, reassure and facilitate, and had admired the skill. He was perfectly disarming. Who on this earth would ever aim a kick at a Labrador, after all?

And yet … and yet … Some sixth sense, buried so deep Joe would scarcely bring himself to acknowledge it, whispered coldly in his ear whenever he had dealings with Hunnyton that here was a man who had every right to rail against fate and hold a grudge against the gods. Joe was familiar with Freud and his theories and critical enough to dismiss half of them as bunkum. He knew that the deepest truths of men and their motives had been laid bare by much more ancient and wiser men. Homer had plumbed the depths in the *Odyssey*, Aeschylus had turned over stones in the *Oresteia*. The horrifying revelations of this three-part tragedy of family-destroying curses, murder and revenge, once understood and accepted, lurked forever in the darkest corner of the mind. But whenever the monster stirred and growled and threatened to break out, it could be called to

heel by the ancient playwright's hint that destiny might still
be overcome by human free will.

Adam Hunnyton was the living evidence of this eternal
ambiguity, Joe thought. A man anyone might have considered Destiny's Experiment, Fate's Plaything. He'd told Joe
his own story with disarming candour, slapping it down in
front of him for consumption along with steak pie and ale
in his London club. The illegitimate son of an aristocrat with
lands in Suffolk, he had had an unusual amount of good luck
for one born with his disadvantages. His maidservant mother
had been married off in double-quick time to the head horse-
man on the estate and the boy had taken his name. Taken
his freely-given affection also and his centuries-old knowledge of horses and farming tradition. All would have been
well and life would have bumped along in its familiar ruts
in the accepting country way, had not Adam grown up the
spitting image of his true father. The boy was also intelligent
and interested in the running of the estate that would never
be his. A characteristic largely lacking in the brace of younger
legitimate male offspring. The old man had favoured, though
never acknowledged, this by-blow, and had educated him
and sent him off to Trinity College in Cambridge on a poor
boy's scholarship to take a degree in economics. All in
preparation for his becoming steward to the estate. The war
intervened and, like many ambitious young men returning
from the battlefields, Adam had craved more excitement in
his life than was offered by crops, herds and account books.
With a degree and an officer's swagger stick in his pack, he'd
joined a police force depleted by the war and desperate to
employ and promote men of calibre. A happy and successful
man, you'd say. A man confident enough to raise a

two-fingered salute to the power that was alleged to prede-
termine future events.

No, Joe would not share his doubts or his information
about Hunnyton with Adelaide. His job was filthy enough
at times and getting filthier. He had no intention of passing
any of the suspicion and the fear on to her.

"Now kindly put Adam back in his box and come over
here and give me your attention, Adelaide." The door closed
behind the superintendent and Joe continued briskly, "You
know very well what we're going to find in the murky annals
of the Victoria Vice, I think. You've been exposed to some
pretty grimy aspects of London life in your career, I know
that. Yet I still have a strange compulsion to edit out some
aspects of my job when I talk to you. 'Not a suitable subject
to air in front of ladies . . .' and all that, I was taught. It's an
ingrained reaction, I'm afraid, like leaping to my feet when
a lady comes into or goes out of a room. You can only try to
re-school me."

This was invitation enough for Adelaide. "The woman
had been—possibly still was—a prostitute. That was clear
enough. There were signs that a doctor would note, but they
might well not be obvious to an uninitiated policeman. But
we must wait for the results of the official enquiries to be
certain. The puzzle is, Joe: Why was she dressed for dinner?
Who else was at that dinner table, making merry while one
of their number was writhing in her death agony, secreted
away in a room at the back of the house?"

"Funny sort of dinner party, I'd agree. If that's what
Pertinax was throwing. I don't believe it was. Not what *we'd*
call a dinner party—all RSVPs, place cards and polite conversation. Oh, I don't doubt that a fine meal was eaten and

fine wines consumed by guests who would appreciate them, guests with names known to the editor of *Tatler*, perhaps . . . or *Debrett* or the *Almanach de Gotha*."

"Probably sent up from Fortnum's in hampers," Adelaide said knowingly.

"Though the guests arrived by limousine, I understand." Joe grinned. "And *there* might lie a few clues for Hunnyton to get his teeth into. If he can find a talkative footman who knows his motorcars, he could establish some identities. I don't see Pertinax volunteering to hand us a guest list."

"And who delivered the tarts?"

"Ah! There we have it! Plural, Adelaide? We only have evidence of one woman of suspect provenance. You were allowed no sighting of the dinner guests."

"No. But I heard them. I told you: piano playing and laughter. But it struck me even then that there was something a bit off about it. The gaiety was . . . oh . . . open, raucous even. Public bar at the King's Head on a Saturday night rather than the Palm Court at the Dorchester. You know the way upper class women laugh, Joe? Hardly ever. If a laugh should escape them they smother it in a lace hanky. A musical trill is the loudest expression of amusement they permit. Now can you imagine me standing up in court and delivering a statement as snobbish as that? I'd sound like a complete idiot and alienate everyone on the jury."

"It would be interesting to discover what other women were involved, how many, how they got there and how far they travelled."

"A professional service?" Adelaide suggested bluntly. "By van? With lettering on the side? '*Bonnes Bouche*s, *Purveyors*

to the aristocracy of after-dinner entertainment. Est. 1892.' It
doesn't sound very like Cambridge to me."

"Oh, I don't know . . . University town . . . The young
male population vastly exceeds the female and lives in
monastic conditions, confined to their college fortresses by
iron railings, bulldogs and dinner gongs. The only females
they see are the master's elderly wife—from across a crowded
refectory—and their bedders—women chosen for their
maturity of years, their marital status and lack of allure. Some
colleges go so far as to specify that applicants for the position
of bed-maker to the young gentlemen must be 'of hideous
appearance.' There's bound to be a yearning, if not a demand,
for pretty girls."

"But no local supply of goods, Joe. And you'd need a
supply as well as a demand to make a market. Girls desperate enough to think that's a way out would catch a train to
London. They wouldn't risk their reputations in a local
involvement, would they?"

"Another question for Victoria Vice. Are they aware of a
travelling branch? Who is the Thomas Cook of extramural
entertainment for the gentry in the shires? Sounds unlikely
as I speak, but I shall ask. Carry on speculating, Adelaide."

"I'm thinking that perhaps after the brandy, the dinner
descended into an . . . orgy," Adelaide offered, round-eyed.
"Am I allowed to say 'orgy' or is that too rude?"

"Banquet degenerating into carousing of a drunken,
debauched and sexual nature?" Joe suggested in the shocked
tones of Lord Chief Justice Sir Archibald Bodkin. "Let's just
stick with 'orgy.' Makes me smile but it will have to do. I
can't think of any other word to express the depths of deprav-
ity I'm guessing at. Though, for me, it will always have rather

jolly schoolboy connotations derived from translations of no-doubt-expurgated Latin texts. A suggestion of Trimalchio's Feast about it. You know, the lavish binge put on by the nouveau-riche Roman freedman with more money than taste—goblets of Falernian wine served by beautiful boys, dishes of honeyed dormice and suckling pigs, obliging girl acrobats, guests eager for any sensuous experience their host can afford to offer them."

Adelaide shuddered. "Though one of the guests—did you know this, Joe?—who traditionally appeared at Roman orgies was a skeleton. A real skeleton at the dining table!"

"Imagine being put to recline on a couch opposite him!"

"When I was a student, I remember the tame lab skeleton they kept gathering dust in a corner disappeared. It reappeared two days later with a laurel wreath drooping on its brow and the fag-end of a Turkish cigarette clamped in its jaw. Someone had borrowed it for a dinner party."

"It's a rather grim reminder that Death is with us even in the midst of throbbing life. Our show-off friend Trimalchio followed the bony finger-wagging tradition but had the bad taste to acquire *his* skeleton, not from a bone merchant operating in a back street behind the Colosseum like any other Roman host, but from a silversmith—a piece specially cast for him. I wonder which style Pertinax favours? Off the peg or bespoke?"

"It's not amusing, Joe. Goings-on went on and Death paid a visit. I believe he was invited in. Women were abused in some way in that house last night."

"I'm sure that's the case. We have an enquiry to make without bias to sex or class," he agreed quickly. "You don't need to remind me."

Adelaide sighed with impatience. "I wasn't about to deliver a feminist lecture. You can dismantle those defences you seem to have erected—I wouldn't waste time preaching to the converted. I've met your sister . . ."

". . . and admired the work she's done on me over the years?"

"Joe, there's precious little energy left for stamping about defending my feminist position in the face of the ignorant, shell-backed males who seem to lord it over our society. I'm a pragmatist. I save my energies for fighting every day to patch up, clean up, heal and repair whenever I'm presented with a case of suffering, whether it's a woman, man or child who needs it."

"A noble sentiment. You'll hear no arguments from me."

"Not noble. No—naïve. It sounds, even to my ears, like childish idealism. At my age I should know better than to be showing shining eyes and a soft underbelly to the world. I ought by now to have grown a tough hide, a seen-it-all leer and an ability for accounting. But doctoring's my mainspring. It's hard to explain to anyone who's not experienced a vocation. It's not a profession I've chosen. It's a life that's chosen me. A job I was born equipped to do."

"Of course I understand! No need to be so lofty!" Joe's tone was more acerbic than he would have wished. No fool, he was interpreting this heavier-than-required statement as the prepared prologue to the phone call she had been sidetracked from making earlier in the day. Her answer to his simple question, "When will you marry me, Adelaide?"

For all sorts of reasons he had already anticipated, he rather thought his answer was to be: "Never."

"I understand because I could swear I also march to an

imposed rhythm. I can't say policing's in *my* blood stream
… an inherited compulsion. We're farmers and fighters and
everyone in my family thinks I'm nuts for taking on the job.
But there it is—I use my energies to combat injustice and
crime. I'm not going to negate the value of that by calling it
naïve. Present me with a corpse and it hangs around my neck
like the Ancient Mariner's albatross until I can find release
by identifying the killer."

"Whether the corpse is in another man's territory or
not?"

Joe pretended to take a moment to consider this. "Whoever. Wherever. For as long as it takes."

Adelaide looked at him steadily. "You're going to pay a
visit, aren't you? You're going out to Madingley to introduce
yourself to Sir Gregory Pertinax, the Host from Hell?"

"Not introduce myself. No. We're already known to each
other, Sir Gregory and I. We have an acquaintance in common. I shall be dropping by to say hello. I'm quite certain he
will not have forgotten our last meeting." He smiled and
murmured, "I shall just have to hope he's forgiven me. He
has a famous collection of paintings including one or two
gems by Watteau, and he invited me to call in and view them
whenever I was in the county. He'll be surprised to see me
taking him up on this but can hardly send me away."

"You risk muddying the water for Adam, don't you?"

"There's always that. But *I'll* run the risk, if risk there
be. I'll leave my visit until I hear that Hunnyton has done
his stuff and cleared off, then I'll dip my toe into whatever
polluted pond he's left behind. I was planning to spend some
of the afternoon at least doing what I was summoned here
to do and learn more about Aidan's death. I want to go back

with you to All Hallows. Along with the constable who helped you."

"PC Risby?"

"Yes. I've arranged with Hunnyton to release him for a reconstruction of the scene at three this afternoon. It begins to look as though the only way I can get you into church is to march you down the aisle under police escort. Pity!"

CHAPTER 8

"Mr. Barnes! Didn't I say I was not to be interrupted? I have a pile of mail to get through before lunch. I say again, old feller, I'm not to be interrupted. If the Prince of Wales has come a-calling, tell him to come back at tea-time."

Dorothy Despond gave her butler a smile so vivid and teasing he had the courage to persist. "I had understood your instructions, miss, and have, indeed, been following them scrupulously for the last two hours. But there is a gentleman trying to contact you as a matter of some urgency by means of the telephone. Mr. Joseph Sandilands of Scotland Yard presents his compliments and would . . ."

"Joe! Why didn't you say? Is he still there or have you cut him off?"

Dorothy was already on her way out of the morning room and did not see Barnes's sly smile or hear his, "I left the assistant commissioner dangling on the line, miss."

By the time she lifted the receiver in her father's study, her voice had recovered its usual blend of warmth and composure. "Joe, are you still there? How wonderful to hear from you! It must be six weeks since we last met . . . Arabella Coombes's ball, I seem to remember. You were looking radiant in a peacock blue cummerbund."

"Sadly no contact, Dorothy, but I've been following your progress through the English social calendar via the pages of *Mayfair Miscellany*. I like to keep a discreet eye on the villains in my patch. The 'Forthcoming Marriages' section of the *Telegraph* is likewise a pretty reliable guide to the exploits of the rich and scurrilous. But—I'm puzzled not to have read a single announcement of an engagement of yours to some unfortunate aristocrat since early September. I thought you must have gone off to Paris to bother the French."

"Do you imagine I would ever again dare to announce my matrimonial plans in the press for the world to see? You'd arrest the poor bloke I had in mind and stick him in jug! I've seen the way you operate."

"Come, come, Dorothy! The last fate worse than death I saved you from was sighted only last Tuesday playing an accordion for pennies in Trafalgar Square. At liberty. Unmasked, perhaps, but unjugged."

"Well, I haven't been to Paris. It was New York. Business."

"Good pickings?"

"I'll answer that when I've put them through the auction room. Nothing you can afford so don't get excited."

"There is something you might help me with though, Dorothy. Just a little matter . . ."

"There always is but it's never the right matter and it's never little. You want the low down on some poor chap?"

"Please! And as low as possible."

"Who is it this time?"

"Pertinax."

"Same to you!"

"It's a surname. Not a curse. Sir Gregory Pertinax of that ilk. If indeed that ilk exists . . . Where do you look for the territory of the Pertinaces? Are they a tribe? I've never come across it on map or in the telephone book."

"You won't. His number is ex-directory, though I can let you have it if you really want it. The name is borrowed or stolen, the lands bought, not inherited. By his grandfather, I believe. The founding father suffered from delusions of grandeur. His origins are obscure—eastern European like my own. Up towards Russia it's thought. A place where the skin is lily-white, the eyes of ice and the soul of steel . . ."

"Don't forget the red-hot temper, Dorothy."

"Or the ambition. This refugee made a lot of money (or arrived in London with his pockets already full) and treated himself to all the trappings."

"The first trapping being what he considered a good name."

"Well, a strong and imposing name at least. 'Good' is debatable. It belonged originally to a Roman emperor, I think. Long dead and in no position to dispute possession. I can't give you any dates. But Pertinax was the first of the five emperors in the year of the emperors, Sir Gregory told me when I enquired. I'd no idea what he was talking about."

"The knighthood . . . baronetcy . . . or whatever he has? The 'sir'—where does that come from?"

"It's an inheritable title. Something to do with suspenders or garters . . . I'm sure you know the one. Well worth having. Duly bought—something you could do in those days if you knew the right political pocket to stuff with your contribution—along with a house in the country, a mansion in London and a seat in the House of Westminster. Lavish parties, shooting, fishing and all that razzmatazz followed. Your rackety Prince Edward—the one before the present one—was a regular visitor."

"Can't say I blame him! Would you have wanted to spend a quiet evening at home with his mama?"

"When Pertinax died, those days were largely over. His son chose to lead a quiet life, becoming thoroughly English and doing what an English gent would do on inheriting a fortune in those spacious days before the war—he enjoyed it. The enjoyment consisted of spending quite a lot of his father's resources on—I'm delighted to say—art. He had an eye and used it at a time when pictures were going for a song or a glass of absinthe. He's rumoured to have done very well. So the Pertinax dynasty can't be all bad, I suppose. Gregory—Pertinax the Third, the one I introduced you to at the Snettishams' dinner party—continues in the art collecting tradition, which is why you found him paying court to me so busily—and then warned him off in your inimitable way."

"Awful cheek, Dorothy! I know you can look after yourself and I should have minded my own business . . ." he began.

Dorothy Despond was the daughter of a formidable and fashionable American art dealer, also a young lady wealthy in her own right. Beautiful, well-travelled and unfettered by any tradition she chose not to respect, Dorothy inevitably invited comment. She was held (by the London cognoscenti) variously to be a scandalous woman never encountered outside a nightclub, a bluestocking able to out-talk the president

of the Royal Society or a dangerously modern woman striding out under a banner in Pall Mall. The cognoscenti, on
this occasion, had it just about right. He could have added—
to the eligible gentlemen who elbowed themselves hopefully
into her orbit—a tease, a challenge and the answer to all
their prayers.

She was quiet for a moment and then said, "Not at all,
Joe. I was grateful for your intervention. I assumed at the
time you had some special knowledge of the man and were
concerned that he shouldn't get too close to me. It was the
only reason I could think of for your spilling a glass of claret
down his dress trousers . . . and then escorting him from the
room to help him change. What a nerve!"

"Least I could do to preserve the honour of a woman for
whom I have the highest regard. My wine-spilling hand is
eternally at your service, Dorothy. Besides there are a hundred other good reasons for putting Pertinax out of
circulation. The man's a menace."

"He's crossed swords with my father on occasion in the
sale room. Pa's opinion is much the same as yours."

"I wouldn't worry about his business deals. It's his personal life . . . his morals . . . Oh, dear! I can't say much and
what I am allowed to say will make me sound like a Dutch
uncle lecturing his wayward niece."

"It's okay, Joe. I've met men like that before—roving
hands under the tablecloth. That's always a bit of a clue. But
here at Castle Despond, it's not the ones who appear at the
front gate with a battering ram I have to defend myself from.
It's the sneaky smiling rogues who know where the sally port
is located that I need to keep an eye on."

Intrigued by the notion of Dorothy's sally port, Joe was

for a moment robbed of words. "Um ... well ..." He collected himself and rushed on, "Speaking as a sneaky, smiling rogue in search of a sally port—not yours, Dorothy—I was wondering if you'd mind awfully giving this chap a ring on my behalf. I'm seeking an entrée. I need to brazen my way into his house and speak to him. That's Madingley Court up here in Cambridgeshire. I'm here as the Met helping out the local CID with a possible murder case. But undercover, you understand. You find me installed in the station enjoying their hospitality, especially their phone line."

"Adam Hunnyton has a problem, has he? Oh dear! I wouldn't like to think of sweet Adam going a single round with ghastly Gregory! Glad you're there to help him, Joe. It takes a villain to catch a villain, I've always thought. I'll give you whatever I have but, being a female, I don't have the kind of information you may be looking for. The dirt that sticks kind."

"No, Dorothy, it's information you *do* have I'd like to pry from you. I've got a notebook here. It's his art collection I want to hear about. At the Snettishams—do you remember? Before the wine was spilled, I was trying unsuccessfully to divert him with my own smart-aleck arty remarks. He wasn't really listening as his attention was entirely on you. But he was distracted enough to mutter at one point—before he had to shuffle off to change his trousers—that if I was ever in the county I might like to see his collection ..."

"Oh! Yes! I remember! You mentioned ... was it Watteau? He has one or two good ones. Got it! Do you have a pencil in your hand? Right then, I'll mark your card. I'll tell you all I can remember about his collection, which may well be more than he knows himself. But take it with a pinch of salt, will you? The information comes from my father who is not an admirer, and he never forgives a man who beats him to a bargain at auction. With the exception of you, of course . . . You'd be surprised, and not a little embarrassed, to hear how often he tells the story of how he was done down at Christie's by your low cunning. A cunning that gets lower with every telling."

Joe scribbled down a fascinating mixture of inventory, deals, prices, opinions, suppositions and sale room scandal as it flowed from the girl's capacious memory.

Coming to the end of her information, she added, "Never forget, Joe, that in this game—and it is a game—your judgement of a picture is all that matters. I've heard you holding forth, and you can be very convincing. Wrong—but persuasive enough to make *me* think twice. You can do this. If you're going into the arena with Pertinax, all you need is bags of guile and a loaded Browning, and I know you have both."

She listened to Joe's rush of thanks with dismissive murmurs and finally, "But do understand that the man's a stinker. The Roman connection is unclear to me and probably just a laughable bit of arriviste posing, but I do remember one disturbing thing he told me—the motto of the Emperor Pertinax. It seemed important to him. The man sets some store by his family's adopted slogan, Joe. They've even had it put on their coat of arms apparently and that's a clear statement of who you want to be, what you want to achieve, I've always thought. This one's more like a battle cry. It's: *Militemus!*"

"'Let's be soldiers'? 'Let's go a-soldiering'?" Joe struggled with the translation. "I shall take that as 'Let's fight!'" He chortled his approval. "How pertinent of Pertinax! I'm sure I can oblige!"

"Fisticuffs at dawn? How exciting! Well, good luck! Remember to throw sand in his eyes. I'm here in London for the next two weeks if you should need a shield-bearer. Be sure to let me know how round two goes." Then, tentatively: "Joe . . . ?"

He sensed she was teetering on the edge of telling him to take care of himself. Womanly warnings were not what he needed or expected from Dorothy. Something a little more sinew-stiffening was required, and she'd already handed him what he wanted: the silken token of her favour to tuck in his breast pocket and the brisk, unsentimental words of a Spartan mother, unspoken yet suddenly coursing through his mind: "Come back *with* your shield or *on* it!" This was a good moment to break off the conversation and as lightly as possible.

"Mon ange! Dorothée, tu es mon ange!" Joe purred in the silken accent of Maurice Chevalier. "And you smell heavenly too! What *is* that perfume?"

"It's *Mitsou* . . . Oh! You clown!" She put the receiver back on the hook, giggling.

Which she always did when that policeman called, Mr. Barnes noted as he passed the open door.

THE SMILE FADED on Dorothy's lips and she picked up the telephone again and requested a Cambridge number.

"Gregory? Dorothy Despond here . . . No, this is business . . . Listen. I know I can always interest you in making a tidy sum for no effort at all . . . The Watteau—yes, *that* Watteau! Time to move it on, I recall your saying, I think? You remember the policeman who ruined your best ..." Dorothy held the telephone slightly away from her ear, riding out the storm of abuse that followed. "Have you finished? You know I don't listen to rude words and shouting, Gregory. Behave yourself! You may be able to do a deal with him ... Oh, come on! ... Candy from a baby ... No, no percentage necessary—just think of it as reparation for the trousers ..."

CHAPTER 9

Smiling, Joe put down the receiver of the telephone in Hunnyton's office in the police headquarters in St. Andrew's Street. He crossed Dorothy off his list and addressed himself to the next name. He picked up the receiver again immediately and asked the operator for another number.

The receptionist at the Garden House hotel greeted him with pleasure, real or feigned, but there was nothing feigned about his recollection that Joe had stayed with them on previous occasions over the summer. The suite he preferred—room 201—was remembered, declared immediately available and would be made ready for his instant occupation. And the assistant commissioner's assistant? The young lady in room 206? No, no. She would not be accompanying him on this occasion, but garage room for a motorcar would be welcome.

The next call secured the occupant for the garage space. Mr. Simpson of Simpson's Car Hire down Mill Road would be delighted to supply him with the Lagonda M45 that he'd hired in the summer. Would he be requiring the services of a chauffeur? Joe politely declined. Would he like it delivered? To the Garden House again? The keys would be left at the reception desk. No trouble at all, Commissioner. Out of season Cambridge, Joe thought with a smile of satisfaction. He wouldn't have wanted to be making these arrangements in the spring. He'd have been reduced to an attic room in Hunnyton's digs and a clapped-out Morris.

So, he had a motorcar and a room, comfortable and central, and—most importantly—a room with its own outside telephone line, a desk where he could do his work and enjoy a calming view over river and water meadow. He looked about him with disfavour at the conditions in which Hunnyton toiled. The Victorian exterior of the modestly sized building just south of the centre was ugly and unimposing. The Victorians might well be out of fashion, but they had built with swagger and solidity, sparing no expense on their public buildings—in every city but Cambridge, apparently. Here, centuries of elegant university architecture took centre stage, occupying the prime position of the old Roman site on the river Cam. The town itself, which both supplied and depended on the university, lapped deferentially about the gleaming classical colleges planted in their acres of green lawn.

Joe reckoned that if architecture was frozen music, as it was fashionable to say, the stock of domestic buildings in Cambridge called to mind the dirty-grey debris deposited by some ancient glacier, and it was playing a finger exercise. Out of tune. The town was built largely of cheap, off-white local brickwork and showed little sign of civic pride or civic investment. Rows of dingy terraced two-up, two-downers housing the college servants filled in the gaps left by the rich landowners, spreading eastwards from the river, while workshops, reeking chimneys and gasometers were pushed out to the marshy outskirts well out of sight of the white turrets and columns of Academe. Just like the *vicus*, the native village attached to a Roman fort, it served its purpose and knew its place. The Romans, Joe reckoned, had not gone away. They were still there in spirit, there in the centre of things. Quiet, manipulative, empowered, self-regulating. And some of the old buggers were still speaking Latin. No one was showing much concern for civil law enforcement if this building was the best they could do.

The ugliness of the façade was echoed in the interior. The ceiling of this cell of an office was high enough but the brick walls were painted in shiny green gloss paint. Easy to clean—had anyone tried—but depressing to the spirits. The floor was covered in brown linoleum and the furniture was turn of the century, between-two-styles heavy, dark wood, designed by someone who had paid a flying visit to Heals in the Tottenham Court Road and reckoned it could all be done more cheaply. The desk was clear of papers, sporting only the black Bakelite telephone, a pot of pens and a blotter. The filing cabinets around the room were closed, some locked. Joe tugged at the handle of the one marked P–S. Locked. He looked in vain for the pictures or posters Hunnyton might have put up to cover the bleak walls or express his own character. Nothing but a pin board carrying the week's roster. If this was where the boss operated, lord only knew what the actual lock-up cells looked like.

"Hunnyton, where do you have your being, man?" he asked himself.

In a spirit of mischief, he opened his briefcase and took out a sheet of paper. He'd torn the page from a recent copy of *Punch* magazine, intending to share the joke with Adelaide. She'd been following Joe's progress as advisor to Lord Trenchard as he'd struggled to convince the commissioner of the importance of requiring a certain level of educational

achievement as well as physical condition in the Metropolitan Force. For years he had been irritated by the attitude
of the press towards the average British policeman. Their
stereotypes were a bumbling, tubby, red-cheeked country
constable eternally ready to tug his forelock for the gentry,
or a rat-like city policeman as corrupt as the villains he was
paid to catch. Realistically, if sadly, Joe had to admit that,
although these pictures came from the extreme ends of the
spectrum, they rang a bell with the public and with their
concerned superiors. Now that he had the authority, Joe was
losing no time in working for improvements both to the
reality and the perception.

Successfully. The new educational standards for recruits
had been announced in Lord Trenchard's latest annual statement and had been duly lampooned by the *Punch* cartoonist.
But so gently lampooned that Joe took it as a complimentary
salute. A handsome uniformed young bobby in tip-top
physical condition, clearly fresh out of police college at
Hendon, was shown directing the traffic in the middle of
Oxford Street. His elegantly extended left arm was detain-
ing at his back a phalanx of apoplectic taxi and bus drivers
while the right hand held an open book which was absorb-
ing all his attention. The reader's eye swivelled eagerly to
read the title. *The Odes of Horace.*

Joe decided to sacrifice the page in the interest of frivol-
ity. He found four drawing pins and fixed it to the notice
board, adding his own heading along the top: "Dead Poet
Stops Traffic."

A SAMPLE OF the Cambridgeshire Constabulary was
waiting for Joe at the door of the ancient church of All

Hallows when he arrived five minutes before the given time. Joe scanned him. Smart in his constable's uniform, tall and gangly, with a brisk salute. Red eyes in a weary face . . . ah . . . this must be . . .

"PC Risby, sir. Pleased to welcome you to the scene of the stabbing. If you'd like to step inside?"

"Two things, Risby. First, call it the 'event' or the 'occurrence,' will you? Not the best English, but we never know what ears are wagging, especially in the centre of the city. Every tombstone could be concealing a gentleman of the press. We don't want to attract a crowd of ghouls. Secondly, I prefer to take a look about the exterior first. That way I have a framework for the interior occurrence. Walk around with me, will you, and give me the benefit of your local knowledge? Oh, and thirdly, you look shattered, man. Have you had any time to get your head down?"

"Sir! Yes, sir! No, sir. Well, not much. I conked out for four hours at home and got here early. I'm feeling fine. I always look like two yards of pump water, my ma says."

Joe walked around the church, establishing that there was the usual second door giving access to the vestry at the rear, where a path led through thick undergrowth that passed for a graveyard. This small wilderness backed on to a street Risby named for him as "Peas Hill."

"Peas?" Joe was intrigued. "Did they grow peas here or sell them? Do Cambridge folk have a particular fondness for peas?"

"Not the vegetable, sir," Risby corrected. "No. This was the old fish market. We used to use it every Friday back before the war. 'Peas' is a corruption of *piscis*—the Latin for fish. At least that's what we were told at school. The master was very keen on local history. A Cambridge man himself."

"Your school was . . . ?"

"The Old Grammar School. Very strict they were. But it suited me. I stayed on as long as was possible, but we couldn't afford the weekly charge after father died, however many hours my ma put in scrubbing. Still I'd done enough to get me into the police force."

"Are you enjoying it?"

"I like the exciting bits like last night. Most of the time it's dull routine. But it's always worthwhile in spite of the pay. Anyhow . . . the harder you pound the beat the faster and further up the ladder you go, my old ma's always telling me."

Joe was satisfied. Though he rarely gave one himself, he appreciated a straight answer and he was developing quite an affection for the lad's doughty mother. "I want to get my bearings and hear about the church before the vicar joins us. I've got him lined up for half past three. Tell me what happens around this church in the four quarters of the compass."

"You know what's to the west, sir—that's the alleyway down to King's Parade." Joe noted that the boy didn't need to wave his arms about and squint at the sky. He knew which way was up. "To the north is that row of private buildings— the second-hand bookshop and the rest down to the tea shop on the corner. There's student rooms on the floors over the commercial establishments. To the east you've got the Corn Exchange and the Guildhall leading to the Market Place where you'll find the Tivoli cinema, tobacconists . . . pubs . . . To the south there's university buildings—the Cavendish Laboratory." Joe could have sworn that the constable's back grew straighter as he added with pride, "The best in the world, they say, sir, Cambridge scientists."

"Well hooray for Cambridge!" said Adelaide, who'd approached them unheard as they stood, parting shrubbery and peering around gravestones. "Sorry I'm late! I heard your voices and took you for tourists. You'd forgotten I was coming, hadn't you? But looking at the place again from here in the daylight—are you thinking what I'm thinking, Joe? It's a sieve! Exits everywhere! I'm guessing Mr. Mountfitchet was probably not alone last night and whoever was with him could have made his way off into the town, any part of the town, unobserved. But what sort of man sneaks away, leaving a man dying an agonising death?"

"I'd agree. If anyone did share his last moments, he didn't wait about to render assistance or an explanation. He was off like a rabbit into a burrow. In any point of the compass."

"True, sir," Risby said. "But you could look at it from the other point of view. Ease of access from any street in the town centre. One moment you're walking innocently along to Bacon's for a packet of cigs, the next you've disappeared into the shrubbery. The door's always open. Anyone could have got in. Good meeting place. It's a hub." Encouraged by Joe's nod, the constable announced his conclusion: "We're looking at a control centre for nefarious activities. Plenty of those going on in Cambridge."

Joe looked at him shrewdly, sensing he was being pointed in a particular direction. "What sort of nefariousness do you have in mind, Constable, if that's a word?"

"There's student high jinks, sir. Raggings and de-baggings, dunkings and dog-fights, even bare-knuckle fights. A bunch of Bede's men rolled up the carpet and turned the aisle of this church into a skittle alley last St. George's Day. To nark the landlord of the Eagle who'd chucked them out for rowdiness. They nicked his skittles and set them up in front of the altar."

At Joe's gentle smile, Risby cast a glance at Adelaide, apologetic yet challenging. "But there's worse. Arrestable offences, sir."

"Which you wouldn't like to mention in the presence of a lady? Go ahead, Constable. The lady is a doctor. She's seen more of life in the raw than you or I."

Risby gulped. "I did say—meeting place. For rendez-vousing. Gentlemen coming together with like-minded gentlemen for purposes of . . ." He ran out of euphemisms.

Adelaide was shocked. "What! Blokes having it off with other blokes? Here? In church? I can't believe that!"

"Happens, miss. There's a sort of devil-may-care Hellfire Club on the loose. Different people every year. The members come and they go, the name changes, but the club goes on. We log all the changes to show we're alive and interested, but, really, sir, I think they're just working their way through a thesaurus." Risby sniffed his disapproval. "Gehenna, Hades, Hell Fire, Inferno, Tartarus . . . Every intake of Freshers, straight from their posh schools, eager to kick over the traces—they'll sign up for anything that sounds a bit racy."

"I think we'd better continue the conversation inside," Joe said. "Has a search of . . . ?"

"All done and dusted, sir. Superintendent Hunnyton's orders. Every last cigarette end bagged and labelled. Inside likewise. I switched the lights on already for you to take a look round."

"This is where he died, Joe." Adelaide led him to the

pew and outlined the events of the early morning with confirmatory nods from Risby. The kindly light streaming in
through the western window and the full illumination from
the electric bulbs banished any sense of mystery or horror
from the scene. They were in a dusty old church redolent of
wax candles and incense trapped in the folds of ancient
woven hangings.

"We'll have to wait for the postmortem results and the
report on the other forensic evidence, of course . . ." Joe
began.

"You're not easy with the suicide bit are you, Joe? I can
see why, but it couldn't be clearer. The constable and I heard
his confession. There was no one else around. What's worrying you?"

"Aidan just wasn't the kind of man who would kill himself," Joe said, and instantly pulled himself up short. "Lord!
The number of times I've heard *that* from a grieving friend
or relation!"

"You knew the gentleman, sir?" It wasn't Risby's place to
question an assistant commissioner of the Metropolitan
Police and, the question having escaped, he blushed and
waited for a reprimand. But the spirit of the man so recently
dead still lingered, bonding the three most closely linked
with his death. Joe's response was immediate and subdued.

"Yes. For many years. Since our army days," Joe said.
"Not intimately, but we were always pleased to see each other.
Always kept in touch. He enjoyed everything he did, whether
it was legal or illegal. He had many friends, laughed a great
deal, drank a lot but never too much. He was well travelled.
A historian. He was writing a book about Russia, where he
spent some time during the revolution, I understand. The

military exploits of Peter the Great." He paused for a moment. "And he was, I'd have sworn, glad to be doing some research for me on the quiet, Risby. Keep that under your helmet. It was all a bit of a game for him but, old soldier that he was, he was giving it his best and relishing it. You don't kill yourself if you have an immediate goal in life or if—as in Aidan's case—there's one more book to write, a pretty girl to meet, a picture to admire, a symphony to hear." Joe heard his own voice beginning to sound plaintive and he fell silent.

"That's well understood," Adelaide said, sensing his distress. "You can be perfectly sound in mind and still kill yourself. Have you thought, Joe, that he may well have been *physically* ill?"

"Ill? He'd have fought back. Aidan would have cursed death and gone down fighting."

"I was thinking of an illness that might have been over-whelming . . . not to be tolerated . . . one which he . . ."

"Wouldn't have cared to tell his mum about?" Risby finished for her.

"That's right. A venereal disease of one sort or another. I've come across cases. Men who couldn't bear the shame of their family hearing of it."

"It's certainly possible. Let's leave it there. No need to speculate—I asked for a full autopsy so we'll know more tomorrow. Now, let's do some serious detecting! Risby—how many candles were alight when you came in?"

"One," they said together.

"The one at the end. It was on its last legs and had lasted longer than the others on the altar because it was in a more sheltered place, out of the draughts," Adelaide remembered.

"But when were they lit, I wonder?" Joe went to the altar,

picked up one of the unused ones, weighed it in his hand and interrogated it.

"Ah! I can tell you that, sir. Eight o'clock the previous evening or thereabouts."

"How do you know that?"

"I got here early. Mrs. Peterson, the daily, was in to do her chores. She usually comes in the morning but the super had told her to hold off and leave everything as it was so she was just wandering about grumbling. I caught her and asked her about the candles. She unpacks them when they arrive and cleans up the altar after services. She told me the thin ones last the length of a service—five hours—and these fat ones last ten hours if they're in glass jars. They can get two evenings' use out of them if someone remembers to blow them out. They're always from the same church supplier and consistent in performance. The vicar lights them before he gets going. So there would have been a service starting at eight o'clock last evening."

"Oh!" Adelaide exclaimed and fished about in her pocket. "I meant to give this to Adam! I took it off the front door when I arrived last night. It was pinned up with a couple of drawing pins."

Joe took the postcard from her and read it, frowning.

"Good Lord! What an evening's entertainment! What is all this nonsense? Distrust? Doubt? Depression? Death? You can add another 'D' to your list; Aidan would only have attended such a piece of indulgence under Duress."

"After suffering a symposium on the black humours, anyone would be feeling suicidal . . . or murderous. You must ask the reverend who else was at the grisly meeting, Joe. They were long gone by the time I arrived."

"Have you met the reverend?"

"Never."

"Well now's your chance. I think I heard the back door opening. Ah! Reverend Sweeting? Right on time! Good of you to see us. Distressing time for you . . ."

Feeling like an invading Viking caught by the abbot enjoying a day's pillaging in Lindisfarne, Joe realised he was striding about, putting the vicar at ease in his own preserve, and he stood still and lowered his voice. He introduced the three of them to the man who had slipped in through the vestry door. Making a modest entrance was a difficult trick to pull off when you were wearing the full regalia of a Church of England vicar, but Sweeting managed it. Joe had expected the day-to-day clericals—dark suit and the obligatory dog collar—but the vicar had gone the whole hog. Floor-sweeping black cassock with frothy white surplice and over and around his neck a richly embroidered stole of purple silk. He should have been an impressive figure, but the man inside the costume wore it awkwardly, like an understudy thrust without warning into the part of St. Thomas à Becket. The weight of the costume seemed too great for the man's narrow shoulders.

He must have caught Joe's speculative eye on him, as he smiled, shook out a fold of his surplice, fingered his pectoral cross and explained, "You will judge me overdressed for the occasion, gentlemen . . . madam. I thought in the circumstances I'd push the boat out and conduct a special service this evening. The vestments are demanded by the solemnity of the occasion. However you look at it, Commissioner, a sinful crime was committed here in these holy surroundings last night and a ceremony of cleansing is called for to rid us of the pollution and render God's house fit for His presence once more. All lingering traces of maleficent spirits must be swept away and directed to the place of evil and torment they themselves have chosen."

It was Adelaide's voice, calm and cool, that answered, "Well. Perhaps when you've finished your holy housework, Father, you'll find time to say a prayer for the soul of the much-lamented Aidan Mountfitchet, who was taken from us last night. I'm quite certain that God is even now enjoying his company. They met as good friends, forgiveness for sins asked for and granted. Pity you couldn't be there at the last to give him a leg up, Reverend. But he seemed to know the way."

Constable Risby, with impeccable sense of propriety, walked quietly away to take up a sentinel's stance at the door, and Joe was left to put himself bodily between two instantly formed and implacable enemies. The church might have witnessed dog, cock or bare-knuckle fights in its day but they were insignificant compared with the potentially volcanic spiritual tussle about to break out.

"Ah well! That's Aidan for you!" Joe heard his own voice, jovial, a touch desperate, out of place. "First class in orienteering with the Scouts, don't you know! If there was a way, he'd find it!"

They both turned to stare at him.

"Unfortunately, in these days of medical ubiquity, *souls* of the dying are frequently reduced to receiving improper and unskilled guidance in their last moments on earth," Sweeting said with waspish regret. He actually wrung his hands, Joe noted. He didn't believe he'd ever encountered that gesture before in real life. Either the man was drawing attention to a magnificent amethyst ring he was wearing or he was nervously playing a part. A full check on Sweeting and his curriculum vitae had moved to the top of his list.

"Lucky old souls!" Adelaide drawled. "They always know a doctor is on their side, fighting to keep them alive and not prepared to consign them to the flames, even the imaginary flames of an imagined hell."

"It's Aidan's last ten hours on earth I'm keen to get in focus," Joe said hurriedly. "He spent them here under your roof, so to speak, Sweeting. At eight o'clock the candles were lit for your symposium—was that the word you used?—on the darker emotions. We've lived through turbulent times and, in these enlightened days, many of us have a deeper understanding of the human condition. Men are learning to un-stiffen their upper lips and lay bare their souls in a way they would never have contemplated before the war." They were at least listening to him as he burbled his calming platitudes. "I would be surprised to hear that my friend was entertaining such doubts but you never know. Tell me, Sweeting—was he present from the beginning of the session?"

"Yes, he was. Everyone appeared on time."

"Everyone? How many would that be?"

After a slight pause, he replied: "Eight."

"I shall need to know their names."

"There were two groups of four. It was well balanced."

"Balanced by you? I note that your card specifies 'By invitation only.'"

"Naturally. Personal matters are not discussed in front of an audience of any rag-tag-and-bobtails! The members of this particular group were sympathetically chosen. By me."

"But you let in a man you considered a sinner?" Adelaide was keeping up the pressure and avoiding Joe's narrowed eyes.

Sweeting smirked. "Of course! A group of eight happy, virtuous believers—now where would you find those? A mixture is the best composition for a helpful debate. Mountfitchet played the Devil's Advocate quite admirably."

"You're saying you used Mountfitchet as an awful warning?"

"He was that indeed. But a good speaker. Trained, I'd have said, in argument and rhetoric. Equipped also with a certain devilish wit and charm. Laughter, I've always suspected, is an unacknowledged tool of Satan. If you wish to seduce, lubricate your Primrose Path with laughter."

"Thanks. I'll try to remember that," Adelaide said brusquely. "Now what about answering the commissioner's question?"

"You were about to give me the names of the other seven guests . . ." Joe prompted.

"No. I was not. This . . . doctor . . . will tell you that the consulting room is sacrosanct, as is the lawyer's office, the banker's books and my church. I cannot be made to give up the details of my congregation." The blue eyes flashed with a martyr's fervour, inviting further intimidation.

"That is, indeed, your privilege, Reverend, and the fact that you choose to invoke it speaks volumes," Joe said dryly and turned to Adelaide. "I fear they were not gathered here to knit socks for Albanian orphans," he confided.

Turning once again to Sweeting, he extended a hand in farewell. "We'll continue this conversation at a later time when I have at my fingertips the results of the tests on the forensic evidence these premises have thrown up. Copious and fascinating is my first assessment. I look forward to sharing the revelations with you. Well, we'll say goodbye and leave you to your ecclesiastical charring, sir."

At the gate, Joe turned to Risby. "I'm going to ask the superintendent to release you from duties to accompany me about the town for the next two days at least. Do you see any problems with that arrangement? Any objections?"

As the constable mumbled his astonishment and willingness, Joe asked further, "Look, this is a long shot, but are you able, by any chance, to drive a motor vehicle?"

FROM HIS SUITE at the Garden House, Joe settled in to make several more telephone calls. His first was to the Mill Road garage. "Simpson, do I remember you offering me the use of a chauffeur along with the Lagonda? You did? Good. Is that still available? Well I have rather a particular request . . ."

CHAPTER 10

Joe returned to his hotel room the next morning following a solitary walk along the towpath to Grantchester. The beauty of the light slanting down from the intense blue sky and through the leaves to the green gloom of the river below seemed to reduce his problems, easing them into to a more accurate perspective. His thoughts were calmed. Thoughts that always returned to Adelaide. Why would any woman in her situation give up this peaceful place and worthwhile life to join him in the smoke and bustle of London, was the question he repeatedly put to himself.

Adelaide had given him a blatantly invented excuse for not seeing him the previous evening in spite of Hunnyton's skill in persuading Easterby to cancel her evening duties. A locum had been engaged and the shifts redistributed, though Adelaide had insisted on taking one of the daytime duties herself. A duty she could on no account neglect, she'd said. Joe had just caught her swift, dismissive explanations, "Work for the public good . . . children's philanthropic clinic . . . no business of yours, Joe . . ."

Her edginess had reduced him to silent acceptance. The girl probably needed a good night's sleep, and she was sensitive enough to want to avoid distracting him from what was developing into a complex and puzzling case, Joe told himself without conviction. Though an internal voice whispered back that he was deceiving himself and that she was still in turmoil when it came to a consideration of her future with him, with all its drawbacks. Professional women were expected to give up their careers on marriage; snaring a husband from among the much-reduced male population was quite a coup, the crowning moment of their lives. But not all women reasoned in this way. Increasingly, women were forging ahead and enjoying jobs previously undertaken only by men. They were insisting on retaining them against much social pressure.

Who made the rules? Could a lady doctor be a married woman? Joe had never thought to ask. It seemed to him that this might be the one profession where the married state could appear as a real advantage. The experience of marriage doubled a woman's knowledge, surely, and therefore her value to society?

On returning, he had a bath and put on his best Savile Row suit, choosing a lavender silk tie to spark it up. Rather daring. Twice thrown away by his sister—"It makes you look like a gigolo, darling!"—and twice rescued by him. He decided that this was its moment. If he was to play the role of art connoisseur, he ought perhaps to signal his London sophistication. Out of habit, he checked that his Browning was ready to go. Worryingly, he'd been given clearance by his superiors—indeed, urgently advised—to carry his gun when confronting Pertinax. Any resulting messiness would be instantly swept up, he'd been reassured. "National emergency" had been invoked, but no one had located the line between emergency and civil war.

Too late now to put in for one of those nifty little Italian pistols. He weighed the Browning in his hand, suddenly seeing the disadvantages. Though well-maintained with a soldier's precision, it was hardly ever put to use and it looked bulky and dated. Too big to conceal about his person, it would be spotted by anyone with the slightest suspicion of his intentions. In his briefcase, then? By the time he'd opened the straps, scrabbled about, taken the safety off, aimed and fired, his target would be halfway down the drive or beaning him with a poker. Anyway, he was just playing a part, planning an innocent cup of coffee with a like-minded art admirer. Watteaus and lavender ties jarred with the blunt ugliness of the revolver. He settled down to read again the art crib sheet dictated by Dorothy over the phone, his mood lightened by the memory of her eager complicity.

"It's a game, Joe," she'd said to encourage him. If only it were!

The views of the small committee convened to brief him in Whitehall some five weeks before had been quite another. Joe winced as he remembered the way he'd been set up, handed a tin opener and a can of worms.

JOE HAD GRUMBLED to his secretary on being handed the summons.

"Sir, you can't wriggle out. It would appear to be a national emergency," Miss Sturdy, interpreting the Top Secret heading and the eyes only cast list, had told him firmly.

"Then it's the fourth one this month. The first three ran happily into the sand. So will this one."

"The security service will be present," she added cunningly. "You'll want to hold your end up."

"Huh! Fine security service that announces its appointments two days in advance! They'll be taking out an advertisement on the front page of *The Times* next. How many people have seen this?"

"Oh, I think it's very civilised to let us know, sir. Gives everyone a chance to reschedule. I'll put the Wormwood Scrubs visit back a week, shall I?"

FOUR PAIRS OF eyes had turned to study him as he entered the room set aside for the meeting at the Foreign Office, expressions ranging from the warmly welcoming to the coldly suspicious.

At the table had been the reassuringly familiar features of his commanding officer, the Commissioner of the Metropolitan Police, Lord Trenchard. The commissioner was the most imposing of the four grandees present, Joe thought. Authoritative, brisk and tireless, the man had Joe's respect for the many reforms he'd made in a short time to the failing police service. A severe taskmaster, he was acknowledged to be hardest of all on himself.

He greeted Joe with a twitch of his bushy eyebrows, which hid a pair of surprisingly warm and humorous eyes. Trenchard was a man of few words but all those words were caught, noted down and moulded into rolling prose by the man seated at his side: Howgrave-Graham, secretary to the Metropolitan Police Force. This man had Joe's trust and affection. His post was a civilian one, but Joe regarded Howgrave-Graham as the heart, mind and filing cabinet of the Yard. Ranged up opposite this pair were two men who, awkwardly, did not see eye to eye with each other.

Put in to bat for MI5, the protector of state security, was

Sir Vernon Kell's deputy, Maximilian Knightly. Elegantly grey-haired, clever and suave, he was the man frequently chosen to be the face of the Secret Service when it had to take off its mask for government. The fourth man was technically their host, the foreign secretary. Sir John Simon's bland, shiny face under a high, round forehead and sleek hair correctly reflected his high intellect but gave no clue as to his humble origins in a bleak, northern town. A self-made man, he should have had Joe's approval. Such, however, had been his soft approach, and so uncertain his handling of foreign affairs, Joe was reserving judgment. In Joe's eyes, running down the British military whilst simultaneously underestimating the rising menace of Fascist Germany was a disastrous policy.

Joe had been invited in his capacity as head of the Special Branch of the Metropolitan Police, reporting back to the Home Office. Of the assembled company, all Savile Row suited, coiffed and manicured, Joe was the only one who knew how to fit a pair of handcuffs and bark out an order. His war years had equipped him with that quality so sought after by branches of both State and Military Intelligence— "training acquired in the school of experience." If there were villains to be exposed and interrogated, charges to be laid and prisoners to be carted off to the Tower, Joe and his Specials would be there at the sharp end.

In the public's imagination, it was all done by muscle power and steel-capped boots. Joe knew that it was more often courage, patient surveillance and intelligence that got the unpleasant tasks done. MI5, constantly undermanned and underfunded, battled on gallantly, recruiting agents mainly from among friends, family and chaps they were at college with: "They tell me your cousin is something of an Arabist, Fortescue . . . He must have lunch with me at my club—I may have something for him . . ." Even women, it was rumoured, were being used as agents. But it was in the quality of MI5's file-keeping, Joe reckoned, that their real strength lay. That and their judiciously dispensed gossip. And at least they were willing to share information with him when necessary.

They seemed to trust him but he knew their trust was about as deep as that of the owner of a half-trained Staffordshire pit bull for his dog. Show the beast respect but carry a heavy stick and be prepared for it to bite your ankle. "Watch him! Joe Sandilands has previous," was probably the first comment that came to the mind of his superiors. All too true. He'd taken on the great and the not-so-good, refusing to sweep dirt under the carpet, examining and dealing with the unpleasant writhing creatures he'd discovered under stones in the home counties. He expected no gratitude and was well aware of his vulnerability.

Some figures in the British establishment were above the reach of common law and order and any policeman threatening to topple one of this élite group would himself be sent spinning base over apex before he could do any harm. Joe's letter of resignation was lodged permanently in the drawer of Trenchard's desk as a gauge of his independence and determination to uphold the law without fear or favour. The men assembled on this occasion were all well aware of that. Sandilands was not "One of Us" nor yet quite "One of Them." Might even prove to be a loose cannon.

Unsmiling and watchful of his reactions, the four men had outlined for Joe a political nightmare.

The very worst scenario, they'd called it, and—inevitably—a national emergency. He'd remember to tell Miss Sturdy. Joe was not, at first, alarmed. The press announced a fresh one of these every day, but, looking round the table, he saw a quartet of men who were not given to exaggeration. "Of course," the foreign secretary had added shiftily, taking out a bit of insurance in case it blew up in their faces and they were accused of hysterical overstatement, "it could all turn out to be no more than the licentious behaviour of a degenerate maniac whose idea of fun is to ensnare and ruin the more gullible amongst the ruling classes. These, sadly, are always with us," he pointed out, "on the fringes, ripe for enticement—the daredevils, the disaffected, the experimenters, the ones lacking in moral fibre, the second sons . . ."

Ouch! Joe calculated that, having scored four out of five on this gullibility yardstick himself, he'd better keep his head down. And—"degenerate maniac"? Plenty of those about. Which one did they have in mind?

This was worrying enough, the foreign secretary declared, but was something Sandilands and the Met could cope with relatively easily given the instruction and the backup. Right now. Before the fire got out of hand. No need to alert the armed forces as yet.

Armed forces? Christ! Where was he going with this? If this wet lettuce of a foreign secretary had been startled into action, trouble really was brewing. Was Hitler assembling an armada? Was Mad Mosely planning an armed coup?

Everyone had learned the technique of containing a solitary fire in an oil drum, Sir John Simon had claimed mysteriously. (Joe wondered briefly what on earth this useful skill could possibly entail and where you could acquire it.) It could, on the other hand, Sir John had suggested, hedging his bets, in the light of present European turmoil, be leading to a problem of huge national and international proportions. With three ruined careers and two suicides already to be accounted for, questions were being asked. The *Daily Herald* was beginning to make connections. Communist-backed rag, of course, its cash blatantly being piped in from Moscow, it could create mayhem if it got at the truth.

And then MI5's man Knightly had pulled his nasty little rabbit out of the hat. "And there's always—perhaps primarily—the *Cambridge* connection." He had spoken through gritted teeth. "We had feared the worst of that place," he added to Joe's bemusement, "and it begins to look as though our fears are well-founded." He cast a sideways glance at Joe. "I say, not a Cambridge man yourself, are you, Sandilands?"

Joe knew that this sharp operator would already have ascertained as much from the file in his cabinet and was just underlining Joe's neutrality for the benefit of the others by eliciting the response, "No, sir. I'm an Edinburgh man. Law. Fusilier and Military Intelligence in the war, and the rest you know."

"Glad to hear it. One of our two most ancient and prestigious universities is shaping up to be a hotbed of intellectual communism, if that's not a contradiction in terms." Knightly looked around, gathering approval. When he'd collected sufficient nods, he pushed on: "Now, a certain amount of flirting with 'socialism' doesn't ruffle many feathers. A weary but indulgent sigh would be our response. That's youth for you. Privileged youth that has only a cerebral conception of the working man and his needs and rights, and he grows out of it if ever faced with the gritty reality. No. This is more serious. It's a well-funded and organised assault on the British way of life. They already have daily newspapers in their pay and the next line of attack is through our intellectual institutions. The universities which are, even as we speak, educating and forming the country's future leaders are being fed a radicalised version of their philosophy. But in palatable form. No burning flags, no resounding anthems, no High Street marches and proletarian nonsense of that sort to worry anyone. *Café communism* is the fashionable term for it, I believe ..."

The foreign secretary interrupted. "Come now, Knightly! The tea shops and coffee houses of an ancient city at the heart of England are, we are asked to believe, the hatcheries for pernicious, destructive philosophies?"

"Oh yes, Sir John! 'Two lumps and a splash of Bolshevism with your café noir, sir?'" Knightly enjoyed teasing the minister. "But, I'll allow—this frivolous picture does demean and distract from the truth. We have to recognise that the disease runs deeper and higher than the chirrupings you hear at café and refectory tables—the rebellious views of callow youths are always with us. I remember exchanging much the same sort of rubbish with friends over a cup of Earl Grey in the Daisy Tea Rooms back in '97 when *we* were callow youths. We can ignore it! But some of us will remember the Trinity College Two ..." Encountering blank looks all round, he'd explained further, "Ten years ago. The Office had to open a file on two Trinity men in high positions—one of them a professor and himself a student of Ernest Rutherford's at the Cavendish Laboratory, the other one an economics tutor. Unashamedly, outspokenly Marxist, the pair of them."

"Great Scott!" the foreign secretary made the connection. "Are these men still in place? If they got together and combined their skills and knowledge, they could make and market an atom bomb! Sell it off to the highest bidder! Wasn't there something in the news recently . . . ?"

"The fourteenth of April last year." Howgrave-Graham supplied the facts. "Nineteen thirty-two was an outstanding year for Cambridge science. *Annus mirabilis*, *The Times* called it. Two gentlemen at the Cavendish split the lithium atom with a proton beam. Cockroft and Walton."

"Knowledge worth having, I'd have thought. Especially to anyone interested in war work. These communist chaps, I ask again, are they still out and about in Cambridge?"

"Yes indeed," confirmed MI5. "Still in post. The economist, one Maurice Dobb, holds meetings for fledgling communists at his home: somewhat appropriately called 'The Red House,' north of the river. The physics professor is still working at the Cavendish."

"God help us! This physics feller—do we have evidence of Russian sympathies?"

MI5 replied after a suspenseful pause through lips tight with amusement or embarrassment. It was hard to tell. "Professor Piotr Kapitza *is* Russian. By birth."

"A Russian! What the deuce is he doing exploding atoms in an English laboratory in the middle of an English city? Has the country gone mad? Someone must defuse this jackanapes. At once."

"He has an outstanding talent, I'm afraid," MI5 explained ruefully. "Born in St. Petersburg and educated there as far as they could accommodate his genius. When he'd outgrown Russian resources, he came to England. We set him up with the best facilities the world has to offer, and he and his team—who themselves are of various nationalities—have achieved some remarkable results. His boss Ernest Rutherford, the driving force of all this, is, you will remember, a New Zealander by birth, educated in Canada."

"Oh, Rutherford? Then it's most probably in safe hands. It's well known he can't be doing with any of that communist rubbish. I'm told he always has a stern word or two to say to his new assistants on the subject when he takes them on. Besides—he's Lord Rutherford now, you know. Baron, is he?"

"Indeed, he is, sir. Baron Rutherford as of two years ago. Member of the House of Lords, President of the Royal Society and countless other honours," Howgrave-Graham murmured.

"Mmm . . . I shall have a word with him. Look here—it's this Kapitza chap who concerns me—any signs of . . . um . . . extracurricular activity?"

"Oh, yes. Lots! He's a sociable type. Charismatic is the word often used to describe the charm he exudes. Witty, warm, an egalitarian, gives generous encouragement to the younger generation. Everyone loves him. He runs a lively association called 'The Kapitza Club' that meets on Tuesday evenings after dinner. The world's best scientists make their way there to join in the discussions. As popular as the Kit Kat with some, I'm told. But they are vastly more choosy as to membership, of course. I hear they stopped Einstein at the door before someone realised . . ."

Joe only just held back a: "Sounds fun!" response to that.

"May I ask what measures we have in place?" Trenchard demanded. "We *do* have measures in place?"

"We have inserted penetration agents at both locales," MI5 was pleased to reveal. "Watchers who alert us to the professor's movements, contacts and, indeed, his plans to some extent."

"Plans? What's he planning?" Trenchard's eyebrows signalled alarm.

"We know that he's planning a trip back to his home country next summer. Nothing concealed or furtive about our breezy professor. He's applied for the usual travel permits in the regular way."

The foreign secretary was shocked. "What nonsense is this? I haven't been informed! Are his travel documents in order? He must be stopped!"

"I'm afraid, Sir John, you will, like the rest of us, be told to reach for your rubber stamp and lengthen his lead. The chap's Russian! He can go back to Mother Russia if he so desires. Indeed, he takes his family to St. Petersburg—or Leningrad, as we have to say these days—every summer holiday. We are not a concentration camp or a gulag. Permission for his exit will be granted, and this comes from the very highest level of government." Knightly cast a glance full of meaning and perhaps warning at the commissioner. "Not a job for the police force, Trenchard. You must sit on your hands."

"Nonsense!" came the rumbling objection.

To deflect a harmful altercation, Joe relieved his boss of the need to rattle his sabre. "Quite agree! The security service and the minister surely need no reminder that the police decide when it's a job for the police and our decisions are scrutinised and judged by our courts of law. The Met does not exist to serve government. We retain the right, indeed, to arrest members of the government should the need arise. We serve the people. And I, for one, wait with bated breath to hear how I may best do that. I've heard nothing yet to make me decoke my pistol and polish my knuckleduster."

"Make a note, Sandilands," said the commissioner. "If the Law, in its idiocy, allows this walking disaster to return to a foreign, politically hostile and unstable country, we shall at least need to be satisfied that he is not taking anything of value away with him. Equipment, notebooks, blueprints . . ."

"We can't check the contents of his head, unfortunately," MI5 pointed out. "But I'm sure in this particular case there's no need to get hot under the collar. He always comes back, you see. He managed to get out of the Russians a document guaranteeing him free passage out of the country whenever he wished to leave. He won't stay. Nothing to keep him in Russia. They have nothing in the way of equipment. You simply can't get the helium liquefiers up there, you know."

Joe groaned. "If he asks politely, perhaps those nice people at the Cavendish will consider packing up one or two and sending them on?"

Howgrave-Graham flashed him a look which said, "Don't push it, Joe!"

The MI5 man made an effort to reassert his authority over the group. "Be that as it may . . . that is not the principal reason for calling this meeting today. Something more serious has reared its head. The Trinity Two and their tea party chums are not our immediate concern. Merely background. A little local colour . . ."

"Red . . ." sighed the foreign secretary.

"Their inclinations are, if not excusable, at least containable. Inside ivory towers where perversions belong. But, gentlemen, pernicious notions have been leaking out from Cambridge. And from a hitherto unsuspected source in that town. Deliberately spread, perhaps? They have reached the corridors of power. Next, the front pages of the London newspapers. After that, into the streets." MI5 had an aversion to the press. And a sinister knowledge of the private lives of the barons who owned the papers.

"Oh, come now! From the secret, claret-sipping enclaves of Academe to the raucous beer-swilling crowds of the . . . er . . . Tottenham Court Road, that's quite a stretch, Knightly," Sir John objected. "The man in the street doesn't give a tinker's cuss for anything the scholars of our universities might be thinking."

Lord Trenchard's secretary however, was, Joe acknowledged, the most far-sighted and the most level-headed man on the Force. Bold, too. He now responded, beating Joe to the comment by a short head. "I think, sir, we would do well to remember the outcome of the Oxford debate of February this year . . ."

"We were all, even we beer-swillers, startled—no, shocked to the core," Joe picked up the baton. "This seems as good a moment as any to remind ourselves of the motion the Oxford Union set itself: *this House will in no circumstances fight for its King and Country.*"

"The motion being carried by 275 votes to 153," supplied Howgrave-Graham, who didn't even need to refer to his notes. He looked at Joe, quietly inviting him to advance further. Further down the path that leads to the chopping block, Joe thought. Ah, well. In for a penny . . .

"Not fight? We ex-soldiers were ashamed of the younger generation," Joe could speak for the common man, he reckoned, being the commonest man at the table. "Our brightest and best young men, the future leaders of our country, by an overwhelming majority had declared themselves pacifists and traitors. The sensation created was tremendous. It was published worldwide. All the Empire watchers took due note: The Irish, the Japanese, the Russians, the Germans ..."

His words triggered a response from Sir John. "Useless, of course, to try to explain to Johnny Foreigner that it's just an English game—debating—and not to be taken as a serious statement of British foreign policy. They may leave such things to me," he finished with a sly smile.

"The Greeks would have understood, naturally." Joe had discovered that at such meetings any reference to the Greeks elicited an understanding nod and raised the stakes of the man who'd invoked their authority. "But modern men were only too happy to take it literally. Wilfully so, I believe. People tried to explain 'whimsicality.' A thankless task! Objectors spoke up against the lack of spirit and the disloyalty. They were hissed and heckled! Churchill, the old warrior, gave his views. He was stink-bombed! 'No, we meant it!' came the shout from a war-weary, undernourished and contrary nation. And they did! At that moment, they did. For once, the educated élite was speaking for the common man and woman. I understand, but I don't condone. It's a national disgrace, I agree, and has set a dangerous precedent. This is an age of fast communications and jittery politicians and we have to allow that the distance from the lecture hall to the street is not as wide as once it was."

Joe saw that all eyes were on him. He'd been pontificating.

Getting above himself. "Though, to its credit," he added in an attempt to lighten the proceedings, "Cambridge University did threaten to pull out of this year's boat race against Oxford."

Dry snorting guffaws greeted this.

"Good for them! But too late to undo the damage. Sandilands has it right! A young friend of mine was hiking across Germany this summer," Trenchard made his down-to-earth contribution. "Very embarrassing! Of course, the one thing every German he met wanted to know was: 'Is it true? That you English have gone soft?'"

MI5 confirmed the fear expressed. "Just what the Fascist nations want to hear, of course. That Italian lout, Signor Mussolini, chortled that the Oxford men had just shown that 'Britannia is just a frightened old lady!' And he took it as a cue to redouble his attempts to infiltrate Abyssinia. Arms are being shipped in and stock-piled, a fort is going up as we speak. The man greets every British protest with a two-fingered salute, a reference to the Oxford debate and a hollow laugh."

With the imagined sound of Italian derision ringing in their ears and creating a unity of purpose, the meeting seemed to be coming swiftly to a resolution.

PRACTICALITIES HAD FOLLOWED thick and fast.

The whole problem had to be eradicated. But tactfully. Flash-bulb arrest scenes and public trials at the Old Bailey would unsettle an already anxious country. What with bloody old Ireland to the west, the Red Menace from the north and now this alarming Fascist state growing like a cancer to the south and east, the British public had enough to worry about. The suspicion that their own society was crumbling into immorality right under their feet would lead to collapse of confidence, disorder and riot. If ever calm was called for it was now. This was no case for a squad of Sandilands's heavy brigade. The Branch should be held back and only used as a last resort. Could all then agree that for the time being the matter should be put in the hands of the assistant commissioner, who'd shown repeatedly in the past his ability to bring such nefarious activities to a discreet end?

They could.

It was not until this moment that, belatedly, a name was put before Joe.

"*Pertinax.* That's our—now *your*—problem, Sandilands."

Joe had the unsettling feeling that the meeting had suddenly come to a rolling boil. All the flummery about the Trinity Two and their high jinks was merely scene painting and now there swaggered on stage the central character. The charismatic physicist and the hospitable economist did not merit direct action from Joe apparently, apart from ensuring customs checked their luggage for blueprints, but this new presence seemed to bewilder and alarm the company to the point where they were handing him the information in short, sharp blasts. Pertinax was a hot potato being hurriedly passed from hand to hand:

"Not a university man, though he graduated from Trinity."

"Rich. A man of influence."

"Origins uncertain. Could be Russian?"

"Potential for mischief enormous."

"Possible connection with this Kapitza bunch? We need

to know. Sandilands, that's where you come in," MI5 said decisively.

The hot potato had landed in his lap. "Do we have any facts about this chap? All I've heard so far is speculation," Joe said calmly. The potato moved on round the table again.

"Known to be a generous contributor to the new laboratory they're all so pleased with up there. That's a fact. Oh, yes! Hand Sir Gregory a request for microscopes, spectroscopes, dynamos and all the other paraphernalia and chances are that he'll get out his chequebook. Could it be that he— or some other Johnny—has the lab in his pocket? If so—precisely what expertise are they buying from these gents in white coats?" Knightly was getting into his stride.

"We know they're using enough electricity to power a large town and with all the stainless steel equipment, the freezers, the liquefiers, the cookers, they might well be searching for the secret of the perfect Victoria sponge! We'll give you what we have. Over to you, Sandilands! Tell us what you propose and what we may supply."

Final landing of overcooked vegetable. Four pairs of eyes turned on him, waiting to see him flinch.

"Shopping lists," he said firmly. "I shall need to know exactly what has been supplied to the laboratory over the last five years and I shall need at my elbow an expert to help me to make sense of them. I'm assuming, sir," he spoke to Knightly, "that you have a man in place on the inside . . ." He waited in some suspense for the nod.

"Let's call him 'Hermes' for the purposes of this discussion, shall we?" Knightly smiled, pleased with himself.

Howgrave-Graham chuckled. "God of science and guide into the underworld? Is that what you have in mind?"

"Indeed!"

"I shall need to meet him. Organise this however you will. At some point I shall have to have access to the building. I'm quite familiar with Cambridge. I've seen the Cavendish from the outside. It's a fortress. An elegantly architected but formidable fortress. I shall need a Hermes as my guide into, through and out of the Temple to Science. As for Milord Pertinax . . ." Joe smiled to see the varying degrees of anxiety and alarm flicker over their faces. "We are already acquainted. I have met the man. I shall remind him, for he has most probably forgotten, that the last time we met he gave me an open invitation to visit him at his Cambridge seat. Last, but not least—though I'm sure I shall think of a further hundred things I need—a dozen or so signed arrest warrants to tuck away in my briefcase wouldn't be a bad idea."

At this point, the commissioner had given the table the benefit of his rare but sweet smile. The company had begun to relax, sighs and grunts accompanying slurpings of cold coffee from the bottoms of cups. Only Joe's back had remained rigidly straight. He put his hands under the table and clasped them together to stop the trembling.

"WITH THE BRIEF that Sandilands is to find out what the Pertinax nuisance is up to and make him stop it," had been the commissioner's blunt stipulation.

"Without bloodshed, explosion or scandal if at all possible," was the foreign secretary's smooth rider.

"Make the problem disappear—get him off our books, away from our shores, but not before you've found out who his friends and connections are," was MI5's concern.

The meeting had broken up and, with the relish of military men who've made their point and consigned the dirty work to another pair of hands, they had given their "problem" a code name. *Operation Imperator* had been settled on. Nothing like giving away the full extent of your knowledge in a word, Joe had objected. He'd suggested *Operation Humbug*. He'd been overruled.

AIDAN MOUNTFITCHET, THE cousin of one of the naval gentlemen at MI5, had been approached, though an amateur, and had cheerfully agreed to put himself into a dangerous situation, poo-pooing the risks, because he was superbly qualified for the job. An old boy of St. Benedict's College, he had gained the trust of the new master, who had invited him to take a room in the college to pursue a project of mutual interest. Aidan had acquired something of a reputation in his field, being a skilled and entertaining writer with a searching eye for the truth. He had offered (and the offer had been eagerly accepted) to research the war records and military successes of members of the college during the recent war for publication before it began to fade from memory. "While their medals are still bright!" the master had enthused. "Too many have dropped off the twig already. The problem is always getting them to talk at all about, er, events. They'll open up to a fellow soldier."

"I fit the bill exactly!" Aidan had reassured Joe, leaving his first briefing meeting with his MI5 handlers. "I paraphrase of course—do they always talk in that obscure way?—but I gather they need a blackmailable, bribable, adventurous rogue to shoot headfirst into a sort of Hellfire Club. They don't come much more roguish than yours truly!

Can you imagine that some sort of aristocratic throwback to an earlier age is indulging in such ludicrous licentiousness? What's wrong with the 99 Club in Regent Street? Can't you just give him a suitable address, Joe? I'm sure you have dozens on your books. He's gathered together a cohort of scoundrels like me. What on earth is this Pertinax chappie planning to do with us? Stage a performance of 'The Rake's Revenge' at Drury Lane?"

He'd laughed so much at the expense of the security services, Joe had been obliged to speak to him soberly and carefully. Aidan had listened and nodded his understanding, finally saying quietly, "You're the last man on earth who trusts me, Joe. Probably the only one I haven't betrayed. I'll get you what you want. If I should fail, you'll just have to fall back on your second choice. I'm sure the Prince of Wales will come up with the goods rather faster than I can."

POOR, DOOMED AIDAN. Remembering his laughter, Joe wondered again if it was his fault that his friend had died. Could this appalling Pertinax fellow have somehow engineered his death? Joe would use all his skills to find out.

And here he was, ready for round one. He was sitting, his arrangements made, clutching his briefcase in the backseat of the Lagonda as it purred northwards up Queen's Road following the river towards Castle Hill. The chauffeur's back view was reassuring. Mr. Simpson of the Mill Road Car Hire had chosen a restrained beige-coloured whipcord for his firm's uniform, with a little red piping and brass buttons. A peaked cap was set perfectly in central position on the head, which sported a military-style short back and sides haircut. Really, a chauffeur to drive you any-where. There were no outward signs that the vehicle and driver were part of a vulgar commercial enterprise. The academics and upper class parents of undergraduates who made use of the service demanded the utmost discretion.

"By the way, we call all our drivers by the name 'James,' sir," Mr. Simpson had told him as he handed over the goods.

"As in, 'Home, James, and don't spare the horses!'"

"Exactly, sir. Clients are most likely to remember the name however doddery they may be. They rather enjoy the joke."

"It's left at the top, James," Joe instructed his James for the day.

"Certainly, sir. I was aware. Cambridge man born and bred, sir." The tone was weary but amused.

"I can't be certain how long I shall stay. If things go badly, I may be thrown out in five minutes. If they go worse, I may have to stay for lunch. Will you just go wherever chauffeurs go—round the back somewhere?—and I'll have you paged when I'm ready to leave."

"I'm sure the cook will be pleased to supply a slice of fruit cake in return for city gossip, sir. I always enjoy a cup of kitchen tea and a good natter with the ladies. They like to entertain a man in a smart uniform."

Joe realised that this was the second time he'd gone over his arrangements for the benefit of the chauffeur. Nervous-ness?

"We are now entering Madingley village, sir," James announced in the reassuring tone of a tour guide. "The inn on your right is the old 'Horseshoes.' They keep a good ale. The church ahead is of the fourteenth century and you'll find the Court a hundred yards north and on your left."

Adelaide, in the middle of her distressing story, had found time to express admiration for Madingley Court. She'd had it right, Joe thought as they approached. James idled at the entrance to allow him to enjoy a view of the house down the long drive ending in a swathe of thick shrubbery that skirted the carriage sweep and softened the tall, leaded Jacobean windows. The rosy red brick and elegant proportions were alluring to the eye; a succession of architectural styles managed to complement each other in a pleasing way. Clearly the overriding good taste of some ancient owner—or series of owners—had known when to hold off, when to repair and when and where to innovate. Money was no problem in this establishment, Joe guessed. The grounds—what he could see of them—were in excellent shape, lawns freshly trimmed, gravel raked. In the distance deer moved through a Capability Brown landscape. A mile or so away, a keeper's sporting rifle cracked twice. Lucky old Pertinax, Joe thought, to have this heaven to come home to.

CHAPTER 11

The Lagonda turned without stirring up the gravel and backed into a space next to a Rolls-Royce. The front door was opened, surprisingly, not by a uniformed butler, but by Pertinax himself! Lord! The Threat to National Security, the Scourge of This-World-As-We-Know-It ambled out, barely recognisable in loose shirt, cravat, cord trousers tucked into boots and a wide smile.

"Sandilands!" the man bellowed, striding towards the Lagonda, arm outstretched. "What a treat! I'm afraid you catch me underprepared for a luncheon party but then—it's a very late arrangement we made. You *are* able to stay for lunch? Good man! I dropped everything. To think I might have been about the estate somewhere gralloching a stag or whatever unpleasantness they perform on the poor beasts at this time of year!"

"De-antlering and worming, I think, Pertinax. You're well out of it, man! And I'm dressed smartly enough for both of us. I put on my best Lyon silk tie in your honour."

"Charmin'. Charmin'," Pertinax muttered with a country aristocrat's automatic acknowledgement. "Let me take your bag." He eyed the briefcase with some surprise. "Lord, man! You're here for coffee, not a conference!"

Joe politely waved away the helping hand. "Busy day. I'm

squeezing you in between two meetings. Don't trouble. I'm used to fending for myself."

"Glad to hear it. You're going to have to today! I've given the butler the morning off. Most of the staff in fact—there's some kind of a domestic event on in the servants' hall . . . A funeral of one of the domestics. We'll manage. Two old soldiers that we are, I thought we could mess together with no fuss. This your man?" He turned to James, who threw him a crisp salute. "Go round to the back will you? The housekeeper's expecting you."

Sir Gregory kept up chatter in the same vein as they walked along the corridors. "It's so pleasant—unseasonably warm, don't you find?—I thought we'd take coffee outside on the terrace at the back and admire the wonderful autumnal colouring in the woodland while we can. The leaves are hanging on valiantly. Just calling out for a Corot, you'll see! Painter yourself, are you? No, same here. Tried it! Useless! Still it makes you really appreciate those blessed souls who can really do it. What!" He pointed out interesting architectural details and identified paintings on the walls as they went.

Pertinax's combination of bluff charm and knowledge casually imparted were setting Joe completely at his ease. The old uncles from whom he'd inherited a good deal of artwork had rattled on in the same manner. If this was to be the style of conversation, he was confident he could hold his own.

Coffee was served in a silver pot on a tray brought out to them by a maidservant. Pertinax dismissed her, grasped the handle and took charge. With an expression of teasing reproof, he announced, "Now, Sandilands! If any pouring of liquids is to be done I rather think I'll do it myself. All's forgiven and well understood, by the way. I mention it now so that it won't hang between us. I hadn't realised the girl Dorothy was of personal interest to you."

"She isn't," Joe replied easily. "No more, no less than any member of the female sex. In any case she is, I've discovered, well able to take care of herself. You escaped lightly!" In response to the raised eyebrow opposite, Joe added: "The last man who annoyed her had a brandy thrown in his face . . . glass and all."

Pertinax chuckled. "A risk worth taking. She can aim a glass at me any day. She is extraordinary! All that wealth and intelligence and on top she has the looks of a Botticelli angel."

"Do you think so?" Joe's surprise was genuine.

"Dark gold curls, blue eyes, marshmallow mouth," Pertinax sighed. "You can't not have noticed."

Great heavens! The man was enjoying a good gossip and evidently little Miss Despond was a subject who'd caught and retained his lascivious interest. Well, Joe was here to play a game. Thankful that his sister was a hundred miles away and not able to tick him off, he launched himself into it. "I'd have said: brown hair, grey eyes and rather more lip rouge than is permissible in an unmarried girl." And, confidingly: "Tidy little figure though. Dance a tango with her and you'll know you've been danced with! I ached for a week! Not entirely unpleasantly." Joe looked about him with sudden misgiving. "I say, Pertinax! No . . . um . . . Lady P. in the picture, is there, to overhear our risqué remarks?"

"Not at all. The position's open. No takers, I'm afraid. Though I am on active lookout. Yourself, Sandilands?"

"Fancy free still. Intending to remain so. I'd guess we're about the same age. Late thirties?"

The speculation gave Joe an excuse to study the features of the man opposite. Though looking rather creased and weather-beaten for his actual years—the forty-three attributed to him by MI5—he had retained his good looks. Dorothy's dismissive words came back to mind: the pale skin, the icy eyes of a northern clime . . . Something of the sort . . . Yes, Pertinax had a Scandinavian air about him. She hadn't mentioned the decisive nose, the threatening anvil of a chin that made Joe's fist curl in automatic alarm or the thin lips which could twitch unexpectedly into a seductive smile.

"The forties—that's the best time for marriage, they tell me."

"There's no good time for marriage," Joe said firmly, adding silently, "Forgive me, Lydia. Forgive me, Adelaide." He decided to change the subject. Time to be arty. "Ah! I see it!" he exclaimed, raising a forefinger. "You mentioned Corot just now. I can see the exact spot where Corot would have planted his easel and the scene he would have put on canvas. That tree over there . . . ash? . . . No, willow . . . drapes itself over elegantly to the left in a pose I've seen before. In Paris."

Pertinax smiled and waited for more of Joe's nonsense.

"It's one of his more important paintings. A transitional piece . . . *Une Matinée* . . . That's it! Known to us English as *The Dance of the Nymphs.* The natural arch of the tree enfolds two mysterious female figures like a stage set. But are they nymphs or are they a pair of drunken bacchantes coming straight towards us?" Joe tried for a lecherous leer.

"Either very welcome, I'm sure! Crack open the

champagne, here come the ladies! You know, I've often thought of staging the scene," Pertinax mused. "Next Midsummer's Day perhaps? A fancy dress party in the wood? String band on the lawn and a flute or two in the shrubbery. Red caviar on iced dishes. Everyone to come as a character from a fête champêtre painting. You're invited, Sandilands! May I suggest you appear as a satyr? Now I have you properly in focus, I see you have the face for it. In fact, I have your portrait upstairs in my gallery. I knew those slanting black eyebrows were familiar!" He shook with silent laughter. "Now, if you've finished your coffee, why don't you do what you really came here to do?" The lively features had frozen into an expressionless mask as Pertinax picked up and handed his briefcase over to Joe. "Good Lord, man! What on earth are you carrying about with you? Ball and chain for emergency use? Luckily, I know you policemen don't go about armed or I might suspect you had a naughty handgun stashed away in here."

Joe grinned. "Nothing more sinister than a flask of coffee. Take a look if you're nervous, it's not locked. The Garden House makes up a good brew to get me through my day. I couldn't be sure of my welcome, Pertinax," he added disarmingly. "You might not have been ready to ply me with your best Blue Mountain."

THE "GALLERY" WAS the width of a room and the length of three, and it was crowded with pictures that made Joe gasp, snort and sigh.

"Little yips of pleasure I hear but no wise words of appreciation or connoisseurship," Pertinax said archly after a while. "Come on, man! You've done the circuit of the room three times, chuffing like a toy train. Are you ever going to give me your opinion? Which, I'm given to understand, is worth having."

"You don't need my opinion. When I can get my breath back and my vocabulary together I shall comment on individual pictures perhaps, telling you nothing you didn't already know. For the moment, I'll tell you this is the best private collection I've ever set eyes on. There's probably more lavish ones over the Atlantic and there's a whole house in Florence stuffed full of goodies but this is . . . surprising, enchanting . . . uplifting."

"My father would be pleased to hear you say so. He had a remarkable eye for talent."

"Inherited by his son, I note. Some of these would have been acquired after your father's death. The Picasso on the west wall changed hands only three years ago. I wondered what had become of it." He added a silent, "Thank you, Dorothy!"

"I like to keep the collection fresh. The main body: the Quattrocentros, the Rubens, the Rembrandts, the Van Dykes and the Impressionists are the solid and unchanging core, but I add new pictures as they take my fancy and sell off those that have pleased me enough. I have paid as much as a million dollars and as little as a shilling and enjoyed the two extremes equally."

"You have great confidence in your own taste. Do you ever discuss potential purchases with an expert?"

"Oh, you're thinking of Dorothy's father. Despond. Rapacious swine! The words 'price' and 'value' are interchangeable for him. No, he's the last person I'd consult. His daughter, however, is a different kettle of fish. She looks at a canvas and sees paint, skill and mind. Not a price tag. I fell in love with her while we stood together in front of the Corot over there."

Was he joking? Joe was for a moment struck silent by the embarrassing admission. How was he to respond to a known villain who showed impeccable taste in art and now women?

They strolled over to stand and gaze at what Joe considered to be an untypical, even disturbing, Corot. No leafy, idyllic landscape here. Pertinax had experienced his *coup de foudre* for Dorothy looking at a spare Italian interior, the austere background for a spectacular female nude.

"I had just bought it at an auction in a French provincial town. They had no idea what it was." He put on a convincing French accent. 'Typical amateur painting-class nude. Sprawling acreage of flesh and undersized head. Nice addition to a single gentleman's study, however,' the auctioneer told me, sticking a sly elbow in my ribs. 'I expect to be offered a thousand francs at least,' he added. Another dig of the elbow. Twelve hundred and a swift removal from the sale did the trick, and she came home with me."

"But . . . but . . . she's in the National Art Museum in Paris," Joe said, mystified. "It's Marietta. The model he painted on his last visit to Rome."

"*One* of his Mariettas. Or 'The Roman Odalisque' as they have it labelled. Such a different style from his equally lovely neoclassical landscapes."

"And Dorothy took one look and pointed out that you'd been sold a fake? Hardly endearing behaviour, Pertinax. Surprised you didn't show her the door instead of falling to your knees."

"*Au contraire!* She was intrigued. Peered at it, looked at the back and the sides. Held it to the light and even produced a magnifying glass. She rattled on for a long time about frottis, varnish, visible pencil lines, choice of colour and finally she stood back and pronounced her judgement: 'You'll need to get a laboratory investigation done, of course, as my word counts for nothing, but my first impressions are that it's a genuine Corot. The twin of the one he painted in Rome. You did well to buy it. The colours are right: the ochre pink of the flesh, the pale green contrast, the unusual frottis technique is spot on ... and she has a lovely arse.'"

"Yes, I see what you mean—you'd simply *have* to fall in love with a girl who knows an authentic derrière when she sees one. Her father would never have made that point," Joe said. "Dorothy has an unusual vocabulary which she uses judiciously and adventurously. Yes, if ever I buy a nude I'll be sure to consult Dorothy."

Pertinax seemed pleased with his contribution. "Odd, isn't it, Sandilands, the way a man responds to filthy words from a rosebud mouth? I see we share a taste for salacious seduction ..."

When Joe was a small boy he'd been having lunch with a corseted great aunt and on his best behaviour. Eating up his salad, he'd inadvertently speared a caterpillar lurking under a lettuce leaf. The forkful was half way to his mouth and the aunt's beady eye on him. The conflicting needs to avoid putting the still twitching creature into his mouth, to avoid being sick and to avoid upsetting his aunt came back vividly to mind at this moment. He'd resolved the situation clumsily by throwing down his fork, faking a coughing fit and running from the room. None of these reactions was available

DIANA'S ALTAR   131

to the mature man, but he revolted in the same visceral way at the sudden attempt to slide a parasitic thought into his head.

The antidote was everywhere around him. "Now, Pertinax," Joe looked at his watch, "much left to see and lunch time is almost upon us. I'll follow at your heels, trying to keep up while we look at these gems one at a time until you get bored."

"THE GONG! WE'RE bidden to lunch," Pertinax announced with no sign of relief that they had come to the end of their allotted time. Art lovers, like dog owners or stamp collectors, never wearied of showing off their possessions, Joe found. He didn't think he'd bored Pertinax; he'd been a genuinely interested and admiring audience. Armed with Dorothy's insights and wicked subtleties, he'd managed, he was sure, to impress and even amuse the undoubted authority he was fencing with, though the effort of putting on an act of amiable, silly ass with aspirations of art connoisseurship had taken its toll. It had left him feeling a little limp and dying for a stiff gin, but Pertinax had further to go.

"There's just one more item," he announced. "You came here ostensibly to see my Watteaus, if I remember correctly. There's one you haven't even noticed yet. A double portrait in which you, Sandilands, play a starring role! Up there over the door where it was designed to hang."

Joe looked up and stared in surprise. "My God! It's *Zeus and Antiope!*"

"Or the *Satyr and the Nymph*, as I prefer. It's never a bad idea to mask your identity if you're a god."

"When you're on mischief bent," Joe added, peering more closely. "The horns are a good touch."

The picture fitted well into its allotted place in the oval-shaped gap over the door. Entering the room you were not aware of its presence and, once blinded by the richness of the delights on display at eye level, it went unremarked. Why on earth would one want to hang a superb Watteau with such reticence? Cynically Joe believed there could be a good reason for the positioning.

"Do you see him? Your alter ego?" Pertinax was chortling. "Could this be your Dorian Gray moment, Sandilands?"

A dusky satyr (or Zeus in disguise) was caught in the act of peeling a diaphanous fabric away from the sleeping form of a nymph (or Antiope, daughter of a river god). Joe checked the male figure's undercarriage for the sure sign of satyrism—a pair of hairy goat's legs—but his lower limbs were hidden in shadows and left to the imagination. Only his muscled upper torso was on view. The traditional horns were almost concealed amongst the tangled vine leaves of the wreath around his head. The two bodies echoed the oval shape of the frame and filled it with a symphony of subtle colour. The satyr, long, sinewy arms extending from power-ful shoulders, could have been seen either as protective or lecherous, his sun-darkened skin and his black hair a contrast with the sugar mouse pinkness of the nymph. She was fast asleep, one arm tucked under her fair head; he was very much awake, handsome in his way and sharing an evil leer with the artist. And, yes, he had Joe's eyebrows. And, yes, he had Joe's empathy.

Joe burst out laughing. "It's a fair cop! 'e caught me bang to rights, tool in hand, M'Lud!" he said in the voice of a

London thug in the dock. "That's me for sure but who's the strawberry blonde?" Then, more carefully: "I know there were several copies made of this painting at the time, but wouldn't you say this is a copy of a copy? Why are you displaying it here amongst all these good pictures? Aren't you afraid it might detract from your bona fides?"

"You scoff too soon, Sandilands! I've always considered it one of the original works. Doubt was, however, cast a while ago by none less than Despond senior. I went to the best for an opinion. Ha! Damn him! No one would dare support me in my claim if it meant contradicting the Master. Can you imagine how many collections would have to be unpicked and at what expense if Despond himself were discredited? He's made himself an impregnable authority and his nod is the most solid guarantee in an uncertain and scurrilous art world."

"The art world closed ranks?"

"Inevitably. So that's an end of it. Pertinax is in possession of a fake. The word was out. The best description Despond could come up with was pretty weak: probably from the studio of Watteau . . . by a pupil of the master . . . Blah, blah! Whatever its true status, it had little monetary value. So I hide it over the door. No one knows he's up there but me. We exchange a wink when I walk by. And now *you* know." He shrugged. "Who cares? I like it and I know it to be *right*. But I have to say, Sandilands, you put your finger on it when you said you fear for the rest of my collection. One bad apple is all it takes . . ." He went silent for a moment, in deep thought. "Look here," he said finally. "I've been thinking about this for some time. It isn't a rash decision. If you would like to make me a reasonable offer for this painting I'll accept it."

"Me? Why me?"

"One can't put such a disputed canvas up for auction. One can hardly sell it to a friend without being accused of unfair influence and scurrilous double-dealing. Men who have clubs get drummed out of them for much less."

Joe thought he detected a passing bitterness before Pertinax fixed him with a smile full of challenge and excitement. The face of a man about to land his fish.

"But if a man with a certain position in society, a man acknowledged to know his art, a man hard-nosed enough to carry a gun in his briefcase were to recognise its quality and name his price . . . ? What do you say?"

"Well, as your gun-toting, nonfriend, I say two hundred pounds."

"Two hundred guineas and the nymph is yours."

"Done! With one proviso—the usual paperwork. In my line of business, I have to be meticulous, as I'm sure you'll understand. My Browning is nestling next to my chequebook and a bill of sale. The work of a minute to fill it in and sign after lunch."

"Well, bugger me! Is this how you always do business, Sandilands?"

"No. Sometimes I have to apply Browning to temple," Joe said baring his teeth in what he was sure Bulldog Drummond would have called a vulpine grin.

CHAPTER 12

"Let me help you with that, sir."

James, who'd been waiting at the open door of the Lagonda he'd carefully parked by the front door ready for take-off, hurried forward at the sight of Joe staggering from the house hefting a brown-paper-wrapped parcel. A yard long but of shallow height, it just about fitted under his arm.

Pertinax followed on, jovial and smelling lightly of brandy and cigars, offering a useful pair of hands and advice for the chauffeur. "No! Not in the trunk. Inside, man! It's not a shove ha'penny board in here! Put it on edge along the backseat . . . Yes, like that. Sandilands, sit next to it and support it."

Brisk farewells followed. From Joe, a cheerful, "So I'll put a date for next Midsummer in my diary. I shall start working on my costume. It may take me some time to locate a goat's hide supplier."

"Do that! Meanwhile, you could start growing the horns. But I hope to see you again before then. In fact, very soon. I know where to send the invitation."

A MILE DOWN the road, Joe pointed to a cart track screened from the road by a tall hedge. "Pull off the road and park there, James—er, Constable, I suppose I can call you again now that's all over!"

Risby grinned and removed his peaked cap. "Just as I was getting into the role, sir. Trousers a bit on the short side but I don't think anyone noticed. Mr. Simpson's son's on to a cushy number with this chauffeuring business! I'm thinking of applying for a transfer. Driving this beauty, stuffing my face with Victoria sponge, flirting with ladies who don't see a real man from one year's end to the next! Whew! I've had a lovely morning! You, sir?"

Joe was digging about crossly in his bag, finally producing a flask of hotel coffee and two silver cups. "Bloody awful! Three hours of torment! Face to face with one of the world's ghastliest rogues and being made a fool of. I remind myself I wasn't there to do any serious detecting. I was just setting myself up as an Aunt Sally for his shafts of rancid humour, an audience for his preening egotism." Joe shuddered.

Alarmed by the unexpected rush of emotion from the assistant commissioner and putting it down to an excess of alcohol taken, the constable reached over and took the flask from Joe's shaking hands. "Shall I pour, sir? Don't want you scalding yourself," and, lightly to defuse Joe's anger, "That bluff old stick? Seemed nice enough to me . . . jolly like . . . Can't see as I'd like to meet him halfway down a dark alley in Newmarket, mind! Did you see the hands on him, sir? Boxer's hands!" After a few sips of coffee, Risby jerked his head at the parcel. "Well you seem to have got something out of it at least, sir."

"A forged painting. Not worth a tenth of the price I paid for it. Must have been mad! Still—that was the point of the exercise: to persuade him that the man he was dealing with was an impressionable nutcase. What better way to do that than by chucking two hundred quid at him on a whim?"

Risby gave a quiet whistle. "Two hundred? Oh, well, I expect you can always claim it back on expenses, sir," he said comfortably.

"Sadly, no. Can you imagine the enquiry: 'So you think your ventures into the art world should be subsidized by the public purse, Sandilands?' I'd be a laughing stock! Is my reputation worth two hundred pounds, Risby? That's what I have to decide."

Risby gulped and gave him a puzzled look. "Is it a *nice* painting at least? You might like it when you get it up on the wall. And who'd know the difference? Pertinax is never going to split." He eyed the parcel with curiosity.

"No. You're not going to take a look at it. Your ma wouldn't like you to be exposed to a scene of debauchery, even though I could describe it as an elegiac composition of characters from classical antiquity disporting themselves in a woodland setting."

"Oh! That sort of picture! Plenty of those in the Fitzwilliam. There's a Sickert I'm particularly partial to . . ."

"It's still—no! Sorry, Risby. Farting about and indulging in salacious old gents' chatter for three hours leaves me feeling soiled and . . ."

"A bit overwrought?"

"I was going to say drunk! He keeps a damned good burgundy and pours with a generous hand. The things I do for England! But I've survived at least. That's the best I could have hoped for. Now . . . I hardly dare ask . . . tell me how you got on. You roused no suspicions?"

"Nah! They've entertained Jameses before. The house-keeper came to check me over before they let me in . . ."

"Housekeeper? Did you catch her name?"

"Mrs. McGregor. Marsha. Fifties. Tough. Bossy. Face like a boot. She gave me the once over, decided I'd probably not come for the silver and told me to wait in the kitchen. Then I had a stroke of luck. The cook, nice woman, told me to take my cup of tea with one of the maids. Little thing called Pearl. When Pearl came trotting up I thought I'd blown it. A girl from my school! A year below me but she remembered me. Canny lass! She said nothing while the cook was in the room but when we were alone she said, quiet like: 'How're you doing, Rex? Thought you were going to join the police."

"Nasty moment. What did you tell her?"

"I said I'd thought about it but discovered the pay was too low and the hours too long and given up the idea. She believed me. Well, why wouldn't she? I blathered on a bit about how good the tips were in the driving business and how I'd do anything to get my hands on a steering wheel. I switched as soon as I could to her situation. She wasn't easy. She went quiet on me in fact and it took a bit of glad eyeing and reminiscing to get her to open up. She doesn't like work-ing there. Scared of the master, the butler, the housekeeper. Plain scared."

"Did she say why? And why would she stay?"

Risby was almost scornful. "It's a job. Nothing else she could do. Recessionary times, they tell us. Country's debts to pay off and all that. It's people like Pearl who are . . . Never mind. She keeps her nose down and sees and hears nothing. Sir Gregory at least pays well. Over the odds. But he expects total loyalty from all his staff. Any hint of insubordination or talking out of turn calls for a sacking. Or worse."

"What's worse, Risby?"

"Not easy to understand her. She knew she was going too far and started burbling a bit. She only confided as much as she did because I was a familiar face and I think she always fancied me at school. That and I was totally unconnected with the house . . . There was a footman. The footmen are never local. They're always brought in from London, though I think 'London' was Pearl's way of saying anywhere but Cambridge. They're always good-looking she says."

"The usual thing. Tall, handsome blokes are guaranteed a footman's position. Good wages they get too. Twins command a particularly high price."

"This one died suddenly. Got above himself, Pearl says. One day they hear the master bawling at him, the next they find his body in the wood. Shooting accident. One of the keepers pulled the trigger. The man's own fault is the general opinion. They're always warning the staff not to go gallivanting out on the estate."

"Name of the footman and dates?"

"Got 'em, sir. Jeremy Newcombe, last August. The week after the shooting season opened. There was a big house party in full swing."

"These house parties, Risby . . . any comments forthcoming?"

"Interesting for the reaction, sir, when I put a careful question. Clammed up at once. 'A whole lot of extra work for the staff,' was all she would share with me."

"Mmm . . . Well done, Constable. It's not much to work on and I expect he's covered his tracks, but it's a start." He sighed. "Did your girl have any information about the visitors to the house? Would that be too much to hope for?"

"Far too much. I didn't even try. I knew she wouldn't tell me and she'd be suspicious and scared if I asked." Risby waited for the glow to dim in Joe's eyes before adding with a sly smile, "But I've done better than that, sir. I've saved the best for last!" He fumbled in his pocket and took out a small, grubby, dog-eared diary.

"What's this you're handing me?"

"A year's worth of visitors! Everybody who's been to Madingley Court since the first of January."

Joe took the book dubiously and riffled through the pages.

"These aren't names in here, Risby. Every date filled in but with . . . What the hell! Oh! Crikey! Is this the gold mine I think it is? How did you get your hands on this?"

Expansive with quiet triumph, Risby began his succinct and modest account. Making his way round to the back on arrival, his eye had been caught by a stirring in the shrubbery. Using his police training, he'd whistled his way past, made a swift turn on his heel and dived on the shadowy presence. A very alarmed small boy had been caught in the act of writing down the number of the Lagonda in his notebook. Risby explained, "It's a harmless hobby, sir. Kids are mad about cars. They write down the number and make. It's like train spotting." With Joe's encouragement he pressed on. He'd reassured the lad, who was the son of Pertinax's own chauffeur, by embarking on a chaps' chat with him about cars, confiding a driver's impression of the Lagonda, asking what the best car in the boy's collection was and so on. He'd ascertained that the boy, who'd been given the diary as a

Christmas present, had used it to record not his day-to-day activities, which ceased to feature after the first week, but the more enthralling comings and goings of glamorous motorcars. He was skulking in the shrubbery because no one was supposed to hassle the guests. Visits were private and if anyone found out he'd even clocked their cars he'd get a hiding and his dad would get the sack.

"Here *we* are, Risby," Joe said. "November the second. Lagonda 45 and the number." He worked his way back through the pages. "My word! We're small fry. Have you had time to look at the contents? Rolls-Royces, Hispano-Suizas, Mercedes, Dodges ... Laundry and fish-delivery vans make regular visits, Mondays and Fridays respectively. Ah, here are one or two cars with diplomatic plates. Lord! While I was stepping my way delicately through a minuet upstairs in the gallery, you were downstairs unearthing—did I say a gold mine just now? Snake pit, more like! But utterly fascinating. Pour us another cup of coffee, Risby. I want to drink to your success!"

"Can you trace all these people at the Yard?"

"No bother at all. I can have the owners of the vehicles named over the phone. Who precisely was travelling in them is less simple. But this is wonderful! It may not put me on the inside of the bend, but it puts me on the track at least."

Joe closed the book then re-opened it at the front page. *Samuel Smith. His Diary 1933*, he read. "How on earth did you get Samuel to part with it?"

"I told him I was an enthusiast. I specialised in Rolls-Royce numbers. If he lent me the book to copy them I said I'd buy him a new diary for next year. I promised I'd get it back to him by next Friday, ready for the weekend arrivals.

Don't worry, sir. Young Sam's got every reason to keep quiet and besides—he's a cub scout with good field craft. We've agreed on a drop spot for the return. All part of the game. Leave that to me, sir."

"The game? I wish I'd played my hand half as well as you have, Risby! I'll say it while I can, shall I? Home, James! Oh, and don't speak of this list to anyone, will you? Not even to the super."

Joe couldn't imagine why he'd said that, but Risby seemed to take it in his stride.

"Understood, sir."

CHAPTER 13

"Sandilands, come in!" Hunnyton welcomed him into his office at the station with his usual good humour. "Where on earth have you been? Calls for you have been stacking up all morning. I feel like your secretary. 'I'll be sure to ask him to return your call, sir, just as soon as he gets back from wherever the hell it is he went.'"

"You're sacked! You should know that I'm always with the home secretary to colleagues, at the barber's to my friends. You'd be a bloody useless secretary."

Still under the effects of a bottle of burgundy, Joe found himself grinning back in great good humour at the superintendent. He remembered his sister once crossly commenting that the more Joe drank, the jollier he became, and he resolved to reach for a little restraint. He dumped his briefcase on the floor and sat on the hard chair on the opposite side of the desk. "Now then, Hunnyton! Cards on table. I've just been to lunch with Pertinax. Much to report. I thought it more tactful to wait until you'd had a go at him. No wish to queer your pitch. So. You first. How did you get on yesterday?"

Just for a moment, the blue eyes across the desk glowed with the fierce flame of a Bunsen burner and Joe sat back in his seat, fearing a scorching outburst.

In the disconcerting way he had, Hunnyton gave a softer than expected response. "No danger. It was never my pitch. I didn't even get as far as the Manor of Mystery. I told my senior officer—the chief constable of the county—of my intentions. We keep each other informed of what we're planning out here in the sticks in our old-fashioned way." The reproof was unmistakable. "He was horrified. No way was I to contemplate trampling about Madingley enquiring into the death of a servant of the household. Surely I had better things to do? These things happened. He understood—and perhaps you'll wonder, as I did, how he caught on so quickly—that all the paperwork was in order. Death certificate duly signed by a reputable medical practitioner who was present at the death. A burst duodenal ulcer, if he remembered rightly. Where was the problem in all this? It was dashed unpleasant and couldn't have happened more inconveniently for Sir Gregory, who was entertaining a selection of luminaries at the time. A minor royal, two knights and a bishop were all named for me. Straight up. I didn't need to ask. God-awful party that must have been!"

"So, are we supposed to think they were the ones being entertained by the ladies—the ones Adelaide heard laughing?"

"Well, they weren't there to play chess, though with that lineup they could have stepped their way through a game, I suppose. My mind boggles!"

"Pertinax was not aware, then, that he'd attracted the attention of the local force in the matter of Mrs. Denton's death? Ah! I thought he seemed very relaxed. Or perhaps assumes he has blanket protection from the county chief of police? But this is a problem, Hunnyton. You're implying—no, dash it!—you're accusing the senior officer of the county of partiality—no, dash it again—of cover-up and possible corruption. Of being in Pertinax's pocket. Serious stuff, Superintendent! What steps do you propose to take?"

Hunnyton shrugged his shoulders. "You tell me, mate! You've been fighting corruption in the force for years. I can see you're not exactly surprised to hear we have a sniff of it in Cambridge. I've never found myself in this position before. Arnold Baxter (knighthood pending in the New Year's Honours List) is the highest authority as far as I'm concerned. Where else can I take my complaint? It begins to sound a bit feeble even to my ears when I replay it. Can I risk my career kicking shins, calling foul, tooting whistles? I'd be out on my ear before the end of the day. You know how it works. Everything done by rank."

The superintendent got to his feet and walked to the notice board. He took down Joe's cartoon and handed it to him. "Cheeky bugger! Trenchard and his new assistant commissioner seem to be working well together. Sweetness and harmony at the Met, it would seem. These are your ideas, aren't they, Joe? Higher standards, education, cleansing of the stables? Well I approve of running a tight ship. But it's not like that out here in the sticks. Here, no one steps out of line."

"Rubbish, man! You must. And I'll tell you how to do it. You report your chief constable for obstruction in the fulfilment of your duty along with suspicion of conspiracy to divert the course of justice, and you do it on a command from me. You give the information to me, your superior and associate at the Met. I, in turn, judge that there are reasonable grounds for complaint and pass it up to Lord Trenchard who has a word in the ear of our overlord, the home secretary, who consults the foreign secretary and Military Intelligence. They mutter together mentioning the name of *Operation Imperator* and the need for kid gloves and then the whole nasty business gets kicked back to me. I'm the representative of the Plod with his eyes and ears and feet on the ground and a pair of handcuffs in his back pocket. I'll tell you—my brief is stark. Comically simple, in fact. It's to find out what Pertinax is up to and, if I judge his activities to be counter to the interests and well-being of the people of Britain, make sure he disappears. But not before handing MI5 a useful list of his friends and associates. I think we can short-circuit a week's bureaucratic paper-shuffling and start our list right now. The first name on it will be . . ."

"Bloody old Baxter!" His chuckle fading, Hunnyton settled back at his desk again and added more soberly, "Sounds good to me, but, Joe . . . Let's have a care. Let's play them at their own game. If you start jumping out of the bushes shouting, 'Gotcher!' and waving arrest warrants they'll just retreat, covering their traces and start up again when we're looking the other way. I recommend we keep it all quiet and wait for a better moment. Relations with the top brass are a bit delicate at the moment."

He frowned and, in response to Joe's raised eyebrow, said carefully, "I've had some pretty iffy responses from him lately—just run-of-the-mill requests for permissions and warrants but odd enough to give concern. Whenever possible I avoid consulting him. But I have it in hand. So, please tell me you won't go hauling old Baxter off his golf course and accusing him of some dire crime."

He waited for Joe's response.

"Very well. I'll put it in writing if you wish." Surprisingly, the offer was not waved away.

Hunnyton's next comment showed equal caution. "If I read their mind-set aright, they think they've got the measure of me: just a minion. At Baxter's beck and call."

"They? Who are *they*? Are you in possession of something so useful as a cast list? A roll call of elected members of this vile club?"

"You know I'm not. He? They? Pertinax and whoever is supporting him. We both know one man can't run the kind of enterprise we're contemplating without the usual lieutenants and squads of foot soldiers. He'll be the capstone on the pyramid. It's never the emperor himself who pours a dose from a poison bottle. He has hands, feet and trigger fingers at his disposal."

"So—they have you stuck on a page in their specimen book with a pin through your middle. *Lictor Cantabrigiensis corruptibilis*, or some such, I expect you're labelled," he said with casual invention and a suspicion that he was slurring his words. "Can you see yourself parading through the streets, bundle of rods and axe over your shoulder, supporting the forces of law and order? But freelancing for a price?"

"*Lictor*, would you say? Nothing so grand! I'd have put me a little lower on the public order scale ... *Vigil venalis*? Night watchman cum fireman? 'I've got the buckets. I'll put your fire out, guv, but it'll cost you. Ten denarii be okay?' How about that?"

Joe sensed it again. The irritability and scorn that ran just below the surface of Hunnyton's bland civility. A true friend would have taken more lightly the throw-away remark of a slightly drunken colleague and not returned it waspishly, corrected in red ink. Joe knew he could be annoying and decided to avoid provoking the man further until the day came when he was obliged to confront him. With fists? Guns? The full weight of the Law? Joe had no idea but he knew that the day would come.

"What about me? Do you see me pinned up on the opposite page?" Joe said cheerfully. "I must say—Pertinax gave no indication that he thought I was visiting for anything other than personal and social reasons."

"He wouldn't. But don't deceive yourself—he's aware. They're just waiting to see which way *you* jump. How much you know. They can't possibly be certain. Today's lunch would have been an exploratory affair. Pertinax is clever. He'll have found out much of what he wants to know about you even though you thought you were eating, drinking and topping his funny stories. If you're lucky he'll have decided you don't fit his collection and he'll be working on the best way of getting you out of his orbit. Squashing you under his heel? Bribery? A call to a friend in Westminster? But—this *Imperator* business? Ha, hum! Sounds serious to me." His twitching moustache, achieving a level of cynical amusement Douglas Fairbanks would have envied, gave the lie to his words. "Oh, a touch *Boy's Own Paper* starring Daredevil. But that's what they're like, our security services. Or what I suspect they're like. Can't say I've met many of the high and mighty you bump up against . . . the leaders of the nation you find yourself playing Figaro to. Dashing here, dashing there, whenever they snap their fingers. Perhaps you'll tell me one day whether you actually do keep a cut-throat razor at the ready in your back pocket." He gave a mock grimace.

"Awfully glad you're in my corner! Your other 'Special' friends, I think, are probably too rough to be allowed to play games with a deuce Cambridge boy like me." He gave Joe a long, speculative look. "I'm concluding that you shouldn't have told me all this, Sandilands, and you'll probably regret it when the effects of the burgundy or whatever it was he plied you with have worn off."

"Quite right. Regretting it already. If you weren't a pre-sworn-in policeman I'd have to make you sign the Official Secrets Act. I may do that anyway. I said our two enquiries might at some point flow together. They have, Hunnyton. You and your Cambridge bobbies are in this up to your necks. I merely went out to lunch with Pertinax today. That's it. That's all. Just lunch. We spread our peacock tails, trying to outdo each other, as you've guessed. You'd have been nauseated to hear the talk. I asked no intrusive personal questions. He can't have suspected he was undergoing a covert interrogation because he simply wasn't! I let him bilk me out of two hundred quid so now he thinks I'm ensnared . . . engaged . . . interested. I certainly find myself invited to join him in various dubious activities. But real detective work *was* done this day! By one of your force: PC Risby. He went backstage dressed up as my chauffeur and got some valuable information out of the ladies in the kitchen."

Hunnyton listened to Joe's tale, making the occasional note. He whistled in satisfaction, Joe thought, when he mentioned the previous death on the estate. "I don't need to look that up. Jeremy Newcombe, thirteenth of August," he said. "I dealt with the case. Death by misadventure. Thought there was something a bit wrong there but, again, it was plausible. Just. And Chief Baxter was tut-tutting and breathing down my neck. We'd had a series of killings of ladies of the night—on Midsummer Common—and that took priority."

"Can you remember the details? Of how Jeremy the footman died? Apparently it occurred out in the woods on the estate to the north of the house. And that's odd in itself. Footmen don't wander far from home in their buckled kid shoes as a rule."

"They do if they're having it off with a maiden from the village under a Harvest Moon," Hunnyton explained. "It looked like a clear case of mistaken identity. One of the keepers—there were three of them working as a team—took young Newcombe for a wild boar."

"You thought that wasn't suspicious?" Joe blinked.

"Funnily enough, when I heard the men's story it didn't even cross my mind. Pertinax fancies himself as one of those landlords who is concerned about ancient English breeds. He has deer wandering about all over the place, a few fox-hounds, Old Spot Gloucester pigs, Herefordshire cattle, you know the sort of thing. He keeps a home farm so dinky you expect to catch sight of Marie Antoinette wending her way from milking parlour to dairy with a milk yoke across her shoulders. Money down the drain!" The estate steward that Hunnyton had been in earlier days shuddered at the extravagance.

"He also has some square miles of old oak woodland. What better than to re-stock it with some traditional wild boar to mop up the acorns? He nipped off to northern France and came back with some evil old buggers and let them loose. After a nasty scene when one got out and killed a couple of pet dogs on the green in Dry Drayton—right next to the village school—he was persuaded to put up some stouter fencing and cull the herd. It became a sport for the weekenders. Those guests with strong stomachs. They go off at dawn after the boar with dogs. Finish the beast off with a rifle shot if it's lucky, knife through the throat if it's not. They butcher it there and then with the full primitive mumbo jumbo, spray of juniper stuck in its mouth, a prayer in ancient English for its valiant soul recited over its twitching body. They send the liver straight off to the kitchens. It's then served up in thin slices with brandy and mustard and cream on a chafing dish for breakfast."

"Sounds delicious," Joe said. "Just so long as it wasn't young Newcombe's liver they carved out by mistake."

Hunnyton grunted. "Damn nearly was! According to their story, a boar had been wounded by a shot the day before and had made off into the woods. Well, you can't leave an injured creature lurking out there. It might attack a guest. So a team of experts was sent out to finish it off. A few minutes into the woods they saw it. Low shadowy shape grunting and squealing behind a tuffet of thick brambles. They shot at it and ran to check their target. Newcombe was lying dead with his trousers round his ankles and a girl was running away screaming in terror."

"Ah. All too plausible." Joe said. "I can see that. Tell me, Hunnyton, did anyone ever trace the girl and check her story?"

Hunnyton gave a bitter smile. "I checked the scene myself. Not much to learn. Tidying up had been done. No sign of a girl's footprints though it had been a dry August so I wasn't at first suspicious. There was, however, an incontrovertible piece of evidence of a female presence at the scene. A pair of knickers. All the women of the household were accounted for. This was clearly someone from outside the estate. Now what was I supposed to do? Go round the village knocking on doors looking for the owner of the abandoned undergarments?"

"Like Prince Charming's equerries? 'Pardon me, Mrs. Goodbody, but does this item fit any of your daughters, by any chance?' I can quite see why that would be awkward. I'm sure Adelaide would ask, 'No helpful label?'"

"A label. Local Woolworth's. A hundred pairs sold that year, sixty of them pink as these were. But, Sandilands, there was something odd that didn't register with me at the time. They still had ironed crease marks in them. There was no sign of wear. No helpful material to be found on the fabric to interest forensics and, in view of the recent presumed activity, one might have expected it. With hindsight I give myself a rap on the knuckles."

"Clearly a plant. So we'll chalk that up as a possible murder. Poor chap. I wonder what his offence was. So dire it called for a bullet."

"Three bullets were fired. One from each gun."

"So that none of the shooters knew which one of them made the lethal shot?"

"Right. One lucky shot to the head did it. I dug the two remaining ones out of trees. Had all the rifles examined."

"Execution-style killing, are you implying?"

"Yes, I'd say so. Though there were no signs of restraint on his arms or legs. Take someone out to the woods and shoot him, away from prying eyes. We've seen that often enough in the war but the cover stories were never so elaborate and entertaining, the motives never so complex."

"Thinking of labels, Hunnyton . . ."

"Ah yes! Some luck on that front. Fenwicks was very helpful. They brought to the phone the assistant who'd made the sale. She remembered the dress. Thought how well it suited the woman who bought it. Her description chimes with what Adelaide gave us of Mrs. Denton. Paid for by cheque. Bank, for once, helpful. It hadn't yet gone out of her account."

"Her account? Whose, Hunnyton?"

"Mrs. Clarice Denton, if you can believe it. All open and above board. Knightsbridge branch of Hampton's Bank. I'm trying to get a warrant to have a sight of her full account, but in view of the boss's decision on the case I'm not sure I can."

"Leave that to me. I know I can. I'll get my superintendent at the Yard to oil it out of them."

"While we're tying up ends, here's another bit of confirmation," Hunnyton said, reaching for a file on his desk. "Remember the bottles of fluid Adelaide managed to bring away with her from Madingley? Just as she diagnosed. The lab confirms: arsenic. Useless to us as evidence, of course. I had to tell them to dispose of the stuff. The telephone call the butler made to the hospital seeking help—a pretence. No calls are on record. No accidents on the Huntingdon Road. So we know we're looking at murder, but an unprovable murder. What steps would the Met like me to take?" His smile was bland, unreadable.

"None. For the moment. Mrs. Clarice Denton's body has been cremated. The servants, I was told, were holding a wake or some such ceremony to mark her passing as I was sipping coffee on the terrace with his lordship. You can officially let it go. I'll give written confirmation of that—I know you like to keep a clean sheet. But—I have no intention of laying Mrs. Denton to rest until I understand her story and know why she died. Her killer will answer to me."

His words sounded hollow even to his own ears, though he spoke nothing but the truth. He deserved a derisory, "Ooh, er!" from Hunnyton, but the man merely looked away in embarrassment and changed the subject. "There's always Adelaide to consider, Joe, mixed up in this as she is up to her armpits," he said. "It wouldn't do her much good professionally to have her name dragged into a murder case. The phrase 'accessory after the fact' comes to mind."

"What are you suggesting, Hunnyton? That sounded a little ominous. Out with it, man! That's an order." Faced with Hunnyton and Pertinax side by side, Joe would not have known which to smack on the jaw first.

"Well, two corpses all too literally in her hands in suspicious circumstances in one night . . . Were you quite happy with her account?"

At least Hunnyton had the grace to look uncomfortable as he trailed his question. He usually did when speaking of Adelaide. He got to his feet and went over to the notice board where he straightened quite unnecessarily one or two notices, his face turned away from Joe. "Look here—I'd rather she spoke to you herself. Not knowing how things stand between the two of you, it's difficult for me . . ."

"Nonsense! This is a professional matter, not a personal one," Joe said briskly. "So clear that away."

Again, Joe sensed a calculated retreat in the face of his brusqueness and a change of tack.

"Hasn't it occurred to you to wonder how she came to

be in Cambridge, employed in the practice of that arsehole Easterby?" Hunnyton asked, beginning to stride uneasily about the room.

Joe was taken aback. "No. Her father paid a goodly sum, I understand, for Adelaide's junior partnership and it's conveniently close to her Suffolk home. Entirely reasonable and commendable."

"Easterby's outfit is doing well. It has a splendid location in the middle of a flourishing city. His list of subscribers is wealthy and growing. He didn't need the encumbrance—as he would see it—of a woman partner. Indeed, if you were to get to know him better, you'd realise that he actively dislikes women. One of life's eternal bachelors. He can't see the point of 'em."

"All the more reason for passing on his female patients to a female partner," Joe said. "I suppose some of his male clients have wives, sisters, daughters who seek advice and I'd further suppose they would have been only too relieved to be diverted to the care of lovely Adelaide." Joe shuddered. "A paunchy bloke with boiled-egg eyes, nose hair and bad breath—not what you want poking about in your underpinnings!"

Hunnyton grinned. "You could hear the sighs of relief from here to Newmarket! I agree that employing Adelaide would be a good device for keeping a happy family practice. But it's not Adelaide's involvement with the happy families that concerns me. You'll have noticed I'm not indifferent to the lady. I've got fond of her, Joe, and would go far to protect her person and her good name. Easterby is vile. He's involved in a vile business."

"He's known to be medically involved with some

influential people," Joe ventured a neutral answer to give himself time to absorb the import of Hunnyton's comment. So matter of fact in its delivery, yet surely it amounted to a declaration of intent? Of overt rivalry? Joe wished his wits were not so befuddled. He was dealing with a man whose motives and morals were largely unknown to him, and he was struck again by the feeling that he'd climbed into the wrong ring and found himself squaring up to an opponent fighting above Joe's own weight.

"Yes. And one or two of them have recently, mysteriously, come to sticky ends." Hunnyton steamed on calmly. Not, apparently, expecting a slap across the face with a glove. "None of them was clutching a pot of the good doctor's pills—oh, no!—nothing so obvious! The master of a college, a candidate for the Nobel science prize, a dean of the Church—and that's just the ones we're sure of—have blown their brains out, jumped from rooftops and so on."

"The Cambridge Connection." Joe nodded sagely. Why couldn't those buggers at the Home Office have briefed him fully? Warned him? Provided him with some names? Feeding their addiction to secrecy as usual, he decided, or protecting friends and relations. Send in Sandilands and have him rootle about and confirm our suspicions. Deal with the outfall with discretion. It's all got too much for us, like an attack of dry rot you know you should have dealt with years ago.

Figaro, here, Figaro, there . . . Figaro every-bloody-where! Hunnyton was right as usual. Damn him!

"You'll have to find the proof, but I'm sure Easterby is in cahoots with that gang at Madingley. He probably met Pertinax as a patient. A patient suffering from a sexually transmitted disease."

"You're right. It's the dreaded syphilis, I'm afraid. Adelaide's seen his notes. Seems to be in the clear for the moment but you know how these things go, Hunnyton."

"How they go and how they come back again. Yes. It's a terrifying diagnosis. Inexorable decay of private parts, possibly extending to other soft tissues including the brain. I don't suppose you've ever seen a syphilitic brain, Sandilands?"

"I have. Several. I don't shirk the autopsies. More to the point, I've dealt with the murderous consequences of such a brain while the body it inhabited was still alive and able to wield a knife and a hammer. 'Dashed bad luck! Caught a dose of the clap,' I've heard men say. Passing it off like a bad cold in the head. 'Join the club!' his friends give him the ritual reassurance. It really doesn't convey the enormity of the situation . . . the mental and moral putrefaction that goes on inexorably, often for years. It's a long, painful descent into madness and death."

"For which there is no cure, what's more. If Easterby is telling his patients there is, he's lying. I've made it my business to find out." Hunnyton resumed his seat opposite Joe and fixed him with his "Honest, guv, nothin' but the truth" expression. "Joe, Pertinax is not the only one on his books with problems in that quarter. And Easterby sees the foul condition as something of a gold mine. He's travelled to Germany, Austria and Scandinavia and come back with the best theories and medical science the world has to offer in that field. Indeed, his dedication and initiative deserve our respect and admiration, not our sneers. His reputation as a discreet solver of gentlemen's problems has spread."

"I can see that it gives the practitioner a certain power too. When your skills and your very particular knowledge

are all that can preserve a patient from a very nasty death ...
well, that conveys an incalculable value. But I can't see why
this medical bonanza should require him to take on a female
doctor," Joe said in puzzlement, risking another pitying
glance.

"He can afford to offload his day-to-day doctoring to
concentrate on his rich male patients with very special needs.
The other two medics are his front, his disguise."

"Sounds like a sensible and economic allocation of time
and skills," Joe suggested.

"Yes, but there's a decidedly uneconomic aspect to these
arrangements," Hunnyton murmured. "The Saturday clinics."

"You'll have to explain. But I'm guessing this involves
Adelaide in some way, seeing as she's forever engaged at
weekends," Joe said in a voice heavy with suspicion. "Too
busy to see me anyway!"

"It's a free service for the poor and needy of the town
who turn up in droves and receive diagnosis and treatment
from Adelaide, courtesy of a charity that sponsors her work.
It's not at all what Easterby would want, as the exclusive
Harley Street image is the one he strives for. She told me
once that she'd made it a condition of her employment. No
free service—no Adelaide."

"And there I was picturing Adelaide punting up and
down the Cam to the Orchard Tea Rooms in Grantchester
with some frisky young don in her time off," Joe said.

"Time off! The girl gets no time off! Easterby cuts her
no slack. No hours off in lieu. Can't you see how strained
she's becoming?"

Joe ignored the intended criticism. "Tell me, Hunnyton—what charity is involved with these surgeries?"

"I wondered if you'd think to ask. It's the Red Heart Foundation." He looked at Joe, waiting for his reaction.

"Never heard of it. Something on the lines of the Red Cross?"

"*Nothing* on the lines of the Red Cross we all know and love! But that's the image the name is meant to conjure up: starched nurses, cups of tea and tins of Queen Mary's chocolate! This group is quite recently formed. Everything above board, legally registered and professionally run. Some big names on the Board of Directors. Admirable service supplied. It really fills a disgraceful gap in our unequal society. Money is genuinely given for the relief of the poor and suffering of Britain. The students here in the city made a wonderful contribution last year—proceeds of their Rag Week stunts. And that's all right. I'm a contributor myself!"

"But?"

"Red means 'Red,' Joe. I investigated. For Adelaide's sake. I didn't want her involved with some dubious outfit, and, as we were dealing with Easterby . . . Well, you never know. Anyhow, making innocent routine enquiries of a 'public safety order . . . police need to know . . .' nature, I discovered that the cash, which flows freely into the coffers, comes mainly—about eighty percent—from Russia."

"Good Lord! The buggers are everywhere! Does Adelaide know this?"

"I told her. She told me to sod off and not bother her with such nonsense. She didn't give a toss where the cash came from so long as it was curing her patients. Boils, rickets, broken limbs and miscarriages healed whether the money was red, blue or green."

Joe groaned and stayed silent. He had no idea what

Adelaide's political stance was. Did she even have one? They'd never discussed it. Why on earth hadn't she asked his opinion, his advice?

Hunnyton began to sum up, "So, someone in an office in Whitehall, troubled by the suicides of old friends, family members, perhaps, up here in Academia, put two and two together . . ."

"Or were tipped off by a victim . . ."

". . . and the powers that be decided to get to the bottom of it. By sending in their pet factotum. And here we are. Waiting for Figaro to make his move."

He looked at Joe—slightly drunk, somewhat disorderly and in retreat—with satisfaction.

THERE WAS ONE more piece of local knowledge Joe wanted to winkle out of Hunnyton before he left. With no reference to the Whitehall briefing he'd received, he asked, following on the Red Heart revelation, what were the superintendent's views on the so-called Red Menace. Was it a problem on his patch? Could Pertinax possibly be involved in any way? And the laboratories where the Russian scientist was working—the Cavendish—had Hunnyton ever had cause for concern in that quarter?

Hunnyton laughed. "I'll tell you the extent of police involvement with the labs! I mean apart from helping the young gentlemen on their way after closing time at the Eagle. One day last year. April it was, I think . . . Our beat bobby on King's Parade spotted something odd. A young man on a bike was wobbling down the Parade, shouting at passersby. Drunk as a skunk, the bobby decided and went to investigate. When he got close enough to hear what the chap was shouting, he heard: 'We've split it! We've split the atom! We've split it!'

"The constable passed a fatherly arm around the bloke's shoulders and helped him off his bike. 'Never you mind, sir,' he said. 'I'm sure you bright fellows will be able to stick it back together again tomorrow morning. On your way now.'"

"I intend to approach the laboratory and make enquiries and fully expect to get the polite brush-off. But can you, here and now, Hunnyton, tell me what projects the Russian scientist Kapitza and his team are working on?"

The question provoked a sly smile and a raised eyebrow. "About time someone asked! Why has his name suddenly come to your attention?"

"Four good reasons. Kapitza is in contact with the ARCOS offices in Moorgate. That's the All Russian Co-operative Society and it's not somewhere you'd go to buy a bag of sugar. Not this Co-op! It's the front for communism in Britain. Heavily financed by Moscow. He is also close to Maurice Dobb—the doyen of the communist fraternity at Trinity. Thirdly, his name has been handed to us by a Cavendish scientist who insists his colleague is passing information to the Russians. A spy. Fourthly, he is known to be planning a trip back to St. Petersburg in the summer vacation. Leaving his family behind for once. He has two young children, I'm told. Changes in pattern of behaviour are always interesting. With the mischief-making propensities of Pertinax popped into possibly the same crucible, someone at the labs rang the fire alarm."

"About bloody time!" Hunnyton rasped again. He rose from his chair and stamped around his desk in his agitation. "It's been bothering me for some time. Nothing the CID can do about it! All those science boys are perfectly law-abiding. I'd love to get one or two of them to face me in the cells, but they don't even spit in the street! Not one of them is on my watch list. But I try to keep abreast of politics. I love the country that I damn nearly died for and if someone blows the bugle again (heaven forbid!) I'll be there in the front ranks. Shoulder to shoulder with you most probably, Joe. When I sniff the wind and scent danger, I take notice and I take action. Those labs worry me. Remember how in the last lot we came close to being finished off by the infernal invention of a scientist? Bloody poison gas! If it all happens again—and I'm one of those who think it will because Europe hasn't done with the blood letting—the outcome will be engineered in some smart, modern, innocent-looking labora-tory. If we're lucky it will be the one round the corner here in Cambridge . . . but if we're not, it will be the new one that's planned for Leningrad or the one in Göttingen."

"Not so much stinks as bangs to expect next time around," Joe said. "Atoms. Smashing them to smithereens in magnetic chambers to see what they're made of. Neutrons . . . nuclei . . . electrons . . . or some such. Dangerous business. Huge potential, I understand, for fuelling what MI5 calls 'war work.'"

"War work!" Hunnyton chuntered with disgust. "What a phrase! Infernal inventions feeding the arms manufactur-ing industry. An expensive business, too. Have you noticed, Sandilands, that the smaller the subject of study, the larger and more elaborate the apparatus required and the space to do it in?"

Hunnyton took a file from a drawer and glanced briefly inside it. "I'm no physicist and I hardly understood a word of what I was being told when I cornered one of the Cavendish scientists in the pub one evening. Not a big fish. Lower echelon, research assistant I think. A college tie and a jar or two of ale loosens their tongues. Gawd! It was like inviting a sewing circle to indulge in gossip. I risked being swept away by the outpouring! The tittle-tattle! The wrist-slapping and hair-tugging! What Blackett thought of Kapitza. What everyone else thought of Blackett. How Rutherford gave the damned Russian everything he asked for. Spoiled bastard. Things had improved since that nutcase Oppenheimer had buggered off to Göttingen in Germany to study theoretical physics. And good riddance, eh? Did I know he'd tried to kill Blackett with a poisoned apple? And do away with himself? Pity was, he'd failed on both counts."

The superintendent sighed. "Spiteful little sod! But—the stuff they're doing in there!" He began to read from his notebook: "Radio-activity physics . . . nuclear physics . . . cloud chambers . . . electromagnetism . . . low-temperature physics . . . superfluidity . . . and here's one that'll stand your hair on end—cosmic ray physics! Can that be as alarming as it sounds? Sorry, Joe! I could hardly get my pencil out in the pub so I had to do my best to remember the terms and write them down later. And the lad was three sheets to the wind at the time. So I may be offering you gobbledegook, I'm afraid. Or his version of the latest episode of *Buck Rogers* in *Amazing Stories* comic. But I tell you, these blokes travel about, flitting from country to country like honeybees, fertilising and spreading ideas. And it's useless checking their luggage for blueprints; give them a blackboard and a stick of chalk and they can reproduce anything, anywhere. This

Kapitza is, in addition, a dab hand at engineering. Designs his own labs and equipment as well. He has undoubtedly the skill to design weaponry. To convert the equations on the blackboard into actual explosive devices or death rays that some bugger can manufacture. With his knowledge he could set up anywhere in the world to work on a new-fangled armoury. Not every country encourages science purely for the sake of scientific advancement. Not every country is as benign, open-handed and trusting as our own. I tell you, Joe, it's all very disturbing."

"I'll tell you what else is disturbing—living within a hundred yards of these laboratories!" Joe said, stricken. "Oppenheimer? Good Lord! 'Unstable' is the last estimate I had of him, on top of 'clumsy in his conduct of experiments in the laboratory.' Even MI5 had got wind of the psychiatric help he was being given here in Cambridge a year or two ago. Brilliant in his field, however, and now you're telling me this chap has gone off with all the experience he's acquired here to lay it at the feet of Herr Hitler's alarming government?"

"You can add to that the Japanese bloke whose name escapes me. He's gone sailing back home with his mental blueprints. Do the Japanese love us? Who would know?"

Joe was suddenly starkly sober. "These men are swanning about the globe, carrying with them the means of destroying the world. We just smile, stamp their passports and wish them bon voyage."

Hunnyton nodded. "They'll tell you in justification that you can't stop the march of progress, and that the larger the number of political powers in possession of the nasty secrets, the less likely it is that the world will be threatened by the domination of a single power. If every industrialised country possesses the means to blow the others to bits, then not one of them will give the order for fear of reprisals. The globe in flames and all the rest of it. Have you ever heard such twaddle? Might just work—barring accidents—as long as you could guarantee that each power is run by a sane and civilised ruler. But you can't. Scum rises to the top and in most of Europe it's scum that has its slimy finger on the detonator. You look at Hitler, Mussolini, Franco, Stalin and what do you see? Power-hungry upstarts, sprung from nowhere salubrious. Crass, ruthless, supported by gangs of like-minded thugs. They appear overnight like full-blown fungus in the forest and they grow most easily on the trunks of rotten trees. A healthy stout oak tree has defences that shrug them off. They thrive amid aged, decaying roots and timber."

"Decaying empires? Italy, Spain, Russia, Germany . . ."
Neither man dared voice his next thought.

Disturbed by his own vehemence, Hunnyton checked himself and finished more lightly, "It's enough to make you head for the hills to build a bomb shelter! Personally I've always thought the men who argue that science should be encouraged to travel the globe without impediment are indulging in a bit of arrogant self-foolery. Scientists are infected with the annihilation virus and they're spreading it round the world, in my book."

"And, as with syphilis, there's no chance of an antidote. One wonders why the government has been so complacent. Have they any qualms?"

"They haven't! These lads make utter fools of them. Twist them round their little fingers. They open up new magnetic labs and suchlike at vast expense and who do they invite to a champagne opening and launch? Not Royalty, whom they despise, but prime ministers (where the power and the purse strings lie) and ex-prime ministers (where the prestige and the honours come from). I was invited to one of these do's as the token civil law and order presence, put to stand next to the mayor in his regalia. The occasion was the opening of that new laboratory of theirs—the Mond—last February. I was covering for old Baxter who couldn't be bothered. One of these jokers—the Russian you've just mentioned, I think—was smarming away with Stanley Baldwin, ex–prime minister and chancellor of the university, who was present to cut the ribbons and declare the place open. I overheard our Russian charmer answer a question from the old grandee and add with a grin Mephistopheles would have been proud of, 'Oh, you can believe me, sir. *I'm* not a politician.'"

"Bloody cheek!"

"Baldwin laughed. That's the kind of attitude you'll be dealing with if you try to get aboard. This new intellectual élite is more exclusive and arrogant than the old aristocratic sort. Frighteningly—a good number of them qualify on both counts. Many have private means and ancient families. They seem to owe allegiance, not to their own country, but to each other and their science. Science is their god."

"And they're quite prepared to offer up humanity on his altar?"

"I don't doubt it. We've seen it happen, Joe. The thing that disturbs me is what's in the minds of these men of science. Or rather what's not. Geniuses, we're told they are worthy of not only our breathless respect but bucket-loads of the country's cash, when some of them—to ordinary blokes like us—appear to have the moral sense and reasoning of a three-year-old infant. There's a great gap where you would expect, well ... wisdom ... a certain social awareness ... allegiance and respect for their alma mater. They show a naiveté that would have had my mother say they had a tile loose. I'll tell you a story ..." He sat forward, claiming Joe's slightly out-of-focus gaze and gave a wry smile that promised humour or surprise.

"There's a well-known Cambridge story that did the rounds a year or two ago. It originates from my old college—Trinity. One of these scientists making a name for himself, a St. John's fellow, was invited to dine on High Table. Problem: this chap was notorious for his lack of small talk and his awkwardness in company. A genial Trinity gent was selected to sit next to him and warned, 'You might find him a bit sticky. Do your best to draw him out.' Turning to his silent fellow guest to open a conversation, our cheerful chap essayed, 'I say, have you seen any good films lately?' To which the response was a puzzled silence, then: 'Why do you want to know that?'"

"A good story. I don't dismiss these folk tales—they have a way of hitting the nail of truth on the head," Joe said with a smile.

"I was that genial gent, Joe. My silent scientist was Paul Dirac. You may have noticed he won this year's Nobel Prize for Physics? Believe me, it was an uncomfortable two hours. But enlightening. This man who discourses and swaps ideas with Einstein, one of the select band who may—how would we know?—have the expertise to blow up the world, has the social skills of a hermit with a bad stomachache."

"Was there nothing you could say to get him going?"

"One thing. One of the subjects you're not supposed to raise at the dinner table. Nothing else was working so I thought I might just as well plunge in, defy tradition and ask him what I really wanted to know: Did he believe in God?"

"Oh Lord, no!"

"Oh Lord, yes! I'd pressed the right button. I'd calculated that all scientists must be prepared for this. Suddenly eloquent, he explained that God is a product of the human imagination. God is a useful notion for keeping the lower classes quiet. Quiet people are easier to govern. I challenged him on this, 'You're hinting at an alliance between God and the State?' 'Oh, yes. Both rely on the illusion that a kindly God rewards—in heaven, if not on earth—those who have done their duty without fuss or complaint.'"

"Sounds familiar. I've heard similar views being shouted from soapboxes in Hyde Park. Karl Marx? Crikey! Religion and politics in the same response! It would take me a week to unpick his assertion. Not that anyone would be listening. Opinions like that tend to flow from people with cloth ears. One-way traffic! What on earth did you say?"

"How does a humble historian argue with a quantum mathematician's view of the universe?" Hunnyton finished hopelessly.

"How do you account for this . . . detachment from reality . . . always assuming a definition of 'reality' can be agreed on? How do you test for it? Has anyone invented the science that will test the scientists? *Should* we? Have we the right? Who are '*we*'?" Joe wondered aloud.

"If anyone thought it fit to measure scientists on a scale for morality or sociability, they'd have to reject three quarters of the world's geniuses as unviable. I have that insight from a physicist. One of the sane ones," Hunnyton said grumpily. "Some of them are aware of the problem."

Intrigued and encouraged by his colleague's ventures into the scientific world, Joe pushed him further. "They seem not to acknowledge national borders and patriotic conventions either. What *do* they care about, Hunnyton?"

A question Hunnyton had evidently already addressed as his reply came with swift decisiveness. "The pursuit of knowledge, the ready cash to support that pursuit and the winning of prestigious prizes. That's it."

"Emotional ties?" Joe asked. "Family, friends, native land?"

Hunnyton snorted. "Nothing you can count on. That arsehole who gave us poison gas—Haber—was begged by his wife to stop his ghastly work. Just after the second battle of Ypres where sixty-seven thousand of us had died as a result of his infernal concoction. He refused to listen to her pleas. In despair, she shot herself in the heart with his service pistol to make her point. The next day he went off, leaving behind his thirteen-year-old son, who'd discovered his mother's body, to the Eastern Front to gas the Russkies. As though nothing had happened."

"What's one death when you're planning millions? I can't begin to understand them."

"Yet this Kapitza has a family here in Cambridge: Russian wife and two children. As far as I know, he's devoted to them. He takes them everywhere with him."

"Except to St. Petersburg next vacation. Hmm . . . Doesn't want to expose them to Stalin's hospitality? Offer up political hostages? Trigger a 'Do as we require and then your children may avoid being offered accommodation in some Arctic gulag' situation?"

Hunnyton grunted. "Too complicated for the CID! Give me a Stourbridge Common Strangler any day. Anyhow—to get you back on track again—I've been sent the police lab results of your friend's death scene. Mountfitchet in All Hallows Church. Everything in Adelaide's and Risby's accounts is confirmed. Puts your mind at rest, I should think. Personal not professional motive. 'Suicide while the balance of the mind was disturbed' will be the coroner's decision. Pity he had to top himself with his job incomplete, but there you go. Perhaps he'll have left some indication of the state of his mind in his college rooms. St. Benedict's. I ordered the master to have his rooms sealed off and left untouched until you gave the say so."

He handed Joe an envelope that had already been opened. Joe took a few minutes to glance through the material. "No prints other than the victim's own on the knife. There's the clincher."

"Had you expected anything else?"

"No, I hadn't. But I always check. The knife itself . . . good lads! They've traced it! Not one of Aidan's own. But he could have helped himself to it in preparation for his own death because it comes from the college itself." Joe looked up at Hunnyton. "Silver handled and stamped with the college arms, sharpened, six-inch-long blade . . ."

"A game blade. Used on special occasions at High Table. At banquets when one of the courses is a joint of challenging meat. The things they get their teeth into! Swan, boar, haunch of venison, sometimes all rolled up together in a bloody great medieval sausage! You need an electric saw to get through some of the concoctions!"

"Aidan appeared on High Table last week at the

invitation of the master. He was an old boy, of course, so that courtesy would be expected. He could have hacked his way through his *paupiette de Gargantua* or his roast neck of swan, wiped his blade off on his napkin and dropped it down the sleeve of his gown and made off with it. Premeditation. But why? The doctor gives him a clear bill of health. In perfect physical condition, apparently. No diseases, no growths, all organs in good shape . . . Definitely not one of Easterby's specials, I'm relieved to note! The life he led—there was always that fear. Yet . . . He had intended to kill himself before he set off for All Hallows. He wasn't tipped over the edge of reason by the Reverend Sweeting and his doom and gloom merchants at least. I don't need to think *that* badly of my friend. But why pick that place to die?"

"There's little in the way of private space in this city. Mountfitchet was a gentleman. He wouldn't want to put anybody out. The clowns who jump in front of trains and leap from buildings cause an awful lot of mess and trouble for others. He sounds like the kind of bloke who would have sought out a quiet, spiritual atmosphere close to his Maker where he wouldn't be disturbed and he'd be no bother to anyone else. It's what I'd have done. The only human he risked startling was the Reverend Sweeting and perhaps he didn't mind that."

"Makes sense." Joe sighed. "He'll have left his affairs in order too, I suppose I'll find when I contact his lawyer in London. He named me his executor. But he has failed me in one matter: we haven't had his report back to HQ, Hunnyton, and that's a concern. I know he was told to report weekly, but MI5 have had nothing yet. I'll go and search his room. He may have left an account of some sort." Joe got to his feet. "Don't ring ahead. I'll just slip back to my hotel and change my tie. I don't think I'd get past the porter dressed like this."

"A gargle with Doctor Smyth's patent mint mouthwash wouldn't come amiss either, Sandilands. Let me know how you get on."

CHAPTER 14

I t was a soberly dressed gentleman with firm tread and impeccable breath who offered his warrant card at the porter's lodge an hour later.

"Been expecting you, sir. Do you know the college, may I ask? . . . No? . . . I'll ask George to conduct you to Sir Aidan's room. It's not straightforward. George!"

Wondering how he was going to find his way out of this stone warren when he'd finished, Joe dismissed the footman on arrival at Aidan's door. Hunnyton had told him the room in the visitors' staircase had been sealed off, but there was no sign of police tape or Keep Out notices. Merely a hand-written sign drawing-pinned to the massive door, saying OAK UP. Probably much more effective, Joe judged. People could never resist the challenge of trying to get through police barriers. This door was barred by eight hundred years of college tradition.

He left the notice in place when he entered and shut the door behind him. He stood, as he required his detective squads to do on entering a strange room with crime-solving in mind, back to the door, looking around carefully. Then, notebook of squared paper sheets in hand, he began his professional scene-of-crime inspection. A disproportionate reaction, he knew, but it gave a formal framework to his search, validating a distasteful rummage through a friend's life.

At least it was speedily done. The guest room was almost devoid of Aidan's presence. Conscious of the clandestine nature of his spell in the college, he had clearly brought very little in the way of personal belongings with him. Such as were on display: alarm clock, coffee flask, electric torch, books and newspapers, Joe noted down. He looked for the photographs every man carries with him into strange territory. Or battle. Wife, sweetheart, children, spaniel? There were none. No familiar face welcomed him back to his lonely room. Joe remembered that Aidan had had no family left to speak of. A second cousin in the navy he rarely saw, an old uncle with whom he'd long since lost touch. A succession of girls but never a steady one. Joe saw loneliness. The fate of every black sheep born into a respectable English family. But Aidan had shown no signs of feeling any disadvantage. His quickstepping path through life had seemed charmed and was the envy of many of his more steady-going friends.

It was a spartan room space. Joe compared it with the fine rooms stuffed with elegant belongings Aidan kept in Albany in Picadilly, the brief shaft of sympathy extinguished by the further thought that Aidan was used to hard living. He'd been a student here until 1914, a boy at boarding school before that—he was used to deprivation of a scholarly nature. He'd just graduated from this place when, as most boys had, he'd left the academic life at the age of twenty-one and taken up a commission in the army. No nonsense in those days of refusing to fight for King and Country. Downy-faced boys had made hard choices: Army? Navy? The new Royal Flying Corps, perhaps? Which regiment to join? Surely grandfather had served? Family history and tradition were suddenly invoked and men looked to their roots to direct and inspire them.

Had it been the making of Aidan or had it wrecked his life forever? He certainly voiced no complaints. Active, lucky, harum-scarum and downright scurrilous on occasion, he'd been a man Joe had always expected to burn himself out at an early age like a shooting star. He'd never have imagined death would overtake him alone in a dim church at midnight. Death by his own hand. The Curse of Pertinax? Joe wondered fancifully. Had it struck his friend so soon after contact? Had, indeed, contact been made?

How would they know? Damn it! They'd run Aidan on too long a lead. He was clever and confident about the whole thing, but, still, an amateur. A puppet who'd been left dangling between the two strings of MI5 and the Branch, each assuming the other was the secure and guiding hand. Joe could have taken steps, managed things differently, preserved his agent's life or sanity. His death was Joe's fault and, standing here in the man's room, the sharp steel of guilt cut him to the core. He could do nothing now but, belatedly, his job. More thoroughly.

Joe checked the desk and the bookshelf first of all. No documents. The blotting pad was unused. Apart from the college handout of essential reading matter: a history of the college, a Bible and the works of Shakespeare, there were four books of Aidan's own. Joe smiled to see the latest Wodehouse, snatched up at the railway bookstall and still in its wrapper, a slim volume of French Romantic poetry, with improvements in pencil in the margins, the works of Aeschylus (Greek on one page, English on the opposite) and a cheap edition of a Dickens novel. Ah. *A Tale of Two Cities*. The first spy novel? Finally, a joke—or at least a grin— shared with Aidan.

Joe checked methodically through the wardrobe and the bedside cupboards. The pockets and linings of the spare tweed suit, the evening suit, the officer's trench coat, the pockets of the shirts, brought to light nothing but ticket stubs and handkerchiefs. No more than the search through the overcoat and dark suit he'd been wearing on the night he died had produced, according to the police report.

Aidan's lightness of touch belied the seriousness with which he'd undertaken the preparation for his task. He had been taking the spy's role very seriously apparently. To a professional level. He had insisted on being given a course in fieldcraft by the bloke at MI5 who was interested in that sort of thing. Joe had thought to provide a few extra—and more practical—life-preserving hints by fixing him up for an afternoon in a gym with his Special Branchman, Bacchus. Hints involving use of concealed weapons, locating the jugular in the dark, a neat back-breaking trick, silencing guard dogs and manoeuvres for shaking off a tail in a city environment had featured. Bacchus couldn't be doing with dark glasses, holes in newspapers and invisible ink, and any agent-in-training who made the mistake of bending to tie up a shoelace would get the Bacchus boot up his backside as a corrective. Joe's lieutenant had never been a Boy Scout in practice or in philosophy. Get the job done, make sure you're the man left standing and get out, just about summed up his attitude to his clandestine work. Bacchus, Joe recalled, had been favourably impressed by Aidan's ability. The professional soldier was evolving smoothly into the professional agent.

Mattress and pillows followed in his search. The bed had been made up most probably on the morning of the day he died and had not been disturbed. The bedder? Worth having a word with her? Yes. Just occasionally, distraught or careless young men living a solitary life confided things they should not have confided to their bedder who was, after all, the only civilian, uncritical human being they came into contact with every day. For most students they were a faceless army of automatons who came in, made the bed, sometimes got them out of it, picked up socks from under it, washed up the dirty teacups and disappeared, telling no tales. But Aidan had loved to talk. People were easy in his company. They told him about their family, their pets, their troubles and triumphs, and Aidan remembered the details. Perhaps, thinking he was on the trail of some other inhabitant of the college, he might have asked a few penetrating questions of someone who knew all the ins and outs and much of the gossip. In the same circumstances, Joe would certainly have made a point of getting to know his bedder.

He interrupted his search to scribble a note and, hearing feet clattering down the corridor, dashed to the door. "I say! You fellows going past the porter's lodge, are you? Jolly good! Look, could you drop this in on him and mention that it's really rather urgent? Thanks awfully!"

He turned his attention lastly to the suitcase which Aidan had retained and pushed under the bed. Locked. This was not a problem for Joe, who carried a set of lock picks in his pocket. He had it open in seconds. Disappointingly, it contained nothing more than a bag of apples, two Mars bars, a packet of Senior Service cigarettes and a pair of gold cuff links bearing his familiar stag's head crest. Joe hesitated before reclosing it. It had been locked. Why? On account of the cuff links? Possibly. But, running a hand around the silk lining he felt a slim shape hidden in the side of the case. This, when he'd managed to disentangle it from its hiding place, proved to be a diary.

A university year book for the academic year, only three weeks of entries. He'd started his diary immediately on his arrival in college on the 8th of October, the beginning of Michaelmas term. Joe followed the entries eagerly, curiosity roused.

But only to be dampened.

The man was taking his role-playing very seriously. Arrivals and departures were noted, times meticulously written in. The state of the weather merited two lines each day. The people he'd met were listed, further meetings had been entered. Even the menus for each meal he'd taken in college were painstakingly recorded. By no means had every evening been so occupied; on ten occasions, no mention of his whereabouts or activities was offered. His visits to the college archives where he was ostensibly spending his days researching the wartime exploits of the alumni were logged. There was no code known to Joe in all this. It was tedious beyond words, but all completely innocent as far as he could judge. Had Aidan invented a new enemy agent deterrence technique—bore the buggers to death? "I catch you reading my diary! Okay, mate—I'll make you suffer!"

The very last entry was made on the 31st of October: "8 P.M. All Hallows." Joe was on the point of giving up and closing the book when his sharp eye caught the aberration.

Same pen, same hand, but words surely more carelessly or hurriedly written?

At the end of a tiresome entry for the 28th of October, following drivel about the unseasonably warm weather . . . how the lawns were crying out for rain . . . roast beef and Eve's pudding for lunch, there it was. So lulled was his brain by the repetition, and so eager to reach the end, it had at first reading passed smoothly over the single line:

I saw him. At dinner. There can be no doubt.

Unfathomable. This entry was out of step with the rest. Why was it written down at all? Aidan couldn't have known that Joe was going to read this. It wasn't directed at him. Communication with headquarters was by quite other means, the drill made perfectly clear to the agent. Joe had the impression that it was a personal comment, the emotional outburst of a man isolated and taken by surprise. If a man stubs his toe in an empty room, he still yells and curses though there is no one to hear. If a solitary agent claps eyes on the Angel Gabriel or the Devil himself in the course of his undercover enquiries and he has no one near him to share his shock, then a single line in a diary might be his sole outlet.

None of Joe's reasoning satisfied him, but the single scribbled line had the unsettling quality of a yelp of pain. Aidan seemed to have been excited—or alarmed—by the sight of a man he did not name. A man who had been present at the college dinner table. That comment at least would reduce his area of search. If Aidan had been given a place at High Table, which seemed to be the usual arrangement, according to the diary entries, then the stranger would be one of no more than a dozen men. And someone, somewhere, would have a list of their names. Easily followed up.

There was no sign at all in the room of any useful notes

for the perusal of MI5. Perhaps he'd already sent them off in accordance with prescribed practice? Joe resolved to ask Bacchus to chase this up. Meanwhile he put the diary and Aidan's cuff links into his own pocket and locked up the suitcase again.

A sharp knock on the door rang out as he pushed the case back under the bed. George the footman was standing there, a piece of paper in his hand: Joe's own message for Mr. Coulson, the porter.

"Your reply, sir."

Joe was impressed. This was quicker service than the Yard could provide.

He asked the man to wait in case he should wish to send a further message.

Here was his answer, written on the back. The bedder on this corridor was a Mrs. Alsopp, who attended, unusually, twice a day as the occupants were "specials." 7 to 9 A.M. for the regular service, and 6 to 9 P.M. for the turning down of the sheets while the guests were in the refectory. Mrs. A. was a long-standing and trustworthy employee whose service dated back to the period before the war. Exemplary character. She would even now be making her way to the college for her evening stint. Mr. Coulson would ask her to pop up and see the commissioner before she started on her duties.

Joe looked at his watch. Five forty-five. He thanked George and sent a verbal response. "Excellent! Please do just that. I will await the lady here."

MRS. ALSOPP HOPPED into the room with the energy of a small brown robin and cast a bright and searching eye over what she clearly regarded as her territory. The arrangements seemed to pass muster. Joe was thankful that he'd made no mess.

He introduced himself and gravely set about announcing the news of Aidan's death.

She sat down heavily on the chair Joe quickly pulled forward, seeing her unfeigned distress.

"Oh, my Lord! It's true then? We'd all heard the rumour but no one could be certain and Mr. Coulson's lip is always buttoned."

She began to look anxiously about the room again and Joe interpreted and responded to her fear. "No, don't be concerned! He didn't die in this room, Mrs. Alsopp. No traces physical or spiritual left to clear up here. He wasn't on college premises at all when he met his death."

"They're saying he was murdered, sir."

"No. We think he killed himself."

"No! Gerraway! I don't believe it. Why would he go and do such a thing, then? He was a lovely man. Always laughing. Liked a joke. Clean and tidy and no trouble. He left me a tip at the end of every week. A gent. It's not right!" She began to fish about in the capacious front pocket of her overall, turning up only a yellow duster and a bag of mint imperials. Guessing her problem, Joe hurried to offer his handkerchief.

He watched the tears begin to trickle their way uncertainly down the rough terrain of Mrs. Alsopp's cheek to disappear in the folds of the crisp white cotton. Bloody old Aidan! Guests of the college came and went in their hundreds, skivvied for by a battalion of Mrs. Alsopps, instantly, perhaps thankfully, forgotten by them, but Aidan left a memory and a loss. This unattractive, barrel-shaped, elderly lady with her unexpected show of grief had crashed through Joe's professional veneer of unconcern as no one else had. He swallowed to ease his constricting throat, sniffed and turned away.

"Friend of his are you, sir?"

"I am," he said. "I'm here to clear up his affairs. Excuse me, Mrs. Alsopp, tears are catching it seems! No, no. Hang on to it, I've got a spare so we can sniffle together in harmony. I met Sir Aidan nearly twenty years ago. Very brave soldier."

"Thought as much. The way he carried himself. It always shows."

"Now, I'm hoping you can help me to understand what was in his mind on that last day. I see the bed was not turned down so you didn't come in for the evening service. Is that right?"

"Yes, sir. I did him out in the morning as usual. He was here at his desk writing a letter but he stopped when I came in and we had a good old chin-wag. Cheerful as ever. He passed me a bit of scandal about the master. That was the last I saw of him . . ." She paused to dab away a fresh outbreak of tears. "When I came back in the evening, his oak was up."

"Tell me, Mrs. Alsopp, was there anything in particular Sir Aidan asked you about? The college, the city, the people here, perhaps? Anything that struck you as unusual?"

She gave the question her full attention. "Nothing out of the ordinary, sir. Just chit-chat, you know. He was interested in everything. Why do you want to know? He wasn't in trouble was he?"

"Nothing of the kind."

"One of you then? A policeman?"

Joe smiled. "Not his style at all. No. Sir Aidan was a good man. Believe me, Mrs. Alsopp, he was on the side of the angels. That's why I want so badly to work out what went wrong for him. I want to know why, instead of propping up the bar at the Eagle and having a good laugh with him, I shall be going to his funeral next week."

After a few minutes' exchange of comment and remembrance, Joe thought there was probably nothing further he could draw from her and she'd already told him the very thing he needed to know. He was about to start making the polite sounds of dismissal but he hesitated at the sight of her face, saddened but straining with a need to be of some help, wanting more from him. He had never met a witness so ready to show cooperation. He made a last shot, taking a more precise aim. "Did he ever mention a scientist, perhaps? Or a local member of the aristocracy?"

She shook her head vigorously. "Nothing like that. He was no show-off. He only talked about things he thought I'd be interested in. He asked me how Mavis was getting on. She was the only one he mentioned from his student days."

"Mavis?"

"His old bedder, sir. Fancy remembering after all those years, but he did! Mavis and I started here the same term in 1905 as soon as our kids were old enough to go to school. I had two, Mavis had three, and we were free to go out to work. They're very particular about who they take on, sir. You've got to be a steady-going, married woman of a certain age with a good reputation. Kids are no problem. They expect you to have got kids and a lot of women pass the job down to them. Keep it in the family." She grinned and shrugged. "And it helps if you're no film star."

"Is Mavis still in employment here? What were you able to tell him?" Joe asked.

"Oh, she's here. Still bedding. She does staircases A to C. We've never been close—she's always been a bit uppity with the rest of us. Thinks she's too good for the job and keeps herself to herself. That's not hard to do when you live out in Ditton."

At the mention of the name "Ditton," Joe was unable to prevent there springing into his mind a line or two from Rupert Brooke's poem about the Cambridge villages. The young poet, an undergraduate at the university, had carelessly, naughtily, characterised the inhabitants with undeserved epithets.

And Ditton girls are mean and dirty.
There's none in Harston under thirty . . .

"Did you tell her someone was asking after her?"

"'Course I did. She looked at me as though I had a screw loose and said she'd no memory of anyone by that name. I pointed him out to her as he was crossing the quad one morning. 'Look, Mavis,' I says, 'That tall, fair bloke—that's him as was asking after you.' Same thing—never clapped eyes on him. Well, you can forget the names, however strange—they get all sorts coming through here and it is nearly twenty years ago—but the man? You wouldn't forget a man like that, would you?"

"No, you wouldn't, Mrs. Alsopp."

"I expect it was Sir Aidan got it wrong then."

JOE CLOSED THE door thoughtfully behind her.

So, Aidan had been writing a letter. Using, Joe assumed, the most spy-proof form of communication—the King's

Royal Mail. Swift. Secure. Unremarkable. As recommended by Bacchus. It was probably waiting in the in-tray on his desk in Scotland Yard right now. He decided to make a phone call from the Master's office when he took his farewell.

His second thought turned on Mavis the bedder. Joe was intrigued and concerned. Aidan didn't make mistakes of that nature and it was entirely in character for him to have made pleasant overtures. Less likely that Mavis would have protested that she had no recollection of him. Mrs. Alsopp had instinctively known that something was wrong. *She* would have remembered Aidan with fondness even without the very generous ten-pound note Joe had thought to press into her hand. "No, really, Mrs. Alsopp! It's what he would have wanted and I am his executor, you know. I insist! And thank you for taking care of my friend."

What care had Mavis taken twenty years ago? Surely not? Aidan had always been a randy old bugger but he'd never have taken advantage of the staff. And taking Mrs. Alsopp's dates into account, the said Mavis must, in 1914, have been in her early forties, married, mother of three and 'no film star.' Hardly a temptation for a twenty-one-year-old undergraduate. That was the whole point. The college authorities knew their business and they understood their undergraduates. A false trail and an unworthy suspicion, Joe decided. He knew when he was being distracted by his affection for his friend and over-intrigued by the mystery surrounding his death. He had to keep his mind on the main event.

THE MASTER WAS all smiles and welcome. Already begowned in preparation for college supper, he asked Joe to step into his parlour for a glass of sherry and an exchange of condolences. In a few swift sentences, he had established exactly Joe's position and his reasons for wanting access to Mountfitchet's room. Joe made the required speech of thanks and added a résumé of his search. He ended with a statement that he had finished his task and the room was ready to be put back into the system once more. There were no residual problems for the college.

"I've packed his few belongings, including his books, into his suitcase and—"

"My dear fellow, I'll have it sent straight round to you at your hotel. The Garden House, was that?"

Joe had only two requests to make: Might he be provided with a list of the guests at High Table on the night of the 28th of October, and might he use the telephone to make a private phone call to London?

In relief at finding that there was no scandal to be chopped off at the neck, and beguiled by the policeman's easy and cultivated manner, the master readily agreed that Joe could make free with his telephone. In the study next door. Where he would also find a copy of the guest lists pinned to the notice board. Would Joe be so good as to help himself? He really had to scoot now. Oh, before he dashed off—perhaps the commissioner would accept an invitation to dinner tomorrow evening? Evening dress, they'd provide a gown.

"It might be of assistance," he'd added, "if you were to take your friend's place at the table. You will meet the same company. No new faces, apart, of course, from the four undergraduates who take their seats on High in rotation. You will have one on your right hand. Can't predict whether it will be an enjoyable experience. Some are tongue-tied with embarrassment, some overly voluble." He'd smiled confidingly at Joe. "I think you'll manage."

BACCHUS PICKED UP the phone at once. "Frank? Is that you? Ernest here."

Joe picked up the message and groaned inwardly. This was to be one of their frank and earnest business discussions, unintelligible to any of the ears that might be listening in over an open line. Occasionally the chat was not entirely intelligible to Joe but he tried to hang on. He appreciated the necessity for caution. Telephone operators galore sat in ranks, plug in hand, ready to overhear any conversation that took their fancy. It was claimed that there were even plants in some of the offices at the Yard. They'd been known to sell tip-offs to the press. Bacchus, his senior executive at Special Branch, never overplayed his hand. If Bacchus was doing some nifty footwork then Joe had better pick up the step and follow his lead.

"All going well up here in the Midlands. Unseasonably good weather. Just ringing through to check whether there's been any post for me."

"Yes, there has. That report you were expecting—it came yesterday. Hope you don't mind—I took the liberty of looking through it."

"Good man. Anything of interest?"

"Yes. Indeed. That rep you appointed last month—the one you have in place for the East Midlands—he's a crackerjack! He's opened up some interesting avenues. You'll want to follow them up straight away, I imagine. I've sent a copy up to you by motorcycle messenger. It should be arriving within the hour. The original I've passed up to Head Office for info and filing."

"Got it! Thanks, Ernest. Love to your girls!"

Well, at least it had been good to hear the crisp London voice. Familiar, responsive. Joe didn't think he could have coped with the loneliness and uncertainty of a spy's life and wondered, again, how Aidan had managed nearly a month of cheerless isolation. He next addressed himself to the problem of finding a particular sheet of paper amongst the press of papers and notices on the master's board. After a minute or two, he began to work out the system and turned up a term's supply of dinner lists. There was Aidan's name on the sheet for the first week of the term and continuing through at intervals to the night he had died: the 31st of October.

There was a pattern. He located the four ever-changing undergraduates, marked by a (U), and discounted them, the remainder being college dignitaries with the odd invited luminary. Joe noted that "Sir G. Pertinax" had attended a week after Aidan's arrival. His name appeared again five days later, on Friday, the twentieth. Contact made, apparently.

Joe wrote down the dates and turned his attention to the night of the twenty-seventh. A Friday. He could see nothing special at this dinner when Aidan had clapped eyes on his disturbing man. An intensive check told Joe that all the diners had appeared on previous occasions and none therefore would have surprised him by making a fresh appearance. Odd.

BEFORE LEAVING THE college, Joe called in at the porter's lodge. Information flowed through here constantly, and Joe could not afford to neglect a last check.

Mr. Coulson was very ready to help but had little to offer. Joe applied his usual technique of pinpoint questioning when faced with genial fuzziness. "You must have been the last person to see Sir Aidan when he left college on the thirty-first, Coulson. How did he look?"

"Yes, sir. I was on duty. Seven forty-five P.M. I clocked him out. Everyone else was still in hall. He looked his usual self: chirpy. Exchanged a few words, hoped I had an untroubled evening—it being Hallowe'en—grinned and told me not to wait up. He marched off in that 'out of my way' swagger that he had."

"So, nothing out of the ordinary."

"No, sir . . ." The porter hesitated, and then, into Joe's expectant silence, added, "There was something three days earlier. Nothing to get excited about! Last Saturday, the twenty-eighth that would be. He came out and asked me what time dinner was expected to finish on All Hallows'."

"He knew the routine by then?" Joe said doubtfully.

"He knew there was a change in routine. Dinner was due to start at the regular time but as so many young gentlemen had either signed out or wanted to get off early—parties and junketing going on—it would be over pretty sharpish. I told him the hall would be cleared by eight and the domestic staff were expecting to get home by ten before the lamps went out. Nasty night to be caught out in the dark, sir."

"Why did you think it was a strange question, Coulson?"

"I didn't at the time. Just the normal query of a gent sorting out his timetable. But then I discovered that he was already signed out anyway for All Hallow's Eve. He'd made plans to eat elsewhere. He often did. So why the questions about the timing of dinner in hall?"

"I agree, Coulson. It doesn't make a lot of sense. I'll ponder on it."

Ah, well. Joe looked forward to his own appearance at dinner here the next evening. To sit in Aidan's place at the table might well reveal a fresh perspective. Or an old, familiar face?

CHAPTER 15

Bacchus's package arrived at the reception desk of the hotel, where Joe had been waiting for ten anxious minutes. He signed for it, tipped the motorcyclist and bolted upstairs to read the contents.

The sheets of A4 paper were a typed copy of the original that Mrs. Alsopp had seen Aidan writing on the morning of the day he died. Transcription smoothly organised by Bacchus. Bleak and official with the usual office stamps at the top and dire warnings of an "Eyes only. For the sole attention of . . ." nature. Joe would have much preferred to read the sheets written in his friend's handwriting with blots, crossings out, underlining and all, but the character shone through the impersonal typeface.

Joe! Greetings! And to any other poor lug who has the job of reading these ramblings—good luck, mate. I did my best! I gave my all in the service of the State such as it is.

First communication. Report on first three weeks, 8–31 October, follows. I hope it was worth the wait. Take a comfortable seat. I've set the whole morning aside to write this!

Joe was alarmed. At a quick glance, this communication was decidedly improper. What in hell had got into Aidan? He'd been meticulous to this point. What possessed him to present an official report that might find its way to the desk of the prime minister himself in this devil-may-care style? Complete scorn for the security services? Embarrassed braggadocio? Coercion? Gone over to the enemy? The one predictable consequence of this outpouring was that serious questions, and possibly the resignation, would be asked of the assistant commissioner who had put this joker into a sensitive position.

Joe slumped down at his desk and read on in a turmoil of conflicting emotions.

Characters in order of appearance:

The Master. As expected. In post for just two years. Youngish for the job. Finding his way, making his reputation. Sees my promised research when published as a feather in his cap. Establishes him as a man who cares about the past and the welfare of his college men. Couldn't be more helpful. I have full access to the college records and permission to interview any old dodderers still in possession of their memories. Hardly any of these remain after two decades and a world war. None, sadly, who knew me as a student. But I did receive permission to work with P.'s old college, Trinity, where I had more success jogging memories. Perhaps P.'s constant injections of cash to his Alma Mater keep his memory bright! Material unexpectedly useful! See later note.

Other dons: none significant. They wander on and

off stage muttering obscure warnings like a Greek chorus. Polite but wary. No approaches made to me of a political or social nature.

Pertinax. First contact 17 October. Both guests at High Table. He was warmly welcomed by other dons. Behaviour exemplary. A good man to have at your table. Chatty and has a fund of funny stories. Many at the expense of other colleges where he appears to be a welcome guest. But he's clearly not a professional academic and a breath of fresh air on account of that. I liked him. He sought me out after dinner and we spoke more intimately over brandy in the Combination Room. I liked him even more. He established that I was a single man who enjoyed cards, music, hunting, gambling—the usual gentlemanly pursuits. Suggested that, after a week of monkish seclusion toiling in the archives, I might be ready for a bit of lighter entertainment. Did I enjoy jazz bands? Good claret and French food? Pigeon shooting? Pig-sticking? Other delights of the autumnal country- side? What could I say? He invited me to dinner at Madingley Court the coming Friday to 'further the acquaintance.' I accepted.

Friday dinner turned out to be a long weekend. Toothbrush and all other material comforts provided. Back in college much the worse for wear. Condition passed off as a bout of the 'flu that's doing the rounds.

Madingley guest list: six congenial gentlemen on pleasure bent whose names I shall not commit to paper but undertake to whisper into Joe's ear when next I see him, and eight ladies ditto. The latter had arrived as a group during the afternoon I discovered, not in taxis, which would have attracted local attention, but by van. Yes, van! Shipped out from Cambridge in a conveyance labelled 'East Coast Fish Co.' (Friday delivery, you see.) The van has undergone interior re-appointments and the ladies are collected on Monday mornings by a similarly restyled motor which is ostensibly and appropriately, a laundry van. ('Dimity's Personal Laundry Services.') They load and unload round the back so never raise local eyebrows. Joe, this enterprise is run with martial precision and a sense of mischief.

The girls are young, pretty and stylishly dressed` and perfectly able to join the gents at dinner and hold a conversation. It's not High at St. Benedict's but it has its points. My dinner partner dazzled me with her views on the after-effects of the Versailles Treaty (the French got it all wrong), greyhound racing (not in favour of the electric hare) and the works of Dashiell Hammett (The Maltese Falcon, highly recommended). I think I proposed marriage between the fish and the game. And again during the dessert. The ladies are recruited in London and seem to be under the direction of an older woman of considerable address whom they refer to as Minerva. Really, I don't think the Goddess of Wisdom herself would begrudge the use of her name! I overheard her conducting a little verbal fencing with Pertinax and getting the better of him with style, brevity and wit. A formidable lady.

I spoke to each of the girls in the course of the evening (no suspicions raised, normal behaviour in this company) and established that none were local girls. They spend their time when on manoeuvres in Cambridge at an

address in Cherrystone Road, number 50. I have inves-
tigated on foot and confirm that number 50 exists. It is
on a secluded corner spot, a capacious Edwardian villa,
and the beautifully-executed name board outside
announces: 'Minerva Milton Secretarial College.
Instruction to Diploma Level for young ladies in short-
hand, typing and general office skills.' As far as my
informant was aware, the maison has never had a visit
from the local constabulary. Not, at any rate, in its for-
mal capacity. Make what you like of that!

La directrice. I shall call her 'Minerva' though she's
probably on your books under quite another name. I
knew at once I'd seen her before and I think she recog-
nised me. It's this silver-gilt hair of mine! It signals my
presence like a flashing lighthouse beam. As anti-vice
supremo of London Town, Joe, you must be aware of an
establishment called the 'Satin Slipper Club' or some
such—the names change—in Regent Street. It is patron-
ised by the highest in the land and is owned and run by
a formidable dame called Mrs. Meyrick. She's usually
one step ahead of the Met but occasionally your vice boys
catch up with her and mount a raid. She's been in and
out of jail for years but carries on valiantly with the
enthusiastic support of some of her illustrious clients.
When I last called at the Slipper, some five years ago,
one of the dance hostesses was a spectacular woman,
going by the name of . . . I think . . . 'Circe.' It was Per-
tinax's associate, Minerva. (Still working to a classical
theme, evidently.) Having served her apprenticeship
with the best, she's graduated to running her own show
in Cambridge.

I spent the night with Prudence (no kidding!) because she seemed to me to be the youngest and therefore least likely to be wise to the ways of the world and in particular of Milord Pertinax's corner of it. And so it proved. Prudence liked a joke, good manners and flattering attention. I searched the room thoroughly according to instructions given. I discovered no illicit camera holes or anything else to rouse my suspicions and douse my ardour.

Down shame! I sweet-talked Prudence into revealing that—yes—sometimes she was aware of clandestine filming going on. Indeed, those encounters were quite sought after by the girls since it was seen as promotion and the rewards were greater. Such sessions were always staged in one particular room, the one at the end of the corridor in the east wing, identifiable by its yellow door.

Saturday started late. Exhausted gents met for breakfast at midday, avoiding each other's bleary eye. It's like sighting an old friend in the nude through the steam in a Turkish bath, I suppose. A moment's embarrassment, then it's 'Pass me the sponge, old boy . . . Nice to see more of you . . . Ho! Ho!'

Country sports filled the afternoon. I remember some shooting and some dashed dangerous pig-sticking on foot. Quarry—wild boar, can you believe! Pertinax keeps a small herd of flint-eyed, leathery creatures he's rustled from the Ardennes Forest and a small army of flint-eyed, leathery keepers to chase after them. I counted a dozen of these. Excessive for a small estate? All, I suspect, judging by their demeanour, are ex-army. And not necessarily our army. I overheard cursing in

Romanian, Russian and Italian. The men are far more dangerous than the beasts. The boarhounds (six of these) are the most dangerous of all. A foreign breed, not, I think, recognised at Crufts. They are vicious and barely under control. Spiked collars and terrible teeth! Guests were warned that they are allowed to roam freely after dark as an anti-poaching measure. I pass on the warning in case you or your friends should be caught out after dark in the environs of the Court.

The evening was a repetition of the previous one but even more jolly with an all-change general excuse-me going on to the strains of a rather good jazz band brought down from a West End club. The after-dinner friandises in bonbon dishes along the table were, on this occasion, accompanied by small, silver boxes containing white powder which seemed to have an instantly restorative effect on the gentlemen who sampled it. The jazz band called itself 'The Limehouse Sextet.' I wondered whether, with their declared connection with a dubious locale, they were responsible for bringing down the exotic substance. More work for B.?

When the music stopped, I found myself in the company of 'Constancy' in the room with the yellow door. Sorry, folks! An indignity too far! When the moment came, I opted out of the What the Butler Saw treatment—incidentally it was the bloody butler! Very nifty with a film camera, Prudence had told me the night before. He's a thug who should be investigated. Goes by the name of Jennings. Picture a warthog in black tie and tailcoat. London man. Thirties, six feet tall, sandy hair, brown eyes, hands of a prizefighter. Well, one hand. Half *his left is missing. Blown off in the war? Chewed up by a guard dog? I'd like to think so! And, if you're looking him up, don't bother riffling through the annals of the Junior Ganymede Club in St. James's; he's no butler. Try the guest list at Wormwood Scrubs, filed under 'Grievous Bodily Harm.' He has a knife scar under his left ear, extending down to his collarbone.*

I wouldn't have found the filming device, so carefully was it camouflaged by an exuberant William Morris wallpaper, but at a moment of calculated maximum distraction (which I'll leave to your imagination) I glimpsed Constancy, with a swift bit of léger de main, move a picture an inch or two to the left. The minx! I promptly re-sited it. So the first and last image of the evening's drama will have been a close-up of my grinning face. Really! The Mountfitchet bum is in pretty good nick still but not for public exposure. For future reference: the picture is a particularly unattractive Picasso of a woman (?) with two heads on a brown background. Sorry! Cover blown, I'm afraid, but I'd done what you'd sent me to do. Though I think I was never fooling the man. He's one step ahead of us all the way. I hardly expected to survive the night. Perhaps I flatter myself? Was I indeed his main prey on that occasion or just a cheery and reassuring fellow guest who had the title, the aplomb and the dance steps to make the evening go with a swing? Though, if so, why did I qualify for the Yellow Room treatment? Insurance for good behaviour or a reciprocal favour at some future time? I count myself banked!

I should declare at this point perhaps that between them, Pertinax and Minerva played their roles with panache and their organisation was meticulous. They had many players on stage with wildly differing handling requirements and they managed to send everyone but yours truly home feeling ecstatic, valued or, at the least, rewarded. Their names should be put forward if ever another Delhi Durbar needs to be staged! I can see how men less worldly than I am could be totally ensnared . . . enchanted . . . by this taste of a glittering, sophisticated, devil-may-care world that knows exactly how to cater for their suppressed desires. And how desperate they must be when they realise they have been betrayed, that career and good name are shot to pieces, those dearest to them shocked and alienated. I see things now from the victims' perspective. I cannot refurbish my own image but I can stop it from decaying further.

I beat a hasty retreat in the early hours of the morning. A clichéd departure involving ivy, drainpipe and extreme loss of dignity. Getting too old for all this nonsense, I'm afraid, though it loses none of its excitement. Exit was not straightforward but, with B.'s training, I managed. It's really quite quick back into the centre of Cambridge on foot when you're running from the Devil.

Joe broke off in alarm. "With Bacchus's training . . . ?" In silent killing? "Oh, Aidan what have you done?" he muttered. He fought down a surge of nervous laughter at the picture of Aidan fleeing back down the dark lanes in his evening suit.

Pertinax was present on a further occasion at college dinner (24th). We exchanged cold nods across the table and he made no attempt to contact me. Excusable froideur, in the circs! I had committed two unforgivable social gaffes: I'd neglected to send him a bread-and-butter thank you note for his hospitality and left him with a dead dog on his hands.

So there you are! That's how they catch their fish! Though I can't imagine why P. would want an insignificant flounder like me gasping in his basket. Your suspicions are confirmed. I hope I've been of help. Now follows the truly interesting stuff! The stuff you ought to have told me to concentrate on.

THE SECOND PART of Aidan's report, dated the previous week, was rather more what Joe expected of an agent-in-place. The writing was less dashing and the single sheet was formally addressed. At first glance it looked reassuringly dull and fact filled. Not an exclamation mark in sight. Yet what had Aidan just called it? The truly interesting stuff?

Intrigued, Joe began to read:

Research conducted at Cambridge and London into the life and career of Sir Gregory Pertinax.

There follows an amalgam of evidence from college files, from conversations with elderly alumni and from details I extracted from contacts of my own in London. The name Mountfitchet still opens doors and jogs memories in military quarters. I can provide sources, names and dates, if you require them.

Being an old boy, Pertinax has his own dossier in college records.

He was an undergraduate (Politics and Economics) from 1907–1910. Left Cambridge before war was declared to join the army of his ancestral country, Latvia, which was at that time held by the Russians. Peter the Great invaded in 1710 and annexed Latvia into the Russian Empire. The capital and port, Riga, is—or was before the war—a splendid city. A map will reveal that it is close to the Russian frontier and St. Petersburg is only five hundred miles distant. Russian became the official language in 1891 but this was much resented by the Latvian inhabitants. Many of these— and I have an idea Pertinax the grandfather may have been one of them—regarded themselves as the descendants of the medieval Teutonic Knights of Riga, a military aristocracy with a chip on their shoulders. 'Brothers of the Sword,' they call themselves.

Pertinax went straight to Riga and signed on with the Latvian Rifles, an élite outfit. They were eventually to fight alongside the Russian 12th Army against the advance of the German 8th Army under Oskar von Hutier, the dashing Prussian general. Our subject was there in the battle on the Dvina River in September 1917 when the German storm troopers, far outnumbered but better equipped, blasted their way through the Russian and Latvian ranks. He survived the artillery, the flamethrowers and the clouds of poison gas and somehow avoided being taken prisoner. It might be interesting to ascertain how the man saved his skin. The Russian losses were twenty-five thousand to the Germans' five thousand. Perhaps our man was even present when the German forces marched in triumph and immaculate order through the streets of Riga on the seventeenth of September?

I see that the Pertinax coat of arms has as its base a black cross on a white ground. This is the emblem of the Teutonic Knights of Crusader days who in turn have it from St. George—the dragon-slaying hero. Interesting to see that the masters of the Livonian Order of Teutonic Knights all have German names: Gottfried, Otto, Hein-rich, Willhelm. And their device is in German: Helfen. Wehren. Heilen. (Help. Defend. Heal.)

Some confusion of loyalties here, I think? One of your Baltic specialists may be able to advise.

Worth reflecting, I think, on the family shield. That usually announces to the world who you really are. When your enemy's shield is surging towards you on horseback, with deadly intent only inches away on the other side of the jousting rails, you need to know if you're facing an eagle, a lion or a boar. There's always a message there. No animals for P. Just the stark St. George symbol. (Sketch below.)

Joe considered it. He snorted in disbelief. It couldn't have taken the College of Heralds more than five minutes to draw up the design. He found himself hoping Pertinax the Elder had negotiated a special rate from the Rouge Dragon Pursuivant. Was this an almost blank canvas waiting for embellishment? Not quartered by any female insignia on marriage, he noted. Didn't Pertinaxes have wives? he wondered. Was this some Templar/Teutonic Knight tradition they were working to? Did they marry their serving wenches? Were they self-generating freaks?

Aidan also appeared puzzled:

Why St. George? I asked myself. What qualities of this saint fix the attention of Pertinax? When I investigated him, the saint proved to be astonishingly popular. Odd how we English assume he's ours and ours alone. Good old St. George of Merrie England. Not a bit of it! He's also claimed by the Russians, the French and the Germans. He must have had a perplexing time during the last lot with all the combatants seeking his saintly support. The number of causes and orders and societies who vie for his attention are astonishing in their number and variety. He was the patron saint of Boy Scouts, of cavalrymen, of Portuguese sailors, syphilis sufferers, even those afflicted by the toothache. And now, if I interpret the heraldry aright, we can add to his list: Pertinax and his self-propagating line. Complete with a suitably warlike motto: Militemus! We can't say we haven't been warned! Nutty as a fruitcake. And that's the most dangerous kind.

Additionally: Pertinax gained an upper second class degree. Respectable. Did well considering how very little work he put in, is the view amongst the old fellows at Trinity who remember him. They put it down to natural intelligence, not diligence. This achievement was accompanied by sporting honours. He's a good marksman. Rowed a bit, mainly skulls. Not a team or a crew member, I note. Boxing blue.

Your servant, sir. A.M.

And, hurriedly at the end: *Keep your guard up, Joe, and, if you have to—fight by Seven Dials Rules! If you need a second, you know where I am!*

SEVEN DIALS! THE roughest, most lawless part of London. In other words: "No rules." No, Joe didn't think the memory of the chivalrous Marquess of Queensberry would prevent Pertinax from delivering a low blow.

But would the villain, could the villain, have engineered Aidan's death? It might well have been his intention to kill him, but it was impossible that he had brought it about. Adelaide and Constable Risby had both heard Aidan's confession.

The dying man had claimed his sins had found him out or some such, but apparently, the sins, whatever they were, had not ambushed him until some hours after he'd written the letter in Joe's hand. There was nothing of the penitent in this bouncy, insouciant prose. There were indications in Aidan's account of a "Let you know ... When I see Joe again ..." nature that showed he was not at that point contemplating killing himself.

Something had occurred between Aidan's original attempt at sober reporting and the free-flowing account in tongue-in-cheek style for Joe's eyes. His focus had changed. The spying world with its dark duties, its conventions and expectations had become suddenly tedious and risible. Something to be shrugged off, but lightly, because he remained aware that he was writing for his friend. In some unspoken way, Aidan's life had changed. Joe had the distinct feeling that Aidan had reset his compass and was moving on.

Joe put these perplexing thoughts to one side and read again the fountain of practical information on the man he was hunting. Bacchus was also in possession of the information and was even now looking through mugshots, contacting the Vice desk and planning a raid, perhaps. He would have plans of Madingley Court, estimates of strength of the defences and enemy man power. He would have a small, selected squad preparing for the assault. Joe thought he could see exactly how it might be accomplished. The only way to storm a fortress. He thought of Dorothy and smiled. A sally port and someone on the inside to open it. Never failed.

It also helped to know the nature of the enemy. Who exactly was on Pertinax's side, willing or unwilling conspirators? He settled in to make a few phone calls from his room, having decided that the young lady on reception was too busy to listen in at this moment of the day and that, on the whole, the line was probably more secure than the one at the police station. His first call was to his deputy, Superintendent Cottingham. Taking the small book containing the car registration numbers from his pocket, he explained his needs.

Ralph Cottingham took the strange request in his stride. "Ouch! That's a lot of numbers! Can you send us the book? . . . Back by Friday, eh? . . . Understood. So how can we do this most efficiently? Look, if you can bear it, why not just read the numbers out to me right now. That's the easy bit. I'll divide them up between four sergeants—one per season—and get them to come up with a complete list including the dates and times. Do you want them to trawl through for frequency and clustering? Right. I'll ring you to say when I'm handing them over to the motorcyclist. They should be with you for breakfast. Well, the delivery arrangements seem to be working out all right. Straight from the officer's hands into yours. Not left lying about in pigeonholes. Now, anything else while I've got my ear to the phone?"

"As a matter of fact, yes—one or two items." Joe began to reveal his shopping list.

"Who's on the Vice desk at the moment? . . . I have a question for him.

"From the ridiculous to the sublime—what connections do we have with the Church? . . . Regarding the qualifications and past history of one of their vicars? You know a dean? That should do it . . . Right. I'll dictate a question for him.

"Lastly, for the moment: Pertinax, Sir Gregory. Can you track his club memberships and find out whether he was ever blackballed from one?

"That'll do for now, Ralph! Why don't you pour yourself a whisky, sharpen a few pencils, lock your door and ring me back in five minutes for those numbers?"

Know your enemy. Joe was building up a picture of Pertinax, but nothing was clear. He was struggling with a web of conflicting impressions. He'd learned from interrogations that it was sometimes a single throwaway remark that burst uncensored from a suspect, seemingly insignificant or unconnected, that gave him a clue to the man's or woman's character and motives.

"Men have been drummed out of clubs for much less . . ." Pertinax had grumbled with some bitterness.

He'd been relaxed after lunch when he spoke, certainly less than sober as he'd plied Joe with wine and topped up his

own glass, drinking along encouragingly. Not a wise strata-
gem when your companion is an astute, large-boned
Scotsman. It had been a fleeting remark and Joe was probably making too much of it, but some resentments run deep
and can affect a man's outlook and behaviour.

He next squeezed in a call to Easterby's surgery. A short
and unproductive call. Dr. Hartest was not available. She was
out attending to a premature birth and naturally they were
unable to say when she would return. Would he like to leave
a message?

CHAPTER 16

J oe was leaving the dining room at seven-thirty the following morning when the call came through to reception.

"I'll take it here," Joe said. "Ralph! Good morning! No, speak freely. Though, as I'm standing in reception, expect some deliberately wooden answers from this end."

"Got it. Parcel ready to leave the office. Rider reckons two hours at this time of day. It took longer than expected, Joe. We were at it most of the night. I kept the four sergeants in separate rooms and told them they were traffic violations we were dealing with. One of the lads was sharp though! 'Cor, guv!' he said. 'Who took these numbers? Where was he standing with his notebook? Outside Buckingham Palace? On a Garden Party day?' I've annotated them. Black underlining equals a single visit. Red: multiple visits. I've put the frequency in brackets after the names. One or two of the contenders appeared together more than once. Likewise marked. I ran them through the sporting and social calendar . . . racing at Newmarket, June Balls in Cambridge and so on. No strong connection observed.

"Now, your list of questions from yesterday . . . but before I kick off I'll give you the contents of a scrap of paper Bacchus pushed under my nose five minutes ago. The butler, he says, is ex-army and very recognisable from the description Aidan gave. Royal Engineer, a Sapper. Pre-war work digging on the London Underground led to his recruitment as a 'clay-kicker.' That's a tunneller. Was wounded in action at Messines Ridge (in the hand) and sent back to Blighty. Spent some years in jail for various petty crimes until he entered into employment with P. His real name's Herbert Jennings.

"Next up, the vicar. My source was too careful to dish the dirt, but he did say in a meaningful way that the bloke has moved or been moved about a fair number of times in his career. Lucky old All Hallows is his present perch.

"Now, the clubs. The editor of the *Tatler* owed me a favour and spoke freely and entertainingly about the black-balling. Was our boy ever blackballed! I'll say! From several clubs but, Joe, this unpleasant tradition doesn't necessarily relate to the kicking out of an *existing* unsatisfactory member. The term is more likely to apply to someone seeking membership. Which is the case with your chap. He never even had the chance to be sacked! He was 'blackballed' and his father and grandfather before him, when he put his name forward for membership. The Pertinax men joined a list at Whites, the Carlton, the Athenaeum . . . all the usual. These clubs do have long lists, but generally a man can be sure of getting in eventually because he's recommended by one or two existing members who put pressure on the rest to accept their friend. No such accommodation for the Pertinaxes. Roundly rejected by all the top clubs. A social stigma that's hard to live with and it's been the ruin of many a good man. Now you or I would say: 'Huh! Stuff you lot! Your loss!' And forget it. Reminding ourselves that these members who do the voting have some quite extraordinary ways of arriving at decisions."

"But would they have the insolence to turn down a Knight of the Realm?"

Ralph laughed. "Did you hear about the Garrick, Joe? The club for actors and the entertainment world? Their membership is so nutty they had the gall to blackball Henry Irving! The best actor of the day, the first one to be knighted for the glory he brought to the profession. Worse still— there's the example of the Travellers' Club! Their measure of suitability is that members should have travelled a minimum of a modest five hundred miles from London, and whom did they find lacking? None less than Cecil Rhodes, the explorer, discoverer of the Victoria Falls and most of central Africa!"

"Mmm . . . I'd love to have a glimpse of their rejection letter! What *did* they come up with? 'Cecil really must widen his horizons'? But what reason did—let's say—White's give for turning down our friend?"

"Some starchy formula about the applicant's incompatibility of background and character with the established ideals and values of existing club members. 'Foreign,' you see. And not even from a country anyone can point to on the map. India, Prussia, the United States as country of origin might be acceptable, but . . . 'Latvia'? Isn't that the same as Lapland? Frozen north? Pine forests full of reindeer and dangerously close to those tsar-killing Bolsheviks?' Better take no risks and write, 'I do not think so,' against his name on the proposal form. Pop your black ball into the slot in the drawer on voting day and you've kept your club safe from bad influences."

"That would account for the explosion of displeasure I sensed. Any particular action taken?" Joe asked tersely.

"There's no record of White's being firebombed, if that's what you're getting at! But we're looking at a chap who doesn't snort and stamp when thwarted—he takes revenge. He opened his own club! After he got back from the war he bought a dilapidated hotel in St. James's, refurbished it, installed a French chef and kitchen staff and invited disgruntled gentlemen who'd been similarly rejected by other clubs to join 'The Oddballs Club.' At a time when many London clubs were having their kitchens exposed by the authorities as unhygienic, rat-infested death traps, Pertinax made something of a show of the superiority of his own culinary arrangements. Press cameras were invited in to record the gleaming fixtures and smiling foreign gents in chefs' hats and chequered trousers. Probably calculated to distract attention away from the illicit gambling that goes on in the upper back rooms! Whatever he's up to, they tell me it's thriving and has the best cellar in London. A good number of the founding members, being swashbuckling adventurers by nature and genuinely deserving of a sound blackballing, had actually done well out of the war and were minded to invest their ill-gotten gains in a scheme that cocked a snook at the society that had rejected them. They became shareholders, Joe! It would be interesting to see a list of the members, but they'd never supply one."

"But—action in general?"

"Ah. Against the establishment, you mean? Now here it all ceases to be mildly amusing. When you've had a look at his guest list you may conclude that he's attacking English society at the roots. You sent us one year's worth of social engagements, Joe. That's bad enough, but we should ask the question: What has resulted from an accumulation of previous years of seduction, defilement and coercion? Are his victims all around us, exercising pressure, running departments? Young men who've climbed to positions of influence in their field and who owe their continued security to the whim or plan of Pertinax—are they, with a nervous smile, sanctioning decisions he's made? With a coalition government presently in power and apparently practising self-destruction, crumbling before our eyes, one does rather wonder . . .

"Um . . . it's a ludicrous idea, Joe, but once it's lodged in your head you begin to see perfidy everywhere. Irrational acts and statements that in the ordinary way you'd put down to no more than the usual carelessness and stupidity suddenly appear in a different light." Ralph gave a snort of disgust. "Even to think like this can be seen in some quarters as a mental derangement . . . Are you signalling for the men in white coats yet, Joe?"

"Ralph, the word you're trying to avoid saying is 'paranoia.'"

"I try to avoid any word that might have been used by Freud. But I do ask myself: Do we risk becoming two of those jittery johnnies who see treachery behind every closed door, continually startled by their own shadows?"

"Two new recruits to the ranks of MI5, are you suggesting? Never! If I see something moving about surreptitiously in the shadows, I arrest it for lurking with intent. And I know—so do you, old friend."

"But, Joe, where do you start to unscramble all this?"

Ralph had been putting Joe's worst fears into words.

"I know what you mean. It's like being asked to unknot a skein of wool that's been played with by a litter of cats."

"You've no doubt been given your orders, Joe. The way I see it, there's only one way out of the problem. Remember that trigger-happy young lout, Alexander the so-called Great? I'm not an admirer but I do approve his short solution when faced with an outsized, knotty problem."

"So do I! 'Pass me my sword, squire!' I shall say and cleave through it. Thanks for the sinew-stiffening, Ralph!"

WITH TWO HOURS to wait before Cottingham's papers arrived, Joe was left agitated and wondering which of the threads to tug on next. He'd keep the sword solution as a last resort; slashing through a tangle of evidence and theory went against custom, character and Scotland Yard rules. As it was still very early, he'd have to leave face-to-face interviews for later and spend his time gathering information.

He decided to see if his face would open gates at Aidan's old college. He'd shown his warrant and made himself known to the chief porter the previous day but couldn't guarantee that Coulson would be there in his lair. Some other under porter who wouldn't know him from Adam might well deny him access.

There was enough light in the morning sky when he arrived at the gate to show his smiling features. Joe took out his warrant and prepared to explain who he was, only to be cut short by the porter. "That's quite all right, Commissioner. We thought you'd be back. The library, sir? Classics collection? Yes, of course. I'll send a boy with you. Here's Sam just on his way to the kitchens. He'll do. Hey, Sam!" The only suggestion that this was a ridiculous hour to be invading the library was a mild, "Well, at least you'll have the place to yourself, sir!"

He followed the bleary-eyed buttery boy down cold

corridors and across two quadrangles where a sudden flare of red Virginia creeper enlivened the grey stone. At the end of a colonnade, they climbed a staircase leading to a surprisingly large and airy east-facing room. All the walls were lined with bookshelves, and further stacks projected into the room at right angles, providing secluded spaces with tables and chairs for the comfort of readers. After taking a moment to get his bearings in the silent space, Joe spotted a well-stocked classics section and headed towards it. He ran his eyes along the shelves packed with familiar Greek and Roman writers but failed to find what he was looking for. Had he been grumbling his frustration aloud? A voice from the adjoining section made it clear that he had. "May I be of some help?" the dry and cultured voice wanted to know.

"Terribly sorry!" Joe said, darting around the stack. "Forgive me, sir—I thought I was alone."

"Never a wise assumption in St. Benedict's," the old man said. "Tell me why you're startling the Ancients with your very modern vocabulary."

"I'm looking for something on the Roman Emperor Pertinax, who died in the year 193. I thought perhaps Edward Gibbon might point me in the right direction, but I can't find him."

The figure was alarmingly ghost-like, an apparition from the medieval age. Paper-thin skin blotched with brown and a monastic fringe of grey hair were framed by the bunched black gown he wore about his shoulders like a stole to keep out the draughts but the eyes twinkling over the top of a pair of half-moon spectacles gave out a ray of warm humour. "Ah! Thinking of writing a volume yourself are you? An excellent thought! I've often had the same one myself. Always rejected it on the grounds of overstimulation! Too exciting a subject for a man in his eighth decade. Cool scholarship and Gibbon's prose are what I was brought up on. To launch into an account of the year of the six emperors would have the effect of feeding a life-long vegetarian a rare sirloin steak. No stomach for it. Death and vice are much better left to the younger generation. Is that what you're after, young man? Murder, greed and lechery?"

For a moment Joe was robbed of words. Transfixed by the quizzical eyes, he felt he was undergoing the last stage of an oral examination. "Yes. I confess: exactly that. And treachery. You may add treachery to your list, sir."

The stranger nodded, seemingly pleased to receive a direct answer. "Then you've hit on a fruitful, if neglected, period in Roman history." He peered more closely at Joe. "I say, young man . . . you're not one of these historical novelist chappies are you? Latter-day John Buchan? All flash and bang, sword and dagger, heads on pikes?"

"Not at all, sir! I'm a guest of the college doing a bit of personal research into a character who interests me. An elusive chap! And no one here is coming forward to help me with my enquiries." Joe grinned and extended a hand. "I'm an assistant commissioner of police at Scotland Yard. Joseph Sandilands, sir."

"Professor Deerbolt. Hubert Deerbolt. How do you do?"

The hand that took his was as fragile and as brown as an autumn beech leaf, and Joe was afraid it might crunch to dust in his own strong fingers.

"I'm delighted to meet you, Commissioner. If it's unsolved crime you're after, there's no shortage on these shelves, but unfortunately you come two millennia too late.

And you've got the wrong man in your sights. Why Pertinax? His predecessor, the evil young menace Commodus, committed crimes so foul even a Scotland Yarder could not envision them. His successor, Didius Julianus, was a corrupt killer who bought himself the Empire and indulged in human sacrifice. Much more interesting to a policeman, I'd have thought. Or a psychiatrist. You're looking in the wrong place, what's more. You're amongst the poets. History is in this alcove over here. Gibbon chapter four should come up with the evidence. But why not get it straight from the horse's mouth? Always go for the primary source first, my boy! Put Dio Cassius in the witness box! Do you read Greek?"

"No, not well enough."

"Then take this copy." The old scholar struggled to his feet, shuffled over to a bookshelf and, with unerring aim, prised a leather-covered book from a row of similar volumes. "Book seventy-four. Dio Cassius was a Roman but, like well-educated men of his day, he chose to write his history in Greek. You'll find the original text on the left, English on the right. The author was a contemporary of Pertinax. Knew him well. An admirer. A senator and an entertaining writer of history. Strong meat for some—I warn you."

"Admired by Dio Cassius, did you say? And Edward Gibbon?" Joe was taken aback. "I was picturing one of the series of bloodletting, perverted maniacs who held Rome at the point of a sword."

"Nothing of the kind. Pertinax was described as 'an excellent prince' by no less an authority than David Hume." He looked at Joe, waiting for a reaction to his mention of a Scottish philosopher of the eighteenth century. Testing.

Academics! Game players! Joe knew he was bound to

lose the traditional sparring with this intimidating old man, but he would play the game to the end in good spirit. "Then I'm convinced, Professor. Any friend of Hume's is a friend of mine!" he replied lightly. "Though we must take heed when he also warns us that, 'A wise man proportions his belief to the evidence.' I have that in poker work above my desk. You see me ready to adjust my belief if you can only present me with evidence."

Deerbolt smiled with satisfaction. "Then you will enjoy Dio. Dio clearly loved Pertinax and much regretted his early demise. Even the people of Rome publicly demonstrated their sorrow at his death. A dangerous thing to do—many were butchered by the soldiery on the orders of his successor. Gibbon says of him, 'He distinguished himself by the firmness, the prudence, the integrity of his conduct.' All accounts considered and at a distance of seventeen centuries, I judge Pertinax to have been Rome's last chance to survive and thrive and perhaps to save the known world from the worst excesses of the Dark Ages that followed. Europe would have been a different and better place had he lived long enough to consolidate the state, weed out the corrupt elements and bring the military to heel."

Catching Joe's look of disbelief, he shook his head and pressed on: "Think about it for a moment, young man! A strong Rome at that time would have made a recall of the Roman army from Britain unnecessary. The Roman influence in our islands would have strengthened. Their civilisation, which has left imprint enough, would have left an even stronger stamp, and we might well have been speaking a form of Italian now, with a continental view of the world rather than the insular one we have affected."

"You must excuse my unwillingness to accept this, Professor—I'm what the Romans would have judged a hyperborean, some rough moss-trooper from beyond the known world, safer kept on the far side of a dirty great wall."

The old man smiled. "A Scotsman. I had guessed as much. Though, in the tradition of Empire, the centre draws in talent from the fringes, and I observe that you have adopted the language and habits of the capital. Your bearing and profession, to say nothing of your battle scars, mark you out as a member of the Praetorian élite. Your figure and countenance would look convincing under a red-crested helmet and a silver breastplate. The Praetorian Guard were the Metropolitan Policemen of their day—were you aware that they had a special section they called the 'speculatores,' a unit given over to spying and clandestine operations?" He gave Joe a sidelong assessment.

"They're still with us, your speculatores! We call them the Special Branch." Joe grinned, entertained by the comparison. "And I'm glad to say they report to me."

"Use your power carefully, Commissioner!"

"The very reason I'm here, sir, speculatively pursuing Pertinax."

"Ah, yes. Pertinax. Your quarry was emperor for three months only and yet he had overhauled the tax system, halved the price of bread, righted a multitude of wrongs and begun to refill the empty coffers left by his dissolute predecessor, when he met his death at the hands of elements of the Praetorian Guard. This spoiled, licentious crew who held the office of emperor in their hands were demanding more and yet more pay and favours from a bankrupt city. Pertinax made them as fair an offer as the straightened times would allow."

Joe found he didn't want Deerbolt to tell him more. He was developing a fellow feeling for the crusty army veteran who appeared to have felt more concern for the state than for his own safety, but an ignominious death was on the cards and the professor was determined to tell the tale with full storytelling glee.

"It wasn't enough! A group of three hundred guards stormed the palace and—whereas any other emperor would have locked the doors, called up his body guard or slipped out the back way, the brave, old warrior went out boldly to face them down, armed only with words. He was sure they would respond to reason when they heard it. He very nearly talked them round. They put their swords back in their scabbards and looked at their boots. With the exception of one soldier.

"This arrogant fool, who knew not what he did, lunged towards the emperor and delivered a lethal sword thrust with the words, 'Take this from the army.' They cut off his head, stuck it on the end of a lance and paraded it about the city to the horror of the people. From that moment, Rome was lost."

"I had no idea!" Joe confessed. "Where did he spring from, this good Roman?"

"Come with me and have a look at that map," the old man invited. Joe put a steadying hand under his arm as he crossed the room and they went to stand, master and pupil, in front of a map of Europe extending from the Arctic to the north coast of Africa, from the Caucasus Mountains to the Atlantic Ocean. In the centre was the boot of Italy symbolically stamping its heel into what, on this map, appeared as *Mare Nostrum*. Our Sea. In the centre of the boot was a large black blob labelled: Roma. This was the known world of the Romans, and the various countries clustering about the blue expanse of the Mediterranean bore their Latin names. Instinctively, Joe's eyes went north to locate his own birthplace. The land of the "Caledonii," according to this view of the world.

A quivering hand drew his attention to northern Italy. "Publius Helvius Pertinax was born in Alba Pompeia in Northwest Italy. Humble origins—slave family. His father was a freed man who paid to educate his son well. The boy was talented and after some years teaching grammar he broke out and entered the military. He rose quickly through the ranks thanks to his ability, his engaging character and—not least— his influential patronage. Now let's take a look at the extent of his sphere of influence . . ." The hand wafted north and west to Britain. "He served on the Wall, indeed, he became governor of Britannia." The hand circled round to the east. "Procurator of Dacia and the eastern provinces along the Danube . . . Down to Syria, which he also governed. And to the southerly shores of the Mediterranean, where he became proconsul of Africa."

The hand repeated the circle with a conductor's flourish. "So, it was a man of courage, intellect and experience encompassing the whole of the known world who, well into his sixties, returned finally to Rome. To Rome where he hoped to enjoy a useful retirement serving in his senatorial capacity." The old man smiled. "A sort of easy spell lolling on the red leather benches of the House of Lords, you might say. But he was to be disappointed. The senatorial benches were an uncomfortable and dangerous place to sit! Commodus had conceived a hatred for the senators, who were powerless to restrain him in his excesses. One by one, the most vocal of the emperor's critics were being assassinated. And Pertinax was an avowed critic. When Commodus was finally strangled to death in his swimming pool by an athletic young man on his own staff, a contingent of the guards climbed into their armour and set out for Pertinax's house before news of the emperor's death got about. It was, not unreasonably, assumed that they had come to kill him on the orders of Commodus. When this fearsome crew stormed in, Pertinax prepared to die. Instead of death the Praetorians offered him the Empire. The very same outfit that snatched it back from him three months later. He was handed the task of rebuilding a bankrupt, lawless and ungovernable hellhole. A Hercules would have balked at the task and Pertinax was no demigod—he was a tired old man with bad feet."

They fell silent, taking in the huge size of the world that Pertinax had marched around, known and governed.

"But he so nearly pulled it off," Joe murmured. "The son of a slave rose to be master of the Western world. Can there be a message here?"

He had been speaking to himself, but Deerbolt answered. "For our own time, do you mean?" He shuddered. "Undoubtedly. What do you see when you look at today's Europe? A rotten, worm-eaten apple! Countries in turmoil, peoples on the move, borders redrawn and disputed, poverty and debt everywhere. Dissolute tyrants who feed on this decay are growing strong. They are recruiting masterless men to their cause. They welcome the poor and disaffected along with the rich and mischief-making. Europe is beginning to march to the tune they have chosen and the tune is a martial one." Deerbolt sighed, then with a grimace that managed to combine despair and humour said, "I say, Commissioner, do you happen to know a sixty-year-old soldier with bad feet?"

Joe replied with an attempt at cheerfulness. "I can't answer for the feet, but I know a sixty-year-old soldier with a dislocated shoulder. He also has courage, intellect, foresight and a certain gruff eloquence. Not much use to anyone at the moment, I'm afraid—he's been run down by a New York taxi and he's recuperating. And you must look elsewhere for someone to tap him on the shoulder and invite him to leave the red leather benches—the gift of Empire does not rest in my hands. The Praetorian Guard serves the people these days, sir."

"Mmm . . . the many are governed by the few with surprising ease, as you know. But who chooses the few? Too often they are self-selected. The people do not know them. The guards have fallen asleep. Time to change the guard and bark an order, Sandilands. What do you say?"

Deerbolt turned to face Joe with a playful smile. He retrieved a fold of his dusty old gown and flung it back over his shoulder with a gesture that turned it into a senatorial toga. He raised his right arm, palm down in an ironic sketch of a Roman salute. *"Custos novus!"* he snapped. *"Ad signa!"*

There was only one possible response from a new guard called upon to fall in and rally to the standard. *"Ad victoriam!"* Joe said, returning the salute.

CHAPTER 17

"Your continent needs *you!*"

Did Sir Gregory Pertinax think the continent of Europe needed him? Had he seen the imperious finger pointing at him? Or had his father and grandfather, sensitive to shallow roots in a condescending society that was prepared to be impressed by their cash but not their birth, prepared him all his life for an assumption of power of some sort? Political? Military? Joe had no idea. At what moment would he make his strike? In years or in weeks?

Of one thing Joe was certain now—the name was badly chosen. He could imagine David Hume's pithy summary of the character of the present-day, would-be emperor. It did not amount to "an excellent prince." No honest warrior with the good of his country at heart (whichever country he chose to support) would go about establishing power by covert and immoral means. Or would he? Joe forced himself constantly to question his own judgement, lit as it often was by the warm glow of patriotism. But did the honest warrior exist? Had he ever existed? Joe's mental list registered Cincinnatus, King Alfred, the Duke of Wellington, George Washington and ran out. Though he recognised that every man was a hero or a potential hero in his own estimation.

The professor had been intrigued by Joe's quest but not

deceived. In the quiet of the academic backwater, Joe had let his guard down so far as to enquire into what was a well-known name hereabouts. Had the connection been made between the names? Of course it had. A policeman of his rank enquiring into the provenance of a local nabob would have sounded the alarm bell. The shrewd old bird, working comfortably within the framework of history and philosophy, had warned Joe and roused him to action. To use his imagery—the old guards had fallen asleep on duty and a potential tyrant was even now stepping over the snoring heaps to seize power with the connivance of his faction—willing or coerced. No need for crude measures, as with Guy Fawkes and his gang, who'd laid down barrels of gunpowder under Parliament, literally to blast their way to power. No, no. Simply drug the guard, disarm your opponent, suborn the senators, and be sure of where you were going, and the rotten state would fall at your feet. In the upcoming elections, Joe had no doubt that the name of Pertinax would feature on the ballot papers. After his election it would be a short step to seizing the reins of power. Manufacture an emergency, a national threat of some sort, put yourself in charge of a war cabinet and the state was yours. It had worked for Oliver Cromwell nearly three hundred years before. The people had thanked the Lord for, at last, a strong leader and had overlooked the uncomfortable fact that he had signed their king's death warrant.

Joe hoped his thoughts were wild and ridiculous. But then he was struck by an even more alarming speculation: How far and how wide did his support extend? All the way to the Baltic? Over the border into Russia? The Roman map came back to mind. The islands of Britain were a wondrous foothold in Europe. Geographically they stood, the cockpit of the continent, insular, defiant and disdainful. When visibility was poor over the English Channel, *The Times* had been known to declare: FOG OVER CHANNEL. CONTINENT CUT OFF. Its navy, harboured in ports from which the world's oceans were instantly accessible in all seasons, was unsurpassed. Recently victorious over Germany—its only competitor in Europe—Britain remained, in spite of its current poverty, a politically powerful plum which, if offered up to the Bolshevik Empire (as an ally?), could furnish the new and untested potentate in those northern realms, Joseph Stalin, with the keys to a continent. He would be able to consider himself the Lord of the World, challenger to the increasing might of the United States. Frowning down over Europe from the vastness of his northern lands, opened up to the Atlantic and the west by a compliant Britain, his multitudes could sweep down unopposed through central Asia to the east and take over India as the British had long feared was their intention.

Joe was alarmed by his vision. Everywhere he'd turned in this enquiry he'd stubbed his toe on the same sinister words: red . . . Bolshy . . . Communist Society . . . Russian scientists . . . Only to be soothed by the constantly repeated, "But good old Ivan is our friend. The Russians fought against the Germans, on the side of the Allies, did they not?"

He called a halt to his fervid imaginings. He was a policeman, for God's sake! Not a politician! Evidence. He'd work away, building a case or demolishing a case according to the evidence. That was his job. Then he'd chuck his report onto the lap of MI5 and it would do the rounds of Home Office, Foreign Office and War Department. If the country still had a War Department. It would, as he'd explained to Hunnyton, bounce right back at him while a good deal of ministerial hand-washing and back-turning went on. Sandilands would be the one left wielding the sword. And, like the bloodthirsty numbskull who'd assassinated the Roman Pertinax, his head would roll in revenge the moment the next man came to power. Joe had learned some lessons from history, one being that assassins rarely got away with it.

"Ad signa!" certainly. He'd vowed: *"Ad Victoriam!"* Yes, he was ready to shake out his plumes, polish up his breastplate and fall in for one last effort. But he would tread a careful path.

JOE HURRIED TO his room with Ralph's package under his arm and settled at his desk to make sense of the car numbers.

He poured out a cup of coffee from the jug he'd had sent up and lit a cigarette, his hand trembling with anticipation.

The agreeable tension he was feeling was that of a hunter who hears the hounds call from two fields away, the stab of excitement of a copper on stake-out who sees a light go on in the window he's watching or the elation of a man turning to the *Times* crossword to find that he has the answer to number one across. He laid out the ten sheets in order, one for each month, January to October, and calmed himself sufficiently to give them an overall appraisal.

Red lines, green ones, blue and black. Dots and numbers. Christ! It was like looking at a piece of Fair Isle knitting! Whilst he admired the hours of work Ralph and his small crew had put in, he was at first stunned by the complexity of the result they had produced. All this from a scruffy little book compiled by a child!

After a while, priorities suggested themselves. Patterns began to emerge. Where to start? Joe controlled the moment of panic and reminded himself that the list, whatever it revealed, gave him his sole objective view of the situation, though this represented a mere ten-month slice of a portion of the problem. It did not include the guests who had arrived by train and taxi, for instance. Or bicycle. Cycle clips on a pair of evening trousers? Possible but unlikely. He would just have to take what he had so unexpectedly been offered and work on the evidence.

The names now linked to the vehicles stunned him. After a while he began to compose a working list of his own, categorising the revellers according to status and occupation:

Politicians: including two—*two*—cabinet ministers. Handily one on each side.

Aristocracy: making up about 50 percent.

Ambassadors and State officials: Russia, Germany, France. Always singly, not competing for attention, clearly.

Armed forces: thinly represented. Army and navy.

Entertainers: baritones and jazz pianists heavily represented.

Newspaper men.

Law and order: one high court judge—surely too old to have survived the Pertinax experience?

Other.

He marked down the repeat performers and bracketed the ones who made a single appearance only.

He was particularly interested in the latest session of hospitality when Clarice Denton had writhed in agony, dying despite Adelaide's attentions, well away from the revelry in the company rooms. Pertinax and his ex-sapper butler had, he believed, administered a fatal dose of arsenic. Not difficult to do when your chosen poison is tasteless and odourless and much fine wine is being drunk in a convivial setting. But why? Some rift in the relationship? Had Mrs. Denton represented a threat to the Madingley establishment? He turned to the last entry on the night she died, checking the Rolls-Royces and Daimlers against their registered owners, and his pencil dropped to the floor as his body shook with a sudden surge of horror. With his forefinger he traced again the name that had so startled him. A name he knew well. A name that his worst imaginings had never offered up as a possible victim of Pertinax. Though it had occurred—albeit glancingly—to a prescient Aidan, he remembered from his friend's briefing.

He retrieved his pencil and entered a further devastating category on his sheet: royalty.

If Pertinax had worked his evil magic and achieved his aims on the weekend Mrs. Denton had died, if he had photographic images in the can, still or moving, then all was lost. The conjuror had dealt himself the winning card.

He forced himself to move on—to turn to the second date of death. The footman, Jeremy. August the 13th. Yes, there had been a party assembled that weekend. A three-day shooting party, to mark the opening of the season, Joe assumed. He checked the owners of the grand automobiles and saw there men he would not himself have been pleased to spend any time with under a roof or on a shooting field. Dubious characters. "Degenerates," his sister Lydia would have called them. They were known, for the most part, to the police but, protected by their status, had always evaded a face-to-face run-in with the Met. Influence and cash kept their names out of the papers. A ghastly suspicion began to form in Joe's mind. He did not rein it in but followed where it led. He resolved to gather evidence and take it as far as circumstances would allow.

A few more minutes of careful study and he saw the anomaly. The dropped stitch in the pattern.

A single entry which he'd bracketed and discarded in the month of July snagged at his attention. A modest motor-car, the only one in the entire list that did not speak of wealth and influence. A Morris. Joe was surprised that the boy Samuel had considered it worthy of being recorded. He opened a further category on his list. Scientists: one only.

The owner of the Morris, a Doctor Humphrey Page, had arrived on July the 20th. Nothing further. Had he decided the scene was not for him? Another ivy and drain-pipe job or a quick dash after breakfast? Joe checked Ralph's additional notes. Bless the man, he'd found time to check up the name. A Cambridge man, address given. Physicist. Working at the Cavendish Laboratory. Was this an attempt by Pertinax to find a wormhole into the scientific world? What was special about Page? Why had he visited only once? Was he perhaps known to MI5? Oh, Lord! Was this Hermes? Joe looked at his watch, made a further entry in his schedule for the day and reached for the telephone.

NUMBER 50, CHERRYSTONE Road, Aidan had said. Joe told his taxi to park well short of it and around the corner. The driver was to stay put until he returned.

"Cost ya!" was the annoying response, and the driver left the engine running.

"No, mate!" Joe said, flipping his warrant card at the man. "It'll cost *you*! Possibly your license if you don't cooperate. Now turn the bloody engine off! You'll be paid what you earn. When I get back. It may be two minutes, it could be thirty."

"Ha! You're a quick worker, guv!" the driver jeered.

Joe walked on, straight past the large city villa on the corner, and peered back at it from a distance of thirty yards. There was a large front door and, he guessed, two others, a side and a rear door. It backed on to an area of grass and trees that Joe took to be parkland. In the distance a duck squawked. As he watched, a nanny pushed a pram down the narrow ginnel by the side of number 50. Off to air the baby and feed the ducks, doubtless. A gentleman being hauled along by two matching Labrador dogs took the same route. Joe wondered, with a wry grin and a suspicious mind, whether the establishment provided a hitching post for dogs at the rear while their masters were otherwise engaged.

The area was suburban and very quiet at eleven in the morning. A few maids appeared at doors and windows in the imposing houses, flapping dusters, shaking mats and scrubbing steps. No one appeared at number 50. Joe did, however, catch a glimpse of two students of the Minerva Milton Secretarial College busily working away at typewriters, backs to the central front window. Window dressing? Joe thought so.

He walked back and strolled up the short black and red chequered pathway to the front door. He tugged on the bellpull and listened as footsteps scurried down the hall. A parlour maid in a mobcap answered mechanically, almost without looking at him. "Sorry, sir, the college is closed for business today."

"Not my business, miss," Joe said with a smile. "I don't wish to see Minerva Milton—or do you know her as Clarice Denton? Fetch any one of the students I see you have on the premises. One of those in the window will do. I'll wait here. Impatiently."

He looked about him, not much admiring the outdated décor: dark red, flocked wallpaper; patterned, deep pile carpet and a portrait of Queen Victoria on the wall. The freshly-polished surface of the mahogany hall table was taken up with a display of knickknacks of a traditional nature set out with precision. Matching silver-framed coronation photographs of King George V and his queen, the ever-glowering Mary of Teck, faced each other at a slight angle. "George and the Dragon," Joe's sister called the royal pair. Between the two, in pride of place on this shrine to the British monarchy, was a study of the six offspring of the marriage. Six! An heir and five spares. Probably taken some twenty years ago. Joe recognised Albert, with his serious and engaging features, looking dutifully at the camera; Edward staring insouciantly into the distance, wondering when this boring session would be over; and the daughter Victoria tricked out in white dress, ribbons and pearls, an uncanny echo of the Romanov princesses, her second cousins.

Joe stopped himself from trying to identify the remaining children, realising that he'd fallen into the trap. The trap of reassurance, familiarity and respect for British convention. Leave a man in this hallway for five minutes and he'd be singing the national anthem.

Looking aside, his eye was caught by a suitcase, a large going-away-for-some-time suitcase awaiting pickup at the bottom of the stairs. A not-unassociated coat was draped over the bottom of the banister rail. He approached and read the bold handwriting on the luggage label attached to the handle of the case. *Miss Beatrice Stewart, 106 High Street, Templeton, Surrey.*

The first rat leaving the sinking ship? On an impulse, he threw back his head and yelled, "Beatrice! Beatrice! Where are you? Taxi's here!"

A distant noise of running water and a door banging at the end of the hallway announced the arrival of Beatrice.

"Who the hell are you?" a pretty, dark girl wanted to know as she grabbed her coat and struggled into it and, suspiciously, "You're no cabby!" She had the aplomb to adjust her fur toque in front of the hall mirror and check the contents of her handbag, keeping him waiting. When she bent to straighten a stocking seam Joe decided he'd had enough. He picked up her case, smiled and announced, "I have your taxi just outside, if you'll step this way. Said your goodbyes have you, miss?" He whisked off through the door.

Puzzled and fearful, the girl stumbled on high heels in pursuit of her suitcase, protesting as she tried to catch up with Joe.

When they reached the taxi, Joe opened the back door and pushed her case inside. "Get in," he said and shut the door. Turning to the driver, "Smoker are you?" he asked. "Good. Buzz off and leave us alone for a bit. There's a wall over there. Go and sit on it where I can see you. Smoke two cigarettes before you come back to the taxi for further instructions."

Grumbling and scowling, the man shuffled off, settled himself and took a packet of Woodbines from his pocket.

The girl was pale with fear, Joe realised, but she held her head high and managed to ask again haughtily who the hell he was. Beatrice had the right eyebrows to express haughtiness. She could have been one of the Russian princesses the photograph had brought to mind. Doomed but spirited and on her way to Ekaterinburg in the hands of revolutionary thugs. She smelled of toothpaste and cologne.

He hurried to reassure her. "I'm not from Madingley, Beatrice. You're in no danger from me. But you may well be in danger. I'm here to help you."

"What do you want?" was the abrupt response.

"Cut the flannel do you mean?"

She nodded.

"Well, you're right. We haven't much time. You have a train to catch. There is something I want. Information. I know who you are and what you do. I'm not talking about the typing. I want some information on Mrs. Denton. Clarice Denton."

She shook her head and seemed on the point of panic. "Nothing to say! Let me out! You *are* one of them."

He pushed on. "Mrs. Denton died in agony, of arsenic poisoning, last Tuesday at Madingley Court. I believe you were on the premises at the time, engaged in entertaining Sir Gregory's guests."

"You can tell your boss I wasn't there. I heard and saw nothing because I wasn't there. Got that? Leave me alone. I'm on my way to my auntie's down south in Surrey and I've sent her a letter saying if anything happens to me she's to tell the police. I've sent her the full story. So get off my back!

I've got a ticket for the twelve-thirty King's Cross train and I'm going to be on it."

Admiring the girl's pluck and sure by now of her stance, Joe judged the moment was right to produce his warrant. "Why not tell me to my face, right now? I'm from Scotland Yard, miss. Joe Sandilands."

She took the card and inspected it with care then stared back at him. "An assistant commissioner? You sure? Blimey! You had me going there! Big, ugly bugger with a scarred face and a slouch hat—I thought you'd been sent to take me for a ride. Thank God for that! I can't be certain the local plod would ever have listened to my Auntie Vera. Chicken-nicking and apple-scrumping is about their limit." She gulped and drew in a lungful of air in her relief. "Well, here we are then. This is it. Go on. What do you want to know?"

"For starters: Why did she die? I'm sure that she was murdered and I need to understand what brought it about. What was the state of the relationship between Pertinax and Mrs. Denton?"

He'd shown his hand, but he couldn't be sure of her reaction. To his relief, she turned a calm face to him and replied with composure.

"They were never the best of buddies but they'd known each other a long time, I think. They got along. She did her job well, Mrs. D. Always. Treated us girls well too. Saw to it we got paid a fair amount and made us keep a bank account. Just in case." She clutched her handbag in an instinctive gesture that told Joe one of its contents was most probably a post office bank book. "Ran number 50 like a business with professional instruction and everything. She got someone in to teach us typing and shorthand. Proper little finishing school she had going! She could take us anywhere. Our table manners, French pronunciation, conversation, are all as good as any debutante's. That made us feel a bit better about what we were doing. The blokes up at Madingley had no cause for complaint. Until that last evening. Gawd! Did the feathers ever fly!"

"A row?"

"I'll say! Before it all kicked off. We'd got there, in our best frocks, made up, revved up . . . you know . . . They run it like an army manoeuvre—briefings and profiles and tactics . . ." She rolled her eyes. "Well on this occasion—All Hallows' Eve, wasn't it?—he'd told the girls to dress in something cobwebby and spooky just for a laugh. Mrs. D. had gone to town on the costumes—masks, the lot! We looked pretty good. It was then, the butler, Mr. Jennings, told us who the guests were going to be. We never knew in advance. To cut the risk of gossip, I suppose. Not that we'd have dared. He liked to keep the names quiet . . . some fellers' names we never knew . . . but on this occasion there was someone . . ." She paused, unable to voice the name. The rules of silence still weighed heavily on her.

"Someone every girl would recognise immediately? From a hundred press photographs? A household name? Let's call him 'H,' shall we? No names, no pack drill. Just 'H.'"

She sighed with relief. "Right. Jennings reckoned forewarned is forearmed. He didn't want any fainting fits or panic attacks when some girl realised what she'd got on her plate. So he came out with it. Well! Who'd have thought it! H! We were all excited and ready to have a giggle but Mrs. Denton blew her top! Life she's led—I mean she's seen it all!—you'd never have twigged that she's a raving, patriotic royalist would you? Was, I mean . . . But then, her room here is a dead giveaway. Full of mementos, souvenirs, Wedgwood plaques . . . She can—could—recite the line right back as far as William the Conqueror. My granny was as bad. It's like a religion with some women. We should have realised."

"What precise objection did she voice?" Joe asked carefully.

"Ooh, hark at you!" Joe was glad to hear the joking jibe. She was beginning, at last, to relax and relish her story. "She gave him a right tongue-lashing! She ranted and raved. It sounded to me like the cork popping out of a bottle that's already had a bit of a shaking. Pressure building up . . . you know . . . And by then the first of the guests was coming down the drive. No way was this illustrious personage whom she so admired going to be defiled (defiled!) by a bunch of tarts. (Tarts!) Pertinax had gone too far this time. Was he planning the Yellow Room treatment?" She looked questioningly at Joe, who nodded his understanding. "That amounted to treason! He deserved to be beheaded on Tower Green and she'd volunteer to wield the axe! She'd go to jail before she'd cooperate! She and the girls were getting straight back in the van and going back to the city.

"Well, Pertinax must have been listening. He rushed in and shouted at her. Clarice went for him! In front of us girls. Couldn't help herself.

"'Bloody foreigner!' she yelled. 'You're betraying the nation that took you in! You come over here, grab everything you fancy, then kick us in the balls! You coward! You didn't even fight for us in the last lot! Somebody should've stuck a white feather up your bum! You're a traitor and I'm not standing for it!'

"I think, honestly, that was the clincher. Ouch! He went pale and very quiet. Then he grabbed her with those great hands of his . . ." Beatrice shuddered. "He bundled her out of the room and into the study next door. Never heard anything like it! He slapped her loud enough to hear clear through the wall and shouted and stormed. Then the noise stopped and that was worse. Jennings came back in and told us to just get on with it as normal. Mrs. Denton wasn't feeling herself. She'd gone for a lie-down and a few aspirins. That's the last any of us saw of her.

"In the laundry van on the way back we were all warned to keep our mouths shut and stay on at number 50 until someone else came to take over the business."

"Beatrice—the girl who drew the short straw—do you happen to know . . . ?"

"That was Clemency. No, I can't tell you how she got on with H. Or even *if* she got on with H. She didn't come back with us. 'Got a lift back to London with one of the nobs, lucky girl!' is what the butler told us."

"How likely was that?" Joe pushed her further.

"Not impossible. It actually happened to one of the girls. A client was so taken with Honoria he smuggled her out and down to London and married her. No—straight up! We've seen her in the *Tatler*! She's a lady now. But on this occasion . . . ? No chance!"

"Ah. And that's when you decided to flee, Beatrice?"

"Wouldn't you?"

"Death and disappearance at the Court—it's not the first time you've encountered it, is it?"

"No. Pertinax has previous. That's why the girls are all so scared."

"Were you here in August?"

"I wasn't, but my friend Marie was. She told me about the footman who got shot. Jeremy, I think. Is that what you're talking about? A really handsome bloke, she said. What a pity."

"Did Marie have any suggestions to make about the cause of his death?"

"You bet she did! It was one of those weekends when the girls weren't really required, if you know what I mean. A gents-only swing round. Jeremy was new and a bit clueless and hadn't rightly understood what Pertinax sometimes required of a footman. And he was a bit full of himself, Marie says. Bad combination. He was heard being stroppy with Jennings, saying as how he'd never signed on for stuff like that. What did they take him for? Someone, and it might well be *him*, ought to report it to the police. You can get jail for that. Well, no one threatens Jennings."

"And someone mistook the poor reluctant Ganymede for a wild boar and put a bullet through his hide?"

"Right! That's what they said. Look—your driver's finished his first cigarette. Woodbines! They don't last two minutes!"

"Beatrice, I'm thinking that you know or have worked out more than it's healthy for you to know about the Madingley mob."

"I've figured that out for myself, thanks very much," she said with scorn in her voice. "They don't like loose ends. Why do you think I have a ticket to London?"

"Listen. I may be a bit over-careful but—had you thought that leaving a suitcase with a name and address on it for all to see is a pretty ropey way of taking off incognito?

They'd only have to ask at the house, and someone would recite it for them. They could even be waiting at Cambridge station to push you under a train to stop you telling me what you've just told me. It's a Friday—there'll be a milling crowd of young gentlemen fighting to get aboard the 'Fornication Express' as they so charmingly call the afternoon train down to the flesh pots of the West End."

She turned to him with a smile, weary and knowing. "Look, mister, my name isn't Beatrice and the address I've put on the label is the address of my auntie's local police station. Seemed a safe enough place to direct my things in case I get lost en route. Give me your notebook and I'll write down my real name." As she scribbled her details, she commented, "I'll have to take my chances at the station. I'll hang about in the ladies' waiting room until the train's ready to leave."

"Well, I'm not taking chances." Over the summer Joe had learned by heart the timetable of the trains between London and Cambridge. He knew which were fastest and which had buffet cars, having a personal preference for the 11:10 from Liverpool Street, which had both advantages. "You must take this taxi, not to Cambridge but to the next station down the line . . . the other line . . . Audley End, I believe. From there you can get on a train to Liverpool Street station and disappear into London." He dug in his pocket and took out some notes. "Here. That'll cover the fare. Ready to say goodbye to Cambridge?"

"You bet!" She looked about her at the lines of prim houses and clipped hedges and shrugged. "Nobody here I'll miss! Except perhaps the doc. I'd have liked to say goodbye and thank you to her."

"I beg your pardon?" Joe was nonplussed. "What was that?"

"The lady doctor. It's her morning for her weekly visit. I was hanging on waiting to see her but she's running late. Oh, well . . ."

"Have you been sick, er, Beatrice?"

"No! Fit as a flea! But—well, you know what I do, and this Pertinax chap has a thing about disease. Fanatical. Can't say I blame him. The type of client he entertains . . . well . . . wouldn't want those grand fellers to catch anything worse than a cold, would we? There'd be some explaining to do!" Beatrice smiled with a secret satisfaction at the thought. "He pays to get us all checked over regularly whether we need it or not. The doc they've found to do it is a real lady, thank God! Knows her job. Has a laugh. We all look forward to her visits. She's a touch with real life and she never treats us as though we're less than human."

"Doctor Hartest, would that be?" His voice was controlled. Mildly interested.

She nodded. "Adelaide. She likes us to call her Adelaide."

"I'll tell her you mentioned her," said Joe, barely aware of what he was saying. Seeing the cabby putting out his second Woodbine with a Music Hall flourish, Joe took a blank calling card from his pocket and scribbled on it. Passing it to Beatrice he muttered, "Ring this London number if you're having trouble. You'll get my deputy or his secretary. Open by saying my name, Sandilands, straight away. Say the message is for me and add that it's to do with the emperor. They'll listen."

He'd felt a bit theatrical doing this, but Beatrice seized

on it gratefully, looked at the number, lips moving, and tucked it away in a deep recess of her handbag.

"One last thing," he said. "Tell me the parlour maid's name, will you? I'm going back to the house and I'll do what I can for your friends. I know the doctor. Perhaps she'll be able to help."

The driver approached the taxi cautiously, looking up at the sky and whistling a jaunty tune. "Have you two done?" he asked, arching his eyebrows to indicate he knew very well the nature of the business conducted at number 50 and, in some way, was questioning the two cigarette length of the exchange.

"All sorted out, thank you," said Joe. "Change of plan. In which you are involved so listen carefully, Cabby Number 5302. Jealous husbands!" Joe rolled his eyes. "What a load of bother they cause! You are to take this young lady to the station but—the station at Audley End on the Liverpool Street line. I said Audley End. Yes, I know it's outside the city limits and, yes, it'll cost me! Wait until you see her get safely on the train. If any strange gentlemen approach, ring the Cambridge police. Here's the taxi fare." He handed over two ten-shilling notes. "That should do it and cover the tip as well."

Beatrice had recovered her spirits sufficiently to enjoy the game and, seizing Joe in a fond embrace, she planted a smacking kiss on his cheek for the cabby's benefit. "Darling!" she breathed, in a cut-glass accent. "You worry too much. I'll be fine! I'll give you a ring from Liverpool Street to say I've arrived safely. And if you see Gerald before I do—give him a kick in the crown jewels for me, will you?"

CHAPTER 18

The same parlour maid recited the same message when he rang at the door of number 50.

"Sarah! It's me again! And you've got me for longer this time." He stepped in and handed her his hat. "I'm waiting to see Doctor Hartest, who is due to visit any minute now. In fact I'm sure I saw her cycling down the road a moment ago. Now, Sarah, show me to the room where she conducts her surgery and I'll make myself comfortable. When she arrives just tell her she has a visitor, will you?"

The small room at the back of the house was freshly painted and furnished with a modest set of chairs and a table. East-facing, it must once have been a breakfast room, he guessed, as it was still lit by a late-morning autumn sun. The centrepiece of the room was an incongruous chaise longue, capacious and recently reupholstered in a dark green, plush velvet fabric. Joe had time to open up and check the contents of the two cupboards built into alcoves on either side of the chimney breast. Freshly laundered sheets in piles, towels, enamel bowls, jugs and medical paraphernalia. Within seconds, this unexceptional room could have become a working surgery.

Hearing the bell ring, he went, with a grin, to stretch himself out on the chaise longue.

The door was flung open and a breathless Adelaide shot into the room. Red hair windblown and flaring aggressively around her head, she bristled with anger. Or was it fear? A combination, Joe decided.

"What in Heaven's name? Joe! How? Who ... ?"

"Darling! Hello!" Joe shot to his feet. "You just missed young Beatrice. I told her I'd say hello and pass on her gratitude and warm wishes. Sensibly, she's just on her way to London. I expect the rest of your little nest of patients won't be far behind. I do hope they all make a safe retreat. I'm doing my best to facilitate it."

Adelaide opened her mouth to speak. "Well, bully for you!" she finally managed. "Why can't you mind your own business, Clever Clogs?"

"Helping an innocent girl—well, a girl undeserving of any violence—to escape this vicious net and get safely back home is any gentleman's business," he said stoutly. "I'm only surprised that their doctor was not able to be of more practical help. I do wonder that you, Adelaide, feminist that you avowedly are, did not take steps to lance this particular boil weeks ago. Why, have you condoned—I'm trying not to think connived—at it?"

"Come off it, Sir Lancelot! You're supposed to be hand in glove with MI5, in the pocket of the commissioner, dangling from the watch chain of the home secretary—if one of those didn't tell you, you ought at least have been able to work it out."

"That my fiancée is a thirty-bob-a-week spy? What do they pompously call them ... ? A 'penetration agent'! Is that what you are, Adelaide? Can you be sure which faction you're working for? Can I be sure you're not a double agent?"

"Wrong on all counts! I'm not your fiancée and it's not thirty bob a week! Is that the going rate? What a nerve—they offered me twenty! And they haven't paid up yet! It goes straight to charity if they ever do. The Cambridge anti-rickets campaign is . . ."

Evasion. Joe cut it short. "Who recruited you?"

Her lip curled. "You don't seriously expect me to give you a name? I'm hardly a professional spy, but I'm not stupid. I'll tell you what I can, though you have no right to ask. You remember the state I was in when you met me last June? I was out of work, desperate to join a practice and being turned down in favour of men I knew to be worse qualified and less able than myself. I even toyed with the notion of joining young Alexander Truelove in his mad scheme to go to Africa and impose himself on the Africans. Luckily, in the nick of time, I was invited to a meeting in London by . . . an old army friend of my father's. Over tea and cakes at Fortnum's, he slipped onto the table the lure of a plum posting to Cambridge, which he somehow knew was my first choice of location . . . Halfway between you in London and my father in Suffolk. There was a condition. A specialist was required to"—She stretched her arms out, encompassing the room—"to check and guarantee the healthy condition of this group of women. Of course, my first instinct was to square up to the chap who briefed me and say, 'How dare you treat your countrywomen—or any woman—like this? Set them free from this disgusting slavery at once! How can you tolerate it? Worse—*exploit* it?'"

Joe cringed, wondering which poker-faced smoothie MI5 had fielded to counter Adelaide in full flow.

"Some silver-haired smarm merchant, heavy with years

and honours, was persuaded to put down his *Wisden Crick-eters' Almanack* long enough to invoke King and Country, the British Way of Life and all that." She looked sheepishly down at her shoes for a moment, then raised defiant eyes. "He didn't actually have much of an uphill task in getting me to agree. You know as well as anyone, Joe, that if ever called on to go into battle again, I'd race you to the trenches. Any fool can wave a flag and sing the national anthem, drink a pint on St. George's Day . . . I had a useful talent to offer up. I could do something valuable towards averting a national crisis. I signed on the dotted line. They convinced me that I would be working towards a goal that would, in the end, be the saving of many more than this small group. Even here, I could do some good. They hadn't made provision for that of course but I was in a position to extract a few concessions."

Joe flinched at the thought of night watchman Knightly put in to bat against Adelaide's bouncers.

"I protected the girls as best I could. Issued them with the latest birth control equipment . . . At State expense!" she added with a nasty grin. "I reckon they earned it. I helped one, who was particularly distraught and missing her home, to get away. Safely and without reprisals, I do believe. The girls, in turn, fed me with quite a lot of valuable information about the Hellfire Club, which was the point of the exercise. Names of members, when they knew them, dates of forth-coming parties. I did my job. Better than anyone had expected."

She looked at her wristwatch pointedly. "And now I'd like to get on with it, if you don't mind." She looked with suspicion at the sofa. "Have you had your feet on this? Make yourself useful. Go and fetch me two sheets from the cupboard over there."

"Adelaide, how did you get this information back to your handlers? Was Aidan involved?"

"Good Lord, no! I'd no idea he existed until I came across him dying in church." She gave him a calculating stare then shrugged. "It was the church that was involved, not a person. All Hallows. A contact point. I handed my messages over to the vicar. If he's not there I leave them tucked into that big Bible that's always lying open on the lectern. I can't stand Sweeting, but he does what's required of him. He has a stinky sort of past, and the Intelligence Service got hold of this and required him to perform certain services to save himself from being unfrocked or whatever it is they do to dispose of the clergy. They tut about blackmail and coercion but—my goodness!—they could teach Pertinax a thing or two, those old goats in Whitehall!"

"Mrs. Denton?" Joe asked as he helped her throw and tuck and smooth, turning the sofa into an examination couch.

"I could never be sure how loyal she was to the organisation. I was told that she was Pertinax's willing lieutenant and I worked on that assumption. It seemed safer. She kept her distance and was always cool with me. When they killed her, I decided that—let secrecy go hang—someone ought to know. No idea *why* she had to die but I told you and Adam exactly what happened. I even brought you clues, for God's sake! Samples of bodily fluids . . . the tag from her dress . . . I couldn't believe how slow the pair of you were being! If they'd trusted me further than they did I could have had the whole nasty business exposed so much sooner! How many more must suffer while our security services play hop-scotch with each other?"

She elbowed him out of her way and began to set out her instruments on a table.

Joe looked at her face, spirited, defiant, scornful and bright. Oh, Lord! He had a feeling that he would always find himself a large, ungainly presence coming between Adelaide and her tasks. But worse than that—not only did he now have to overcome the distance between them, the demands of his job, the demands of her profession—he was faced with a woman who had tasted excitement, the dark pull of undercover work. Work which she knew she was at least as well suited to as Joe. He understood why, though claiming to love him, this lively girl had turned aside all his suggestions that she should marry him. She had once light-heartedly conjured up the trite but truthful picture of a house in Hampstead which they would share with two retrievers until the children "came along," as the phrase was in the women's journals. "As though they just toddled in through the garden gate one day. House-trained and shoes shined," Adelaide had said scornfully. He had always known that her plans had never meshed with his.

As he stared, a page turned, a book closed, the second shoe dropped.

An image he'd heard his sister call up on hearing of the end of a friend's affair came into his head. "Another moth sizzling in the candle flame! Have they no sense! So lovely, so alive and yet they go circling in deliberately to a nasty death and—flash! bang!—it's all over in a second. You'd think Nature would have equipped the creatures with the means to detect and resist a life threat, wouldn't you?" Joe had sizzled in the flames before. He recognised the moment. And—no, Lydia!—he had never seen the moment coming. He took stock and understood that he was still alive and buzzing with shock and dismay, but would his scorched wings even have the strength to carry him away from the bonfire? At this moment he just wanted to move far and fast from the scene of his crash landing.

"I'm sorry, Adelaide. To have been such a lumbering disappointment to you professionally. For having overestimated the value of what I had to offer emotionally. For undervaluing the work you are doing and the woman that you are. At least this time I don't need to make excuses for my preoccupations. Nor do you. You'll have worked out exactly how important all this is. Our own dreams and delusions are pretty insubstantial when weighed against the 'national emergency' as they've labelled it. Though that hardly begins to cover it . . ."

Joe heard his flat policeman's tone creeping in and fell silent. He remembered how she hated it. He stood for a moment, defeated, nothing more to say.

Seeing an equal dejection and acceptance in Adelaide, he opened his arms wide in a last instinctive gesture and, to his surprise, she moved swiftly towards him and hugged him tightly. Joe recognised the farewell hug of a concerned friend.

"Shall we agree to talk about our own affairs when this is all over, Joe? Much to do. Now, tell me—do I take orders from you, from Adam, or from those chinless wonders in Cromwell Road? I like to be clear about these things."

He replied with equal composure. "From me. My first order is—on no account return to Madingley Court or meet any of the inhabitants. You would be putting yourself into danger. Secondly, do what you can to clear up things here for the girls. There's no one in charge, and they'll look to you for direction. I'll ask Adam to post a guard here at the house until matters are resolved and to ensure that anyone who wants to return to London is able to make her way there. Thirdly, communicate through me and me only. Do not return to that church. When you've done what you can here, tell Easterby you're taking a week off. That's an order!"

"What about my handlers, as you call them, at MI5? I wouldn't want them to think I'd walked out on them."

"Don't worry. I'll tell old Knightly at Oliver House that I've taken you into stock. Your job here with the girls has folded but I've sent you out on a different but associated task. I'll also mention the backlog in payment."

"This task, Joe?" she began, her voice slow with suspicion.

"Do you know who I mean by 'Clemency'?"

"Of course. She's small, round and dark-haired. Rather roly-poly and innocent looking. Why?"

"Adelaide, I'm afraid we may have another engineered disappearance on our hands. Clemency was chosen to entertain a very important person on the night of Mrs. Denton's death. A person so important any intimate knowledge of him, his behaviour, and the Pertinax connection would have to be snuffed out, gagged, um . . ."

"Oh, no! What can I do?"

"Mrs. Denton ran a tight ship. There must be files here in the house? Details of the girls' real identities?"

"If there are, she didn't share them with me. But—don't look so distraught!—I've compiled a list myself while I've been working here. Any snippets of information that pop out I jot down in my little book."

She produced a school notebook from her bag and began to leaf through it. "Clemency . . . Right. She's Elsie Jones and her home address is in Hertfordshire. She lives with her grandmother and is still in close touch with her. Granny thinks she's really doing secretarial work here in Cambridge. Elsie types all her letters home to show how well she's coming on. She asked me to post one for her one day and I steamed it open before I put it in the box." Adelaide smiled. "The first and only time I've felt like a spy! Are you thinking this might be of some help? It would go some way to making me feel a bit better about this disgusting business."

"Yes indeed! Listen, Adelaide. I want you to go back into town. To the police station. Pick up a squad car and driver to take you down to Hertfordshire. I'll ring Adam from here and set that up. When you get there, interview Elsie. Find out what really happened on that grisly night. Then tell her to go to ground somewhere else, somewhere safe, until you contact her again to say it's all over. If she never arrived . . ."

"Leave that to me. I'll backtrack until I find her," Adelaide said with quiet determination. "If I make contact, I'll put her under my wing and take her back to Suffolk with me and do the lying low there. My father would teach Pertinax a thing or two if he attempted a raid on Suffolk. The house is full of shotguns and with a few phone calls he could raise a small unit of the Suffolk Yeomanry to guard the house. I'm a fair shot with a Purdey myself."

Joe hugged her again and smoothed back the hair that was tickling his nose, feeling utter trust, admiration and a loss so wrenching it tore at his throat. He could raise no more than a whisper to say: "Listen to me, Adelaide, my love. If you're going to carry on doing work for the government, you'll have to get used to ducking and weaving and lying as well as shooting straight. Can you do all that?"

"Oh, yes, Joe. I've had a lesson from the master in self-righteous deception and ruthless efficiency." Seeing his dismay, she grinned. "Come on! How else do you kill dragons? Thank God you're there, Joe!"

CHAPTER 19

Adam Hunnyton dismissed Constable Batty, having given him his orders and a signed chit for the keys to an unmarked squad car.

"It's for Adelaide's safety," Joe had explained. "I want her to be driven straight over to Suffolk. Send someone who can be spared indefinitely, a single man who can stay over if necessary with no questions asked. Make it clear that he's on State business and is to take his orders from Doctor Hartest."

He had not wanted to reveal to Adam that this was the first step in the hunt for the girl Clemency and wondered at his own deviousness. He'd given Hunnyton an edited but substantially correct version of Adelaide's role in the affair and, in bold stokes, had filled in the results of Ralph Cottingham's research into the car numbers, withholding the revelation of the cast list of the final dinner party.

"It's all moving," Hunnyton commented. "Rather faster than you were expecting? Anything else I can do, Joe?"

"Yes, there is. Can you lend me Constable Risby again for the rest of the day? In his Cambridge copper's uniform please. The navy tailoring opens doors that would slam in the face of a slouch-hatted London gent in a trench coat. I was taken for one of Pertinax's thugs earlier today."

"If you insist," Hunnyton grumbled. "While you boys are off junketing, I'm here trying to hold a force together with depleted numbers and bugger all cash, don't forget. Where are you off to now?"

"North Cambridge. I thought I'd cruise by the Red House in Chesterton Lane and try to get an interview with a real-life commie," Joe said cheerfully. "Bolshevism, Hunnyton. That's the key to this whole nasty business."

He hoped the man hadn't detected his lie.

HALF AN HOUR later, Joe, sitting in the passenger seat of the Lagonda, was passing a beef and horseradish sandwich to Constable Risby, rightly anticipating that the lad had missed his regular canteen lunch to drive the commissioner about the town.

"We're heading north of the river. To Chesterton. Do you know of a 'Spring Terrace'?"

"Yes, sir. It's opposite St. Andrew's Park."

"Rather a boring day I have to offer you, Constable. Routine stuff. Now this is absolutely hush hush, you understand . . ."

"Got it, sir."

"What I'm doing is dropping in unannounced on one or two characters whose backgrounds have to be vetted. People in key positions who have to be interviewed from time to time to keep records up to date. There's a big hoo-ha on at the moment about the dangers of communism . . . I suppose you were aware of that?" He waited for the nod and the understanding gleam in Risby's eye. "The Secret Services are seeing reds under beds everywhere in London and their anxieties are spreading to Cambridge."

"Not surprised, sir!" said Risby, suddenly knowing. "North Cambridge, eh? Hotbed of socialism."

Risby pulled up outside number 1 Spring Terrace and sat looking in puzzlement at the modest little Victorian house. It was neat and well-cared for. A baby's perambulator was parked in the tiny front garden and a football had been left on the scrap of lawn.

"Um . . . makes a change from the last place we visited, sir," Risby said dubiously, with the luxuries of Madingley Court fresh in his mind. "Doesn't look to me like a hideout for a bunch of revolutionaries either."

"They roost in some unexpected places, Risby! That's the whole point. Blend in. Establish yourself in a community. But I expect you're right. At least I certainly hope so. Come with me, will you? Flash your reassuring uniform and your sincere smile. Take your cue from me. I've no idea where I'm going with this. I may be wasting our time. I'm simply aiming to have a quiet chat with the householder."

A young woman wearing a flowered overall and a headscarf knotted on top of her head answered when they tugged on the bellpull. The daily cleaner?

"I'll have a pound of haddock today . . . oh!" she began, then, popping on a pair of spectacles that were hanging on a chain around her neck, she caught sight of Risby. "The police? Oh. I was hoping to see the fish merchant. How can I help you, gentlemen? Is there a problem?"

"Madam. Sorry to bother you." Risby smiled his smile. "No problem whatsoever. I'm Constable Risby of the Cambridge police and this is Assistant Commissioner Sandilands from Scotland Yard. Our credentials, madam. We're here to speak to the lady of the house."

Cambridge folk were careful, Joe reckoned. His warrant and that of the constable were properly inspected before she sniffed, tugged off her headscarf and glowered at them. "And about time too!" she snapped. "Belinda Page. How do you do. If you're looking for Doctor Page you've missed him. Again. Better come in."

They followed her down an uncluttered hallway and into a front parlour.

"I was just going to have an after-lunch cup of tea while the children are still having their nap. It's a precious ten minutes in my day. Kettle's just boiled. Will you join me? Kitchen tea all right? Humphrey's at the labs. He won't be back before six. No—don't put on such a po-face! If you've come here about the Cavendish business, I can explain everything—well, most things. Probably not the science."

"I'm not sure I would understand anyway, Mrs. Page." Joe smiled at her. "And yes, we'd love a cup of tea. As it comes—we're not fussy."

He stood, looking around him, enjoying the efforts that had gone into making a comfortable but smart space. In past times the front parlour would have been a cold room, only used for funeral receptions, family gatherings and music lessons on an upright piano. This room had been swept clear of traditional furniture and swags of heavy fabric, allowing the afternoon light to flood in unobscured. It had been painted and furnished on a shoestring, but the refreshing eau-de-Nil green and white colours enlivened by a bunch of gallant, late pink roses turned it into a useful and pleasant place. No nursery things had been allowed in to pollute the sophisticated scene.

Doctor Humphrey Page's wife took off her overall and

showed herself to be a pretty woman in her early thirties, wearing an old Hebe skirt and a silk blouse. Fluffy brown hair spilled onto a round, pink-cheeked and very English face. Her brown eyes (rather short-sighted, Joe guessed) interrogated him sharply. Correctly interpreting Joe's appraisal of the room, she grimaced and said, "It's not Mies van der Rohe, but with two children about the place, I have to have one room I can paint white and keep free of their clutter. This is it. Make yourselves comfortable, and I'll fetch the tea. Mugs be okay? Slice of fruitcake with it?"

They sank onto a low couch covered in zigzagged Florentine-patterned fabric to wait for the refreshments. Risby, taking in the décor with some surprise, said, "Did you see the stairs, sir? No carpet! Painted. Two shades of green. What's that all about?"

"It's all about style, Risby. Belinda Page has it. Raising two children on a scientist's salary can't leave much over and when you're having to compete in a cutthroat academic world with its conventions, its jealousies and its bosses' sharp-tongued wives, you have to make your mark cheaply but with style and humour. I admire it."

In came Mrs. Page carrying a tray and they began to talk politely about Cambridge affairs and the wonderful weather. Joe answered eager questions about Scotland Yard as they sipped their tea.

A sudden clumping on the stairs and a wail disturbed the douce tea party. A small boy, pink and tousle-headed, staggered into the room, fixing a challenging gaze on his mother. "You said you'd take me to the park with my football if I did a good sleep, Mamma, and now you've got visitors."

He glowered at the two intruders.

Summing up the situation, Risby shot to his feet. "And what might be your name, young sir?"

"Timothy."

"Well, Timothy, it's your lucky day! I'm good at football. Play for the police team. Why don't we pick up that ball from the front lawn, nip over the road and practice a few skills?"

"Oh, I say, Constable! Would you? He'd just love that!" Belinda was all grateful smiles. "Off you go then! Remember to have a pee before you set off, Timmy! Tiptoe down the path and don't wake little Freddie!"

"Well now! Tell me all," Joe invited, when the silence returned. "Your husband has some concerns about the organisation . . . the staff . . . at the laboratory where he works. Are his concerns of a political, security-of-the-nation nature? Does he confide in you?"

"Of course he does! Look—can we get one thing straight before we proceed, Commissioner? I am as sharp as my husband. I was a chemistry student before we married and marriage and motherhood have not quite yet softened my brain."

Mrs. Page went on to outline her husband's career in the Cavendish establishment, mentioning illustrious names Joe felt he was getting accustomed to hearing. She sketched in neatly the social problems of working in such a talented and competitive group, hinting that Doctor Page, a specialist in magnetism, had been overlooked for promotion. Plum research projects had been awarded to foreign scientists. He was not the only one to harbour such grievances.

"But things seem to have taken a more serious turn of late?"

"Yes. Vastly more urgent than a scrabbling after

recognition and advancement. We didn't know what to do
... whom to approach. We decided not to go to the Cambridge police. They're hand in glove, Humphrey says, with
the top echelons. The 'champagne coppers' Humphrey calls
them. Always there at celebrations and drinks parties, glittering with gold braid and chests covered in medals. A
college friend of his gave him a number to ring in London.
Humphrey was relieved. Just the words 'Cavendish' and
'Cambridge' seemed to get him interested. It was an easy
conversation he had. He was invited down to talk to someone in the security service. He had the feeling he wasn't
telling him anything he didn't already know. About the spying. Sorry. It sounds melodramatic, but I don't know what
else to call it."

"How long ago was that?"

"Ages ago. In the summer recess. August, I think."

"And the upshot was?"

"They thanked him and told him to keep his eyes and
ears open and they'd contact him when the time was right.
They made him sign a secrecy document of some sort. Honestly I thought they were just fobbing him off."

"Mrs. Page, does the name 'Hermes' ring a bell with
you?"

She smiled. "Of course. A joke! The messenger god in
winged sandals with responsibilities for science and information. Humphrey's code name! Their suggestion. It made me
even more certain that they were having a laugh at his
expense. Playing a game of Send-Up-the-Scientist? By their
rules, I'm half expecting you to tell me you're Zeus." She
sniffed. Peering at him more closely, she grinned and corrected herself, "No. With those stormy eyes, I think I'll make

that Poseidon. I can see you stirring up a whirlpool with your trident. But here you are—apparently sane, sensible and clued up. And—for the moment—peaceful. Please tell me I shall have to eat my words."

Joe decided not to ask disturbing questions about her husband's visit to Madingley, which he calculated had occurred before (and perhaps had instigated) Humphrey's contact with MI5. A delicate matter that could wait until he saw the man himself. But there was something he wanted to establish—an attitude, a moral stance, and this was often best done by playing devil's advocate.

He allowed an emollient smile to ease his words along, "I can see why you were reluctant to expose what you were interpreting as a very grave crime against the State," he began. "Of course I can. But, as in most other countries, our laboratory doors are always open to able men of science whatever their homeland, race or politics. Work done at the Cavendish is not carried out in the shadows—it adds to the scientific knowledge of the whole world. Science has no frontiers, Mrs. Page."

He heard the clichés rolling easily off his tongue and was embarrassed, but they provoked a clear response.

Belinda Page stabbed Joe with a look as sharp as a gimlet and said crisply, "Well thank you for coming. I'll get your hat."

She shot to her feet, then, before he could get up, she rounded on him. Joe had the impression he was about to be attacked by a very angry, brown hen.

"Claptrap! We examined those contentions long ago, Commissioner. Exhaustively. We are still left with the conviction that there's something chillingly reprehensible going on in Cambridge. The centre of the vortex is in those laboratories. That little clique of golden boys bobs along on a small patch of calm sea, in the eye of the storm, making wondrous discoveries, recognised and fêted by the whole world when outside, all around their haven, chaos swirls. Have you any children, Commissioner?" she finished abruptly.

Taken aback, Joe said evasively, "I'm not married."

"I'm sorry to hear it. I have two boys—three if you count Humphrey—and I don't want some years from now to see them blasted to smithereens by a wickedness spawned and hatched here in this town and shipped off around the world to the highest bidder."

"Bravo! My thoughts exactly! I needed to be sure of your conviction, Mrs. Page. Now—to do something about it. It's been festering long enough."

She breathed deeply and sank back down onto the sofa. "Thank God! If this were a boil, I'd say it was coming to a head and about to burst painfully over all concerned."

At that moment the telephone rang in the hallway and the baby outside in the pram woke up and began to cry.

"You answer the phone," Joe said firmly. "I'll fetch Freddie in for you."

He returned moments later patting the back of a red-faced infant drooling stickiness onto the shoulder of his tweed jacket. "There, there, little man! Mamma's right here. Hush now or I shall have to arrest you for disturbing the peace . . . shush . . . shush," he crooned.

Belinda smiled and murmured into the phone, "You heard rightly. There *is* a man in the house, yes. A rather surprising one! He's dark and handsome and seems to be good with babies. You'd better get home at once, Humphrey! No. Wait. I'll put him on. Can you talk?"

She passed the receiver to Joe and took Freddie in exchange. "He's at the lab so he can't talk freely. Fix something up!"

Joe took the phone and, feeling slightly foolish murmured: "Er, is this Hermes? . . . Good . . . I shall be in the Snug Bar of the Anchor at six o'clock. I'll be in evening dress—I'm going on somewhere afterwards."

"I'll put my best sandals on! See you there! Mine's a pint of Adnams if you're getting them in," said a young and hearty voice and the phone rang off.

"ENJOY YOUR FOOTBALL, Risby?" Joe asked when they eventually set off again in the Lagonda.

"I did! That's a good little dribbler for his age."

"I'm guessing you have little brothers."

"Four! All of 'em players! Um . . . sir . . . ?"

"All's well, Risby. They passed my test with flying colours."

"Glad to hear it! Where are we off to now, sir?"

"A quick inspection and possible exchange of information. I think we've got time. Go south of the river again and out to one of the villages . . . Harston. The Old Hall. Do you know it?"

"Calling on his nibs are we? That's where the chief constable lives."

"Right. The 'champagne coppers of Cambridge' is what Mrs. Page called your bunch, Risby. Any justification for that, would you say?"

Risby grunted. "For most of us a half-pint of bitter is a

treat! But the upper echelons . . . well . . . they do like to get their photos in the local rag, champagne glass in hand. Arnold Baxter graces many an occasion with his polished presence," he added with asperity, probably quoting from the *Evening News*.

"The governor? Superintendent Hunnyton? Does he present his impressive profile for the cameras?"

The constable's face softened and he shook his head. "Not so's you'd notice. He can't stand stuff like that . . . smarming . . . masonry . . . funny handshakes . . . As soon as a photographer appears, he turns his back. Mind, he's had to grit his teeth and show his social side lately. Chief Baxter's been taking a bit of a backseat. The super has more on his plate than he ought to have. Filling in for the old feller."

JOE ASKED RISBY to drop him in the village street and he walked up the drive to the front door unaccompanied.

A parlour maid asked him to wait in the hall while she fetched her mistress. The master was out in the garden, she explained, and not to be disturbed, and Mrs. Baxter was expecting some friends for tea. It was not a convenient time. Who was calling? Joe handed over his card.

"Tell your mistress a colleague is calling on the chief constable to pay his respects. Assistant Commissioner Sandilands from Scotland Yard." He noted with satisfaction that the magic words had their usual effect of producing round eyes, intake of breath and scurrying feet.

He was joined some minutes later by an elderly lady in an old-fashioned, lavender tea gown straining over a pearl-swagged bosom. Her grey hair was freshly marcel-waved into narrow furrows all over her head, and she was regarding

Joe with disdain and something else. Joe thought he detected anxiety.

"So? You've come for him at last?" she wanted to know in a voice of doom.

"I should very much like to have a few words with the chief constable," Joe said in a neutral tone.

Her fear turned to anger. "Couldn't you have waited for a month or so? Just until January? What harm could it possibly do? And why do they have to send someone from Special Branch? I take it that's what you are? I've heard about your department and its methods! Grammar school riffraff! Little better than attack dogs!"

Joe listened to the gathering tirade without interrupting. He learned more when people lost control and gave him the benefit of their uncensored thoughts.

"Harm one hair of Arnold's head and I shall alert the home secretary, young man!" she shrilled, bosom heaving. "My husband has forged a blameless career, has an immaculate reputation and I will not stand by and see his achievements ruined at this crucial stage by a graceless, vindictive colleague! There's a Judas at work here! And his name is Hunnyton! Did that upstart send you? Dead men's shoes! That's what he's hoping to step into! He hasn't the authority to remove Arnold himself so he persuades his friends at the Yard to do the dirty work for him."

She insisted on staying at her husband's side while Joe interviewed him, and such was the force of her concern, Joe agreed. He was led through corridors and out through a rear door opening onto a garden still green and ablaze with autumn flowers. Under a willow tree to the side of an extensive lawn, wearing a straw hat and gardening trousers, humming a snatch from the Mikado, sat the chief constable of the county. His head was bent over a copy of the *Times* and he seemed to be busily working on the crossword puzzle.

"Sir!" Joe called a greeting, hurrying ahead of Mrs. Baxter. "Don't get up. I'll join you. Glorious afternoon we're having, aren't we?"

Baxter looked up, his mouth sagged open and, questioning and friendly, he tried to focus on the smiling invader.

"THAT DIDN'T TAKE long, sir." Risby carefully side-stepped asking a direct question.

"Fifteen minutes," Joe said. "The longest fifteen minutes of my life is what that felt like! Poor old Baxter! All's well, Risby! I found out what I needed to know. More than I was expecting, so chalk that up as another success. No, no! He's not a communist. Mrs. Baxter would never allow it. You might have warned me about *her*, Risby! Had you any idea? Now, you can drive me back into town and dismiss for the day. I'm off to the pub and then I'm dining at St. Benedict's. Busy day one way and another. Go home, lad. Get some rest and come and pick me up at the hotel after breakfast tomorrow. Eight o'clock suit you?"

CHAPTER 20

Joe reckoned his choice of pub was a good one. The Anchor was five minutes' walk from both his hotel and the laboratories, inches from the river and fronting a broad expanse of anchorage for boats. A constantly changing flow of students, local people and visitors drifted by.

As Joe approached, he stopped to look out over the Mill Pond, admiring the peaceful scene and passing a little time. Good agents, he reckoned, always arrived early—or late. Dusk was descending fast and the temperature along with it. Though the sky to the west was still warm with the benevolent shades of a good fire, cold air was gathering on the water and a mist obscured the last of the punts bumping and disputing places to tie up in Scudamore's Boatyard for the night. The end of the season. The last punt of the year. Young voices called out wistful goodbyes or invitations to prolong the jollity in the Anchor. In a couple of hours, the place would be buzzing with life and it would be too crowded to conduct a conversation or even raise an elbow, but for now it was perfect.

Once inside, Joe took stock of the other clients. He was pleased to see two other gentlemen in dinner jackets joking with the barman, so he didn't feel out of place. He managed to pick up two tankards of Adnams ale and make his way through to the empty snug bar at the rear of the building. He set them down and settled, back to the wall, to watch for his scientist.

Page came in on the stroke of six o'clock, an eye flicking to his wristwatch to underline his punctuality. He looked around him, raised his eyebrows on spotting Joe and bounded straight over to his table.

What had Joe expected? Anything but swaggering over-confidence. He registered: tall, gangly, a turbulence of curly hair, baggy tweed suit, college tie, heavy spectacles. This must be a disguise, was Joe's first thought, so exactly did his appearance fit the *Punch* cartoons of a scientist. He forced back a smile as Page shook his hand and took a grateful swig of his ale before speaking.

"Poseidon, eh? Mm ... see what she means. You're easy to spot. I, on the other hand," he announced, "am in disguise." He swept off the spectacles. "Borrowed them from Belinda. Makes me look more serious don't you think?"

Joe leaned forward and confided, "Makes you look a complete arse. Now stop fucking about or I'll chuck you in the Cam. This isn't Oliver House, Cromwell Road. A gents' chat over a cup of Darjeeling and a selection of fairy cakes in Fortnum's isn't my style. I'm more the pint of bitter and a knuckle sandwich sort. The tool they use to keep their own hands clean." He smiled with all the charm of a shark and, turning his head to his own glass, gave Page the benefit of the shrapnel scar across his brow. "This is your one chance. Give me what I want or you'll float back to Chesterton tonight."

Page was gratifyingly startled. He took control of his drooping jaw, swigged some more of his ale, took a deep breath and then, to Joe's surprise, looked straight at him and grinned. Strangely, his response echoed that of his wife some hours earlier, "Thank God for that! I do believe you would! I didn't think the fairy cakes at Fortnum's were taking me seriously. Or had it in them to do anything about it if they were."

Joe gave another tight smile. He had Page almost where he wanted him. "It took three murders to concentrate their minds." He paused to let that sink in. "But they got there. Now, let's see what you can do to stop that number rising to four."

"Ah. Oh. Well, then. How would you like to proceed?"

"Quickly. Before the pub gets busy. If we're interrupted, I'll get up and leave. Follow me and we'll go for a walk."

Page gulped and, not much tempted by the prospect of a riverbank tête-à-tête with a thug in a trench coat, he nodded hurriedly.

"No gossip. Facts, not suspicions."

Page nodded again.

"Firstly: give me the names of the men you are mainly concerned about."

Three names were whispered across the table. Two Russian, one German.

"Follow that, will you, with evidence. The harder the better."

"Not difficult," Page said, the strength of his evidence clearly stiffening his resolve. "I can give you names and dates. How about, for starters: Andrew Rothstein?" He threw the name out and watched for a reaction.

Good move. Joe was going to have to reassess this man. From his MI5 briefing notes, he remembered the name of an agent recruiter working for the Bolsheviks under the sketchy cover of a Russian Trade Delegation. He'd been judged too transparent and too amateur and they'd allowed him to go sniffing about the place on a long lead. Too long, Joe judged, but the poor cash-strapped buggers in MI5 didn't have the resources to nursemaid every Tom, Dick and Ivan who entered the country.

"To whom did he speak and what did he want?"

"He spoke to Kapitza and one or two of his department. Not me. I'm too low down the scale." Page took a folded sheet from his pocket and passed it across the table. "It's all in there. Dates and names. Thought it might save you time. Rothstein . . . Is he Jewish? German? Russian? Perhaps you would know . . . Anyhow, the bloke was seeking someone to supply scientific and technical knowledge to Russia. He was especially interested in information on the new plant for the dilution of helium. Helium gas! Seems to be all the go at the moment. Everyone . . ." He caught himself launching into a diversion and hurried to finish, "That's only the bit I overheard."

In response to Joe's raised eyebrow inviting more, he added, "And then there's the ambassadors . . ."

"At the Cavendish?"

"Yes. Official visits if you please! Another excuse to bring out the Bollinger. They love their socialising! The delivery boys drop off as many crates of bubbly as they do of lab equipment. Magnums or magnetometers—they don't stint themselves! Look—I come and go through the labs all the time. Part of the fixtures and fittings, I'm afraid, in as far as the top boys think of me at all. I'm regarded as a sort of superior lab assistant these days. On occasions, I've had to drop what I was doing and take the buggers round the labs on guided tours!"

"Hang on a minute. Ambassadors from which countries?"

"The Russian ambassador has been three times since the new Mond Lab opened last February, the French twice and the German chap twice. Oh, and the Americans sent a large fact-finding party. That was a two-crate do! All logged. You'll see the visits seem to be getting more frequent. There's something brewing. I'm a scientist. I rely on facts. Evidence. I can't possibly justify the chill between my shoulder blades, the mental terror that seizes hold of me sometimes . . ." Seeing Joe's eyes narrow he fell silent.

"Facts. Evidence. Let's stick with those shall we? For chills I'll look to Edgar Allen Poe. Were these officials showing an informed scientific interest?"

"You bet! The Russian bloke even had his chauffeur take the tour with us. He may have been a chauffeur, but he was a damned good scientist as well! Searching questions were put. I resented it. I shifted the responsibility. Played dumb and referred them to Kapitza or the Old Crocodile."

"Old Crocodile?"

"Rutherford. Sir Ernest, now Lord. Cavendish Professor of Physics these last thirteen years, Nobel Prize winner, President of the Royal Society and now—'Crocodile.' It's the nickname Kapitza has conferred on him. They have these little jokes together. He explains it by saying he began to use it when he first came to work in the labs because he found Rutherford so terrifying. In Russian folklore the crocodile is the symbol for the father of the family, he says. Revered but terrifying. It can only move in a forward direction with jaws wide open, ready to eat up anyone in its path."

"Not unlike my perception of science," Joe muttered. "Go on. Are they allies as well as colleagues, the director and the star of the show?"

"Not all the time. There are differences of opinion. No, wait! This is too important to be reaching for mealy-mouthed euphemisms! There are blazing rows! Hissy fits galore! It's like sharing a dressing room with a pair of opera divas. In the end, Rutherford always gives in to his demands. Their families know each other. The director uses his clout with the big bugs in government to acquire visas and documents for Kapitza's Russian wife. Kapitza flatters him and remembers to send him birthday cards."

Joe frowned, not much caring for the scene being laid out for him. He could understand the resentment felt by Page and perhaps others. "So, you're telling me it's possible that certain elements of the physics team are actively working with or, at the least, well-disposed to enemy foreign powers?"

Page sighed in exasperation. "No! I'm telling you that they're bloody-well spying! They're giving away or selling information that could blow this country to smithereens when the next lot bursts over us. As it will. Intentional or not, mischievous or naively deluded, it hardly matters—the outcome will be the same. Universal slaughter of the coming generation. And do you know what the truly concerning thing is? They don't care! They don't give a damn who knows what they're up to. If they were planning to kill the king, they'd announce it openly, have a jolly laugh and move on. It's their *cover*! Scientific arrogance is their cover! How can you possibly be a traitor when you count the whole world your own country? Knowledge is universal and must be celebrated and shared with everyone, mustn't it? In these brave and enlightened days, there are no secrets, no father-land to betray, so where is the problem? If you claim to perceive one, you're ridiculed, relegated to the ranks of the backward-looking; you're last century's man."

Page heard his tone becoming acid, the volume rising, and he stopped for a moment. "Sorry! I get carried away." He took a deep breath and Joe understood that he was about to commit himself to an irrevocable statement. "Look here—it would be worrying enough if the views they express were pure academic, highfalutin theory, and they were all self-deluded enough to believe it, but I think . . . I think the insouciance, the laughter, the charm, the openness are the most enormous bit of camouflage. Bluff. Deliberate deceit. It's a magic show! They calculate that the audience *wants* to be deceived by glamour, spotlights and a roll on the drums. They're complicit in ignoring the tawdriness and the risk." He appealed to Joe. "Am I the only sane man who can see the dangers we're running? Or am I out of joint with the world?"

"Tell me, what is the feeling in general amongst your fellows—the community of scientists that you are a part of? There must be how many in Cambridge?"

"Hundreds. Never occurred to me to count and we're all so busy we don't have time to do much politicking or even socialising. Give you an idea . . . There's a new society just been formed in the university. The Cambridge Anti-War Group. Scientists uniting together against war. Lightly com-munist, I suppose. But nothing to scare the horses. Belinda calls us 'The Pinks.' We have a membership of about fifty already." This last was delivered with a smile of pride.

"Should the forces of law and order be concerned?"

"Probably. Some of the members are planning to stage a demonstration at the war memorial on Remembrance Day next weekend. Some young hotheads, mainly Trinity men, are aiming to disrupt the service. Lob eggs at the wreath-laying old warriors who keep the flame of war alight."

"Shows some nerve!" Joe said. "I wouldn't care to take on those old fire-eaters! They don't care for egg on their epaulettes and they all carry a sword." He wondered if Hunnyton was aware of this threat to the public peace. "This could all get out of hand. Will you be in attendance?"

"Lord, no! I have infinite respect for those who died. I just don't want their sons and grandsons to be called on to make the same sacrifice. You don't achieve that by daubing paint on a stone cross and screaming abuse at old soldiers in wheelchairs."

"Is this anti-war group something the security services would like to know about?"

"They know. I told them! Huh! They'd have been more alarmed to hear the Cambridge Tiddlywinks Club had re-formed."

Joe smiled a genuine smile. "Subversive bunch—tiddlywinkers! Give me honest-to-goodness, cut-throat croquet players any day. So—politically, where does the lab stand?"

Joe listened patiently to Page's assertion that scientists were generally uninterested in politics in the abstract. Practical—that was different. Handing out sandwiches and sympathy to hunger marchers and fighting poverty and injustice was right and human and not the sole preserve of left-wing radical idealists. They enjoyed a good debate as much as the next man, but the vast majority were too focussed on their work to care about who was running the country. So long as the cash support kept coming through, naturally.

Joe decided to follow this line and asked Page to outline the sources of funding. Most came from government, but a certain amount, unknown to Page, came from private sources. Of course the greatest consumption of cash had been the new Mond Laboratory, opened this year in the courtyard of the Cavendish. The Royal Society of Science had donated £15,000 for the project. Kapitza was appointed its director.

"Sounds like a bargain to me," Joe murmured. "What is its purpose?"

"To indulge the director in his enthusiasms," Page said bitterly. "Magnetic research ... Low temperature physics ... Whatever he fancies. He's engineered and installed a hydrogen liquefier—completely new design . . . You must come and see the Mond. Very latest in architecture and equipment. Best in the world. And the bloody thing cost more than the total budget for the rest of the Cavendish. We're all hoping something world-shaking will come of it."

Joe picked up the unspoken concern in his muttered last sentence. "A hydrogen liquefier?" he asked, puzzled. "What does one of those look like?"

"It looks like nothing so much as your granny's newfangled, wall-mounted water heater circa 1920," Page said. "Large tank, wires everywhere and dials so that you can see when it's about to explode."

"Any real danger?"

"There's always danger. We close our minds to it. Belinda

doesn't. She'd be happier if they were magnetising atoms to destruction in the middle of the Sahara. But some bright spark in the architecture department made a clever nod to safety! The liquefier room has a very light roof. It's designed to just blow off and relieve the pressure from underneath in the event of an explosion."

"Splattering the rooftops of Cambridge with body parts?" Joe was aghast. "I should like to see this lab—preferably on a nonworking day."

"You're probably too late to see that piece of equipment. They're planning to install a newer model this week. The parts have been delivered. A *helium* liquefier. Onwards and upwards!" he finished cheerfully.

Joe acknowledged his attempt at a joke with a grimace. "Tell me, Page, this helium gas . . . how . . . um . . . explosive is it? Should Cambridge folk be issued with tin hats?"

Page smiled indulgently and launched into a very brief explanation in words that even a copper could understand. "The lab's interested in passing huge amounts of electricity through a set of metal coils to produce a magnetic field hugely more powerful than any previously known. You need extremely low temperatures to stop the coils from overheating. Liquid helium has the lowest temperature achievable by man. It's a coolant. It's difficult to produce."

"Sounds an expensive business?" Joe speculated and pursued Page further on the funding, inviting him to hand him the identity of the contributors.

A list of financiers and industrialists showing an interest followed. One name snagged at Joe's attention and after a moment he remembered.

"Metropolitan-Vickers?" he said. "The Manchester

company, Metrovick? We had a problem with them back in January, do you recall? The nation was gripped!"

"Of course. Six of their engineers, installing turbines in Moscow, were arrested by the Russkies and put in jug for spying, weren't they? Cause célèbre . . . all over the press."

"Yes. The poor chaps were interrogated, tortured and threatened with execution. It was claimed in the confessions the secret police extracted along with the toenails that they'd attempted to sabotage the turbines they were installing. The Americans stepped up to the plate and joined in the condemnation. An embargo on trade with Russia was threatened. The Yanks must have shaken a big stick because, unbelievably, an apology came from Comrade Stalin: What was all the fuss about? he wanted to know. They must understand that he loved Americans and always welcomed them warmly to his country."

Page shuddered. "I'd sooner be kissed by a cobra."

Joe smiled. "I don't think anyone was deceived. But—riding on the tide of Comrade Stalin's good humour—or possibly the threat of being deprived of the connections essential to get his turbines to light up Moscow, the British engineers were let off. MI5 chalked up a success and attended a cocktail party in Grosvenor Square. What's Metrovick's interest in the Mond Laboratory?"

"They're a huge support. We put a lot of business their way. They supply the machinery. Often specially designed by Kapitza. Did I mention—he's a brilliant engineer. If he weren't billed as a pure scientist they'd probably offer him a job. They do electrical generators, steam turbines, trains, aeroplanes, anything connected with power supply. I'm guessing that they would have a very keen interest in the second generation of bomb-proof, fighter-proof, helium airships that they say are on the cards. A company like Metrovick would want to be at the forefront of any physics research, naturally."

"To the extent of paying for influence?"

Page shrugged his shoulders and fished in his pocket for his pipe. "You'd need to get hold of the books. I won't speculate."

"Is the expression 'war work' ever used in your hearing?"

"Lord no! High science is what we do. Wouldn't get our hands dirty."

Was the man being ironic? Or was he merely spelling out the laboratory management's code of conduct? Joe had no doubt that at least some of the scientific staff were up to their armpits in mire.

"Any more names come to mind? Perhaps local university interests?"

"Yes. As a matter of fact there is."

Joe endured the irritating filling, tamping and puffing process that accompanied pipe smoking. It usually heralded a significant revelation or a confession. He'd learned long ago to value the nose-tingling blast of St. Bruno tobacco.

"There's a local aristocrat who seems to have a finger in every pie," Page finally offered. "You'll have seen his ugly mug in the papers. He's not shy. Sir Gregory Pertinax. Much admired. Generous contributor to the lab. He supplies us with boxes and boxes of valuable equipment. All the same— I can't stand the bloke."

"How well do you know him professionally and socially?" Joe probed.

"I expect in your line of business, you know that better than I do myself," Page said sharply. "Apart from his visits to the lab, he invited me to dinner. Once. Out of the blue. Oh, back in the summer I think it was."

"July the twentieth, at Madingley Court," Joe supplied.

"Er, yes. That sounds about right." Page looked stricken. "Look here—I'd rather not talk about it."

"You don't have the choice," Joe said flatly. "If you clam up we must assume the worst—that he encouraged you to partake in some reprehensible behaviour involving sex and drugs and subjected you to blackmail. Threatened to reveal all to Belinda if you didn't cooperate."

Page turned pale, swallowed smoke the wrong way and began to cough. "Oh, my God!" he wheezed. "That's what it was all about? All that Hellfire Club stuff? *Ama et fac quod vis* and all that! Bunch of profligates! I was supposed to get drunk and indulge in . . . Well, they got the wrong bloke! Belinda would have given them a piece of her mind! 'Publish-and-be-damned' Wellington is her hero. I thought he'd asked me there to check up on me. I thought he suspected I was up to what your boss would call 'clandestine surveillance' . . . that someone at the lab had denounced me. I was expecting Rutherford to pop out of the woodwork and hand me my notice any moment but nothing happened."

"How did you get away?"

"Played the innocent, unworldly scientist! Bored the pants off the assembled company by explaining gravity to them. Rolling oranges round a fruit bowl came into it, I remember. And walnuts on a table napkin." He gave a mischievous grin and went on apologetically, "I, er, showed them a few magic tricks. You know . . . setting fire to macaroon wrappers and exploding eggs. I think I quite lowered the tone. I certainly wrecked the tablecloth. Fearing the worst, I'd arranged for Belinda to ring me at the hall halfway through dinner. She was to tell me our boy Timmy had been taken ill and needed to be driven to hospital. They seemed to swallow it. Glad to get rid of me by then, I think, before the house went up in flames. The butler put the mastiffs on a lead and escorted me to my car. I was never more grateful to hear my old Morris start up. I'd been having problems with the ignition. So—I had a lucky escape?"

Joe decided the moment had come to bolster the man's self-esteem and pin him more firmly into his place as agent. "No luck involved—good judgement and courage, I'd say. Well done, Hermes! Another one of our chaps was not so fortunate. He had to kill one of the dogs in single combat, climb the gate and run back to Cambridge in his patent-leather dancing shoes," he confided.

Page beamed. "Great heavens! What a hero! I say—give him my felicitations when you see him."

"Sadly not possible," Joe said, staring into his beer.

"Ah. Sorry. One of the three you mentioned?" Page said quietly.

Joe nodded. Aidan wouldn't have minded him using his example of derring-do in the cause of a bit of psychological skirmishing, he thought.

Joe's stab of sorrow did not go undetected by Page. "Did he have a divine nickname, this Slayer of Hounds? I think we should drink to him," he said seriously.

"No, he didn't. But if he had, I'd have called him Loki. God of mischief. And fire."

"To Loki, then!"

"To Loki!" Joe smiled into his beer. He was certain enough of Page now to make further use of him.

Page had let his pipe go out. He put it back in his pocket, where the still-hot tobacco proceeded to make another hole in his baggy old suit. "Just tell me what I can do, sir," he said with quiet resolve. Joe had a sudden glimpse of Belinda's third boy: tousle-headed Humphrey.

"Thank you, Doctor Page," he said. "There is something. We're going to play them at their own game! We're going to blind them with truth, innocence of purpose and lashings of oily charm. I want you to arrange for me to visit the labs. An official visit under my own name and rank. The sooner the better—and certainly well before the eleventh of November. It'll take quite a bit of scientific arrogance, fast footwork and conjuring skills on your part. Are you up to it? Ready to give those sandals another outing?"

CHAPTER 21

A hearty "Welcome back, sir! The master's expecting you for sherry in his drawing room before dinner," from the porter cheered Joe. He was beginning to find his way easily about the college and, he was slightly alarmed to acknowledge, to enjoy the feeling of inclusion and acceptance.

Not the first of the High Table guests to arrive, nor yet the last, Joe was greeted with warmth by the master. He accepted a glass of dry sherry and turned his attention to meeting his fellow guests, very much relieved to find that Pertinax was not amongst them and that his new friend Professor Deerbolt the classicist was.

When all were assembled, he looked around the company wondering which of these chattering, civilised men had so alarmed or intrigued Aidan that he'd jumped the security service rails and run amok. Who had so startled him that he'd broken all his own imposed rules and made a terse and impenetrable entry in his diary?

I saw him. At dinner. There could be no doubt.

He would only find out by talking, listening carefully and making himself agreeable.

Joe had long ago stopped quarrelling with the notion that he had effectively taken a course in diplomacy from Sir

George Jardine, a decade before in India. The old servant of Empire, spy extraordinaire and éminence grise behind the viceroy had, early in Joe's career, taken him under his wing, trained him in sugar-coated skulduggery and attempted to seduce him into following a path identical to his own. In Joe he had seen his alter ego, an attractive young man with a silver tongue, a genuine rapport with his fellow men (women, too, and that was a serious advantage in India), physical and mental courage and—above all—an unrelenting patriotism.

On occasions like this one, Sir George was always at Joe's elbow in spirit, a wily and jovial presence. Joe had at first been wary of his position as outsider in this group, knowing the strength and exclusiveness of the academic world. Whatever cultural and social distance there was to be overcome, however, he thought he'd probably conjured up himself. If it had been real, he would never have survived the conversational onslaught of Professor Deerbolt. The elderly academic had greeted Joe with pleasure and had taken it upon himself to escort Joe around the groups, an indomitable icebreaker cutting through the floes of reserve and hauteur, announcing to everyone with pride and innocent excitement the part Joe played in the outside world.

"Lord Trenchard's right hand at Scotland Yard," was his description.

Joe did not attempt a pedantic correction, but smiled modestly, scooped up the ball and ran with it. The very words "Scotland Yard" would have sunk an iceberg. Witticisms, questions, experiences bad and good followed on. Almost all the company had an old uncle who'd once fallen foul of the "Roberts," as policemen were apparently still called in this place. All were eager to establish the identity of Jack the

Ripper and Joe duly revealed it, dramatically swearing them to silence. All rules governing the unacceptability of talking about one's job were suddenly ignored. People wanted to hear more. Joe had a store of scandalous tales of the Yard which he constantly refreshed, polished and paraded on such occasions. Prompted by Deerbolt, he even dropped a few Latin phrases at an appropriate time and felt he was probably earning his place at table.

Not one of the guests reacted in a significant way when Joe mentioned Aidan's name. Several had expressed their sorrow at his death, none reddened with guilt and fled the room with an eldritch screech. His evening, it seemed, was not about to produce the result he'd hoped for. Ah, well. He had dinner to look forward to. A cheerful undergraduate had been put to sit on Joe's left, and on his right (at Joe's request) the domestic bursar, a fellow of the college whose role it was to know all the secrets of the establishment and its personnel. Accommodation, housekeeping, security, welfare of staff and academic members of the college were all within the remit of Dr. Calthrop.

Joe hoped he'd make it through to the end of the evening without disgracing himself or annoying the redoubtable bursar with his questions. Thankful that he'd drunk little of his beer in the Anchor, he sipped his sherry slowly and refused a refill of his glass. He realised he was extremely hungry and lined up with relief behind the master when the gong sounded for dinner.

AN EXCELLENT GAME soup with a deep, dark flavour—Marsala?—was an appetising start to a series of dishes which promised a celebration of the autumn season. The highlights were to be haunch of venison and a blackberry syllabub, the undergraduate on his left confided, adding innocently that the quality of the dishes on High almost made up for the terror of being invited to appear. How had the commissioner enjoyed the food in India?

The soup plates were being collected, and the wine stewards were gathering in readiness to pour out the hock that would accompany the fish, when Joe, in mid-sentence, looked up, scanned the crowded hall with its ranks of chattering and laughing students and saw him.

He saw him. There could be no doubt.

"Sir! Sir! I say, are you all right?" The young man on his left took Joe by the arm. "You look as though you've seen a ghost. Sorry! Silly thing to say! Are you having a turn? Bread crumb gone down the wrong way?"

"No. I'm perfectly well, thank you. But I *have* just seen a ghost."

"Ah! That's all right then. Did you know we have eight here in college? The oldest is believed to be that of the second master who threw himself from the belfry in—"

Joe cut him short, able at last to find words. "Look—the young man at the back of the hall, standing in the doorway—do you see him? I don't suppose you have any idea who he might be?"

The boy peered doubtfully through the candlelit gloom and said in some puzzlement, "No, I'm afraid I don't. But if you'd care to ask the bursar, I'm sure he would. He knows everyone in college, including the ghosts."

"Of course. I'll do that," Joe murmured, and he addressed his question to Dr. Calthrop.

"Oh, yes. I do," the bursar replied. "He's rather

distinctive, isn't he? Everyone knows Hereward. He works for us. Followed his mother into the business, so to speak. He started out as a buttery boy and he's now a wine steward."

"Did you say 'Hereward'?"

Calthrop smiled. "He doesn't much care for it either! Everyone calls him Harry. Harry Melton. Though if anyone could wear the name of a Viking warrior with a swagger, it is he! Was, indeed, Hereward the Wake, our local hero, of Viking origin? Was he Saxon perhaps?"

"Danish, I believe," Joe said, distracted and dismissive. He had suddenly no heart for polite conversation-making.

Calthrop sensed this and went on smoothly, "Do you know him, Sandilands? I do hope you're not going to say you have, er, a professional interest!" he teased. "We're all very fond of Harry, and if you're thinking of carting him off in irons on a trumped-up charge of berserking, you will be resisted in your endeavours!"

"No, no. Nothing of the kind. We've never met before. And I'm sure he's not on the Met's calling list. You know, the French have a much more expressive word for "ghost." It's *revenant*. Someone returning. Coming back to haunt me."

"Harry? Is Harry haunting you?" Intrigued, the bursar looked again at the figure, which now detached itself from the doorway and began a smooth advance down the room, hugging the wall. Halfway towards High Table, which was raised up on a dais at the far end of the room, he stood still and began to rake the company seated on either side of the master, one at a time, with a searching eye. When he reached Joe, he stopped and stared.

The bursar, watching this performance, said dubiously: "I do believe you're right, Sandilands! Strange behaviour!

You may not know *him*, but I'd say he knows *you*. And, what's more, he doesn't like you very much. I say—is he being a nuisance? I can have him removed from the hall."

Joe returned the gaze, barely able to withstand the concentrated force of hatred, scorn and—yes—fear directed at him by those familiar eyes.

He responded to the challenge lancing its way across the room with a curt nod, received one in return and turned with a smile back to his concerned neighbour. "A reaction I've had, sadly, to get used to over the years. People *will* always try to knock a bobby's helmet off. We're not popular. Perhaps I had the bad luck to send his uncle down for roistering twenty years ago? Families bear grudges."

"Well, you can stand easy again. Hereward's got bored with putting a hex on you and he's gone off about his business." Still concerned, he added, "He really is a fine chap, you know. I wouldn't like to think he was in trouble. He works hard and is a credit to the college ... Much too good for us, I've heard it said ... Good sense of humour, considering he's not had the easiest of lives. Brought up by his mother, I understand, the last child of a large family. No paternal influence—his father, a regular soldier, was shot dead early in the war. Bought it at Mons."

Joe looked at him in quiet surprise. "Mons? I was there myself, manning a machine gun. Perhaps, through the smoke and fury, I caught a glimpse of Hereward's father?"

Dr. Calthrop was shaken by a sudden thought. He looked again from Joe to the disappearing figure of the steward and, after a moment, spoke quietly, "Good Lord! I think I've seen your revenant, Sandilands. Though it takes a seeing eye and an accommodating nature to pull both ends together. How very disconcerting! Hereward's father must have been a very handsome man since his mother is no oil painting. Dying, as he did, on French soil, nineteen years ago, he never set eyes on his beautiful boy."

Joe knew exactly why Aidan had died. He could conjure up the enduring pain, the sense of shame and guilt that had swamped his friend at the last. Yet, in the acutest torment of body and soul, he'd still been able to rouse himself to joke and flirt with the pretty girl who'd tried to save him. He'd used Adelaide to establish his own redemption and to obstruct and divert the course of justice. He'd almost fooled Joe.

One more phone call to be made as soon as he was able to work himself free of this confounded dinner party.

This was proving to be a long day, but the worst was yet to come. He hoped he would have the moral strength to do the right thing when he put himself in Aidan's shoes. Excusing himself from coffee in the drawing room afterwards, he wrote out a short note and passed it to Dr. Calthrop, asking him if he could make a delivery within the college before ten o'clock.

The bursar had taken it, looked at the name on the envelope with troubled eyes and said, "Without any difficulty. Grasping the nettle, Sandilands? Always the best way. I never leave anything to fester."

"SAME TIME, SAME place."

The invitation, the summons. Four words. Instantly intelligible to the recipient of the note, if Joe's appalling suppositions were correct. If he ran he should have plenty of time to make the phone call and pick up the evidence he'd put away in his drawer at the hotel. Then, at last, he'd be ready to face Aidan's murderer.

~~

AT TEN MINUTES to ten, Joe approached the church of All Hallows. The last of the unseasonal summer weather seemed to be over. The weathercock creaked as it shifted round in the wind, and a flurry of leaves, torn from the branches in the sudden blast, somersaulted along the tiled path, playing tag with his feet as he approached the heavy door.

Once inside, Joe turned on his pocket torch. He knew where the light switches were, but he wanted to recreate the scene that had greeted Adelaide on All Hallows Eve. Without the corpse in the third row of pews on the right, however. For the moment.

He lit the row of candles which still stood ready on the altar, put out his torch, checked that the knife was ready in the pocket of his coat and went to sit in the place Aidan had occupied in the pews. He said a prayer for his friend and waited.

The cracked bell of a nearby college rang out ten strokes.

One minute after that, Joe heard the latch on the door to the vestry at the back of the church click open and then click closed. Careful steps approached over the flagged corridor leading into the nave. Joe steeled himself for the confrontation Aidan had so eagerly wished for and arranged days before.

The velvet curtain obscuring the door was pushed aside and a man stepped into the candlelit gloom. He stood, not hiding himself, with a defiant tilt of the head that Joe instantly recognised. The candles lit his shock of silver-gilt hair and turned his eyes to chips of ice.

"Aidan!"

Joe could not keep back the word and was dismayed that his voice sounded as cracked as the college bell.

The illusion was shattered when the young man spoke. "Not bloody Aidan! Never bloody Aidan! Hereward Melton to you, scumbag!" The voice had none of the waltzing smoothness of Aidan's. It was rough and full of fear and aggression in equal measure. The coarseness was delivered in a heavy local accent. Suddenly he scarcely looked like Aidan and Joe was assailed by doubt. Had he made a fool of himself? No one else apart from Dr. Calthrop had seen what Joe had seen. But no one else had known the young Aidan as well as the middle-aged one. Had the boy made the connection for himself?

The newcomer must have heard the rawness of the emotion in his own voice, exaggerated by the stillness of the church. He moved forward abruptly and said in a sharper, more challenging tone, "How did you guess? Who gave me away? In any case you have no proof of anything."

"How did I guess? I didn't. I knew. And it was your mother who gave you away, you could say."

"Don't be daft! You've never spoken to my mother."

"She told the world when she christened you 'Hereward.' You may not like the name, Harry, but it's a dead giveaway. It meant a lot to your father. His thesis when he was an undergraduate here was on 'Hereward the Wake,' the East Anglian hero who fought a rearguard action against the invading Normans from his stronghold in the Fens. 'Hereward the Dane' according to Aidan's research. Aidan's family was from hereabouts, and I think he always fancied himself a descendant. Anyone who knew your father in those days would have known that. Hereward was his fascination."

The boy hadn't been aware. Or else he'd exhausted his store of expletives. He eyed Joe truculently in silence.

"And besides . . . I'm one of the few men who knew Aidan when he was young . . . twenty-one? About that when I met him. You must be . . ."

"I'm eighteen."

"Almost the same age. The resemblance is shattering. I can imagine what he must have thought when he looked up and saw himself when young across the hall . . ."

"Himself!" Harry pounced on the word. "Not *me*! Got it in one, copper! You can imagine, huh? Can you imagine how cheesed off he must have been? What a nuisance for poor Sir Aidan to find that the illegitimate kid he'd denied and had forgotten about all these years is still alive and wants to kick his head in?"

"Half a mo, Harry!" Joe spoke sharply. "Let's clear one thing up. He had no idea you existed before he came back to St. Benedict's last month."

"Oh, yer! How likely is that?" the boy sneered.

"It's exact. I was his friend. I remain his executor. He never married. I have been in touch with his solicitor in London who confirms that the man had no idea he had a son. Apart from a second cousin, he had no living relations, or so he thought until a week or so ago. Look, why don't you confront your mother with this? She of all people knows the truth."

"My mother?" The boy appeared dazed. "What the hell do you know of my mother?"

"From the dates, from your family history with the college and your present address, I can deduce that Aidan had an affair or an episode of a sexual nature at the very least with his bedder while he was at college. With Mrs. Mavis Melton. Of Ditton." Joe finished awkwardly. "Then he went straight off to the war and was never aware that . . ."

A raucous chortle greeted this. "Well, deduce me this copper . . . Have you seen Mavis Melton? No? Thought not! She's the dearest woman in the world to me but even she would tell you she's an ugly old boot—always was—and a good twenty years older than Sir Aidan. And they tell me you're a commissioner of some sort!" he sneered. "Bigwig from the Yard? No wonder the country's in trouble. You should stick to finding lost cats, mister."

He stepped closer following up his moral advantage. "Naw! Mavis is my granny, you barmpot! They have very strict rules here about who can and who can't do the bedding. In 1914 money was tighter even than it is now. My grandad's army pay wasn't enough to keep a family of six kids. Gran lied. She needed the job. She lied about the number—they didn't like you to have too many. A distraction. When she got ill or was confined with another kid, and couldn't get in to work, her eldest daughter Alice used to sneak in the back way and do her jobs for her. No questions asked. The stewards in those days were more accommodating. They knew what was going on all right. So long as the work got done, they looked the other way."

"Alice was how old?" Joe asked faintly.

The boy moved down the aisle and stopped just one row of pews away. An arm's length.

"Fifteen. He had his way with her, the dirty old shit! She was just sixteen when I was born. Died in agony cursing the bugger! I never saw my mother."

Joe did not dare speak. The blue eyes were swimming in tears, the boy's nose was beginning to run. Grief was struggling with anger but both emotions were being held back by a need for self-justification.

"My granny took me over and brought me up with her own brood. Told everyone I was hers. Granddad was shot in the war and couldn't argue. She never lied to me though. I've always known who I was. And whose fault it was. I've always promised my gran that if ever I set eyes on the man who ruined and killed my mother, I'd give him a good kicking. But he were a big bloke. Not sure I'd have got near him. He deserved to pay for what he'd done. Bloody nobs!"

Impotence and rage against the upper classes was an explosive brew, Joe recognised, and was wary.

"I thought if I could get near enough I could put a knife in his ribs. He turns up here in college again, bold as brass, asking about his old bedder! 'Remember me to Mavis,' he says to Maggie Alsopp! He was remembered all right! He had the bloody nerve to put his arms out to give me a hug!" Hereward shuddered at the memory. "That gave me my chance. I got in and I passed on my mother's regards as I stuck the knife in him. And I'd do it again!" He fished in his pocket.

"Leave it!" Joe shouted. "You little twerp! I'll have you on your back and in handcuffs before you can—" Horrified, he stopped himself in mid-sentence.

Alarmingly, after a moment of shock, the lad burst out laughing. It was Aidan's laugh Joe heard. "Before you can say knife? . . . How about: handkerchief?" he suggested and, taunting Joe, took a large, white one from his pocket and proceeded to blow his nose.

Recovering his poise, Joe took a deep breath and went on more calmly, "This is the game knife the pathologist recovered from Aidan's body." He took it out and showed it to the boy, who affected not to be interested. "It's been tested and photographed for fingerprints, of course. They got a clear set. It comes from the college kitchens where you work as a steward. You could have plucked it from the washed cutlery tray after work on your way to come here and meet Aidan. You charged him with what you considered to be his crime and stuck it into his rib cage, aiming for, but not quite striking, the heart. You will not know that your father was still alive hours later when he was discovered by a local doctor who did her best to save him. The doctor and the dying man had time to hold quite a conversation before the end came."

"So I did it? I thought I'd admitted that by coming here." The lad was, strangely, unaffected by the evidence Joe had produced. He took a reluctant look at the blade. "But no one's going to listen to you in court, copper, when I tell them *my* story. You know what this church is used for sometimes? 'Nefarious purposes,' the rags call it. 'Clandestine rendez-vous.' Huh! If it comes to saving my skin *I* can spin a tale. I shall tell them that a noble guest of the college had lured me, a poor innocent lad, a college servant, to one of those clandestine encounters in a place notorious for it. I had to defend myself against an evil, old degenerate. There you are! Self defence!"

Joe's guts and his mind were churning, unable to digest the sickening mix of Aidan's handsome remembered presence and the vile thoughts being spat in his face. He fought for control.

"No one's going to believe that disgusting rubbish, Harry."

"Course they're not! Don't matter! You missed out on the important words, didn't you, cloth ears! 'Noble guest . . . St. Benedict's College . . . Hallowe'en high jincks in city church.' Stick that lot together and you've got a headline and a half! A headline that's going to get up the noses of a lot of ponces! You've got the aristocracy, the Church and—not least—the university . . . and they run the town. The Cambridge cops will never let it get as far as the papers. They'll lose the evidence and gag the editors like they always do. Go back to London where you came from. There's nothing you can stick on anybody here."

Joe couldn't leave the matter there. He'd make one last try to get through to Aidan's son. For Aidan's sake.

"Listen. Your father would have loved you if you'd let him live. Do you want the proof? You are the living proof! You're standing in front of me right now showing off, spouting rubbish instead of being marched off to a cell with a capital charge hanging over you. This knife . . ." He held it by the blade. "It had fingerprints on it all right. Not the killer's. Not yours. Aidan, dying, had wiped it clean of your prints, grasped it and left a clear set of his own on the handle. He made a confession to the doctor claiming that he'd stabbed himself and botched the job. There's no way the Crown Prosecution Service would allow the case to come to court. Insufficient evidence."

Harry broke the shocked silence that followed this information. "Why? Why would he do that?"

"Because that's what a father would do for his son. It's what I would do for mine. What a mess! But there's one thing that's clear in this dirty business and let's hang on to it. My friend, your father, was a sinner like most young men. He admitted it. But he had courage and honour and much love in him. Had he known about you, you could have received it and enjoyed it as his friends did. You robbed many people of a wonderful man and not least—you robbed yourself. The case is closed and for that you can thank your father. He showed his love for his son in the only way left to him."

The dam broke and Harry covered his face with his handkerchief, gulping for air and mewling like a kitten.

Tears of regret? Relief? Joe couldn't say. He walked around and joined the shaking figure. He flung a comforting arm around Harry's shoulders.

"Sit down, lad," he said. "I haven't time to wrap this up. So take this in now and think about it. I'll give you my number and you can ring me up to talk about it any time you like. It may take a while to adjust. Anyhow—here goes . . .

"I told you I'm your father's executor. He's had the same unchanged, boring old will for many years now. Suddenly, yesterday, his lawyer, Giles Fairbain, in London got a message through to me saying he'd heard the news of Aidan's death and would I contact him as his executor regarding the will. I assumed this was the usual harrying from a solicitor eager to clear his in-tray and collect his fee, and I didn't jump to answer it. When I saw you in the college this evening and the bursar told me your name was Hereward, I put two and two together. I dashed back to my hotel, skipping the coffee, and rang old Fairbain at home. Dragged him away from his game of bridge and demanded some answers. We coppers can get away with stuff like that. Upshot is, in a new will drawn up last week here in Cambridge, all shipshape, signed and legal, he'd named you as his heir. Don't get too excited—he wasted much of his family money and you're not inheriting a fortune. All the same, there'll be a bit to get you started in life or just make this one more comfortable for you and your gran. Entirely up to you. If you'd like me to take you to see Mr. Fairbain in his office, I can lay that on."

Receiving no answer but a horrified, staring incomprehension, Joe finished, "You murdered a dear man with anger and brutality and will never have my forgiveness, but—sod it!—you had your father's forgiveness, and that's what counts. Aidan made certain that you could not be pursued in law but, believe me, you will be pursued. You're going to have me on your case for the rest of your days. You're going to use the opportunity he's handed you to earn his respect—to earn *my* respect."

The boy went on sobbing and Joe went on grieving for father and son.

CHAPTER 22

"It's midnight, sir, here in Mayfair," Mr. Barnes explained, sarcasm lightly veiled by formality. "Miss Despond retired to her room two hours ago. Perhaps you would like to ring back in eight hour's time?"

"Terribly sorry! Yes, of course." Joe was mortified. Bloody butlers! In his agitation he'd somehow thought Dorothy would pick up the phone herself. She kept late hours and was rarely in bed before midnight. Perhaps she was not alone? He knew very little about her private life although he felt free, because he had never been discouraged, to joke with her in an intimate way. He assumed too much.

"I can offer you *Mr.* Despond. The master is recently returned from New York and is at present in the snooker room entertaining his transatlantic guests."

"No, no. Don't disturb him. Sorry to have bothered you."

"A moment, sir!" Barnes caught Joe a second before he cut the connection. "If the assistant commissioner's call chanced to relate to a matter of business—law enforcement business, that is—I should feel at liberty to count this one of those occasions on which duty might compel me to divert the communication to Miss Despond's own private extension in her bedroom. If she is awake she will answer within three rings. More than that and I would advise you replace . . ."

"Mr. Barnes! Let's enforce a little law, shall we? I'm about to charge her butler with aggravating circumlocution! Will that qualify?"

Dorothy picked up the receiver on the second ring. "Hello. Dorothy Despond here."

She sounded wide awake, as though her day were just beginning.

"It's Joe. I'm in Cambridge. Are you alone?"

"Let me check. Well there's Barnes somewhere about the place but he's not in my bed. My companion for the night is a handsome, hard-bitten (and hard-biting) private eye that my father brought back from New York for me. Hunter is quite sweet but he will call his women 'Lady' and he sleeps in his boots. By page ninety he's beginning to bore me. Give me a moment while I chuck him at the wall, will you? Well, now—it's good to hear from you, Commissioner. I was wondering . . . Are you still upright and holding your shield?"

"No. I'm collapsed on my hotel bed and my shield's as full of holes as my socks."

"I'm sad to hear that. I hope you managed to deflect all the blows?"

"No. Two took me by surprise and got through. I've taken serious wounds in the region of the solar plexus and the heart. I'm pure done in! Not sure I'll recover, Dorothy."

With a trace of suspicion and laughter in her voice, she asked, "So, you're treating the condition with whisky, are you?"

Joe eyed his half-empty glass of Islay Malt. "How did you know?"

"You come over all Scottish. Don't worry—I like it! Slainté! Have another swig."

Dorothy had the knack of making her presence immediate, friendly and forgiving. He did as she suggested, making the glass ring as he picked it up, to oblige her.

"That's better! Now, let me examine your solar plexus . . . Oh, nasty! Who delivered the blow?"

"An eighteen-year-old college servant. A killer who stabbed a dear friend of mine to death and would have dispatched me the same way. No . . . No, I confiscated his knife before worse occurred. It wasn't physical skirmishing that knocked the wind out of me—it was the psychological shock. The killer turned out to be the son Aidan never knew he had. Nearly two decades of poison, allowed to fester, reached bursting point, leaving yours truly to clear up the mess and mourn for two unhappy souls."

"Poor Joe! Have a hug. A careful hug—I don't want to open wounds."

Joe smiled. Face to face, she would never have attempted such an intimacy—one shake of the hand was the only physical contact they had shared, but at a distance of seventy miles a nanny-ish hug to raise the spirits of a suffering man was perfectly acceptable.

"Thank you. Gratefully received and, believe me, it helps. I did my best but I'm left with the backwash. Aidan had been working undercover in this Cambridge affair and he'd set me on the right trail. I'd assumed his death was connected and would unravel the problem of Pertinax but no—it was totally unconnected with our mutual art-loving friend. The motive was a personal one. So now I have a neat solution, but it puts me no further forward with gathering events."

"I shall try to pretend I understand all that. Are you going to reveal your heart wound?"

"No. I've smothered it under layers of bandages." Into the silence on the other end he added lamely, "There was a girl I was hoping to marry. She's turned me down."

"Adelaide Hartest? Well of course she did! Any woman would. Especially a talented and outstanding woman like Adelaide. I'm not a bit surprised that you fell for her. But the man who deserves her has never been born. It's certainly not you, Joe."

Joe gobbled, sat up and took another gulp of his whisky. "Oh. Ah. How do you know about Adelaide?"

"You seem to have blanked out the fact that I was very much present last summer when you demolished my plans to marry Sir James Truelove. You stripped my fiancé, in front of my eyes, of his . . . well, everything. His position, his self-respect, his family, very nearly his life. Of course the man deserved it, the country owes you a huge debt and I'm eternally grateful . . . though there was a moment when I could have cheerfully smashed your skull. You've forgotten I was there—because Adelaide was on the scene. Every woman fades into the background when they're sharing a stage with Sarah Bernhardt, an Iceni queen and the goddess Athena all rolled into one. But, bless her, she's never aware that the spotlight follows her about. *She* noticed me and realised what I must be feeling. She came to see me and gave me some very good advice along with her sympathy. We stayed in contact and we've become friends. She's not my best friend—she would scorn such a schoolgirl notion—but she's the best of my friends."

"Oh, Lord!"

"Yes. It's bad!" Dorothy chortled. "For you, it's alarming! No man wants to hear that the women in his life know each other . . ." Her voice lost its confidence for a moment as she hurriedly added, "I mean, that's to assume I am in your life somewhere. Confidante? Agent? Agony aunt? Whatever my role—do admit—I'm not given to gossip and social stirring. I couldn't do my job if I were. I hear all and say nothing. I only mention it now because I think you need advice from an expert on surviving heart wounds. With my perspective on things from three angles, perhaps I can say—and perhaps, for once, you'll listen: you'll have to think again, won't you? Joe, you're just terrible when it comes to choosing women."

"You're right, Dorothy. I'll never choose one again," Joe agreed quickly, uncomfortable with the direction the conversation had taken.

"You concede too quickly," Dorothy reproved. "Like a good doctor, I'm not going to accept the patient's diagnosis or prognosis. Grit your teeth! Hold on to the bedpost! I'm going to pull out the arrowhead, which is still stuck inside you. Here goes . . . Adelaide is an Acolyte of Diana."

"Eh? What's that? Not another weird Cambridge society? She's already got the Hellfire Club and the Ladies Against Public Indecency vying for her attention."

"No. I was assuming you knew some Shakespeare. *A Midsummer Night's Dream.* One of the girls . . ."

"Hermia or Helena," Joe supplied in an effort to show he still retained a hold on the exchange.

"Hermia . . . is given the choice of marriage to her father's nominee or being a sacrifice on the altar of Diana. Goddess of chastity and the single life. In other words she has to marry a suitable man or renounce all men for ever and become a nun. Now, Adelaide is supremely attractive to the opposite sex and they assume she must be taking her time finding someone worthy of her to settle down with. She finds you and everyone smiles. A perfect match. There'll be a pretty house somewhere green and just out of range of the city soot and fog, a Bentley in the garage, a string of children and a husband who comes home occasionally when the demands of his work and his club permit. With a knighthood in the offing he has to spend much of his time earning it."

"So? You've just described every man's ideal life. Paradise, so long as you include a brace of long-legged dogs."

"But not the ideal of a well-educated woman with very particular life-enhancing—life-preserving—skills. Skills acquired as a result of seven years of expensive and demand-ing work. A career which she would be compelled by society to shelve were she to marry. She's weighed the two choices of Hermia, made up her mind and thrown herself on Diana's altar."

"Nonsense! The nunneries are nearly empty! We're not in the Middle Ages any longer, Dorothy. You've been read-ing *Ivanhoe* again."

"You'd be surprised! I blame the war. The idiocy of men, slaughtering each other in some ancient spasm of rage and blood lust. Ugh! And now the brutes have put themselves in short supply by their efforts. They've acquired a rarity value which they don't deserve.

"I have a wide circle of friends, Joe. Many of the girls my age are bright and well educated. Some of them even have degrees from the more forward-looking universities. I heard something heartbreaking from one of them the other day. Twirling her new engagement ring on her finger over celebratory buns at the Ritz, Lois announced she was marrying one of her fellow students. Leo would be pursuing his career while she would be learning how to make toast until her husband could earn enough money to employ a full domestic staff.

"I asked her why she had worked away all those years to get to graduation point.

"'Oh, it wasn't for the degree,' she told me. 'I wanted to meet some clever and eligible young men. And now I have! There they all were, heaps of them at University College in London! And at least I shall understand what my husband's saying, as we took the same course.'"

"Enough, Dotty! The arrowhead's out. You forced it clear through and out the other side."

"Good. Lace up your corset and pick up your shield again. I want to hear about Pertinax. Did you get the painting? What have you done with it? Did it end in fisticuffs?"

"I got it. I offered what you suggested. It's here in my room with me now, propped up against the wall, a rather disturbing image. Lord knows what the room maid makes of it. I expect she's reported me to the management."

He caught the eye of the satyr leering over the pink innocence of the sleeping nymph. Then he took a deep breath and plunged in. "Listen, Dorothy. Your friend and client Pertinax—were you aware that he claims to be in love with you? This might be the moment to invoke the goddess and run for cover behind her altar yourself because I fear he may have plans to include you in his future."

"Joe! That's the least of your troubles. Gregory has plans to include the world in his future. Haven't you got there yet? I'm flattered and touched that you find the time to think of one woman's discomfort when faced with the brazen hideousness of his schemes. He says he loves me, though 'claims' is more accurate—he doesn't really understand the word. Yes—he's asked me to marry him once or twice. I've refused, but he doesn't expect ever to be thwarted in anything. I was hoping *you* might do a little thwarting. Have you any plans to pull his plug? Do you know where he keeps it?"

"I think I do. And I have to act quickly. There's a clock ticking."

"Ouch! Sounds urgent. Anything I can do? Shall I come up and join you? Sit on Sir Gregory while you tickle his feet with a feather? What are you planning?"

"I can't tell you, Dorothy. Because I don't know yet. I shall play it by ear."

A lie. Joe rarely played any tune or scene by ear. He knew exactly what he had to do and who was going to join him in his activities. Dorothy was definitely not one of them. He wanted her well away from Pertinax's gathering evil.

"Just stay away from Cambridge. That's all you can do, Dorothy," he said in a tone that invited no reply "Now tell me—did you know that Pertinax has acquired another Picasso? . . . Yes! That's the one! All buttocks and bosoms! Amongst the assorted globular hemispheres on display I detected a clear case of chronic carbunculosis. Gave me quite a turn!"

AT ONE O'CLOCK, Barnes made his ritual inspection of the upper floors before retiring for the night. Pacing silently past Miss Dorothy's room, he paused, checked that the coast was clear and put an ear to the door. Girlish giggles. The assistant commissioner was doing his stuff. Barnes smiled and padded on down the corridor.

CHAPTER 23

Constable Risby turned up at precisely nine o'clock to pick up Joe after breakfast.

"Lagonda today, sir?" he asked eagerly.

"Oh, yes. It's going to rain and I don't want to appear looking like a drowned rat. I think we'll arrive in style. Though we're only a few minutes' walk away from our destination."

He checked the officer's appearance. Smart police uniform, freshly brushed helmet, all leather bits and bobs shining. Joe had had his trench coat sponged and pressed overnight. He now slipped it on over his best charcoal-grey suit and put his fedora on at a good angle.

"We should knock 'em for six!" he decided. "We're off to the laboratory, Risby. The Cavendish. You will escort me through the building with a swagger, please. You are my entry ticket. You're there to guarantee that I'm not a paint salesman drumming up business. They know we're coming; I telephoned and made an appointment."

Risby looked alarmed. "The governor's been there. For parties and openings and suchlike. But it's hard to get inside without an invitation."

"Quite right too. But I have an open sesame kit that gets me in wherever I need to go." He patted his briefcase. He was silent on the matter of the various documents it contained:

warrants and special permissions signed by the home secretary himself, documents that he had taken the trouble to extract from the Services under the aegis of *Operation Imperator*. "I could even get into the Strafford Club if I thought that at all an entertaining idea. Come on, laddie! Cambridge is ours for the taking this morning! Now—a briefing—let me tell you why we're stalking scientists in their stronghold."

They parked the car and made their way down the very narrow Free School Lane towards the Cavendish. Following on from the ancient churches, inns and houses in the centre of the city, the buildings of the laboratory were a surprise. For a start, they looked nothing like anyone's notion of a scientific work place in the twentieth century, and to go on, they were not sympathetic to their surroundings. The Tudor-Gothic stone front rose up to three storeys in height, soaring above the medieval rooftops and dwarfing its neighbours by its bulk. The Victorian architect had clearly been striving for grandeur. Heavy oak doors were encased in ornate stone details, windows likewise. Both were impenetrable and set within an unbreachable flat, stone-slabbed façade of dull grey-brown. The place was a fortress, Joe decided, and he didn't care much for it.

Risby's throat wobbled under his chin strap as he stared up at it. "Did we miss the sentries, sir?" he whispered. "I think that's the front door down there. But how do we get in? It's shut. No one about."

"Forward the battering ram, then!" Joe said cheerily.

Risby grinned, took out his truncheon and advanced on the huge door. Holding the truncheon like a mace, the constable banged peremptorily three times. Spotting a bellpull,

Joe tugged on it and repeated the tug. "That should fetch 'em!"

The door swung open and a puzzled steward in a green boiler suit peered out at them.

"Assistant Commissioner Sandilands of the Yard and Constable Risby of the Cambridge Police to see the director," Risby announced.

"Oh. Right. Why didn't you come in the back way like everyone else?"

"The commissioner doesn't use back doors," Risby announced as he shouldered his way through.

They passed small groups of chattering and laughing scientific staff on the way through the building, and Joe decided he would never be able to tell one from another. They seemed to be wearing a uniform, a uniform consisting of a rumpled tweed suit inherited from a not-very-careful uncle who'd bought it before the war intending it to give good service. Pockets bulged with—Joe guessed—pipes, smoking requisites and bags of mint humbugs. All carried notebooks. Half wore spectacles. Two wore ginger golfing plus fours. One of these was a woman. She gave a cheeky whistle as they walked by and chirruped something rude. He froze her with his police stare. Conversations broke off as they sized up the two strangers and, from the level of astonishment, Joe guessed that visitors were not frequent and police officers as rare as hens' teeth inside their redoubt. The jibes came thick and fast as they walked along.

"Game's up, Hugo! They're on to you!"

"Just stick to your story, Julian, and remember—you *can* be in two places at once. Einstein says so. It was your alter ego what dunnit."

All seemed to be working well so far. Now for the next bit of distraction.

The deputy director, into whose office they were ushered, checked Joe's credentials and asked why an eminence from Scotland Yard should be paying him a visit. Joe explained that his position put him at the head of Special Branch and, as such, in liaison with the security service. His presence here today had nothing to do with general policing and all to do with national security. A problem had arisen and it required instant attention.

Dr. Haraldson apologised for the absence of his superior. The director was away in Göttingen in Germany along with a small contingent of German scientists from the Cavendish. Good-will visit, don't you know. Exchanges in the planning stage. Busy time of year. "Will your constable be staying? Make that three cups, Dennis." He sent an assistant off to bring the tea tray he'd ordered and took Joe's hat and coat with a crisp, "Take a seat. Both of you. I think we've been sufficiently intimidated, don't you?" He turned briskly to Joe. "Very short notice but of course I'll do what I can. Now, the commissioner's problem. Can I help resolve it?"

"It's your problem, Doctor," Joe said with a concerned smile. "And you have very little time to deal with it. It has come to our notice that there has recently been formed a society in Cambridge calling itself the Anti-War Group. It has fifty members, a good number of whom are at present working here at the Cavendish." Joe hoped he sounded authoritative. He'd certainly raised the deputy director's bushy eyebrows an inch higher on his cliff face of a forehead. The man was tugging with a finger at his over-tight butterfly collar.

"They have in common a political affiliation," Joe kept up the pressure. "They are communists, either signed-up members or sympathisers. It is now the fourth of November. We understand that a demonstration is planned, aiming to sabotage the Remembrance Day service being held at the war memorial in Station Road on the eleventh. Many dignitaries and distinguished veteran soldiers will be present. The anti-war brigade, aided and abetted by other fun-seeking agitators, are minded to disrupt the proceedings. Paint will be splashed. Red, of course. Eggs and tomatoes will be thrown, trumpets and jeering will interrupt the minute's silence. The press have been invited, naturally."

"A deplorable scene you describe, Sandilands, but hardly the end of the world! Student capers! We are accustomed to them in Cambridge."

Joe had a feeling that he hadn't broken any fresh news.

"Not, I would hope, communist-inspired ones? The government has decided that enough laxity is enough. The Red Menace flows through our revered institutions—none more heavily affected than Cambridge—and it must be stopped before society crumbles."

"Not sure what you think I can do about it. Why aren't you saying this to the city police?"

"Better to cut the nonsense off at source. The police involvement is a last resort. I want a list of communist members of the laboratory and I want them to receive warnings that they face the full force of the law if they take part. There will be government agents in the crowd. They *will* take prisoners. For the sake of your reputation and the careers of your employees, I would urge you to take this request seriously."

"How dare you ask such a thing? In a country that

upholds the right to free speech and the right of its citizens to choose their political stance? I object to compiling a list of names!" He leapt to his feet, moustache twitching with outrage. "What kind of establishment do you think this—" His words ran into the sand as he read Joe's expression and realised where he was heading.

"A generously democratic one. But law-abiding, I trust. Don't be concerned. We won't be shipping the reprobates off to an Arctic gulag without trial on the basis of information received. This is not Communist Russia after all," Joe smiled with sweet menace. "Is it? Your objection is noted. Your objection is set aside. Ah, tea! How very welcome."

They sipped their tea, exchanging conversational platitudes. Business evidently completed, Joe twinkled with polite enquiry about the laboratory. He talked knowledgeably about the architecture, hinting at a dislike for the Victorian pomposity and was careful to show no interest in the world famous physical science to which it gave a stout framework.

"I think you might prefer the starker, more modern attempt we now have here," Dr. Haraldson said, unconsciously following Joe's lead. "The Mond Lab, which opened last February. A daring design, rather in the Bauhaus style. It has been much admired."

Joe at once expressed a keen interest.

Coming to the end of his tea and eager to see the back of his visitors, the director seized on this and said with some enthusiasm, "Look here, why don't you take the tour? Would that suit? Good. You may leave your things here, they'll be quite safe. I'll have someone fetched to show you round."

He went to the door and stuck his head out, preparing to shout along the corridor then Joe heard, "Ah! Hey there,

Page! Here's a stroke of luck. Busy are you, Humphrey? Well, drop that for the moment. There's someone with me who would like to take a look at the labs."

He came back inside leading Humphrey Page, smiling with innocent and polite enquiry.

"I leave you in Doctor Page's capable hands," he said. "Come and say goodbye before you leave, Sandilands. If you take your time, I should have ready my plans for . . . um . . . the ceremony, as requested," he muttered.

They were in!

IT WAS CLEAR that Page had performed the service many times. Showing not a sign that he had ever met Joe before, he went cheerfully through his act, gliding through the parts that he knew would not be of interest. At a point, Joe turned to Risby, sensing the officer's boredom. "Constable—you may return to the car. Drive it back to the hotel for me, will you? I'll walk back when I've done here."

Risby saluted and went off, retracing his steps.

Left alone, Page grinned and continued in his dutiful tone, "Let me show you the more modern facilities, sir. You'll have heard of the Mond Laboratory? Named for Ludwig Mond, who donated money to the Royal Society which, in turn, funded the new building. It's just along here in the courtyard. Interestingly, this parcel of land was, in ancient times, a friary and, after the dissolution of the monasteries it became the University Botanic Garden."

"And is now the world centre of scientific discovery?" Joe went along with the chatter.

"As you say, sir. Blackett, Chadwick, Cockcroft, Watson, many others . . . all at work here, off and on. The Mond is under the immediate supervision of Professor Kapitza. He's not at work today—I believe he's taken his boys to the zoo—but I am able to show you his latest toy. It's just been installed—the last checks on the system were made yesterday, and it will be ready for action on Monday, following the launch."

"Launch?"

"We're going to uncork a bottle or two of champagne. An informal gathering before lunch to wet the baby's head."

"What! Cover everything in fizz?" Joe smiled.

"Nothing so vulgar! We leave that sort of behaviour to the racing drivers."

As they approached the Mond, Page drew his attention to a wall of grey brickwork into which a design had been etched halfway up the façade. Joe stood to admire it, as that seemed to be the expected reaction.

"Ah. Any child would recognise: a crocodile," he said and peered more closely. "Moving forward with open mouth. I wonder if it has an alarm clock ticking in its tummy. Mmm ... I detect the chisel of Eric Gill ..."

"Who is much admired and has many friends hereabouts in Cambridge," Page said with a warning smile, sensing Joe's disfavour. "Watch it, smarty-pants," he hissed in Joe's ear as they stared at the brickwork. He reverted to the guide's tone, "It's a tribute, of course, to our director, the illustrious Professor Rutherford, who is affectionately known as 'The Old Crocodile.'"

"Then I take it the artist had in mind a god of the ancient Egyptians: Sobek, Force of Creation and, equally, Force of Ultimate Chaos." Joe ran a speculative eye over the grooves of the carving, lost in thought. "Creator and Destroyer of the Universe," he murmured.

"We prefer to associate it with Tick-Tock the Croc in *Peter Pan*."

"Anyone would," Joe said dryly.

"The swallowed clock gave, um, timely warning of his appearance. The ring of the director's boots along the corridor performs the same function nowadays."

The heavy-treading director was clearly adored and respected by Page. "A formidable man," was Joe's neutral comment.

"Oh, yes. The heart and mind of the laboratory. Why don't you come along and hear him for yourself? He lectures on Mondays and Fridays at noon. Anyone may attend. You may find him a little old fashioned—the whiskers, the antique dress and Victorian manner—but his subject matter is decidedly modern."

"His subject is?"

"Atomic and subatomic physics. The constitution of matter. You won't understand a word," Page finished, scoring a point. "And here we are. The liquefier room," he finally announced.

Joe was surprised that a laboratory in such a state of chaos would be ready for the undertaking of experiments, let alone the setting for an opening drinks party in two days' time. He murmured as much to Page. There were packing cases lying disembowelled on the floor, boxes of tools standing open, even oil-covered towels.

"It's the morning tea break," Page explained awkwardly. "They're working all day to get it ready, because, of course, no one's here on Sunday."

"Who's doing the work?"

"The Metrovick men who delivered the equipment and

a team of our own. The lab staff here are first class engineers as well as top flight physicists ... best in the world."

"I'll try not to put my foot on anything," Joe said easily. He looked about him and sniffed. "I say—has somebody left the iron on?"

"Iron?"

"Mmm ... I thought I caught a smell of solder."

Joe moved on, his attention caught by a construction of glass and metal. "Oh, here we are! This is it? Are you going to introduce me to the machine?"

He put his briefcase down in a corner and went to examine the helium liquefier at close quarters. His first instinct was to look for a suitable screen to pull out over the unsightly mess. Attached to the wall was a stout wooden board covered in dials of varying sizes, sockets and transformers from which wires snaked up, down and sideways and in front of this— yes!—Joe saw his auntie's Mark One Acme Water Heater. The large metal cylinder was fixed in a housing of metal struts and connected to the system top and bottom by pipes and tubes. The most significant of these sprouted out of the top, made a sharp bend to the right and dived down into an intriguing shiny metal sphere.

"And the moonshine comes out of which pipe?" Joe wanted to know.

Through Page's impenetrable outpouring of "Joule-Thompson inversion temperature ... adiabatic expansion ... piston lubrication ..." Joe was remaining alert for any sound of returning workmen. He caught the new arrival clumping across the cobbled courtyard in hobnailed boots and through the window glimpsed the delivery man heading straight towards the door of the lab.

It was the awkward grip on the package he was delivering that caught Joe's eye. The man shifted his hold on the heavy crate, preparing to lower it to the ground before opening the door. Not many delivery men having only half a left hand would be employed as such, Joe reckoned. He looked more closely. Oh, Lord! What bad luck! From Aidan's brisk but competent description, he had no trouble in recognising Pertinax's lieutenant, butler and old lag: Herbert Jennings. Six feet tall, brown hair, thuggish appearance. The scar under his left ear was not yet visible. Apart from the giveaway hand, he was completely unremarkable in his brown deliveryman's long coat. He was paying attention to the floor under his feet, muttering curses about the state of the place and hadn't taken in Joe and his companion. He had made no appearance at Madingley during Joe's lunch with his boss, having been below stairs leading the funeral wake for the woman he'd conspired to murder two days before, and wouldn't recognise Joe.

Joe was taking no chances. With a quick wink, he grabbed Page's pipe from his breast pocket and stuck it between his own teeth at a jaunty angle. He leaned over the metal monster and, with a swift hand, messed up his hair and loosened his tie. It was a red-faced and irritated scientist who looked up moments later.

"Pass me your screwdriver, will you, Doctor Page?" Joe bent to inspect a connection and tapped about in an exploratory way on the metal frame for a few more seconds. "Someone will have to get up there and check those connections," he announced crossly. "I'm not happy with them. Where are your workmen, Page? I don't expect to have to do every menial task myself!"

Turning, he caught sight of Jennings, who was now lowering his crate to the ground, and rounded on him with a startled, "Oy! What the hell do you think you're doing, feller?" He stormed towards the man and stood an intimidating six inches from his face—definitely a scar below the ear—and yelled again. "Deaf, are you? I asked what the hell you think you're doing!"

Jennings sprang upright with an old soldier's reaction. He looked with the traditional glassy stare straight ahead over Joe's shoulder, and for a moment Joe thought he was going to salute.

Jennings mastered his surprise and just managed to avoid the embarrassing show of subservience. His face hardened into truculence. "Who wants to know?"

Hermes, god of information, stepped forward and informed him. "None of your business. But as we *all* appreciate good manners under this roof—" this was delivered with a measure of reproof aimed at Joe, along with a restraining hand on his sleeve, "I'll introduce Professor Cartright from Manchester. He's representing Metropolitan-Vickers. That gleaming beast"—he pointed to the liquefier—"is the professor's baby."

"And I don't damn well want it cluttered up with crates of . . . What the hell have you got in there?"

"Champagne. Courtesy of Sir Gregory Pertinax," Jennings announced with a satisfied sneer.

"Champagne? Are you having me on? Look, mister, I don't care if it's courtesy of Dom Pérignon himself. Take it away! This is a laboratory, not the rear end of Harry's Bar. Good Lord, there's another of them over there behind the door! I won't have crates in the proximity of the equipment.

It's producing helium, for God's sake! One of the most inflammable substances on earth. Think of hydrogen and double the danger," Joe invented. "If you knew anything about explosives, my man, you'd keep this whole area clear of combustible material. These crates are of light wood—sawdust inside—and the contents have even been known to go pop," he finished in exasperation.

"Sir!" Jennings could bear the insults no longer. "Sergeant Jennings, Royal Engineers during the war! On the Somme. The Big One! Not much you can teach *me* about explosives, Your Professorship!" His voice had lost its London-rough coarseness and taken on a staccato military delivery that was calculatedly just this side of insubordination.

Page stepped in again. "That's enough! Who sent you? Give me your dockets." He reached out and plucked a folded sheet of paper from the top pocket of Jennings's overall. "But—be warned—I'm thinking of putting in a formal complaint . . ."

"Yer! You do that, guv! I do as I'm told. And my orders was to leave 'em 'ere on account of the party. Compliments of Sir Gregory. This is the Mond Lab? Liquefier room?" He looked about him stagily. "Prof. Kapitza has never complained and he's the ranking officer, I think? He may be a Russkie, but he's a gent! Still, if it's not wanted I can always take it away . . ."

"Leave it, leave it," Page said and turned to Joe. "And *you* can stand easy, Professor. There *is* a party planned to celebrate the installation. Monday lunchtime. Very informal. We're hoping you'll be able to extend your stay by a further day and join us."

This seemed to amuse Jennings. "Sounds like a spiffing idea to me!" he jeered. "Your good health, gentlemen! No offence, Professor Cartright."

"Not much taken," Joe conceded. "Now, bugger off! We've got work to do." Turning back to the liquefier, he grumbled on until the man was out of earshot. "Monday is it? And have they thought how they're going to chill the bottles?"

"With a dozen experts in cryogenics about the place," Page joked, "low temperatures shouldn't be a problem!"

"OUF! THANKS FOR that!" Joe said, handing back the pipe and the screwdriver.

"Ten out of ten for aplomb, five out of ten for physics knowledge! He didn't take a shine to you. I should avoid dark alleys. You might even consider fleeing to Manchester."

"Ah, yes. Cartright? Is that going to be all right? These people are nothing if not careful, and they're quite likely to run a check."

"Prof. Cartright *is* in the employ of Metrovick. He was here earlier. You missed him by ten minutes. Anyone who's interested enough to ring up the factory and ask will be told Cartwright is unavailable—he's away in Cambridge. It should hold up." Struck by a disconcerting thought, "Crikey!" he said. "Who's going to go to such lengths? Who or what exactly are you up against that the arrival of a crate of bubbly can send you into a blue funk? What's going on?"

"I wish I knew. You can sometimes get a raw response from someone under unexpected pressure. That man reacted badly to officer bluster and couldn't resist retaliating with sarcasm and veiled threat."

Joe looked doubtfully at the boxes.

"They don't normally drop them off here," Page offered. "They're supposed to go straight down to the cellars under the main building."

"Better safe than sorry. Shall we?" Joe invited, moving towards the crates. "Shall I bother to say: Let's watch our step? That bloke wasn't bragging. He was indeed an explosives expert and his last recorded caper was to blow up half of northern France. He and his fellow sappers rearranged the landscape of the river Somme. The contents of one of these crates could blast your new machine up through that specially light roof you were telling me about! I'll have that screwdriver back. That should do it."

"So that's what it's all about? Sabotage! Who'd go to such lengths? We're in something of a race with Oxford to produce the first liquid helium, but I can't see Lindemann sending someone over to nobble us. A huffy letter to *Nature* is more his style . . . No! Wait! We're not plunging in without an examination. We'll do this with all proper precautions. There'll be tools we can use in the work boxes over there. Now, Sandilands, would you like to check there's nobody about in the courtyard or the corridor? And then you should probably retreat to a distance while I carry out the examination."

The pacifist father of two quietly took off his jacket and stood, white-faced but determined, in his shirt sleeves, sizing up the boxes.

Ten minutes later both men stood upright again, sweating with tension and staring blankly at the contents of two completely innocent cases. "Two dozen, best Bollinger," Joe said. "Just as it says on the delivery chit."

"Does it, though?" Page said. He had unfolded the paper

he'd taken from Jennings and was looking at it in puzzle-ment. "Says here: *three* cases. Where's the third case and what's it got in it?"

"Well, whatever was in the surprise parcel—he's now driven off with it!"

"You went off at half cock, Sandilands. Now he'll have to try again. I say—do you think he will? Or did your snarl-ing put him off? If he's planning to blow up the unmanned machine on a quiet Sunday morning, there's plenty of time for him to arrange a further delivery. We'll have to tell Director Haraldson to set a guard."

"I'd guess he'll be back when we've left the coast clear. He won't want to waste the opportunity. I agree—the direc-tor must be made aware. But Haraldson should know that it's worse than sabotage . . . Far worse. I'm going to share an awful thought with you, Page. It's not the metal beast they're going for. It's the scientists collected together in a tight bunch around it, drinking a toast, they're out to destroy."

Page's voice was slightly hysterical when he was able to speak. "You mean there'll be metal and glass and champagne and helium and human limbs raining down on Cambridge? Why, Sandilands? Why us?"

"I thought your deputy director was a good chap. Shall we go and warn him and see if he can shed some light? Oh, and while we're gone—let's leave a guard on the door, shall we? Nip out and find two strapping lads and set them to refuse and report any unwanted special deliveries."

HARALDSON WAS LOOKING over a sheet of paper in a marked manner when Joe returned to his office.

"I should like Doctor Page to stay for a discussion, if you don't mind, sir."

"If you wish, Sandilands. Sit down, both of you. Now, look here, Commissioner. This is as far as I'm prepared to go to meet your demands." He handed over a typed list of names. "No state secrets there. Names only and they are publicly available to all, though the taxman is the only one who ever shows an interest in us. I refuse—and Page will witness my words—to make any statement or even guess as to the political affiliations of my staff. None of your damn business!"

Joe's approving smile came as a surprise. "I hadn't expected that you would. It's quite all right, sir. I was merely gaining entry to the building and supplying you with a perfectly credible reason for allowing me a police inspection of the labs if anyone asks. My true motive in scrambling aboard is a much more serious one.

"I've discovered something disturbing on my tour— *we've* discovered—Doctor Page was with me and will bear witness. But before I go any further . . . A necessary formality."

A stunned and awkward silence accompanied the signing of the Official Secrets Act documents he handed to each man.

"Now, Haraldson. Page and I have just disrupted a plot to blow up the Mond Laboratory and all who sail in her at the champagne launch on Monday."

Having fixed the scientist's attention, he filled in the details of the encounter with the delivery man.

Haraldson heard him without interruption and examined the delivery docket. "Three dozen . . . 1926 vintage?

What a waste that would be! Pertinax, eh? You're telling me that one of our most generous sponsors—a man who contributed a thousand pounds to the building of the Mond—has now changed his mind and wishes to blow it to bits?"

"Yes. At the very highest level of government, he has been suspected for some time now of being the Russians' prime spy in our country. He's been planted here for years—generations—biding his time. All the signs are that he is about to make his play. His quarrel is not with the architecture. Nor yet with the production of helium. His aim is to kill off the cream of the British scientific establishment at one fell swoop. The crime would never be exposed as a crime because the authorities and the public are predisposed to expect a tragic incident of this nature in this place. 'An accident waiting to happen,' was the local paper's prediction when the news of the splitting of the atom was announced last year. The good folk of Cambridge wonder that you've got away with it for so long."

Joe ignored the slight smile of disbelief creeping across Haraldson's craggy features and passed back the list of names. "I'm not asking for political affiliations, but perhaps we should know precisely which people on this list will attend the ceremony on Monday? Will you mark them for me?"

"Certainly. I have a ticket myself for a ringside seat and so does Humphrey so we'd better get this right." He looked again closely at the list. "We haven't sent out invitations—it's not that formal an arrangement. More of an omnium gatherum with fizz. All welcome. But we can eliminate the nonstarters. I think I told you our director and a selection of staff and students had gone off on a jolly jaunt to Germany?"

Joe nodded, frowning.

"In his party are three Germans, an Italian, a New Zealander and five British, if you count the Scots. I'll put a line through their names." He did so. "Now I'll mark with a cross (believe me I intend no pun) the twenty or so who will be in the lab. That leaves us the star of the show of course, Professor Kapitza, his two Russian assistants and a selection of others (of mixed nationality, if that is important to the powers that be). We're left with a group whose principal interest is in magnetism and cryogenics and their use in the smashing of the atom. Hmm . . . I summarise and simplify, of course."

Joe nodded his thanks for being let off a lecture.

"A good number of these men—shall we call them the Helium Group?—have Communist Party cards in their wallets. Kapitza makes no secret of his sympathy, though he has never been a member."

He looked up at Joe, startled and challenging. "You've got this arsy-tarsy, man! Upside down and back to front! If the nightmare you describe comes to pass, the left wing of not just British but world physics would be obliterated. The *left* wing! A goodish number of couldn't-care-less chaps like me are in the lineup, but predominantly these are the socialists and the communists among us. At least four men who will be in this group are geniuses and I don't use the word lightly. There are two potential Nobel Prize winners here. Russian science, which I think you must be seeing as the ultimate beneficiary of such a plot—yes?—is already years behind everyone else and would be blasted back to the Middle Ages by the loss. Moscow is relying on Kaptiza to design and run their version of the Cavendish in St.

Petersburg. Two gifted Americans of undisclosed political affinity would be caught up in the blast, a Norwegian, a Dutchman . . . Yet you tell me that the would-be perpetrator of this devastation is a Bolshevik agent? I judge your theory not proven. Back to the bench and think again!"

"I believe you're right." Joe was reduced to embarrassed silence. "Though it does begin to look like a good day for *German* science," he said, voicing all their thoughts. "Perhaps we're looking in the wrong place? Is the new Nazi government recruiting? Already?"

The two men looked at Joe in some discomfort. After a moment, Haraldson nodded at Page.

"Göttingen has been building up a stable for some years now," Page said. "It's a three-horse race with Germany vying with us here in Cambridge and Niels Bohr in Copenhagen. If someone nobbles the favourites before the race, those lads are going to have a straight run down the course."

Haraldson spoke decisively. "It's not as uncomplicated as Page makes out. It's not a prep school sack race! Things are changing rapidly. In the political world even faster than in the scientific one. How do you judge form anyhow? By the Nobel awards? It's one indication, though occasionally a baffling and unreliable judgement of achievement. A coarse evaluation might be: of the one hundred Nobel prizes awarded since its inception to the present day, thirty-three have gone to German scientists, eighteen to the British and six to the USA. There can be no doubt that in maths and physics, Göttingen University has reigned supreme for years."

He paused, eyebrows converging in heavy disapproval. "Until very recently. The scientists who have led the world from that city are almost entirely Jewish. The new power in the land does not like Jews. Hitler and his heavy brigade have found ways of persuading the likes of Einstein to resign their posts and flee the country. Albert escaped last year. Got away to the United States and I doubt he'll be back. Göttingen's loss has been our gain, of course. This would seem to be a propitious time to . . ."

"Go fishing?" Joe said. "What a short-sighted chump Herr Hitler must be!"

"The man has a very high view of his own ability." Haraldson shrugged. "They say it approaches the messianic. When someone dared to suggest to him last year that his mathematicians and his physicists were leaving their posts and asked, 'Where, *mein* Führer, are the brains of our country?' he replied: 'I'll be the brains!' Such an idiot deserves to lose his best men. But—surely you would know, Sandilands—does your chump have anything so sophisticated as a spy system established in our country?"

"I couldn't possibly say. But I'll bear it in mind. I know, as well as you do and the whole country does, that the *Bolsheviks* have an extensive and well-funded organisation in place."

Haraldson smiled at the tact and the innuendo. "Whatever the twisted thinking behind all this, we can't let it go ahead, and we must take all possible steps to confound the villain. Look here—I think this is all nonsense. Special Branch has got its knickers in a twist, but I'm not prepared to risk lives by dismissing it out of hand. Let's think like scientists, shall we? Or even detectives? Devise and perform a test. Acquire evidence. Assess and interpret. I don't know about you, Sandilands, but I never accept a theory—it's the same as opinion as far as I'm concerned.

"What have we got? A couple of wine crates, innocent

in themselves but delivered by a known villain with puzzling theatricality—am I getting this right? A possible third astray somewhere. We can put them safely away in the cellar they were destined for anyway and watch out for the missing one ... No! Wait! This is barmy!"

His exclamation disturbed his audience.

"The champagne delivery was a distraction! Evidence: see how we have been distracted and for how long! Let's return to your premise that for some reason Pertinax wants to destroy a company of twenty scientists. The target: One of them? A selection? All?"

"It's their work," Page said. "It's the one thing they have in common. They all have special knowledge of or contribute to work on smashing the atom. We all know what's behind this and, as usual, we're tiptoeing around it. It's war work. What's that German factory called? Krupps? Are they still in business? You should rake through Pertinax's bank statements for Deutschmarks, Sandilands. We pretend there are no such dirty compulsions but out there in the real world, there are. Ostriches! We're ostriches."

"Or—to explore another option—an anti-war faction that's decided eggs and paint aren't really making a strong enough statement?" Joe suggested lightly to relieve the intensity. "Funded by Pertinax, they're going to make a bang the whole world will hear."

Two pairs of eyes looked at him with derision.

"Are you sure you understand this man and his loyalties, Sandilands?"

"No. I doubt if anyone does. I shall have to go back and check my workings. I've only met him twice and I can't express a valid opinion on the state of his mind. Though ...

the state of his *brain* . . . I think I may be able to get information on that by twisting an arm or two."

"Good luck with that then!"

"It may be, sir, that what we have to deal with is a type of madness. We're looking at vicious unreason and the vaunting ambition of a Roman Emperor."

"Mmm . . . Madness, you say? Sir Gregory may have Viking looks but he's every inch the English gentleman. I have heard no reports that he goes off berserking down the High Street on the night of the full moon. I'm not sure how your diagnosis of madness sits with the rather careful planning that you claim has gone on. We'll wait for further evidence on that score. But you've both failed to notice the truly disturbing part of this scenario," Haraldson announced. "If the crates were a distraction—what have they been successful in distracting us *from*, gentlemen?"

"Oh, my God!" Page leapt to his feet, breathing in noisy excitement and dread. "It's in there already, isn't it? He's already fixed the explosive in place! And we didn't spot it! No wonder the bugger was laughing at us."

CHAPTER 24

"It's an old peterman's trick," Joe said. "Fix up an obvious—but not too obvious—distraction and everyone drifts away from the scene with relief, having resolved a phantom problem—only to be caught out by the intended blast when it comes. The old safe-crackers in my patch like to have a quiet time while they're manipulating the tumblers or drilling the weak spot. Nothing they like quite so much as to hear the klaxons of the Flying Squad tearing off up the road a mile away. Whenever I hear a suspicious package has been found in a florist's shop, I check out the bank round the corner as well."

"What do you propose?" Haraldson asked.

"Subtlety and discretion! I want this kept quiet. I want no invitations revoked. The Helium Party will take place. We're not pressed for time at least. It can't have been armed yet. He'll probably go for a twenty-four-hour fuse or detonator mechanism, assuming the eventual trigger man is not one of the group and intent on suicide—planning to press the plunger as he raises his glass. So—he'll get back in to set the timer sometime after lunch on Sunday in a conveniently empty lab. I'll arrange a little champagne reception of my own."

"Never mind the fisticuffs and the manacles,

Commissioner. I'm not running the risk of leaving that bomb—if bomb there is—hidden away in the laboratory for a minute. It has to be removed. At once."

"No rush, but I understand and share your concern, sir. There's an army unit out in barracks down near Duxford airfield. I'll make a phone call to check whether they have a bomb-disposal outfit they can deploy."

The eyes were now staring at him with disbelief.

"Sandilands," the director said, "you forget where you are! This place is teeming with men with the skill and knowledge to perform the task. Pure scientists they may be, but all, from the day they enter, are trained in using their hands to make their own equipment. For the very good reason that the special apparatus they require is not generally available as a manufactured item. You don't ring up a supplier in Birmingham and say, 'I'm intending to split an atom next Tuesday. Send me the appropriate equipment, will you?' Our boys can design systems, reform metal, solder joints . . . they have all the practicalities at their fingertips and all the instincts for safety you could wish for." He smiled grimly. "Our intact roof stands witness to that."

"I had to blow my own glass tubes when I first came here." Page nodded in support. "Removal will be a doddle— it's finding it that will be the hard part. That's a big space and they've given some thought to it. It occurs to me they might even have had some inside information, but that would be one for you, sir," he finished, smiling blandly at Haraldson.

Page was having a good morning on the whole, Joe decided. Scoring all around the wicket.

"I'll make a phone call," Haraldson announced. "But I

won't have any Keystone Cops or Major Disaster stomping about wrecking my lab! One call will do it. To the best engineer in the world! To Piotr Kapitza! If he can't do it, it can't be done."

"Problem there, sir," Page said. "He's gone to the zoo. I had assumed Regent's Park in London as there isn't one locally."

"Nonsense! That was a believable excuse. Sandilands will recognise the device. In any case, he's not gone far—he's at home in Huntingdon Road with his boys, teaching them how to repair clocks. Family hobby, don't you know. I'll try my luck." He picked up the receiver and asked for a number.

Suddenly agitated by a memory Haraldson's words had triggered, Joe hissed across the desk, "*Solder!* I smelled it when we went into the room. Mention to the professor that the concealment may have involved a soldering process."

Not a word was wasted. When Haraldson put the receiver down two minutes later he was smiling. "He's on his way. By motorbike. Bringing his toolkit. Shall we go to the car park and receive him, gentlemen?

HARALDSON ACTED SWIFTLY. He ordered the sounding of the fire alarm and cleared the building with orders to the grumbling staff that they go straight home and stay away for the rest of the weekend. He retained on the premises only the usual stewards to man the door and gatehouse. "We're testing the alarm system, evacuation times and all the other palaver," he announced to anyone querying the sounding bells. "No one will be able to work through the noise we're about to make so you might as well beetle off and take your girl to the matinée at the Victoria."

The three men waited by the door and were not kept waiting long. At the sound of a motorbike engine roaring in through the gates, Joe looked at his watch and raised an eyebrow. "The prof doesn't waste any time," he commented.

"The prof, you'll find, is supercharged. In everything he does," Haraldson said with affection.

The rider parked his Scott motorbike by the back door and Joe took in the neat, low-slung, purposeful nature of the machine. Black with a big brass radiator, it looked almost too modest to be the race winner Joe knew it to be. The Bauhaus of bikes, Joe decided, and if fate ever tempted him to risk his limbs on such a contraption, he'd choose one like this.

The scientist had spent no time putting on special clothing before leaving. Or perhaps he wore a cloth cap with a wide peak and the inevitable tweed suit for every activity? The British-built bike, the outfit, even the pipe tucked away in the breast pocket shouted the message that here was an Englishman and the best kind at that—an eccentric. His face was alive with the anticipation of a pleasantly challenging experience, Joe thought. A game of chess, perhaps, rather than a possible bomb-disposal exercise. He had dark, expressive eyebrows in a handsome face and looked like nothing so much as a very knowing and mischievous elf.

He swung a leg over and went to detach the metal tool case he'd strapped to the back carrier.

"Haraldson!" he exclaimed with a delighted smile. "You have a little puzzle for me? Always glad to have a Saturday morning's diversion." His voice was high-pitched and noticeably Russian accented in spite of his having spent more than twelve years in England.

Introductions followed once they were inside the laboratory and Joe sketched out the events of the morning, filling in his suspicions in broad strokes. Kapitza listened without interruption, eyes flitting over the scene and always being drawn back to his pride and joy, the new liquefier.

"Sorry to drag you out for this, old man!" Haraldson clearly thought the story at second telling sounded even thinner than it had before. "We aren't convinced ourselves, not even Sandilands here. If you can just run a quick check and assure us that we're overreacting to a mundane situation, we will all be delighted."

The physicist went straight over to check his precious equipment. He walked to the far wall where the new installation gleamed innocently, halted ten feet from it and studied it. The others went to stand behind him, taking care not to crowd him.

"Yes. I thought so. Oh, my goodness, me! Thank you so much for drawing my attention to it. Clever! Even I could have easily missed it. Especially with the distraction of a glass of champagne in my hand and a crowd of chattering friends."

"What are you seeing, or not seeing, Peter?" Haraldson asked.

"The dials. Look at the dials."

Joe peered at the backboard accommodating the various glass faces. In differing sizes and lined up in a rather higgledy-piggledy fashion, they were all connected to some other part of the equipment by snaking wires and measured heaven knew what—Joe supposed pressure, temperature and so on. Nothing caught his attention.

"There ought to be—there were when I left after installation—only eight dials. There are now nine."

They all peered again, counting.

"The smallest one—there, do you see?" He pointed. "Almost hidden by the broad pipe—that was not put in by me. It's surplus to requirements and—it appears to be a common or garden clock face. A timer, are we thinking?"

"What's it connected to?" Joe asked the urgent question.

Kapitza moved closer and, with a confidence that made Joe cringe, he stuck out a forefinger and traced the line of the wire leading downwards from the clock. "There, neatly out of sight because hidden by the cylinder itself, indeed, attached to it, is a smaller, slim cylinder that looks as though it could well be a bona fide piece of the equipment. I think, Sandilands, you were certainly right when you said you smelled solder. Metal has been fixed on metal. I shall have to scramble behind to find out exactly how. What a nerve! They could have—may have—ruined my experiment."

Joe approached and verified this. "It's the size of a policeman's truncheon," he called back to the others. "Big enough to cause a sizeable explosion if it's carrying the right substance. I've seen nothing like this. The nearest, I suppose, would be a Bangalore torpedo. We used them in the war. To blast through barbed wire obstacles. Filled with bits of metal and projected by a couple of kilos of Mr. Nobel's best—good old gelignite? Perhaps something we haven't even come across yet . . . They haven't been standing still since the last war ended. You may know more about that than I do. Explosive substances available from Nobel Chemicals in Ayrshire, Scotland."

"Nitrols of some sort, I expect. Whatever's inside there, it's meant to blow to bits twenty scientists standing in a confined space within feet of it," Kapitza concluded. "Death by blast and shrapnel. You can leave this to me. I'll get it out. Would you like to retire to a safe distance while I fiddle with the blue touch paper, gentlemen?"

Three short and decisive statements of intent tumbled over each other.

"Leave you alone with it? No!"

"Not a chance!"

"I'm not leaving!"

"Well then, let's not waste time," Kapitza said. "I was in the middle of fixing the mechanism of a Louis XV carriage clock when you dragged me off. A much more delicate operation. I'd like to get back to it. Now, I can see you fellows will want a witness to the removal. Sandilands, representing the law, is my obvious choice. He can stay if he's willing."

Sandilands stayed. He actually held the sinister black metal tube once it had been removed and made safe. At the moment when Kapitza turned his attention to the small clock face, which had been meant to count out the minutes and seconds to an ugly death for the man now advancing on it with a screwdriver, Joe called him to a halt. Apologetically he asked if the clock could be left in place for a while longer.

"Not only that, Professor. I wonder if I may ask—is it possible to put the whole device back in place, looking as though it hasn't been discovered?"

The imp grinned a conspiratorial grin. Instant comprehension.

"Nothing simpler," he said. "The tube was magnetically attached to my cylinder. I've broken the contact with the timer so there's no danger of an explosion. You are setting a trap of your own?"

Joe explained that the perpetrator would be expecting

to return to the laboratory to set the timing device. Probably at some time on Sunday when the labs would be deserted.

"It would be good to catch him with his fingers in the jam jar! Of course. I do hope you're planning a clean arrest, Commissioner. Rough and tumble in the middle of so much expensive and delicate equipment could do much damage."

Joe promised there would be no breakage. There would be no blood on the floor. He didn't add that there would be no arrest.

HE SOUNDED THE all-clear to Page and Haraldson, who had dutifully stayed on watch in the courtyard, and the three men waved goodbye to Kapitza as he zoomed out of the gate.

"May I ask what you've done with the device?" Haraldson asked, sighing but not letting go of the essentials.

"It's completely safe. Back in place again but all contacts broken," Joe assured him. "When he returns to finish his dirty work tomorrow, I shall be there taking notes."

Limp with relief, they went back into the laboratory.

"Well, I don't know about you fellows," the director said, "but I think, after the mill we've been through, we've earned a reward. Get down three of those glass measuring beakers from the shelf over there, will you, Page? I thought we'd stage a little controlled explosion of our own!"

He rummaged around in one of the champagne crates and produced a bottle. Firm hands dealt with the wired cork and poured a lavish stream of the straw-coloured, almond-scented wine into the beakers. Joe smiled back at his two companions. He shared their euphoria but was careful to keep himself in check. This would be a good moment to push forward his plans, certain that success and fellow-feeling would ease his path.

Once again, the director was ahead of him. "Take notes, you say, Sandilands? I was rather hoping for a swift arrest and carting off to the Tower or wherever you put traitors these days."

"The man who will be lighting the fuse, so to speak, is no more than a tool. I don't want the master alerted by the disappearance of his minion."

"This master—Pertinax, you're saying—will he try again?"

"Yes. It will go on. None of you are safe, the country is not safe, until this man is behind bars or dead."

"Right-oh. Any immediate plans for bringing this about?"

"Yes. I shall need your help. No danger involved, I assure you! But there is something . . . I take my inspiration from Hercules, who had a certain problem with the swamp-dwelling beast, the nine-headed Hydra. Head-chopping didn't seem to be working as they instantly regrew, so he devised a more radical scheme."

"Oh, Lord! I know where he's going with this! He's going to set Cambridge on fire!" Page said, laughing, and refilled the beakers.

"Not the whole of Cambridge," Joe said. "Selected bits. I need to smoke this creature out of his lair. This is England. I can't just put my Browning to his head and pull the trigger, which is what he deserves. I shall have to extract a confession before I can charge him and send him off to London."

"You think he's likely to hold his hands up and say:

'Sandilands! There's something I simply have to get off my chest!'?" Haraldson objected.

"Something like that. A man who believes himself to have been successful in his endeavours, a complete egotist, may be tricked into an incautious piece of boasting. If I can arrange for him to do it in front of witnesses and happen to have a pair of handcuffs in my pocket, I've got him."

The two scientists exchanged furtive glances of something very like pity. As a plan, it had sounded pretty thin even to his own ears. "Don't worry—I shall call in backup of the very best kind. My Special Branch boys are polishing their knuckle-dusters as we speak." They nodded with relief. Such was the reputation of the Branch, the mere mention of its name, delivered with a know-it-all expression, intrigued and reassured.

"Now. The fire-raising. May I use your blackboard?"

Joe strolled to the blackboard, picked up a stick of chalk and drew a map of Cambridge, recognisable from the loops of the river Cam. He swiftly sketched in the central area and the Cavendish. Next, his chalk moved towards the west and he marked with an X the position of Madingley Court. He drew a line from the house to the laboratory. The two scientists strained to make sense of his mutterings: "Six miles . . . woodland . . . hills?"

He turned to his companions. "Is there a piece of public land between here and there? Something on this exact line?"

"No. There's the backs of the colleges and they're private land. There's Castle Hill but that's too far north," Page said.

"Oh, look!" The director stepped forward and took the chalk from his hand. "I see what you're after. Extend the line a bit in the other direction, past the lab . . . here . . . and you've got twenty-seven acres of public land. Parker's Piece." He drew in a square. "Wonderful space for football, cricket, picnicking, canoodling . . . Anyone can use it. It's five minutes away on foot. And in a direct eyeline with Madingley."

"Oh!" Page's eyes gleamed as he understood. "And we've got chemists here as well as physicists. We can take their advice. I'm sure they'll have an exciting element to contribute!" He chortled. "You couldn't have picked a better day! Do you know what the date is tomorrow? No. You haven't got small children at home—why should you? It's the fifth of November!

Remember, remember, the fifth of November,
Gunpowder, treason and plot!
I see no reason why gunpowder treason
Should ever be forgot!

"It's Bonfire Night! Every back garden in the city will have its small fire in celebration of the failure of Guy Fawkes to blow up Parliament. Toffee apples and gingerbread, a rocket or two. The kids love it! As it's a Sunday there have been the usual objections from the killjoys and most people have put it off a day. Until Monday."

Joe grinned. "So no one is going to look askance at anyone hauling timber and building a bonfire where you wouldn't otherwise expect one? Perfect! Right, gentlemen! I think we're ready to put the finishing touches to this plot, involving gunpowder and treason, as it does. Let's pray we end up with the right Guy on the fire."

His next request might be a bit tricky. Joe decided to play his man, using the horse gentling skills he'd learned from Hunnyton. He picked up the champagne bottle to fill the director's glass, then caught himself and put it down again. "Sir," he said, fixing Haraldson with a straight gaze of pure honesty and concern, "I have something to ask of you, and I don't want you to agree because you're too tiddly to say, 'Out of the question!'"

Haraldson listened, laughed and then replied, "Very well! If you've got this all wrong, Sandilands, there'll be fences to repair, egos to smooth. But what the hell! We'll do it from my office. Bring the bottle with you. And perhaps another, why not!"

"**Sir Gregory!**" **Haraldson** exclaimed into the telephone. "This is Haraldson at the Cavendish. How good to hear you! And I'm delighted to find you at home. I'm ringing for two reasons and the first of them is—I've just discovered your gift to the laboratory. Another generous gift! Two crates of the very best! In fact, I have to admit, a colleague and I have just cracked open one of the bottles, so excuse the hiccups. It is excellent, by the way! We're drinking to your good health!"

He listened for a while to the response, seemed pleased by it and went on, "The second is to offer an invitation to an ad hoc sort of rather silly little party the cryologists are planning . . . The new helium liquefier—you remember? Only possible because of the generosity of our sponsors—we never lose sight of that here—and well, the long and short of it is—they're planning a get-together to toast its arrival. With the unexpected, very welcome and totally appropriate Bollinger you sent. It's happening on Monday—a drink before lunch—at half-past twelve here in the Mond. I can offer you Kapitza—you always get on well with him . . . the other Russians and two new faces for you—Americans both and utterly charming. Do say you can come! Late notice, I know, but sometimes these extempore occasions turn out to be the most memorable."

After more intent listening: "Oh, dear! That's a pity! If your circumstances should change—well you never know—just turn up. Our people will be told to expect you. In any case, I'm sure . . ."

He finished with a few polite phrases, a convincing hiccup or two, and put the phone down.

Looking at Page and Sandilands teasingly from under his bushy brows, he announced, "Shame! Sir Gregory is otherwise engaged and won't be able to join us. He's got a party down from London he says. He'll be entertaining them to lunch at the Court. They've got wild boar on the menu apparently . . . Is that what you needed to know, Sandilands?"

WHEN JOE RETURNED to the hotel for lunch, the manager seized on him. A gentleman had rung three times. Sir Gregory Pertinax. He assured him that Joe would be informed the moment he reappeared. Joe thanked him and asked him to be so good as to ring back the number and hand him the phone once Sir Gregory had been passed through. Joe had no wish to speak directly to a butler he'd had a slanging match with only hours before. The voice of Professor Cartwright might still be ringing in his ears.

"Ah. Hello there, Pertinax," he said. "You've been trying to reach me?"

"Sandilands! At last! Nearly too late. I was within a

whisker of signing up an assistant master of a newish, rather obscure college in my desperation . . . I'm having a lunch party on Monday. Here at the Court. People up from London, don't you know . . . I need a sixth at table and I thought of you. How can I tempt you to drop everything and hare over here at short notice? I think I have the lure! Dorothy Despond is here with her father. Yes, the lovely Dorothy! She's particularly asked after you. She seems to know you're holed up in Cambridge and says she'd love to see you again. Despond senior doesn't seem to have any insurmountable objection . . . No, they're not staying, sadly. Dorothy has friends in Grantchester and always descends on them."

Joe had accepted and the connection had been cut before he had a chance to find out who the other couple was. Pertinax had said six.

He went to his room and made a further call.

When Bacchus answered, Joe spoke urgently: "It's on. For Monday. Twelve noon. I need your best boys. At the expected location. I'm lunching with our client and there will be civilians at the scene. So—extreme caution. But, I'm getting ahead of myself. Before that there's a small traffic accident I want you to help me arrange."

HE CAME JUST when Joe was expecting him. At 1:30 P.M. The whole of Cambridge, the whole of England, in fact, was in the middle of Sunday lunch or staggering back from the local pub, hoping they weren't too late to snaffle the outside slice of roast beef. The streets were deserted, the laboratory was very nearly deserted.

Watching from the lab window, Joe saw the small

delivery van approach gently and pull up by the gateman's lodge. Cheerful greetings were offered and a paper waved from the window of the Morris. The gateman, in his long brown overall, put down his racing pages, took the cigarette out of his mouth, put his spectacles on and gave the docket a careful inspection.

"Sorry, sir." He sniffed. "It's a Sunday. No deliveries on a Sunday. Nobody here to sign for it. You'll have to do a turn in the courtyard."

The driver was disposed to argue. Joe could just make out his objections: special delivery from Sir Gregory for the director. So—ring the director at home and check with him . . . No, he'd had orders to take it straight to the lab. The new lab. He pointed.

The gatekeeper hesitated, then reluctantly scribbled on the paper and came out of his cubicle carrying a bunch of keys. He didn't offer to help with the heavy package but strolled across the cobbled courtyard and, with more ceremony than was necessary, unlocked the door.

"Ta, mate!" the deliveryman said as he struggled through the doorway. "I'll be a minute . . . The boss told me I was to check everything is hunky-dory inside the case. This French fizzy stuff sometimes goes off before it oughter. One case in twenty is a bummer. You never know. No need to hang about . . . Have you considered Stephenson's Rocket for the three-thirty on Wednesday?"

The gateman returned to his lodge, licked his pencil and picked up the racing pages again.

Joe gave the visitor a minute or two to commit himself to his task and then slipped into the liquefier lab. So intent on his delicate adjustments was Jennings, Joe had reached the man's shoulder before he became aware of his presence. Joe stepped out of arm's swing and spoke pleasantly to him.

"Twelve forty-five, eh? Well timed! Everyone halfway down their first glass and all eyes on the machinery."

He'd found out exactly what he needed to know.

Jennings whirled around, screwdriver in hand, feet and body instinctively adopting an aggressive stance. A delighted smile rendered even more hideous his unlovely features and he expressed his satisfaction on seeing Joe in front of him. "Well now! Professor Cartright, innit? Wondered if you'd pop up again." The narrowed eyes checked left and right and saw no one but his target.

"Right—I'll play by the rules and ask you, Herbert Jennings," Joe began with a police officer's pompous formality, "if you are going to come quietly away with me now to answer a few questions . . ."

The truncheon in Joe's left hand snaked out and chopped into the wrist of the hand holding the screwdriver, and a split second later his right fist crashed into the undefended jaw.

". . . at the nick," Joe finished, watching carefully as the man gasped and gurgled and, eyes rolling in disbelief, slid to the ground.

Bacchus, still wearing his brown overall, small pistol clutched in his hand, was in the room in seconds. "Blimey, Joe! That was quick!"

"And clean," Joe said, looking around him. "That's the main thing. I promised—no mess."

Bacchus was on his knees inspecting the recumbent thug with a professional hand. "He'll not be out for long. Better move fast. What the hell did you use?"

"A helpful little contraption I confiscated from an old

lag," Joe said slipping the metal off his knuckles. "Cheating, I always think, but I couldn't risk a barroom brawl in these surroundings."

"Mmm . . . It's left an interesting mark. I think he must have hit his jaw on the steering wheel. I'm surprised he let you get so close."

"He wanted me close. Close enough to stick that screwdriver in my ribs." He picked up the tool and put it in his pocket. "Right, he's quite a load of muscle, but I think if we both heave we can get him in the back of his van. The rest I'll leave to you."

Bacchus grinned. "All set up." He stirred the body with his toecap. "How about a few days' blissful peace and quiet, eh, feller? In a safe place. No cops, no nasty explosions to worry about. Better than you deserve, you shit! But first we'll have to mess up your Morris."

CHAPTER 25

Joe drove himself out to lunch at Madingley in the Lagonda. He parked it precisely on the stroke of twelve next to the grand motorcar he recognised as belonging to Guy Despond. He looked at his watch and steeled himself to avoid constant nervous glances that would betray the inexorable countdown in his head as the minutes ticked on to 12:45.

The grand front door opened as he approached and his hat was taken by a hard-featured young man who appeared to be a manservant hurriedly promoted to the position of butler. The poor fit of the jacket gave him away.

Pertinax was swiftly on the scene, warm with his welcome. He vibrated with energy and good humour. "Sandilands! Harbinger of fine weather again! Nasty autumnal mist earlier, but I'm glad to see the skies clear and the sun come out the minute you appear."

"Nonsense, Pertinax. You may ascribe that magic power to Dorothy. She would brighten any day. I see the Desponds have beaten me to it."

"They're upstairs on the balcony. I thought we'd have a cocktail out there and enjoy the fresh air while we still can. Wonderful view from up there, right over the woods between here and Cambridge, do you recall?"

"I do. It must be the best in this otherwise flat county.

A veritable sea of autumn gold!" Joe said heartily. "It's turned a bit nippy, though, since I was here—I hope the ladies are well rugged-up?"

"Cashmere wraps provided. Though you may like to retain your smart Charvet scarf, Sandilands, if you object to the rustic shooting-party look." He turned to the butler. "Cartwright? Stay down here and attend our last guest. Let me know the moment he arrives, will you?"

"Certainly, sir. It's Clive, sir. Cartwright left last week." A London voice.

As they walked along to the stairs, Pertinax turned to Joe and said confidentially, "Churlish lout! I'll speak to him later. New boy. My old butler was, most unfortunately, involved in a road accident yesterday evening. I had a call from Addenbrooke's Hospital to say they had him in custody and were keeping him in overnight for observation."

Joe's expression showed an English gentleman's reaction to a mention of the serving classes: part embarrassment, part hauteur. "I'm sorry to hear that. Servants, eh? Not at all surprised to hear it though. The Cambridge traffic is terrifying even to one like me who dices daily with hell-bent London drivers."

Impervious to the attempt to close down the line of conversation, Pertinax chatted on as they went, step matching step up the grand staircase. "Not so simple as that, I fear! In fact, I'm pretty sure they were deceiving me." He watched for Joe's reaction.

"Oh? Good old Addenbrooke's?" Joe chortled. "Surely not!"

"I had a follow-on call from the police. Ticking me off! Me! As though the chap is my responsibility on his half day off! The idiot chose to spend his time driving out to The Brown Cow. Do you know it? . . . No, why would you? Low haunt on the Newmarket Road. A betting pub." He leaned closer and added confidentially, "Drunk as a skunk! Picked a fight with another in similar state just before closing time, drove off and picked a second fight with a lamppost."

At last he seemed to have Joe's attention. "The police gave you all this fiddle-faddle? Unusually cooperative of them. Not planning to press charges, are they?"

"I thought they were suspiciously informative. I took the trouble to ring the pub and check their story."

"How meticulous of you! When my man gets drunk I leave him in the tank to sweat it out! One can be too considerate, Pertinax. Firm up! You'll have to hope for better with, um, Clive, did you say? And never let him have access to your car keys." After a start of horror, he grasped Pertinax's arm. "No! Don't tell me he'd gone on the razzle in your Royce—or even worse—your sporty little Morgan?" He added silently, "God bless you, Bacchus!"

"Thankfully not. He was driving the Morris van. Here we are. I thought we'd have drinks before lunch in the salon and then step out through the windows onto the balcony." He ushered Joe into the elegant square room at the centre of the house, where a row of tall windows opened onto a magnificent view. Close by the window stood a table filled with cocktail-making paraphernalia—gleaming silver shakers, glasses, ice buckets and bottles of brightly coloured liquids. It struck a modern and light-hearted note that was not echoed by the three solemn people in the room, all of whom looked as though they'd find a dry sherry somewhat frivolous.

"Come and meet my guests. I think you know everyone,"

Pertinax said. "Miss Dorothy Despond and her father, Guy Despond, I know you are acquainted with . . ."

Joe collected two hesitant and rather guarded smiles from the Desponds, and he murmured polite phrases in their direction. Guy, bald patch shining pinkly through thinning grey hair, old-fashioned cravat and collar meticulously chosen, would have given consequence to any gathering. Dorothy was looking beautiful in a clinging emerald green silk dress, the effect rather spoiled by the tartan rug clutched around her shoulders, but her expression was not the warm and ready-for-amusement one he'd become accustomed to encountering. He was dismayed to see that she could not return his eager gaze but looked away, awkward and fearful.

Joe found any response to the Desponds difficult as he'd already set eyes on the third guest, loitering moodily by herself out on the balcony.

"And Doctor Hartest. Adelaide. I understand you two have met? Adelaide! Here's Joe Sandilands. What you probably didn't know is that Adelaide is by way of being associated professionally with the house. She has recently joined the practice of my dear old friend Easterby and finds herself pressed into the service of yours truly occasionally. As I'm sure I don't need to tell you, Adelaide is far too charming and pretty to be constantly hiding behind a stethoscope and should be encouraged to do her duty in enhancing the dinner tables of Cambridge."

"Ooh, steady Pertinax! When you know her better, you'll realise she is no Zuleika Dobson. She will not set out to charm the dons."

As Pertinax turned to the cocktail tray, Adelaide pulled a rude face at his back and looked pleadingly at Joe. Oddly, she seemed to be wearing her cycling skirt, thick stockings and brogues. The cream Aran sweater that covered her top half was practical and seasonal and looked lovely with her auburn hair tumbling down in windblown chaos over it, but it was hardly cocktail party wear.

What a collection! Joe thought. It only needed the Mad Hatter.

Into the uncomfortable silence Joe said, "Adelaide! Charming to see you again. I had understood you were away in Suffolk, spending the half term with your father in Mel-sett."

"I spent the weekend there," she replied briefly.

Joe sighed. This was going to be an uphill struggle in more ways than one, he realised. "And how are things going at the Hall?" he asked, not needing to fake an interest.

"Badly. For the Trueloves. All, apart from the youngest son Alexander, have flown and the house—I see you didn't know—has been sold."

"I had no idea. The land? The stables?"

"Are safe. The new owner has taken them on in their entirety. The staff, the tenants, the flocks and herds carry on seamlessly."

An odd conversation. Joe turned apologetically to the Desponds to include them. "You'll remember Melsett, of course, sir, from your visit last spring?"

"Still trying to forget it, Sandilands," Guy replied with a grimace. "Nothing like it since Rembrandt unveiled the *Feast of Belshazzar* before an unsuspecting public!" He shuddered. "Staring Eyes and Pointing Fingers . . . the Writing on the Wall . . . Death in the Night, and, by next morning, the ancestral home has been seized by the barbarian . . . I enjoy a bit of baroquerie as much as the next man, but I blame you, Sandilands, for slapping on the mars black and the cadmium red and directing the melodrama. Glad to hear the horses are okay though. Got quite fond of those big fellers. You're a horse lover—do you know anything about a painter from down Sudbury way? I'm told his horse pictures are really something . . ."

"That will be Alfred Munnings. Yes, indeed, his horses are the best you'll find and the landscapes they stand in are stunning. I wish I owned one. Had you realised he was a war artist in . . ."

The conversation picked itself up and began to flow forward on the current of Guy Despond's enthusiasm and experience. Dorothy roused herself to help it along. Joe sparkled. Pertinax seemed to think it was all going well enough for him to leave his guests when the summons came from Clive.

"He's arrived, sir. Waiting below in the hall. Wants a word . . ."

"That'll do, Clive. Off you go, I'll be straight down. Will you all excuse me for a moment?"

He had hardly turned his back when, oblivious to the surprised stares of the Desponds, Adelaide launched herself at Joe, grabbed him by the arm and shook him.

"What on earth are you doing here? Have you no sense? Listen—this may be important. Guy, Dorothy, you ought to hear this too! We've all got a terrible problem. He's ill. Very ill. Oh . . . it would take me ten minutes to explain his condition in medical terms . . . Just accept—the man's completely bonkers and dangerously out of control. Easterby's devised a concoction that seems to have a good effect. He sent me over with supplies this morning." She nodded down at the medical bag at her feet. "I gave him an injection an hour ago. He's strutting about like a wind-up soldier, but the effects wear off after a while. Who knows how long he'll remain lucid. It's not my speciality. He insisted I stay. He's up to something and I'm quite scared, Joe."

Dorothy and her father exchanged horrified looks but stayed silent while Adelaide rushed on.

"Something else you should know. I can't make sense of it myself, but . . . but . . . Melsett . . . I know who the new owner is and it's quite surprising. It's been kept a secret. Sale done through agents and so on. But my father had vet's bills—long unpaid—to worry about and he marched off to the Hall to ask for payment. He was met by Alexander Truelove. Drunk as usual but reasonably rational. He told Pa there was no cash left anywhere. His brother James has done a bunk and is mouldering in the stews of Marseilles. His mother has decamped to her sister's in Brighton. All he could suggest was that Pa address himself to the new owner. He gave him the name."

PERTINAX STRODE BACK into the room, leading his last guest by the sleeve.

"Here he is. The coming man of the county. In fact, you have all met him before, but I think this may be the moment to introduce him afresh. Nothing more delightful, don't you think, than to introduce a new friend only to discover that he is already known to your old ones." Pertinax was clearly over-revving. His eyes shone, his speech was faster than normal, his brow was glistening. Even his new guest seemed alarmed and muttered a dismissive, "Oh, I say! No need for the trumpet fanfare, old chap . . ."

"You know him as the chief superintendent of the local police force. With a country estate recently acquired and a knighthood to be announced next month—a reward for services to law and order over many years, you must become acquainted with the future Sir Adam Hunnyton of Melsett in Suffolk."

Thanks to Adelaide's double-barrelled delivery of news, Joe was just able to make his calculations, keep his astonishment in hand and say, "What a surprise! If Pertinax has it right, you are very much to be congratulated, Hunnyton. Squire of Melsett at last, are we to assume? What good fortune for Melsett! The estate couldn't be in more competent hands. I'm sure you'd probably like to have chosen a more appropriate time to make the announcement to your friends and associates but then . . . At least we have on hand a champagne cocktail to toast your success! Come and try one of these, Adam. You'll enjoy it."

Watching Pertinax's quivering hands making a clattering confusion of the glasses and jugs and ice buckets, Joe moved to his side. "Allow me, Pertinax," he said, shouldering him out of the way. "No need to call a footman. I've had the training. At the Savoy. Now then, Adam, what will you have from this lineup? On the menu we seem to have a champagne cocktail with late raspberries squashed into it. That's what the ladies are drinking. And then, what did you say these were, Pertinax?—a 'Gimlet' . . . a 'White Lady' . . . and what's this cloudy concoction in the jug? A 'Coup de Grâce'? It's all the go in London Town—the Corpse Reviver is so passé—but I'm surprised you can get the absinthe out here in the sticks."

"Gin and tonic would do me fine," Hunnyton said, annoyed by the blather.

Somewhere in the distance, a stable bell banged out the half hour.

Pertinax looked nervously at his watch.

Joe topped up the ladies' glasses and covertly assessed the two men he had, for some time now, both feared and strongly wished to thump seven bells out of. He had them, for the first time, together in one shot. Viking and Saxon, he decided, and each as dangerous as the other, in his own way. Pertinax with his sanity hanging by a thread, his strength and his ungovernable temper, was the more immediately threatening. In his overexcited state, he seemed likely to explode into violence first. Joe recalled, with pity and foreboding, the victims of syphilis he'd encountered in his professional life. Far too many of them. The plague seemed to be engulfing Europe. He judged that Pertinax was entering the tertiary stage of devastation by the spirochete bacterium. The parasite, making its way through his bloodstream, was probably laying waste to his nervous system, his heart, his brain. The overactivity in this organ could lead— in artists and musicians—to the production of works of genius in their last days. It could, on the other hand, lead to madness and acts of violence. There was no cure. He wondered what concoction Adelaide had been sent out to administer. Salvarsan? Mercury? Morphine? How long before the effects wore off and the man was left stranded in unimaginable pain and venting his fury on others?

Hunnyton, on the other hand, was all sanity and purpose. In control of himself and controlling of those around him. A large, strong, bluff East Anglian in appearance, he still had the work-worn hands of the countryman. "Fists like hams," one of his admirers had remarked to Joe. A concealed man, conflicted. A man Joe had never understood.

Time to take off the gloves, Joe decided.

"So, tell us, Hunnyton, whatever persuaded the powers that be to rescind the offer of knighthood to your superior, old Arnold Baxter, the chief constable of the county, and hand it to you?"

Joe was satisfied to catch a flash of astonishment on Hunnyton's impassive features.

"Have you met Baxter?"

"Yes. More importantly I've met *Mrs.* Baxter! I made it my business to visit the man who for so long had been making life easy for a politically disruptive force in the city, according to your account. Look-the-other-way Baxter. The old gent has trouble looking in any direction. He had a stroke a year ago and lost most of his faculties. His wife covered up for him as best she could, waiting for the moment when his knighthood should be conferred. The lady desperately wants to be a Lady, you see, with all the kudos the title will bring her in her tea group. His day-to-day organisation he left to you, his thoroughly competent superintendent. If any favouring of criminal activities or dodgy politicking has gone on in this fair city recently, I'm not blaming Baxter. I'm blaming you, Hunnyton."

The superintendent was unruffled. "There's no need to be huffy, Joe. You'll never have to call me 'sir.' I've turned it down. Grateful though I was to be offered it," he said with an alarming and mocking half bow to Pertinax. "You see, I wish first to accept a seat in Parliament. The honours will come later, perhaps."

"Seat in Parliament? What's all this?" Adelaide wanted to know. "There's no election due for another four years. I know you're a patient man but ..."

"There will be a by-election next year in the county. Early next year. The sitting MP will withdraw from government on the grounds of ill health, and I shall win the seat. A Tory in a sea of blue Tory voters. No problem. You've said yourself, Joe, the government is presently in a mess. Coalitions rarely work. There is no strong leader coming forward. They bicker and fail to take the vital decisions which could keep our country afloat. The British electorate will soon be crying out for strong leadership. I intend to respond to their cry. With the backing of key members of the government, elements of the armed forces and, vitally, the popular press, I'd say I had a pretty good chance of achieving my aims. Prime minister within two years, war leader in ... who can say when Armageddon will break out? I shall be ready!"

Looking at his fair, Saxon features, aware of his aura of strength and purpose, the man's ability to trick and cajole and twist, Joe thought he probably had it right. Time to find out which of this pair of impressive men had the whip hand.

"This valuable support, Hunnyton. All supplied by your creature here? Pertinax the insane? Pertinax the diseased defiler of women? Pimp, blackmailer and murderer extraordinaire?"

With a cry that came from deep in his throat, grey eyes blazing, Pertinax clenched his fists and would have rushed on Joe, with or without battle axe in hand. One raised finger from Hunnyton was all it took to stop the man in his tracks. Joe had seen him perform similar tricks on horses weighing more than a ton, and he reminded himself that Hunnyton had shown himself perfectly able to control the assistant commissioner also.

"Calm down, Gregory! He's insulting you with a purpose. Do you see what he did? He's just succeeded in establishing the pecking order between us. I would have preferred him to remain in suspense a little longer. I warned you not to under-ate him. Now, wrappers on, ladies and gentlemen, we'll take our drinks out onto the balcony. I can promise you a once-in-a-lifetime experience."

"Not going to chuck us all over, are you, Hunnyton? The last-of-a-lifetime experience?" Guy Despond asked. Standing protectively in front of his daughter, he glowered at Hunnyton with deep mistrust.

"Quite the reverse, sir. A rebirth, like the phoenix rising from the flames. Be patient. You'll see."

They lined up on the balcony, eyes stonily on the middle distance.

"A moment!" Joe doubled back through the window into the salon. "Ah! There you are, Clive! Thought I heard someone creeping about. We have all we need, thank you. We're waiting on ourselves. You may go back to your pantry."

"Sir. Yes, sir."

Joe waited until a door closed.

"Sorry, Pertinax!" he said, returning. "I didn't think you'd noticed him skulking about. Villains like him standing behind my shoulder blades make me a bit touchy. Right then, Hunnyton, what have you got for us?"

Hunnyton pointed in the direction of Cambridge. "From up here we should have a clear view. Look between the two tall elms . . ."

He consulted his watch again and gave a tight smile. Not entirely the confident showman, Joe thought.

The obliging stable bell sounded the three quarter hour.

It was Dorothy who spotted it first. "Look over there! Isn't that smoke? Oh, my God! That's Cambridge! Is the city on fire?"

"That's no fire!" Adelaide said. "It's . . . it's . . . a bomb! Like the ones they dropped from airships in the war. I saw a Zeppelin drop one on Lowestoft in 1915. It's a single explosion. Powerful . . . see how high it's rising and how fast . . . And how black! What have they hit? Joe!" She turned an anguished face to him in her agitation. "What are we looking at? Are there precious buildings burning? People?"

Through tight lips Joe replied. "Hunnyton is about to tell us both. And, if I'm right, he and the toad Pertinax are about to boast that, between them and with equal guilt, they have just exploded a bomb in the centre of the Cavendish Laboratory. Their man, Herbert Jennings, former Royal Engineer, set the timing mechanism which produced what you are looking at. It was timed to go off in the faces of twenty of the world's most talented physicists. But *why*, Hunnyton? *Why*, Pertinax? And why on earth put us up here to witness the devastation?"

Everything depended on hearing the right answer from Hunnyton. If he chose to back away now, turn his face away from them and wander away as he did with a recalcitrant horse, all was lost.

"Come, now, Joe! A serious step has been taken, I'll allow. You're angry that your attempts to defuse the coup have met with no success. When you understand the reasoning behind it, you will change your mind. Look on this as the first fusillade of the war. We both know the next war is fast becoming the present war. Sides are being chosen. War leaders of thuggish ability are rising to the surface. Italy, Spain, Germany, Russia. We were unprepared for the last one. We will not be caught out tripping over the starting line this time. It will be a conflict of weaponry. Of chemicals and engineering. The scientist who can devise the means of destroying the world will be God of War. The Germans have seen this already, and the Russians. The men who met their fate in that blast just now were well advanced in the planning of a device that will, in a short time, be powerful enough to blast the whole of London out of existence. Or Moscow. Or Berlin. That lot are, for the most part, Bolsheviks. They owe their allegiance to Mother Russia. When they'd sucked us dry of money, equipment and expertise, they planned to go to Moscow and deliver their lethal knowledge to Stalin's doorstep. Even you suspected as much, Joe, so try not to look so innocently aggrieved!"

"What? Are you telling me you're an anti-war group?" Joe probed, needing a clear answer.

"Hardly!" Hunnyton laughed. "Come on, Joe!"

"Are we then to infer from this that you are going to attack Göttingen next?"

"Of course not! By this stroke, we have strengthened their hand. A key selection of Cavendish men are already there. I don't doubt that they will be easily persuaded to stay on. There are many spare places available as Herr Hitler's purges have seen off the previous generation of elderly Jewish professors."

"You're joining the Fascist cause? You swine!" Despond shouted.

"Not at all. They will be joining me. My country will reassert its place as leader of this continent. In a year or so, Germany will have put its house in order, cleaned up its act. The German people will have come to their senses and seen through the mad oratory, the crazed ambition of that strutting little nobody they, for the present, revere. A new empire will be forged. Many on each side in the last lot could not see why we were at odds with each other. The two nations have much in common. The press made a good deal of the camaraderie of the trenches—the football games, the singing, the chivalry. Hoi polloi will not need much convincing when sympathetic editors have spread their propaganda. Many of our sitting MPs already favour the cause, many members of the aristocracy also. Our monarchy, indeed, has German roots. If they were to be offered a supportive, dashing young king, willing to take on the role of figurehead for a new combined nation . . ."

"A man under duress . . . blackmail." Joe was remembering the last motorcar registration number on the chauffeur's son's list.

"Wrong, Sandilands! It won't come to that," Pertinax gave his opinion. "Tell the bastard why he's here, Hunnyton, and get rid of him."

"Enough, Pertinax!"

"No, go on! Do tell me! I'd sincerely like to understand why you assumed I would hesitate to clap you both in irons and haul you off to London on a charge of treason, arson, murder . . . everything in the book?

A pitying smile, then, "Your last chance to save your skin. An offer. I'm building up a base, as you know. I already have people in important positions in government. I inherited a selection when I met Pertinax some years ago. The fool had tried to entrap me, thinking a presence on the local police authority would be useful for him in his endeavours." His glance at Pertinax taunted and dismissed. "Instead I took him over and his little empire. Nothing more than a money-making enterprise in the beginning—the fool hadn't even guessed at the potential. I broadened the power base, became more selective of targets. I have a civil servant or two from the highest level in my pocket. The Crown Prosecution Service is a useful tool, I find, and I'd like now to offer Scotland Yard a place at the top table. You, Sandilands. Commissioner in a very short time? We work well together. Your naiveté annoys me occasionally but that can be ironed out."

"What—no orgy on offer to persuade me?" Joe asked.

"No. We offer recruits what they want. I think you would refuse the orgy. But every man wants power. I offer you power."

At this, Pertinax objected loudly. He had rightly interpreted Hunnyton's proposition to Joe and saw in it his own end. He was being discarded in favour of the assistant commissioner. A fresh, young force, more congenial to Hunnyton was to replace him. His face grew red, his breathing shortened, his body seemed to be going into spasm. A stream of shocking abuse spurted from his lips. He had turned his anger from Joe to Hunnyton and was adopting a boxer's aggressive stance. One temper-fuelled blow from those concrete fists would have sent Hunnyton flying over the balcony. Joe moved out of the way to allow him a clear run at his target.

It was Adelaide who stepped into the bad situation.

She picked up her medical case and waved it in Pertinax's face.

"Sir Gregory!" she snapped. "Time, I think, for your next injection. Will you go to your room and I'll administer it? Come along now! We'll soon have you on your feet again."

To Joe's surprise, Pertinax growled quietly, turned and shambled out, followed by Adelaide.

"Stay where you are, Sandilands!" was Hunnyton's response to Joe's instinctive attempt to follow. "She'll be fine with the patient. At the moment she is the only person in the world who has what he wants. He won't harm her. Yes, you've all guessed, the man is mentally deranged. He has suffered from syphilis for years now. He has his good weeks when he reverts to the perfectly normal for quite long periods and believes himself cured. And then he has his bad moments, dipping deeper into decay and malignity each time. He's dying. He's not long for this world, but as long as he's in it, he's a liability. Sandilands, you must take his place."

Joe had heard as much as he needed to hear. But now the most dangerous moment had arrived. The presence of Guy and Dorothy on the small balcony had not been in his calculations and was a hazard. They were staying calm and quiet and trying to attract no one's attention, but Joe knew that Hunnyton would not hesitate to take one or both of them hostage. He had early established that the superintendent was carrying a gun in his usual favoured position, tucked into the back of his trousers. Joe was unarmed. Hunnyton was an inch or two taller than Joe and of heavier build. Speed and low cunning were Joe's only advantages. Would Dorothy read his mind? How good was her memory? Worth a try.

"You'll have to wait a while for me to absorb all this, Adam," he said finally. "I say—I don't know about you fellows but I'm gasping for a drink. Where did I put my glass?" He picked it up and took a grateful swallow. He reckoned there was nothing more disarming than the sight of a possible adversary with a glass in his hand. "Dorothy! Join me, won't you? This takes me back uncannily to our little scene at Melsett."

If she remembered she showed no sign of it. Sniffing and with tears running down her face, she threw him a look of utter disdain, reached theatrically for her glass and flourished it. Hunnyton smiled, waiting to hear the words of scorn pour from her.

Her screech took him by surprise. The glass she hurled took him in the face.

Joe leapt, one hand extended and smashed it down into a spot behind Hunnyton's ear. It should have felled him at once but he shook his bull's neck, recovered his balance, crouched and launched his weight at Joe. His longer reach landed two swift though weakened blows on Joe's jaw. He followed up with a battery of hard-knuckled blows directed with furious hatred at Joe's face. With no space to back away, Joe was being pushed ever closer to the waist-high balustrade. He felt the stone parapet behind his thighs and pushed back.

To his horror he heard Hunnyton panting in his ear. "Knew it would come to this! Smart-arse! Over you go. Your choice. When I investigate your death, I'll find no bullet holes, just a champagne-sodden, dizzy copper."

His hatred was his undoing. If he'd held his tongue and given one last heave Joe would have broken his bones on the stone slabs of the terrace below. In his overconfidence, Hunnyton had lost sight of Guy Despond. Elderly, round, and dapper, he had been no threat. Now the manicured white hands were gripping a glass jug full of alcohol, his expression of fierce determination a mask of Nemesis. The heavy jug crashed down on Hunnyton's skull with a sickening explosion and the unconscious bulk of the man collapsed on top of Joe.

As Joe scrambled to his feet, awash with alcohol, feeling sick and dripping blood from his nose, Despond stayed to check his victim. "He's still breathing. Shall we push him over while we can? What do you say, Sandilands? A crack to the head amongst the other broken bones will never be noticed."

"I'd say, better leave it right there, sir, and let me deal with the gentleman." Clive appeared at Despond's side, service pistol in one hand, the other one elegantly extended to escort him off the balcony. "You're quite all right now, sir. And the young lady. Will you go with these two officers from the Yard and they'll take a statement?" He turned to the recumbent Hunnyton, drew a pair of handcuffs from his belt and slipped them on with practised movements, passing them through one of the balusters. "There. He'll keep for now. Sorry, sir. That could have been nasty. I was distracted by the other young lady making off with Sir Gregory and splitting the party, so to speak. The right blokes were all in place. We got the confession. The rest of the household's safely stashed away. Cooks in the kitchens, dogs in their cages, keepers locked in the cellar." There was a short, uncomfortable pause and he added, "That just leaves Doctor Hartest to worry about and Pertinax."

"Ouch! Adelaide! Come with me, Clive! Where the hell have they gone?"

"It's this way, sir."

Joe ran after the Special Branchman along corridors and up a flight of stairs until he paused at a closed door. "Wait here," Joe said.

He flung the door open and hurled himself into the silent, curtained room. Pertinax was lying sprawled on his bed, his limbs spread in the defenceless pose of a sleeping baby, his face in slumber relaxed and youthful. Adelaide sat watchfully on the bed at his side. Her bag was open on the floor at her feet. She turned to stare at Joe as he moved to her side and put a hand on her shoulder.

"Adelaide! My love! Are you all right?"

"Not really. Probably never will be again. Devastated. But I'm as healthy in body as ever I was, if that's what you mean. You, on the other hand, look as though you've been through a meat mincer. I'd better give you something for those eyes before you lose them." She passed him a towel.

"That was bold of you—to make off with him like that. You probably saved everyone's life. I got here as soon as I could. There was some opposition, but all's well and in the capable hands of Special Branch."

"Opposition? Are you saying Adam's dead?"

"He's presently unconscious and safely in handcuffs. I think he'll survive if the Branchmen can keep Despond from doing him further damage. How's your patient?"

"Dead. Very dead. It worked faster than I had calculated."

Alarmed, Joe put out a hand and checked the pulse point on Pertinax's neck.

"As you say. Dead." And with foreboding: "Um . . . what worked, Adelaide?"

"Well, as you can see—it wasn't Doctor Easterby's magic rejuvenating potion. I gave him a shot from the second syringe I'd prepared."

"Oh, my God! What was that?"

"It's a formula my father's been experimenting with. He objects to putting animals out of their misery with a gun, and he's trying to perfect a painless injection method. I brought some back with me. I used a quarter of the amount he uses for a carthorse. I'll come quietly." She looked up at Joe with a sad smile.

Joe was lost for words.

Calm and resigned, she bent to fasten up her bag. "He wasn't going to let any one of us get away, was he, Joe? He was gloating, explaining himself. Hunnyton, I mean. Speaking freely to victims he knew would soon be in no position to contradict him."

"I'm afraid you're right. All his nonsense about recruiting us to his cause was a ploy to encourage me to reveal exactly how much I knew and who else was aware. He never intended to let me loose. I believe he had other plans for you. I believe he was truly fond of you, Adelaide. Pertinax would not have survived the day—indeed, any untidy deaths occurring on the premises would certainly have been put onto his account and explained away. The Desponds? I'm not sure what they're doing here but they seem very uncomfortable. Good old Guy nailed his colours to the mast by beaning Hunnyton with a cocktail jug. Appropriately he anointed him with the Coup de Grâce, though I'm sure he didn't have the time or presence of mind to select it."

"God! Joe! What does it take to make you give a serious, heartfelt reply? One man dead, two injured here and twenty blown to smithereens in Cambridge, and you spout frivolities!"

"Sorry, Adelaide! They're all safe. What you saw wasn't the laboratory going up in smoke—it was a giant bonfire built by the scientists themselves, most of them, I suspect, appropriately enough, members of the anti-war group. On Parker's Piece. With a little know-how from the chemistry department, they gave it every appearance of a bomb going off. I couldn't say anything there and then—I was trying to extract a confession from Hunnyton, a wallowing-in-success euphoric state which often loosens tongues. Bacchus and his boys—Clive the butler was one of them—were taking witness notes from the salon."

"How on earth did they manage to get in?"

"Thanks to two agents in place—the right place—*this* place, we had a good enough picture of the defences and how they functioned. You and Aidan certainly earned your infiltration agents' thirty bob a week. I was advised to use the Branch only in dire emergency. I judge the thwarting of a diseased, perverted blackmailer with his hands at the throat of dozens of our great and not-so-good and an egomaniacal Fascist a dire emergency. Just up their street, a bit of infiltrating with intent! God! My head aches! Hunnyton's in worse nick! If he survives, he'll be charged with a list of offences as long as my arm."

"Thank goodness for that! I'm in the business of preserving life, you know. If I had to balance the life of this degraded, diseased monster—and I reckon I did—against that of the Desponds and you and who knows how many others, well, there was an easy decision to be made. I mentioned the name 'Clarice Denton' as I made the injection. I've worked with my father since I was a small girl. Animals sometimes have to be put down. Sentimentality is not part of my make-up so you don't need to talk me through it." She gave him a sly smile, having accurately guessed what his next task would have been. "Now, tell me to whom I should give myself up. I don't think it should be you. You might refuse delivery, Joe."

"Well, there's Bacchus downstairs. He's my head of Special Branch. He'll advise. But I'm telling you, Adelaide, I will not let you be taken in charge."

"Well just make certain I don't have to share a cell with Hunnyton, will you? You know—you got it wrong. Hunnyton is the mad man. This chap here was suffering from brain decay and one can understand and sympathise. Hunnyton is, to all appearances, sane, purposeful, easy and sociable. And yet there's a disconnection there. An inner coldness at his core."

"Come away, Adelaide. We'll leave the clean-up team to do their stuff."

She picked up her bag. "Something you ought to see. On his wall. Waiting for him to die, I had a chance to look around me. Over here. What do you make of this?"

Mounted on a folding screen close to the wall at the foot of the bed and not immediately visible by anyone entering was a grouping of pictures and photographs. A very ancient sepia photograph of a fiercely moustached man in an old-fashioned and, to Joe, unrecognisable uniform glared down at him. Pertinax's grandfather, he assumed. Next to it was a Kodak shot of a young couple, probably on honeymoon, surrounded by the palms and bougainvillea of the south of France. Mother and father? Perhaps most interestingly there was an enlarged reproduction of a press photograph that Joe—and the world—had seen towards the end of the war. A wide view of a broad boulevard edged by elegant classical buildings bore the date and place in gold lettering underneath: *Riga. 3 September 1917. Militemus!*

The German army, victorious the previous day, was marching into the captured city, stepping out with perfect military precision, immaculate in every way.

"He wasn't a Russian sympathiser, was he, Joe?"

"His forefathers believed themselves Teutonic Knights and they had names such as Gottfried and Heinrich," he remembered. "Aidan found that out. The Pertinax coat of arms is a simple black cross on a white background. Waiting for a decoration, Aidan thought. Add to it a swastika and you have an eye-catching little number. Perhaps that's what he was planning. No offspring—for the obvious reason—so this mad line ends here, I'd say."

Adelaide shuddered. "It never ends, Joe. This man's madness. It will have spread already . . . physically, by infection . . . intellectually, by oratory and false logic. The need to grab power and have someone else pay for it."

She took his arm as they began to descend the staircase—more in the interest of keeping him steady on his feet, he suspected.

"I'll drive you back into town, Adelaide," he offered boldly. "What do you think you'll do now? Too soon to say?"

"Thanks but I'll be safer on my bike. First I shall resign from Easterby's practice and then I shall go back to Suffolk for a while. Oddly, young Alexander needs some help. The poor little rat's falling to pieces. Probably the one Truelove who has had no hand in sin and death, but he's suffering on their behalf."

"I think it's this one, cabby."

Joe stopped the taxi and peered out through the gloom of an early London evening. Fog was rising from the river and silently working its way up through the city, gathering smoke and soot into its stinking yellow miasma. The taxi had crawled along for the last mile, navigating by the feeble orange glow of the street lamps.

"Yes, this is right," he decided, looking at the brightly lit house. "Give me a second to get my parcel out, will you?"

Mr. Barnes answered the door at once. He didn't seem surprised to see Joe, but Joe didn't think surprise was in his repertoire.

"Miss Dorothy? A moment. I'll check whether she is at home."

Joe propped his brown-paper-wrapped parcel against the wall and scribbled a note on the front just in case she had decided to make herself unavailable. He wouldn't blame her. Disaster followed Dorothy whenever she met Joe, it seemed. This gift was precious little reward for saving his life, he reckoned.

"From Zeus. For Antiope. With incalculable gratitude," he wrote.

He heard the butler speaking to someone in the distance,

in tones calculated to carry all the way back round the corner to Joe, he guessed.

"Miss Despond. There's a policeman with a big package waiting in the hall to see you. Shall I tell him you're unavailable?"

"How could I resist? Of course I'm available, Barnes! Unless, of course, his name's Sandilands, in which case I left for New York ten minutes ago . . . Joe! Well there you are! On your feet again and . . . Oh! How ghastly! Good gracious! Your face looks like a sunset by Turner! Come and let me see it."

She bustled down the hallway and Barnes moved off, humming to himself.

Dorothy was dressed for an evening's entertainment, wearing a stunning gown in red satin, a diamond necklace and far too much lipstick. She shook Joe's hand heartily, peering at his stitched and swollen features with a cry of concern.

"Oh dear! Your poor nose! Will it ever recover?"

"I don't think so. It's broken. They've done their best. I shall just have to hope it scares the villains. As well as the horses and small children. And now girls in red dresses, it seems."

"Not at all!" Dorothy stood on tiptoe, leaned forward and pressed the gentlest of kisses on the end of his nose.

Joe caught his breath in surprise and wondered if he now looked like a clown.

"I brought you a gift. Spoils of war! I think you'll recognise it. I'll leave it with you and buzz off—I see you're dressed for something or someone exciting this evening."

"No, no. Father is having what he calls a soirée. He's

entertaining some new clients. They won't be here for a half hour or so. We're to start the evening with a warming English punch. Barnes is concocting it in the drawing room. Shall we go and help ourselves before anyone arrives?"

In the drawing room, Barnes was steaming gently—on his third tasting glass, Joe judged—wielding a silver ladle to encourage clove-studded oranges to bob about more vigorously in the punch bowl. Invited to sample the brew, Joe took the glass he was handed and pronounced it delicious. A little more cinnamon wouldn't hurt, he suggested as it seemed an informed comment was expected. Barnes nodded in agreement, selected four more cinnamon sticks and popped them into the mixture.

"Barnes, tell my father when he appears that the commissioner has arrived with a picture for me and he's taken it up to my sitting room to find a place for it on the walls. We'll take our drinks up with us. Can you summon Harry to help with the picture? It's a bit cumbersome."

As they set off up the stairs, following the footman, Dorothy explained, "I have a suite of rooms for myself up here on the second floor. The public rooms downstairs are designed to impress my father's guests. I have no hand in decorating them or choosing the pictures on the walls. I content myself with doing exactly what I want up here in my own rooms."

Entering her sitting room, Joe was dismayed. The furnishings were modern, clean-cut and the ones that didn't bear the "Liberty of London" label had been shipped in from Paris, he guessed. The colours of the fabrics were bright but the walls were covered in a white linen to show off the many pictures Dorothy had chosen to have about her. Her professional work was clearly both centre stage and background for her private life. Most of these had been painted in the last ten years, he judged; a few were classical and he even recognised one or two by very famous artists. One thing was certain. The Watteau he'd brought for her would be completely out of place.

He said as much, adding that he would take it away and try his luck at Christie's.

"If you don't want it for yourself," Dorothy said. "That would be a good idea. Joe—I don't think you realise—that painting is worth ten times what you paid for it. It is the real thing. As right as rain. My father lied to Pertinax to annoy him. I can see why it wouldn't please you to keep it. Bad memories!"

"Dorothy, you've never told me—and perhaps you should—how you and your father came to be involved with the man."

"I was waiting for you to ask. I thought that must be your reason for coming. Father says he wants to tell you himself. I suspect he's not told *me* the whole truth. But—this is as good as any time, I suppose. Art lovers all know each other. They gossip, they play tricks on each other. It's a cutthroat world. My father and Pertinax had dealings that turned sour. Pertinax asked about, exerted pressure in certain quarters and found out about some pretty shady deals my father had done when he was starting out in the business. He could go to prison if anyone pressed charges. At the very least, his reputation would be lost. Blackmail ensued. He never pushed father too hard—he had a good feeling for how far he could go and he sensed that my father had the grit to poke him in the eye if he crossed the line. They had an uneasy relationship, tossing each other the occasional snippet of information, the occasional recommendation. Well, you'll remember how you got involved yourself."

Joe asked her to say no more on the topic. He told her that, following on the death of Pertinax and the incarceration pending trial at the Old Bailey of Hunnyton, there had been many ends to tie up and trails to follow. Inevitably, this unpleasant business had been firmly laid at Joe's door. "Sandilands is aware. He has his eye in. Let Sandilands complete what he has begun." Policy decisions had been taken at the highest level and it had all culminated in a bonfire. But this time an imaginary bonfire. It was about to be revealed in the press that Sir Gregory, who had been suffering for some years from an incurable tropical disease, had recently died at his home near Cambridge. His body had been found in a summer house in the grounds where he had been storing memorabilia of various kinds. Family documents, photographs and filmic records had all gone up in the blaze. The Fire Department had attended the scene and subsequent investigation showed that the cause of the fire was a cigarette left unattended. Sir Gregory used, according to his butler's statement, to be in the habit of retiring to his summer house to smoke his favourite Balkan Sobranies against all the advice of his man of medicine.

As he talked in his top-policeman's voice, he watched her strained features begin to soften and regain their brightness.

"So! There you are! Poof! Up in smoke," he said in conclusion. "Reputations saved. Men all over the country will read that piece, thank their lucky stars, put their revolvers back in the drawer and live to fight another day. You may tell your father. He's in the clear. You're both in the clear. Whatever you've been up to," he added with a teasing snarl.

"They ordered an *imaginary* fire, you said ... Hmm ... Where are the records at this moment, Joe? The evidence on film that he was holding. Who has them?" Once again, Dorothy had gone straight to the heart of the matter.

"Ah. Many would have liked to get their hands on them, MI5 being first in the queue. Bacchus found them. Not outdoors at all but secreted away in a strong room in the house. It was he who peeked at the material and saw there such images from hell he was resolved to set the whole house on fire around it. Bacchus may be a bit of a thug but he's quite the puritan when it comes to such things. That wonderful house! Jacobean! Riddled with rots wet and dry, woodworm and furniture beetle, but all the same—I couldn't allow it! We discussed it and then hit on the notion of putting a match to the whole lot in the summer house I've just described. The fire was *not* imaginary. And the relief felt by the dozens of men he'd threatened and squeezed dry for years will be justified when they read tomorrow's *Times*."

At last Dorothy seemed to feel relaxed enough to sink down onto one of her sofas. He handed her the mug of punch and sat down beside her. He suggested a toast. "Let's drink to Loki, shall we? Norse god of mischief. And fire! I think he's been looking down favourably on us."

"Naughty Joe! You're too freethinking and too free-acting to be a man of law. You're nothing but an anarchist manqué, I've concluded. You should stop pretending to be a policeman, resign and find another job. What would you really like to do?"

"Well if you should sack Barnes, call on me. I could make

punch and growl in the hallway when randy, fortune-hunting gentlemen call on you. I could carry your chequebook for you when I escort you to Regent Street to choose Italian silk for your drapes."

Dorothy grinned. "Oh, would you, Joe? I'd love that!"

She looked at him strangely and spoke again hesitantly. "No, I'm not joking. I really would like to see you more often and father has plans to introduce you to some of his friends. The ones he thinks you'll like. Since he saved you from being hurled over the balcony, he feels rather proprietorial towards you, I'm afraid."

"Gracious! You remind me—your father's party! I must make myself scarce. Dorothy, you clearly don't find satyrs and nymphs the most fashionable subjects to have about the place—I'll take it away." He leapt to his feet and picked up his parcel.

"No, no. Wait." She joined him and began to tear away the paper. "I've thought of just the place for it. It's designed to go above a doorway. Offer it up for size over my bedroom door, will you? Ring for Stanley if you need help—or a chaperon."

She had scurried off through an open doorway into the next room before he could voice his objection. He stood truculently holding the picture before him like a shield, and feeling foolish.

"Oh, come on! You're a policeman. I'm not going to attack you. There," she said. "The very spot. Exactly the right size. Leave it by the wall and I'll have it put up tomorrow." She peered more closely at the image. "Yes, I see it. He does look a bit like you. Before Hunnyton rearranged your face."

Joe was hardly listening. He was looking about him at

this space, the centre of the layers she surrounded herself with. Downstairs, she played the part of London hostess with her father. In her upstairs sitting room, she entertained her smart friends. With a care not to be caught staring, he took in the very different atmosphere. The fabrics here were not meant to impress, they were her own choice, for her own comfort. He had an impression of white linen, patchwork quilt, deep rugs and jugs of blue hydrangeas. A bookshelf was spilling over with yellow-backed French novels. Yet it was the one or two pictures carefully hung that intrigued him.

He admired the Degas riverbank scene and the lively gypsy encampment by Augustus John, but it was the tender and relaxed portraits of mothers and children absorbed in domestic activities that he liked. Fat babies were being dried after their bath, a small girl was being read a story by her mother under a willow tree, another was sitting on a lap counting apples. Not at all the kind of picture a sophisticated creature like Dorothy, a woman with the pick of the art of two continents, would choose.

She answered his thought as she often did. "I lost my mother when I was about the age of that tubby little girl over there. The woman in the portrait is very like her. I cried for two days when I found it. I don't know who the sitter is but the painter is Mary Cassatt."

"I like them. I like them very much," he said quietly. "But then I'm very sentimental."

"I'd noticed that." She passed him a lace handkerchief. "Some would say soppy. I've never known a soppy man before."

"Oh, I don't know," he said, politely dismissive, "I just

react to circumstances . . . I coo over babies, pat puppies, smack villains in the chops. Nothing out of the ordinary."

"And women? How do you react to women who're trying to get your attention?"

"If it comes down to it, I reckon a man has the choice between flight and flight. I generally choose the latter." Joe gave a nervous grin.

"How very rude! And a blatant lie. This from a man who's embarked on and promptly disembarked from two serious affairs in the last six months? You're bidding fair to overtake my record for fickleness!" She took hold of his hands and looked up at him, suddenly serious. "Joe, if I'm careful not to bump your nose, may I kiss you?"

Panic took him by the throat and he heard himself gurgling. "Stitches in the lip . . . decidedly unpleasant experience for a girl . . . Not ungrateful, in fact honoured . . . Later perhaps . . ."

He hurried from the room, dashed down the stairs and let himself out into the London fog before Barnes could catch up with him.

He went to the edge of the road and looked up and down for a taxi. Nothing was moving in the streets. Perhaps if he waited, one of Despond's guests for the evening would roll up in a cab and he could commandeer it to take him back to his apartment in Chelsea. He found he was shaking with emotion and could hardly begin to understand his grotesque reaction. A wonderful girl, whose attention he could never have hoped to attract, had thrown aside convention and her defences and made very clear her feelings for him. What the hell was wrong with him? He was no unworldly innocent to run off in the night like that to the safety of his bachelor flat.

Sudden fear had ambushed him. Dorothy had said it her-self—"You're bad at choosing women, Joe." True enough. And he wasn't ready to compound his mistakes. It was dif-ficult to accept that on this occasion he'd been chosen.

He tried for a measure of calm and asked himself some searching questions. He stopped that exercise when he realised he'd asked the same question six times. The answer was always the same: he wanted to be with Dorothy, looking into her laughing face and snuffling into her hair. He wanted to be exchanging warm looks with her over the heads of her father's guests. He wanted to slip his arms around her slim waist.

He paced to and fro on the pavement, angry and con-fused. Stitches! True enough but what an idiot! He remembered he was still clutching her handkerchief.

It was an even bigger idiot who, a moment later, rang the doorbell, whisked the hankie in Barnes's face and mut-tered, "Awfully sorry, I seem to have walked off with this."

Unfazed, Barnes said in his stately manner, "Perhaps you would like to return it to Miss Despond yourself? I believe you know the way, sir."

AT ONE O'CLOCK, Barnes made his ritual inspection of the upper floors before retiring for the night. The butler was smiling. The evening had gone well. Young Sandilands had not only changed his mind and accepted an invitation to dine, he'd been the life and soul of the party. Sharp enough to hold his own with the master, gracious and amusing with his fellow guests and confident enough to stand no nonsense from Miss Dorothy. He'd do!

Pacing silently past Miss Dorothy's room, Barnes

paused, checked that the coast was clear and put an ear to the door. Girlish giggles. The assistant commissioner was doing his stuff. Barnes smiled and padded on down the corridor.

AUTHOR'S NOTE

TREACHERY AT THE CAVENDISH LABORATORY:
RUSSIAN SPIES IN THE 1930S.

Authors are often asked: "Where do your ideas come from?"

I never thought I'd hear myself say, "From page eleven of the *Tuscaloosa News*, December 24, 1957!"

But there it was—the headline that intrigued me:
BRITAIN GOT CROCODILE, RUSSIA GOT SPUTNIK

That's what happens when you enter the names "Peter Kapitza" and "Cavendish Laboratory, Cambridge" on Google.

In the months of research I did for the book, this headline was the first I came across that dared to make an accusation rarely expressed in my country—England—to this day. It suggests that in the foremost physics laboratory in the world in the 1930s, the group of men who first split the atom (Nobel Prize winners of the future and geniuses who make the *Big Bang Theory* lads look like sixth-formers) were sheltering in their midst a Russian agent. This man, an extraordinarily talented physicist and engineer, would, after thirteen years of working in Cambridge, return to his homeland to present the fruits of his experience to Stalin. He would go on to build Russia's version of the Cavendish in St. Petersburg, exploiting the knowledge he had acquired in Cambridge.

The judgment of the Tuscaloosa journalist in 1957 was cynical:

> *An eight-foot crocodile with gaping, saw-toothed jaws, carved on the brick wall of a Cambridge University laboratory, will remind Britons for generations to come that "Kapitza was here."*
>
> *Yes, Dr. Peter Kapitza, the Russian scientist who designed Sputnik, very definitely was here. I found traces of him everywhere at Cambridge, where he spent 14 years doing atomic research at British government expense.*
>
> *The fruit of that research is the Russian satellite now circling the globe at 18,000 miles per hour.*

The charge would seem to be that the development of the Soviet atomic bomb, Sputnik, the space race all followed thanks largely to Kapitza's double-dealing. And Cambridge was left with his crocodile. The carving was chiselled into the brickwork of the laboratory avowedly as a joking Kapitza tribute to Sir Ernest Rutherford, the Director of the Cavendish, whom Kapitza nicknamed "The Old Crocodile." He was ostensibly linking his formidable boss flatteringly with the Russian symbol for the father of the family. A different interpretation is that it carries the connotation of "hypocrisy."

Rutherford and the scientific establishment appear to have shown nothing but sympathy for their colleague in his predicament when he wrote to them from Moscow (where he'd gone for his usual summer holiday) claiming that he was being held in Russia against his will. Stalin, he told his Cambridge mentor, was making him build up, practically single-handedly, a new laboratory: "The Institute for

Physical Problems." He had the nerve to complain to Rutherford that the resources available to him in Russia were outdated and inadequate. Could Rutherford help?

He sent a list of requirements: the big generator, duplicates of the hydrogen and helium liquefiers, the wiring, the clocks, two top physicists to act as his assistants ... Rutherford replied testily that he'd be asking for the paint off the walls next. And yet—the gentlemen at the Cavendish responded to this plea by packing up the equipment Kapitza wanted and posting it off to Russia.

Why did this man go unchallenged? Was everyone looking the other way deliberately? Where was the British Secret Service in all this?

THIS STORY TAKES the fictional Joe Sandilands into the turbulent and shady world of spying, defection and atomic secrets between the two world wars.

In 1933, MI5, the British Secret Service, was a very sketchy, cash-strapped organisation and not to be compared with the present super-efficient, highly technical body. Its headquarters were in the Cromwell Road in London and though it kept an excellent filing system it was something of a gentlemen's club, running a few agents and keeping tabs largely on Irish terrorists and the increasingly active Russian menace. Hitler's Nazi Party did not give much cause for concern, being considered somewhat distasteful and, judging by the ease with which their agents in Britain were identified and dislodged or turned, hardly a threat to our society. Anti-spy work was shared, not always smoothly, with the Special Branch of the Metropolitan Police. This was staffed by ambitious young men, the cream of the detective force. Linguistically gifted, intelligent and resourceful Branch officers performed any duties involving physical force, such as arrests and interrogation of suspects. The Branch was technically under the direction of an assistant commissioner at Scotland Yard.

Joe would have found himself with a very hot potato in his lap.

The activities of the Cambridge Four—Blunt, Burgess, Maclean and Philby—during the Second World War and the Cold War years are well documented and their consequences understood. These student spies were, at the time of the story, already actively communist. Little seems to have been written about the years immediately preceding their activities but it was at this crucial time— the year the lithium atom was split at the Cavendish Laboratory—that Peter Kapitza may well have done much more serious damage to the West. It was a piece not of spying, perhaps, but of deception and manipulation so blatant that, to this day, Britain has difficulty in questioning and evaluating it.

Our scientists and writers prefer to dwell on the many entertaining stories that came out of the Kapitza years. They were seduced by the young and arrogantly idealistic world created in this academic hothouse and by the gifted Russian at the centre of it. I decided to trail this intriguing man. Amusing, witty, daring to tease and criticise his distinguished employers, Kapitza was loved by all who met him and worked with him. He affected an exaggerated Englishness with his tweeds, flat caps, pipe-smoking and enthusiasm for fast cars and motorbikes. He flattered and fawned and was disarmingly open about his love for Russia and his communist affinities. Hiding himself in plain sight? A man who has no secrets can hardly be suspected of being a secret agent. It's the ultimate cover.

At a time when the British working class was being hounded and imprisoned for communist leanings, Kapitza seemed able to talk openly of his sympathies without attracting suspicion. MI5 noted his links with Communist Party members and associations but no steps were taken to bring him to book. He even stated to Rutherford in a letter from Moscow: "... First of all, I am and always will be in sympathy with the work of the Soviet Government on the reconstruction of Russia, on the principle of socialism and I am prepared to do scientific work here."

He complains of being held a virtual prisoner by Stalin, anxious, lonely and suffering increasingly fragile mental health and yet, for the next decade and beyond, this self-styled victim confronted—even crossed swords with—murderous monsters: with Joseph Stalin and Lavrenti Beria, the sinister head of the Secret Police and Nuclear Weapon Development. Kapitza got his own way and he survived—a feat which could only have been achieved by a man of considerable nerve and incontestable political and scientific clout. This factual evidence does not fit with the plaintive, homesick-for-Cambridge image he projects in his correspondence. He outlived several tyrants, dying in 1984 and—with his sense of humour—probably well aware that he'd had the last laugh.

At the height of his popularity in Cambridge he formed the Kapitza Club, an intellectually adventurous and entertaining gathering of the world's most intelligent men. Einstein, Heisenberg, Dirac, Landau, Chadwick, and Skinner were some of the distinguished members.

The stories about the club abound. The very last meeting was held when he was warmly welcomed back to Cambridge in 1966 after thirty-two years in Russia. Kapitza was staying as a guest in his college and he was invited to sit on High Table for dinner. Discovering that he did not have a gown to put on, a steward dashed off and returned with one that, when examined, proved to have Kapitza's name stitched into it. The college had kept his old gown through the intervening years, awaiting his return.

This politically amoral opportunist is still exercising his charm. He elbowed his way into the story I was writing. I was fully intending to tear off the smiling mask and reveal him for the duplicitous scoundrel he might well have been, but, once again, he roars in on his Scott motorbike, smiles, displays his skills and roars off again. Unchallenged by me or anyone—except the hard-nosed journalist of the *Tuscaloosa News* on Christmas Eve in 1957.

Readers wishing to find out more about this outstanding scientist and social will-o'-the-wisp could dip into some of the following books.

Andrew, Christopher. *The Defence of the Realm: The Authorized History of MI5*. London: Allen Lane, 2009.

Badash, Lawerence. *Kapitza, Rutherford and the Kremlin*. New Haven: Yale University Press, 1985.

Boag, J. W., P. E. Rubinin, and D. Shoenberg, eds. *Kapitza in Cambridge and Moscow: Life and Letters of a Russian Physicist*. Amsterdam: Elsevier Science, 1990.

Quinlan, Kevin. *The Secret War Between the Wars: MI5 in the 1920s and 1930s*. Suffolk: Boydell Press, 2014.

And concerning the London Metropolitan Police at Scotland Yard in Joe's day:

Howgrave-Graham, H. M. *Light and Shade at Scotland Yard*. London: John Murray, 1947.